Inception

THE MARKED

D1360174

BIANCA SCARDONI

INCEPTION, THE MARKED #1

First Edition: September 2015

All characters and events depicted in this book are fictitious. Any similarity to
real persons, living or dead, is purely coincidental.

ISBN: 978-0-9948651-0-6

To my mother, Anna,
for believing in me long before I wrote this.

CONTENTS

Be careful who you trust,
for even the Devil was once an Angel.

PREFACE

The most dangerous enemy is not the one who lingers behind you in the shadows, but the one who walks beside you as a friend. They shape the world around you with well-constructed lies, entombing you in the gossamer of their deceit. You'll never know their true face, for they shed their masks in layers—meticulous and devious, like the skin of an ever-changing snake.

I walked hand in hand with my enemy, allowed their kiss of death to linger on my lips while the world disintegrated around me. I couldn't see through the smoke and mirrors; too consumed with fighting a destiny I didn't want; too afraid to let go of a life I wasn't meant to have. Running only brought me closer to them. Back to where I started. Back to my inevitable fall from grace. One misstep was all it took, and it all came crashing down. And they were right there waiting for it—eager and ready to bury me in the wreckage.

The stage had been set.

The actors were in place.

Everything was a lie, and I never saw it coming.

1. HOLLOW BE THY NAME

The wrought-iron gates creaked open as the black town car glided through the late afternoon fog and took us up the winding driveway to my uncle's house—the Blackburn Estate. The massive, Baronial-style gray stone had been in our family for over a century and had all the trappings of a real life haunted house, outfitted with arched Victorian towers, ivy-clung walls, and a spike-tipped fence that spanned the entire length of the grounds.

It was arguably one of the most macabre-looking houses in town, and for a second I contemplated telling the driver to take me back to the hospital—a thought that quickly dissipated with a brief flashback to the mandatory group therapy sessions and decrepit nourishment they had the audacity to call food.

Anything was better than that place.

I had spent the last six months holed up in a mental institution, suffering from what they called, "a psychotic break from reality due to a traumatic event." That event being the death of my father, and the psychotic break being the part where I claimed to have been attacked by a vampire.

Yeah, I know what you're thinking; *vampires aren't real.*

They don't murder your father in the middle of the night while you're watching on helpless and powerless to stop it. Certainly not if you're living in this little place we call *reality, so* that's exactly what I told my doctors—over and over again like an anti-psychotic mantra—until *they* believed that *I* believed it and finally signed my release papers.

But I *know* what I saw.

The town car came to a stop at the top of the driveway where my Uncle Karl was standing in wait on the front stoop, solemn and watchful like a raven holding fast on its perch. His hands were crossed firmly behind his back—stoic, just the way I remembered him.

He was my father's brother no doubt, and looked every bit the part with the same dark hair and matching charcoal eyes. His hair was brushed back neatly, broken up only by the thin, white edges along his ears that threatened to reveal the age he otherwise carried so well.

It was often said that I looked just like them—a Blackburn through and through—with the same dark hair and lean frame, though my hair was longer and turned in waves all the way down my back, and my eyes were a lighter, more peculiar shade of gray. I used to cringe when people said I looked like him— my father, because I was a girl and girls aren't supposed to look like their fathers. Girls are supposed to look like their mothers, or fairy princesses, or Barbie dolls, or some crap like that.

I plucked the ear buds from my ears and gathered my things as the driver came around back and opened the door for me. My first reaction was to jump back when his hand came out towards me, though I quickly relaxed, realizing he was only trying to help me out of the car and *not* decapitate me by way of an extended palm.

Clearly, I still had some residual issues.

I sucked in a calming breath and shook my hand at him to

let him know that I had this, and then climbed out by myself, dragging my oversized duffel bag with me. The driver smiled back at me unaffected, and circled back to the trunk where he dug out the rest of my bags; one small, russet suitcase.

This was what my seventeen years of life had been reduced to: one duffel bag and a hideous valise. How ironic since I used to be the kind of girl who shopped every week-end and worried about what *so and so* thought about my outfit or if *what's his face* noticed me that day. Lately though, I couldn't find it in me to give a shit. I just packed up the bare essentials and told the realtor to donate the rest to Goodwill.

"Hello, Jemma," greeted my uncle as I made my way up the front steps. He didn't bother with a hug. "Welcome *home*."

There was something strange about hearing that word, like it didn't belong to me anymore or shouldn't be coming out of his mouth. Maybe it was because it made me face reality; that these past six months weren't just some perpetual nightmare I was stuck in; that I wasn't simply waiting for someone to wake me up and tell me none of it was real and that everything was fine. Because everything *wasn't* fine. It was far from fine, and somehow, that seemingly harmless word made it all too real.

The life I knew and loved was gone, and so was my father. No matter how many words I chose to reject.

Inside, the monolithic foyer was fixed with pale, textured wallpaper, mahogany wall paneling, and an incredible grand staircase dressed in a crimson stair runner. Everything about the house was rich, and dense, and rooted. It was everything I wasn't. Even the air, with its distinct smell of oak wood and sage, spoke to its identity and its history. I couldn't help but feel small here. Overwhelmed. Incompatible.

I stood in the space holding my duffel bag, unable to seed myself into the hardwood floors—into the house—and stared up at the elaborate chandelier, drinking all of it in and wondering if I'd ever really be able to feel at home here.

"This way," said my uncle, taking me away from my wandering thoughts. "Let's get you settled in."

I followed him up the stairs to the second floor where we traversed the darkened corridor in shared silence, passing a string of doors and painted portraits of noble men who marked a striking resemblance to my father, until we reached my room at the end of the hall. The grand tour left much to be desired, though I didn't figure my uncle for the tour giving type anyway. The truth was, I didn't really care to see the ins and outs of the house. I just wanted to unpack what little things I had left and settle into anything that remotely resembled a bedroom.

"I hope this will do," he said as he opened the double doors to my new bedroom—a plum colored space at least twice the size of my old room.

I was at a loss for words as I soaked in the floor to ceiling windows, the outdoor terrace, the queen-size canopy bed, and elegant black furniture. It was a far cry from the institutional white I had grown accustomed to in recent months, and was absolutely incredible. "I think it'll *do* just fine."

His staid expression teetered around a smile. "There's school clothes in the closet and the bathroom's been stocked as well."

"You shopped for me?" I asked, discernably surprised. And who could blame me? He looked like the kind of man who couldn't tell a roller from a rolling pin.

"Well, I signed the check if that counts."

"It counts," I said, shrugging my shoulders.

An awkward moment of silence passed.

"Very good then, I'll leave you to get settled in. I'm sure you're quite tired from your trip," he said, adjusting the collar of his dress shirt. He seemed to be in a hurry to leave. "I'll be right down the hall in my office should you need anything."

I nodded, propping my bag up onto the bed as I took in the depths of the walls around me. I wanted to get lost here, to lose myself in this new beginning and forget everything else that happened to me. I wanted to forget the grief and the uncertainty; the terrifying moments that had etched their details into the forever of my mind. I wanted to forget all of it.

"Uncle Karl," I called out as he began to close the door. I waited for him to peer his head back in. "I just wanted to say thank you, you know, for taking me in. I know you didn't have to do this."

He stepped back into the room. "I wouldn't have had it any other way, Jemma. This is where you belong—where you've *always* belonged. With family."

I tried for a smile. "Would it be alright if I made a long-distance call? I'd like to let Tessa know I arrived okay."

"Of course," he nodded. "This is your home now. You can call your sister anytime you wish." His eyes darted over my shoulder as though something had snagged his attention.

Reflexively, I turned towards the apparent distraction. I thought I saw something flicker across the balcony window, but it was gone just as soon as my eyes settled.

"Did you see that?" I asked, turning back to him.

"Did I see *what?*"

"In the window…like a shadow or something."

"A shadow?" His eyebrows pulled together.

"Yeah—or a figure?"

"A shadow or a figure?" he repeated, eyeing me as though maybe I'd been released from the hospital a little too early.

I wasn't sure how to explain what I thought I just saw and the more I tried to answer him, the more ridiculous I felt about it. "You know what, never mind." I shook my head. "I'm probably just tired from my trip."

"Of course. Say no more," he nodded. "Get some rest, and

I'll see you in the morning."

I waited for him to close the door and then shifted my eyes back to the window—watching it as though it could speak to me; as though it would profess its truth.

There's nothing out there, I told myself, hugging my arms for warmth. *Just my eyes playing tricks on me...*

The line rang at least a dozen times before Tessa finally picked up her phone. She sounded out of breath, like she'd been running a marathon or working out heavily...or something else. Tessa was often busy doing something else. Most of the time, I was just grateful for getting through to her at all.

"Tessa! It's me Jemma," I whisper-yelled into the receiver.

"It's good to hear your voice, Jemma." Her breathing was still labored. "How is everything at Uncle Karl's?"

"It's fine. I just got here," I said speedily.

"Where are you? Can you come see me? I really need to talk to you" —I paused and looked over my shoulders, lowering my voice— "about that thing we discussed at the hospital."

That *thing* being the vampires. Vampires that she seemed perfectly comfortable discussing, not at all like everyone else's reaction (such as Suzy Carson, my former legal guardian) which basically consisted of having me committed.

My initial decision to stay in Florida after my father's murder had been an easy one. I wanted to stay close to the people I knew—close to my friends—and since my sister couldn't very well put her life on hold to move in and take care of me, going to live with Suzy had been the next best thing. She was the closest thing I had to a mother anyway, and I trusted her. Up until she had me institutionalized, that is.

"I know, Jemma. We'll talk soon. I'm a little tied up right now, but I'll try to make it out there as soon as I can. Spend some time with Uncle Karl in the meantime. I'm sure he has plenty to talk to you about."

"Yeah, sure," I mumbled, feeling disappointed. "He seems like a real talker."

She laughed, the sound of it raspy yet strangely melodic. "Take care, Jemma. I'll see you soon."

"Right. See ya."

If I don't get killed by a vampire.

I woke up early the next morning to a melancholy sky that seemed to go on forever, its dull gray light encroaching itself in my room through an opening slit in the velvet curtains. Tiny particles of dust danced lazily around my face, beckoning me for my attention as they fought to stay inside the light. I watched their sway through groggy eyes, transfixed by the normalcy of it all, and for a moment, I'd forgotten my place.

Hollow Hills.

That was my place. A sleepy little town tucked away in the rangy coast of British Columbia—worlds away from the sunshine state I used to call home.

I rolled onto my back and looked up at the black cloth ceiling of my canopy bed as reality set in and wrenched me from my happy place.

Even though it had been almost a year since my father died, I still woke up expecting to be in my old room, in my old house, with my father downstairs waiting to fix us breakfast. It usually only took a few seconds to remember—to wake up from my daze, but in those fleeting moments, I was happy again.

It was hard to let go of that; to let go of the life I had before, but the truth was, it was harder for me to stay there inside the pain. I wasn't strong enough to live there no matter how much I wanted to. At most, I could allow myself only a few minutes to cry for him—to grieve our lives, and then I had to push the memories away, burying them deep inside of me once again so that I could function. So that I could go on.

I kicked the covers off my legs and shivered as I tried to summon enough courage to pry myself from the warmth of my bed. The chill was unshakable. Even with the light of day, I could feel the bite in my bones, lingering and unwilling to thaw itself out. The cold would take some getting used to, I realized, as I walked over to the window and pulled back the curtains in search of the morning sun.

I stood there for a moment and watched as my new world roused itself from its slumber with silent promises of a new day—a new start. There was almost something hopeful about it, reassuring, like a forged whisper of hope telling me that everything was going to be okay.

Even if I didn't believe it.

Even if I didn't feel it inside.

The coils in my stomach tightened as thoughts about my day began to surface. Thoughts about my *first* day; in a new town; in a new school; *Mid-semester*. I hadn't even left my room and already my day had taken a U-turn straight to hell.

After a hot shower, I dressed in a pair of fitted blue jeans and a plain white camisole, and made my way to the kitchen where my uncle was sitting by himself at the breakfast nook over by the large bay windows. He had the paper in front of him, but he wasn't reading it. He was on the phone, deep in conversation.

The kitchen, like the rest of the house, was spacious and plump with contrasts—cathedral ceilings and arched doorways on one hand, warm taupe walls and granite counter tops on the other. It was a seamless blend of old-world and new.

I searched through the cabinets for a decent-sized bowl and filled it to the rim with the fruity cereal box that sat on the kitchen island. My uncle turned at the sudden commotion of tumbling sugar pebbles and held up his index finger to me as if to say, "just a minute," even though I hadn't actually said anything to him.

I took my bowl over to the table and dug in, pulling my uncle's newspaper over to me in the process. Some fatal animal attack was plastered all over the front page, but I didn't get a chance to read the details.

"Did you sleep well?" he asked, hanging up the phone.

"Yeah," I nodded through a mouth full. That is, unless we're counting the four times I got up to investigate the balcony, or the nightmare that nearly drowned me in a cold sweat. I was keeping that part to myself, though. "I slept great."

"I'm glad to hear it." He took a slow sip of his coffee, probably ransacking his brain for something else to talk to me about. "Are you looking forward to your first day of school?"

I gave him the kind of look that said, "Are you from this planet?" and he smiled knowingly, confirming that he was.

"You'll be fine. I'm sure."

"Well that makes one of us," I grumbled, unable to hide my doubt. Things tended to go very wrong for me. My expectations were pretty low.

"Are you sure you wouldn't prefer to make it a long week-end—start fresh on Monday?"

"I'm sure," I answered easily. "I'm behind enough as it is. I just want to get it over with." Besides, if it turned out to be half as bad as I'd been imagining it, I would have the entire week-end to plot my escape.

"I thought maybe you'd like to take a little time to settle in…or perhaps to talk."

My face contorted. *Talk about what?* My extended stay at the hospital? My father's murder? I had no desire to talk about either of those things. And definitely not with him. "That's okay. I'm all set," I said with extra fake-sauce on the smile.

"Very well. As you wish."

"So, what's the story with that animal attack?" I asked as he unfurled his newspaper. "Does that happen a lot around here?"

"It happens enough. Plenty of bears and wolves and such."

My mind snagged on the '*and such*' part.

"That reminds me," he said as he reached in his pocket and pulled out a sleek black device. "I picked this up for you last week. I hope it's the right kind," he said, pushing it across the table to me.

"You bought me a cell phone?" I fought back a smile. "You didn't have to do that."

"It's for me as much as it is for you."

"Oh, okay." I thought about that for a second. "Is this like a trust thing?" I wasn't sure if I should be offended or not.

"It's a safety thing."

"In case I go *schizo* again?"

His eyes bulged. "Jemma—"

"I'm kidding," I cut in as I examined the phone with my free hand and scooped another spoonful of cereal with the other. "It's great, Uncle Karl. Thank you."

"You're quite welcome. Well, now that we have that settled," he said, pulling back the cuff of his shirt to check the time, "you should probably get your things together. You don't want to be late on your first day."

"Uh-huh," I nodded, still distracted with my new phone.

"I'll have the town car ready for you outside."

The *chauffeured* town car? *Ugh.* That should go over well.

"Thanks, Uncle Karl, but that's really not necessary. I don't think showing up with a chauffeur is the best way to make a good first impression." When he didn't answer, I enlightened him. "Because they'd think I was a pretentious snob."

"Don't be ridiculous. It's *Weston Academy*," he informed, straightening out his newspaper. "They're all pretentious snobs."

2. WELCOME TO THE GAUNTLET

Weston Academy sat on the hilly outskirts of town amidst a thick tangle of evergreens, resembling more of a cathedral church than it did an actual school building. A narrow, cobblestone road trimmed with pine trees on either side stretched all the way up to the three-story, ash colored building where we took our place behind a row of similar-looking town cars, carrying similar-looking students, all wearing similar-looking uniforms. I couldn't help but feel like I was in a funeral procession for the young and the prosperous.

A thicket of dark clouds burrowed in above us as we reached the front entrance of the school, their presence casting an eerie shadow over the goliath building and blocking out any semblance of sunlight.

"Looks like it's going to rain," I noted, staring out the back window. That, or this was the world's worst omen.

"It usually does," said Henry, the driver who I'd gotten better acquainted with on the way over here. "You'll get used to it."

That seemed doubtful. I hadn't even been here one full day and already I missed the sun.

The knots in my stomach tightened as I continued surveying

the landscape. Everything was so grand, so intimidating. I wasn't sure I could ever fit in here. It took every ounce of courage I had not to lock the doors and barricade myself in the back of the car like a petulant child.

Luckily, Henry was none the wiser when he came around back and opened my door for me.

"Thanks," I said as I climbed out on shaky legs.

"My pleasure, Miss Blackburn." His gently graying hair seemed to fade into the mounting fog.

"Just Jemma," I reminded.

"Of course." He nodded. "Good luck on your first day."

I thanked him again as I straightened out my uniform (a black pleated skirt, crisp white blouse, and a way-too-preppy blazer) and began my walk across the metaphorical plank, butterflies swarming deep inside my belly. I swung my near-empty schoolbag over my shoulder and pushed through the large double doors just as the bell rang out around me.

The bustling crowd thinned quickly as I made my way down the corridor (through the chaos of slamming lockers, excited chatter, and rushing students) and had all but disappeared by the time I reached the main office and coaxed myself through the door. A round-faced woman in her late forties with short, cinnamon red hair peered up at me from behind the reception desk, her glasses resting on the tip of her short button nose.

"Hi," I said as I approached her desk, my schoolbag dangling from my fingertips. "I'm not sure where I'm supposed to be."

"Name, please?"

"Jemma Blackburn. It's my first day."

"Oh yes, of course," she grinned. "Karl's niece. Welcome to Weston Academy, my dear. We're glad to have you with us."

"Thanks. I'm glad to be here," I lied, figuring that's probably what she wanted to hear.

"I'm Candice Tate, but you can call me Ms. Tate, or

Candice, or Ms. T, however you please," she sang, waving her hand in the air flippantly. "You know, I'm sure I had your transfer papers here just a second ago," she said as she rummaged around her desk, lifting and dropping stacks of papers and manila folders.

I waited patiently, racking my fingers on the counter as I pretended to take an interest in the academia posters and public service announcements plastered all over the eggshell walls.

The office door swung open behind me as a tall blond girl walked in with a stack of books cradled in her arm. Her long flowing hair was parted neatly to the side and looked as though it were lifted straight out of a magazine.

"Morning, Candice. I need a late slip for homeroom. Mr. Bradley won't let me in."

"Good grief, Miss Valentine. The day you actually manage to get to class on time is the day I hang up my gloves in here for good," she said in a semi-scolding manner as she rolled her chair back and disappeared below the desk.

The girl turned to me with a mocking face, mouthing the words, "what gloves?"

I couldn't help but laugh.

"You're new," she smiled. It wasn't a question. "I'm Taylor."

"Jemma," I smiled back.

"Cute kicks."

I glanced down and noticed our matching pairs of black Converse sneakers. "Yours are pretty cute too."

"Great minds," she winked.

"Here she is," cooed Ms. Tate, pulling out a pink pad from the bottom drawer and jotting something down onto it.

"What's your schedule look like?"

"I'm not sure yet," I said and looked over at Candice.

She handed Taylor a sheet of paper, presumably my class schedule. "Perhaps you might escort Miss Blackburn to her class?" She eyed Taylor as she wrote. "It is her first day after all."

"Love to," she smiled and turned back to me, her round, denim blue eyes sparkling. "The longer this takes, the better. I seriously can't stand history."

"Me neither," I laughed, and left out the part about how I hated the other subjects too.

All eyes were on Taylor and me when we walked into our first-period World History class together. A short, balding man with a white chemise and beige pants stood at the front of the class, an open book in one hand and a piece of white chalk in the other. He didn't look pleased by the intrusion.

"Miss Valentine," he said, in a low staccato voice. "Nice of you to join us. I see you brought a friend with you."

I felt my cheeks warm as the entire class gawked at me.

"She's a new student, Mr. Bradley," explained Taylor. "I was in the office helping her get registered. That's why I'm late," she added and then turned around with a smirk before taking my transfer papers and handing them over to him.

"Of course it is, Miss Valentine," he said sardonically as he took the papers from her and looked them over. "Very well. Find yourself a seat, Miss Blackburn. Any seat will do."

Taylor waved me off before heading to the back of the class. She took her seat next to a pretty brunette with thin almond-shaped eyes the color of an aquamarine stone who would have been even prettier if it wasn't for that nasty scowl she was wearing; which, consequently, seemed to be directed right at me.

There was a definite hate-on-first-sight feel to it.

I scanned the class and found an empty seat on the other side of the room, mid-row against the wall. I moved to it quickly, avoiding all eye contact as I shuffled down the aisle.

"You can share Mr. Pratt's textbook until you get your own," said Mr. Bradley, motioning to the brown-eyed blond guy with the buzz-cut and industrial piercing sitting beside me. He scooted his desk over to mine and pushed his book closer.

"Thanks."

"No *problemo*," he said, grinning. "I'm Ben."

"Jemma."

"Make sure to see me after school," continued Mr. Bradley, at the front of the class. "We can go through what you need to get caught up with the rest of the class."

I nodded that I would and breathed a sigh of relief when he went on with his lesson, taking all the attention and curious eyes back with him.

All except one, I noted.

He was sitting clear across the classroom, leaning back in his chair with his legs stretched out in front of him like he owned the room, and was staring at me through the most striking blue eyes I had ever seen before—piercing cobalt eyes, like the clearest part of the deepest ocean.

An ocean I had the sudden urge to swim in.

While everyone else was busy taking notes, he sat in front of a closed notebook with his pencil tucked behind his ear and absolutely no intention of connecting the two. His jet-black hair was thick and long. Just long enough to be slicked back neatly, and dark enough that it made his eyes soar out at me from across the room.

I noticed he averted his eyes as soon as I met his stare but they quickly returned, and then it was my turn to look away. Only I didn't. I *couldn't*. My eyes locked in on him, and in an instant, I was embroiled in an entanglement of feelings I was neither ready for, nor prepared to understand.

There was something about him—about those eyes and that stare—something familiar. It was the kind of something that made everyone else in the room fade away into the dark recess of my mind until there was no one left but me and him. He was the picture. Everything else around him was just white noise.

His eyebrows pulled together as he stared back at me from across the room, and then, seemingly despite himself, his expression softened and gave way to a faint smile that caused two of the most beautiful dimples I'd ever seen ignite on either side of his marvelously sculpted face.

Before I had a chance to react, to catch my breath again, the moment was abruptly detonated when the scowling brunette from earlier leaned forward in her chair and pushed herself into my frame of vision, breaking the connection and sending a tirade of daggers over to me by way of her glowering eyes.

It was a warning shot if I ever did hear one, and I knew enough to leave well enough alone.

I turned away quickly and spent the rest of the class with my eyes glued to the lackluster Mr. Bradley whose monotone voice almost put me to sleep on three different occasions, and even though I felt eyes burning into the back of my head, I never once turned back to see whose eyes they might have been.

3. FRIENDS AND RIVALS

The sound of the lunch bell blaring was music to my overstimulated ears. I felt an unmistakable pang of relief when I saw Taylor Valentine walk up to my locker and invite me to eat lunch with her and her friends in the cafeteria. She had already become my favorite person at Weston, and it wasn't just because we both hated history, or liked the same shoes, or because she'd gone above and beyond all day—showing me to my classes, introducing me around, and breaking the ice when it got awkward. We just sort of *clicked*.

That wasn't to say that the other students weren't nice. Most of them were, but in a different way. There was a forced politeness about them, a shallow curiosity about the new girl, whereas with Taylor it felt genuine. She was herself right off the bat and had this kind of, "this is me, take it or leave it," attitude, which pulled me in like a moth to a flame.

The cafeteria was overcrowded and buzzing with heavy chatter and laughter when we walked in together. Thankfully, most of the student body was too engulfed in their own conversations and lunches to bother noticing me as we headed over to the lunch line, though the sentiment was short lived.

"Yes she's new! Get over it and quit staring at her," snapped Taylor at some kid standing in front of us.

He turned around before I could see his face.

"You'd think they never saw a new student before," she said rolling her eyes, and then leaned back against the aluminum divider railing. "So? How do you like Weston so far?" she asked, and then went on in a more hostile tone, glaring at another group behind us. "Aside from all the creepers, that is."

"It's fine—It's great," I said shrugging my shoulders.

"Yeah, I know, it blows," she laughed. "The uniforms suck, the teachers suck, and our hockey team has the worst record in the entire league. If it wasn't for all the cute, rich boys, I would have transferred out of here a long time ago."

At least she had her priorities straight.

"Any of them yours?" I asked.

"Cute rich boys?" she raised her eyebrow. "Nah, not me. I'm far too capricious to be tied down to just one boy."

I couldn't tell if she was being sarcastic or not.

"Meanwhile, I totally saw you and Trace Macarthur making googly-eyes in history," she accused, her lips curving upwards.

Trace Macarthur. His name swept through me like a summer breeze.

"Nikki looked like she was about to go postal on you," she continued, laughing.

"Nikki?" I asked her casually, though I had a fairly good idea who she was referring to.

"Nikki Parker, his *girlfriend.*" She tweaked her eyebrows.

Of course she's his girlfriend. That's just the kind of luck I have.

"They've been on and off since sophomore year," she continued, blindly re-applying her cherry lip gloss. "Apparently they're off-again, but I'm sure it'll only be a matter of time before she gets him back. I mean, it's not like she has any competition. She's freaking Nikki Parker and no one around here is crazy enough to go after anything that *belongs* to Nikki Parker. You know what I mean?"

"I'm getting it." *Loud and clear.*

"Anyway, there's plenty of other hotties just ripe for the picking. And with all that," she said, gesturing over to me brazenly, "you'll have no trouble picking them right off the top branch, one by one."

I couldn't help but laugh with her, though her not-so-subtle heads up was certainly not lost on me.

After paying for our food, we walked back into the main cafeteria where I followed her to a secluded table of her friends; several of whom I recognized from previous classes together, though none more so than Trace Macarthur and Nikki Parker, who stood out at the forefront of the pack.

Nikki was leaning into him, her arm wrapped around his neck as though draping him in a luxurious sheath that was herself. They appeared to be looking down at something—the table, the tray of food, nothing in particular—laughing privately as we walked up to them. If I didn't know better, I might have thought they were still a couple. A happy one.

Trace straightened out as soon as he saw me, like my presence affected his person, while Nikki's stare went arctic. If looks could kill, I would have already been a pile of grizzled bone dust.

"This is Jemma," announced Taylor. "You know Benjamin from History," she said pointing to the blond guy who shared his book with me this morning, and then to the couple. "That's Nikki and Trace. And this is Hannah Richardson, Carly Owens, and Morgan Sinclair," she concluded, gesturing to the slender blond, baby-faced brunette, and the voluptuous red-head, respectively.

"Hi," I said, giving an awkward wave.

"Hello," said Morgan, coolly. Her sea-green eyes shifting up from her Blackberry as she summed me up.

"Nice to meet you," added Hannah, her smile was lopsided though welcoming. "I think we're in chemistry together?"

"Yeah, I think so," I agreed and sat down in between her and Taylor, with Nikki directly across from me. Morgan, Carly and Ben were on her free side.

"So how's Weston treating you?" asked Ben. "Is it everything the brochure claimed it would be?"

"Yeah," I laughed. "It's fine—good. Everyone's been really nice." *Well, almost everyone.*

"Fine? Nice?" he chortled and took a sip of his soda. "Come on, you can do better than that. Grade our paper."

"It's school," I shrugged impassively. "What else is there to say?" I'd moved around enough to know that most schools fell into the "once you've seen one, you've seen them all" category, but I didn't bother saying that part out loud. Maybe he thought his school was more special than the rest of them. I didn't want to burst his bubble.

"Did you go to a private school before, too?" asked Carly. She was twirling a strand of her shoulder-length, chestnut hair around her finger, seemingly disinterested, though her wide set caramel eyes pinned me with their full attention.

"No, it was public."

"I went to a public school once." She said it proudly as though it were this incredibly rare event only few experienced.

"You did not," barked Morgan.

"Yes I did," she insisted. "For like half a semester, before we moved here."

Silence.

Awkward.

"That's nice," I said, unsure of how else to respond.

Nikki stared at me across the way before bringing her elbows onto the table and interlocking her fingers under her chin, feigning interest. "So where do you hail from, *Jenna*?"

"It's Jemma."

"*Jem-ma*," she repeated, exaggerating my name as she said it. It sounded like she was making fun of me, and worse, she was using my own name to do it.

I decided to give her the benefit of the doubt and pretend not to notice. "I was living in Cape Coral before. It's a little coastal town in southwest Florida," I answered nervously, then glanced around the crowd, trying my best to appear friendly—nonthreatening. I wasn't particularly in the market for any more trouble than I already had.

"Why'd you leave?" she asked. Her eyes were a sharp, almost translucent aqua that kind of gave me the creeps. "I mean, you must have been all the rage back in Cape Whatever."

"Nikki," said Trace, reproaching her. It was the first time I heard his voice—smooth and deep, with sort of an edge to it.

"What?" she asked innocently. "I just want to know what brought her to Hollow. I'm sure we all do, right guys?" Her phony tone was starting to grate on my nerves.

My eyes darted around the table. I noticed Hannah stopped making eye contact with me altogether now. It looked as though she was unsure whether or not she could still be friendly with me now that Nikki was clearly on the offense.

"My father passed away. I'm living with my uncle now."

"Don't you have a mother?"

"Jesus, Nikki!" This time it was Taylor who called her out. "Give the girl a break."

"It's okay," I assured her and then turned back to Nikki. "She left when I was two. I don't have any memories of her. I also lost my grandparents before I was born. Both sets. Would you like me to go into my extended family as well?"

"*Saw-ree*," she snipped as though *I* were the one being the rude bitch all day. "Didn't realize you were so touchy."

"Sorry about your dad," said Carly, tucking a piece of her hair behind her ear and looking wholly uncomfortable.

"Thanks."

She wasn't the only one who was uncomfortable. I felt Nikki's negative energy all around me, billowing in the air and suffocating me with its weight. She wanted me gone—away from her, or him, or maybe all of them—and at this point, I wanted nothing more than to oblige. I just hoped my legs could get me out of there fast enough.

"Well it was really nice meeting all of you," I lied, rising from the table with my tray in hand.

"You too," said Carly, half smiling.

"You haven't even touched your food," noted Taylor, the disappointment heavy in her eyes.

"I guess I wasn't that hungry," I told her and left out the part about how Nikki had all but pulverized my appetite. "I'm late anyway. I have to meet up with some teachers to see if I have any chance of getting caught up on all the work I missed."

"Well hang on a sec, I'll come with."

"You don't have to do that, honest. Enjoy your lunch. I'll catch up with you later," I said and jetted off before she had another chance to protest.

By the time the final bell rolled around, I was completely drained, dejected, and ready to get as far away from Weston Academy as I possibly could. The day had been long, the stares exasperating, and the catch-up homework demoralizing.

I crouched down at my locker, struggling to get all my new textbooks into my schoolbag, and realized fairly quickly that it wasn't going to happen. No matter which way I worked them (vertical, sideways, horizontally stacked), the result was always the same: too many books, not enough space.

Eff my life.

I gave up and straightened out, holding the remaining textbooks cradled in my arms just in time to be on the receiving end of a bony shoulder-slam. I stammered back into my locker hard, dropping all my books in the process.

"Watch where you're going," snapped Nikki, her indignant eyes *daring* me to say something back to her. "What a total spaz!" I heard her say to Morgan as they walked away laughing.

If I had any doubt before, it was definitely official *now*: Nikki Parker hated me. I leaned my head back against my locker door and sighed. This was going to be a long semester.

Seconds later, Trace appeared in front of me. His arresting blue eyes spiking my temperature as he bent down before me and picked up my books from the ground, one by one, and then handed them back to me without saying a word.

He didn't even wait for a *thank you.*

I stood there, dumfounded, with my mouth slightly unhinged, staring at his delicious broad-shouldered back as he disappeared down the hall.

"I love watching him walk away, too," said Taylor who was now standing beside me. I hadn't even noticed her walk up.

I blushed. "I wasn't looking at his, I mean, I wasn't—"

"Sure," she laughed. "You don't have to defend yourself around me, babe. Nikki, on the other hand..."

"Yeah. I got it," I said knowingly, pulling my blazer out from the locker and then securing it with the assigned lock.

"So anyway," she said, flipping her hair to the side as we started down the hall together, "I'm glad I caught you before you left. We're going to *All Saints* tonight, and you're coming with. I'm not taking no for an answer."

"All Saints?"

"It's this bar everyone goes to. There's tons of hot guys. And pool tables, and dancing, and decent food if you get there early enough. But did I mention the hot guys?"

"I don't have a fake ID." Besides, I had vampire-research to do and phone calls to make. Mainly to my inaccessible sister who was refusing to cooperate with me.

"You don't need one," she said, waving her hand dismissively. "They'll just stamp your hand at the door."

"Oh." I scrambled for another excuse. "I don't know," I told her, shaking my head. "I'm pretty tired, and I still have a lot to unpack." *A whole, entire duffle bag.*

Her face scrunched up. "You can *so* do that tomorrow. I'll even help you if you want. C'mon, you have to come. Everyone's going to be there. And you know what they say, when in Rome...something or another."

I couldn't help but laugh at her misguided logic.

"Pleeeease!"

She was making it extremely hard to say no. And did I really want to shut down the first friend I made here?

"Sure, why not," I finally said. I had the sneaking suspicion she wasn't going to let up until I agreed anyway.

She squealed and interlocked her arm through mine. "We're going to have so much fun!" she announced, hopping around like an excited bunny. "I can't wait to show you off."

My own smile, however, was short-lived. "So when you say everyone goes there, does that mean like...*everyone?*"

She hesitated before answering. "Okay, alright, so *yes*, Nikki and Trace will be there. But maybe that's a good thing."

I raised a brow at her. "How do you figure?"

"Think about it. Maybe this is your chance to show her that you're not interested in Trace. We can totally scout out some new hotties and flirt with them until she doesn't even remember you exist. It's the perfect opportunity for you to get off her radar."

I wasn't sure if it was the lack of sleep or hysteria from my first day of school, but Taylor's plan was actually making sense. Maybe this was my chance to show her I wasn't a threat to her and that I had no interest in her boyfriend—well, none that I intended on following through with.

Maybe this was exactly what I needed to get her off my back and salvage whatever chance I had left for a nice, peaceful, below-the-radar existence at Weston Academy.

Maybe.

4. DANGEROUS CONNECTIONS

There was a lineup halfway around the building by the time I got to the bar. No velvet ropes or carpet runners, just a messy line of bodies and a single bouncer at the front door, presiding over who gets in and who doesn't. The building itself looked like it might have been a warehouse at one time but had that chic refurbished feel to it along with a lit-up retro sign plastered across the front that boldly exclaimed this was *ALL SAINTS*, lest anyone forgot it.

I sent Taylor a text message as soon as I got there. She was outside within two minutes, waving me to the front of the line.

"She's with me," she said, smiling at the tall, bald-headed bouncer who was manning the front door.

He was dressed in fitted black clothes and stood dauntingly with his mammoth arms crossed over his chest. "I.D."

I wasn't sure which cards he wanted so I pulled them all out and presented them to him like some sort of weird offering.

He made a face at me and took one from the bunch. "Hand."

"Hand?"

"Give me your hand so I can stamp it," he repeated,

obviously annoyed with my rookie mistakes.

"Right. Sorry."

His hand descended over mine. When he pulled it back, the word *underage* was stamped across it in thick black ink, branding me with my own little mark of ageist shame.

Inside, the bar looked just the way you'd imagine a warehouse-turned-bar-and-grill might look. A large, open space painted in sinister colors with dark furniture, stained-glass windows, and floor-to-ceiling brick walls that lent themselves to the whole industrial motif. There was plenty of tables and seating all around the place, pool tables in the back corner, and a space in the middle where people were dancing.

As vast as it was, the place was packed, humming with the reverberations of live music, prattle, and the distinct sound of clinking glasses.

Taylor grabbed my hand as soon as the crowd thickened around us and began towing me through the swaying bodies. We found a spot next to a banquet table filled with purses and personal effects, and of course, that one lone girl—the designated purse sitter. Satisfied with our location, we hung back as people trafficked around us, back and forth to the main bar stationed just a few feet away from us.

Taylor searched the dance floor for the friends she ditched when she came outside to meet me, though she didn't seem particularly concerned with finding them and was mostly just dancing to the music. I stood idly by her, leaning against a brick pillar watching all the faces in the crowd.

It was a sea of uninspiring mugs. Some I recognized from school, but the majority were just nameless strangers I never met before with too-happy faces, glazed eyes, and gyrating body parts that only every so often matched the beat of the music. The whole thing was hard to watch, in an annoying sort of way, because they were all having a great time. And I wasn't. I was just some outsider looking in on them.

"There they are," said Taylor, ticking her head into some non-specific part of the crowd. "I'll be right back, I'm just going to let them know where we are."

I nodded, and went back to contemplating my overall discomfort level when I thought I heard my name being called. It was too loud to really hear anything, and yet, it was as though the entire room had quieted down just long enough for me to hear it. A few moments later, I heard it again:

Jemma.

I looked up into the crowd searching for the source; a waving hand, a raised eyebrow, something—anything that would indicate somebody was trying to get my attention, but I saw nothing like that.

And then everything came to a dead-stop.

Without any warning, the entire room appeared to freeze right before my eyes. The music cut, the light-changes stilled, and every single person in the room stood motionless, completely immobilized as though I were looking at a life-size picture of them and not actually standing in the room myself.

The only sound I could hear was my own ragged breath as my eyes circled the room, frantically trying to blink everybody back to life. It was as though *time* were actually standing still for them—for everyone. Except me.

"What the—"

My voice was swallowed up by the sudden reanimation of the room. Everything around me resumed without missing a beat.

So, apparently, I was losing it, and for real this time because I was certain that what I had just witnessed wasn't actually possible, and therefore could not have happened, which would mean I just hallucinated the whole thing. Perhaps my little stint in the hospital left me with some long-term side effects...like actual insanity.

Or maybe I was just suffering from some kind of sleep deprivation by-product from the night terrors, mixed in with first-day-of-school hysteria. It definitely sounded like a recipe for disaster. I decided I was holding fast to the latter and thinking maybe it was time for me to get home and get some rest.

"Looks like you picked your first apple," said Taylor, appearing beside me again. "And what a yummy pick he is."

I looked back at her, blank-faced.

"Directly across from us." She spoke into my ear without gesturing, her voice soft as honey.

I redirected my eyes and saw him right away, leaning back against the wall just across the way from us. He was impossible to miss in his head-to-toe black clothing and contrasting short blond hair. There was something about the way he was watching me—unapologetically, without reserve—that threatened my inhibitions and jumbled my ailing thoughts.

"Who is that?" I asked her, never taking my eyes off of him.

"That's Dominic Huntington," she said, leaning into me.

"He's so—"

"Smoking hot?" she cut in, beaming. "I know."

"Does he go to Weston?"

"I wish," she laughed. "He just moved back a couple weeks ago. Heard he got kicked out of college," she said and then tweaked her eyebrows mischievously.

Her implications were understood—bad boy.

He looked about nineteen, maybe twenty. I was about to ask her why he got expelled when the girls suddenly appeared beside us, jumping up and down around Taylor as some bubblegum pop song came on that apparently meant something to the lot of them. It only took a few seconds before they were all latched onto her and collectively floating back to the dance floor together.

My eyes went back to Dominic who ticked his head sideways, signaling for me to go over to him. My heart raced at the idea of meeting him, of losing myself in the distraction. Maybe that was exactly what I needed to get my mind off my troubles.

"You don't want to do that," said Trace, crossing his arms over his chest as he rested his back against the column beside me. I hadn't even seen him walk up.

I turned to him slowly, remarking his arm lightly touching my own. "Why not?" I asked, dragging my fixated eyes away from the pulsating link.

"He's trouble."

"He's *trouble*? What does that even mean?" I scoffed, my eyes darting back to Dominic who was gliding through the crowd.

"It means, he's trouble," he repeated impatiently as he locked eyes on mine, making no attempts to explain his warning. "If you were smart, you'd stay away from him."

"*Excuse* me?"

He didn't answer.

I had no clue what this was about. Was he alluding to the supposed school troubles? Or maybe the age difference? Or was it something entirely different and potentially serious?

Whatever it was, he wasn't saying, and I was fast not giving a crap because the truth was, I didn't *want* to stay away from Dominic. Not in the slightest.

My eyes raced back into the crowd in search of him, but he had already disappeared from the herd, leaving me with this unsettling feeling that I had just missed out on something big, something exciting, though I wasn't even sure what that was.

"You shouldn't even be here," Trace went on, barely audible.

My eyes slipped back to him easily.

"And why is that?" I asked, narrowing my eyes as he stared

back at me intensely. It was as though he were trying to read me—to speak to me with his eyes. I didn't understand them but I desperately wanted to know their language.

Before I had a chance to get an answer, I felt someone pluck me off the pillar and shove me backwards, landing me hard on my backside a couple of feet away.

"What do you think you're doing?" screeched Nikki, advancing on me as though she were going to kick me while I was already down. "Stay the hell away from my boyfriend!"

"I didn't do anything!" I defended, scooting backwards on the floor, scrambling to widen the gap between us.

"Did you really think you could just show up here out of nowhere and move in on him?"

"What?" I shook my head, completely stunned. This chick was certifiable. "That's not what I'm doing, I—"

"Listen to me carefully because I'm only going to tell you this once, Jem-*ma*." She reached over and grabbed someone's drink off a nearby table. "Trace is *mine*, you got that? Stay the hell away from him or I swear to the heavens, I will make you regret the day you were born!" She turned the glass over and dumped its contents in my lap.

"Shit, Nikki, what the hell are you doing?" yelled Trace as he pulled her back by her waist, drawing her away from me.

Her boreal, aquamarine eyes diced into me before she turned her insanity on him, the vein in her forehead bulging as she assaulted him with a barrage of words I couldn't make out.

Holy freaking shit.

The stench of alcohol stung my nostrils as I sat there with my mouth agape, soaked and shell-shocked. Taylor ran to my side and helped me up to my feet while the other girls lingered around in the vicinity looking wholly uncomfortable.

"Oh my God," cried Taylor, grabbing napkins off the table and handing them to me. "I can't believe she just did that."

Neither could I. I couldn't even speak.

I took the napkins from her and started patting down my wet pants, trying to dry them as fast as I could as though that might erase what just happened. It *so* wasn't working.

"Let me get some more napkins," she said and ran off in the direction of the bar.

Still in a state of shock, I looked up around the room and realized how many people had just witnessed that. Half the room was still staring at me with wide eyes, o-shaped mouths, and slanted smiles. It was amusing to them. *I* was amusing. Suddenly, I knew the pain of a carnival side-show freak.

My eyes welled up with humiliation, though the idea of crying in front of all these people after what just happened was just too much to take. I threw the wet napkins on the table and bolted for the nearest exit.

The wind bit at my cheeks as I pushed through the doors and started down the empty street, leaving All Saints and all of its *unsaintliness* behind me. The crowd from earlier had all but disappeared with most of the people already inside now, probably having just bore witness to one of the worst nights of my life.

A tear trickled down my cheek as I walked, and then a dozen more fell, and before I knew it my cheeks were soaked with the hurt and frustration of a really bad couple of months. The loss of my father, the hospital, the move, the new school—the new *enemies*—it was just too much to take. Something had to give.

I wiped my cheeks with the back of my hand and crossed over to the other side of the street, desperate to find a main road or boulevard I could call a taxi from. I needed to put this place in a rear-view mirror. Shivering in my damp clothes, I searched up and down the stretch of barren avenue for some kind of street sign or saving grace amidst all the darkened buildings and empty warehouses. And then I saw *him* again.

A faceless figure in the distance, leaning against a building with his foot kicked up behind him—nearly unrecognizable if it weren't for that familiar blond hair and that familiar lean. There was something about him that called to me, something enigmatic, and tempting.

Before I could work out the equation, my legs were moving themselves toward him, walking with what seemed like a mind of their own. My stride weary but considerable, each small step taking me closer and closer to him. I could feel my heart begin to pound as Trace's warnings replayed in my head, and yet, I knew none of that mattered now. I had already made the decision to ignore all of it the moment I saw him standing there, without even making the choice.

What did Trace know anyway? Anyone who could date someone as vile as Nikki Parker—stupid, psycho Nikki Parker— obviously didn't have the sense of a green apple.

Screw him. *No.* Screw them both.

I walked on undeterred and resolved to meet him when a metallic blue Mustang with two white racer stripes pulled up next to me, decelerating to a steady crawl as it kept pace beside me. The sound of its powerful engine growling obscenely as it sliced through the stillness of the night.

I stepped away cautiously as the tinted passenger-side window rolled down. His oceanic eyes were the first thing I saw.

5. THE GOOD SON

"Need a ride?" asked Trace, leaning over the passenger seat.

That was the last thing I needed from him. "No thanks," I said icily and continued walking.

He released some pressure from the brake and let the car move forward slowly, following alongside me.

"Come on, it's late," he pushed. "It's not safe out here."

"I'll take my chances."

"Please, just get in the car."

"I said no thanks!" My voice was laced with the frosty bite of a cold December night.

"Fine. Suit yourself."

I walked another dozen or so steps and waited for him to drive away, but he didn't. When I looked back at him, he was still leaning over the driver seat with his forearm relaxed over the steering wheel—watching me.

"What are you doing?"

"Driving."

"I mean, why are you still here?"

His dimples pinched, though he wasn't smiling. "I'm seeing you home."

"Okay...could you not?" I said, making a face. "I'd prefer not to get run over by your girlfriend when she happens to drive by and see us." And with my luck, no doubt that scene will be unfolding any minute now.

"So get in the car then," he said impatiently, looking at his watch. "She'll be walking out of there any second."

I looked over my shoulder for any signs of Nikki, and then back up to the building where Dominic had been, but he was already gone. Again. The street suddenly seemed a little colder, and darker, without his luminary presence.

Apparently, I was out of options.

"Alright, fine," I said as I stopped and faced him. His foot came down on the break in perfect sync. "But only because I have no idea where I am, and the thought of running into Nikki again makes me want to dry heave."

He nodded, his dimples pressing in as he leaned over to the passenger side and pushed open the door for me. I looked over my shoulder one more time to make sure there weren't any witnesses, and against my better judgment, climbed in.

"See, that wasn't so hard was it?"

I rolled my eyes as I grabbed the seat-belt and tried to pull it across my chest. The stupid thing locked with every tug.

"Let me get it for you," he offered.

"I can do it," I insisted, pulling at it harder.

He waited a whole three seconds before pulling my hand away. I flopped back into my seat as he slinked his right arm around my headrest and then leaned in over me with his other arm. The smell of his cologne—a sort of spicy, woodsy scent that made my stomach pinch—wrapped itself around me like an intoxicating embrace.

I pushed back in my seat, fighting off the sudden urge to do something embarrassing, like lean in and inhale him.

Or worse.

He pulled the seat-belt out easily, and brought it down across my body in one sweeping motion. "There," he said upon hearing the *click.*

"I didn't need your help."

"Clearly." His face was still lingering just inches from mine, his gripping blue eyes grazing over the edges of my face—studying me.

"You probably have it rigged so you can like, put the moves on girls or something," I said, feeling flustered.

"Don't flatter yourself."

"As if I even—" My retort quickly died in the back of my throat as his eyes dropped down to my lips and settled there, making my breath hitch.

Damn, he was close.

Too. Close.

Apparently he thought so too, evidenced by his clenched jaw and hasty return to his own seat. Within seconds, he threw the car in gear and then barreled off down the darkened street, the engine droning as he pushed down harder on the pedal.

I turned my attention outside the passenger window and worked on steadying my breathing.

"Sorry about what happened back there," he said after a few beats of silence. His eyes mapped my body as though he were looking for battle wounds. "Are you okay?"

"Oh yeah, totally. Best night of my life."

I had somehow managed to acquire an enemy *and* an assault, all in one night—without even trying. One could only imagine what I might accomplish if I put forth the effort.

On the plus side, at least she only assaulted me with liquids and not her fist.

"I tried to tell you," he said complacently.

"Tell me what?" I glared at him. "That your crazy girlfriend was about to attack me out of nowhere for standing beside you?

No. I don't think you tried to tell me *that*."

"I guess not." It sounded as though he were smiling through the words, but I kept my eyes fixed outside my window out of fear that I might sock him if I caught him laughing.

"Anyway, she's my *ex*," he corrected. His tone was so low I wasn't even sure he believed it himself. "We're not together."

"Did anyone tell *her* that?"

He didn't look at me when he answered, "It's complicated."

"I'm sure it is," I grumbled, patting down my whiskey stained jeans, certain that I didn't want to be a part of it.

There was no doubt in my mind that there was unfinished business between the two of them. That much I knew. What I didn't know was how I factored into it. Why had she felt so threatened by something as trivial as a conversation between two people? Surely I wasn't the first girl to speak to her boyfriend (ex or otherwise). Did she go around assaulting everyone who spoke to him or was that just for my benefit?

Something felt off about it.

And now he was driving me home, which probably wasn't going to go over very well with the ice queen. I could only imagine the various shades of horror on Nikki's face if she got wind of this. He was taking a major risk by giving me a ride. I couldn't help but wonder—

"Why are you doing this?"

"Doing what?" he asked without looking.

"After everything that happened tonight, why did you follow me out and offer to drive me home?"

He hesitated to answer as though he were asking himself the same exact question. "I'm not going to just let you walk home by yourself," he said finally, almost annoyed by it. "You don't even know where you are."

Fair enough. "But what's it to you?"

"It's nothing *to* me," he said icily, his eyes flicking to me as he shifted gears. "I just like having a clear conscience."

"And driving me home accomplishes that for you?"

"Yeah. Something like that."

"Because...?" I said, pushing for him to elaborate.

He sighed loudly as though I were grating on his patience. "Because you'd get home in one piece and after what happened tonight, I figure it's the least I could do, okay?"

Oh, swell. He felt guilty for what happened at the bar with Nikki so this was his redemption ride (or pity ride), though I refused to entertain the latter thought.

I turned back to the window. "Whatever helps you sleep."

After a few minutes of silence, he turned to me with a strange look in his eyes and said, "You really should try to stay away from all that."

"All of what? All Saints?"

"All Saints, Nikki and them. All of it."

Ugh. Not this again. "What is it with you? First you tell me to stay away from that guy and then refuse to give me a reason, and now I'm supposed to stay away from the entire bar *and* everyone in it? Why don't you just write me a freaking list and tell me exactly who I *can* be friends with? I'm sure it'll be much easier to keep up with."

He scoffed. "Believe me, I would have already done it if I thought for one second you'd actually follow it," he said and then glanced over at me, looking me up and down. "But something tells me you don't follow orders very well."

I felt the heated prickle of anger lick my skin, though I refused to give him the satisfaction of responding.

On second thought, "Get bent."

I went to bed aggravated that night, and didn't wake up any better the next morning.

The sun was working overtime trying to break through the

morning clouds, giving every indication that today would be a buoyant day, only I didn't feel that way inside. Inside I felt tired and achy, like my bones had been grating themselves against the rigid concrete all night as I slept unsuspectingly.

My uncle was already seated in his usual spot at the kitchen table, busying himself with the week-end paper by the time I strolled downstairs. He looked up to examine me as I plopped down into the chair across from him.

"You look terrible," he noted, pulling off his reading glasses. His dark hair glossed back in the dull morning light.

"Thanks," I said and buried my head deep into the crux of my arm. Alas, my ego was still safe from over-inflation. "I think I'm fighting off a bug or something."

"Oh?" he asked thoughtfully. "What sort of bug?"

"I don't know, just regular flu stuff, I guess. Tired and achy. It sort of comes and goes."

"Interesting."

I lifted my eyes to meet his. "I guess?"

"So, what do you have planned today?" He picked up the newspaper from the table and smoothed it out.

"Nothing really."

He blinked disapprovingly.

"I don't know anyone around here," I defended.

"What about your school friends from last night?"

I groaned and buried my head again. "I don't want to talk about it."

"Very well." He continued after a drawn-out pause, "I've been thinking that it might be a good idea for you to get a part-time job while you're here."

My head whipped up at the sudden barrage of odious words. "A job?" I squeaked, my eyes wide with repulsion.

"Yes," he said, stifling a laugh. "You could use the job experience, I'm sure, and it's a good way to meet new people and develop some financial independence. What do you say?"

What I wanted to say was *hell no*! But what choice did I really have here? I was living under his roof, on his dime. If he wanted me to get a job, I was pretty much getting a job.

"Sure, I guess so," I said with all the excitement of a deflated balloon.

"Wonderful." He was obviously unfazed by my own lack of enthusiasm. "I already have something lined up for you—a favor from a friend."

"A favor?" Was I so unmarketable that he actually had to call in a favor for me? The thought depressed me.

"Here's the address," he said as he scribbled something down on a piece of paper and handed it over to me. "Henry will drive you over as soon as you're ready."

Right. Because getting chauffeured to work falls right in with that *real-world* job experience he was talking about.

Not even an hour later, I was in the back of the town car, pulling up to a vaguely familiar building. Trails of fog slithered into the car as I rolled down my window to get a better look. *All Saints*, the scene of last night's crime. It looked different in the light of day sans the flashing lights and people and the intimidating bouncer out front.

"This has to be a mistake," I said, bemused.

"I don't believe so," replied Henry. "Mr. Blackburn gave me the instructions himself," he said and then exited the vehicle. He walked around the perimeter of the car and opened my door for me. "It's a fine place to work, Miss Blackburn. I'm sure you'll be well taken care of here."

"Jemma," I corrected absentmindedly as I stepped out of the car, staring up at the structure. "Thanks, Henry." It came out like an afterthought.

"Have a good day, Miss...Jemma."

"You too, Henry."

I walked in through the unmanned doors, cautious and weary of my surroundings as though I were expecting Nikki to pop out of the shadows and assault me with a coke bottle. I immediately noted how strange the place looked in the light of day. It was freakishly dim inside, hollow of any natural light or souls that might help fill up the palpable void. The place just felt eerie to me, and way too quiet.

I was about to make a run for it when I noticed some movement over at the bar from my peripheral. Someone was there, bent down, stacking glasses and setting up.

"Excuse me," I called out as I walked over.

"Yeah," he answered casually before straightening out. "What can I do—"

My mouth unhinged.

Trace Macarthur stared back at me, wearing an employee T-shirt and an unmistakable look of shock on his face. One that happened to match my own perfectly.

6. UNINVITED

"What are you doing here?" I asked, confused.

Please don't say you work here. PLEASE don't say you work here. PLEASE DON'T—

"I work here," he said, wiping his hands on the white dish rag as he came around the bar. "My dad owns the place."

"Your dad *owns* All Saints?

"Yeah."

"As in, your dad's the boss here?"

"Yeah." He furrowed his brow. "What are *you* doing here?"

There was only one reasonable thing to do here: lie and get the heck out. And I was just about to do that when—

"Jemma Blackburn, I presume?"

I looked up to see a tall, polished man approaching us. He had a full head of dark wavy hair and a pair of striking blue eyes that I immediately recognized. Trace's father, no doubt.

"I've been expecting you." His smile had the same appealing shape as Trace's, minus the dimples. "Your uncle Karl's told me so much about you," he informed and then held out his hand to me. "Peter Macarthur. It's nice to finally meet you."

I forced a smile. "Nice to meet you, too."

"What is this?" asked Trace, ticking his chin at me as he crossed his arms over his husky chest.

Peter smiled at him as he placed his hand on the back of his neck—a gesture that Trace promptly shook off. There was definitely something clambering beneath the surface between the two of them. Some sort of unspoken divide. "Meet our new waitress."

I shifted uncomfortably.

Trace's eyes bounced from his father to me and then back again. "You hired *her*?" he asked incredulously.

"I did."

"She's not working here." A darkness washed through Trace's eyes—something akin to fury.

Okay. Wow. That was rude.

"Well, no, not yet," smiled Peter, unfazed. "But she will be." Before Trace could object again, Peter quickly cut him off. "This isn't your call to make, son. It's done."

An angry choke rumbled from Trace's throat as he chucked the rag onto the table and took off in the other direction, leaving a gust of wind in his absence, and a bitter taste in my mouth.

What a freaking jerk! I thought as I fought off the urge to run after him and slap him in the back of the head.

"Please excuse him," said Peter apologetically. "It's been a difficult year for him. For all of us. We haven't been the same since the death of his sister."

His sister? "Oh. I didn't realize..." A familiar, leaden feeling washed over me, diluting the anger I had built up for him into a pool of nothingness. "I'm so sorry for your loss."

"Thank you." He nodded curtly. "Well," he forced a smile, eager to redirect the conversation back to business. "This is All Saints: good food, good drinks, good music."

"So I've heard."

He wore his pride like a fine Italian suit. "Have you been

here before?"

"Just once. Last night actually."

"And did you enjoy yourself?"

"Oh my God, yeah. I had an *amazing* time," I said, lying through my teeth. I mean, really? What else was I supposed to say? He was my future boss, and my uncle's friend. And besides, I had grown far too good at telling people what they wanted to hear to stop now.

After a few more minutes of idle chit-chat, Mr. Macarthur took me on a tour of the place, starting with the *employees only* area on the other side of the black double doors.

"This is where all the magic happens," he smiled, extending his arm around the pristine silver kitchen. "That's Sawyer, our head cook," he continued, motioning to a man with brown eyes and matching long brown hair secured under a bandana.

I waved awkwardly at him. He smiled back.

"The kitchen's open from Noon until nine p.m., seven days a week," he explained. "After that, we only serve sides."

He followed up with a brief introduction into the comings and goings of the kitchen, like how to give an order in and where to pick it up once it was ready.

The tour continued down the adjoining corridor.

"This is the main office," he said pointing into the medium-sized room that had a messy desk, filing cabinets and scattered chairs. He introduced me to the red-haired, petite-in-stature Manager, April Demarco, who made a brief appearance before hurrying off to tend to some disaster in the lady's washroom.

The last stop in the tour was the employee bathroom and the storeroom. I poked my head into the latter.

"It's your standard stock room. It's got all your napkins, salt, ketchup, and all that other good stuff. Just remember, whatever leaves this room has to be marked here," he said and pointed to an inventory clipboard hanging on the wall. "They'll explain all of this once your official training starts."

I nodded and smiled even though I wasn't entirely sure I was looking forward to all these mundane tasks. I'd been on kitchen duty back at the hospital and nearly expired from utter boredom.

Thirty minutes later, the tour was over and we were back in the main hall, which had now filled up with the lunch crowd. We sat down at one of the corner tables to fill out some forms.

"You can start right away," he offered. "A few hours after school, and alternating week-ends."

"That works for me."

"It's pretty quiet during the week days so you're more than welcome to do your school work here in between service. You certainly wouldn't be the only one."

That was a definite plus. I smiled.

"Looks like we're all set," he said rising from the table and holding out his hand again. "It was wonderful meeting you, my dear. I'm glad to have you with us."

"Thanks for the opportunity. I'll try not to disappoint."

"We're all rooting for your success here," he nodded. "Just leave the forms in the office when you're done, and you can start training with the assistant manager right away."

I nodded once and returned to my form before my head popped up with an afterthought. "Mr. Macarthur," I called after him as he walked away. "Who would the assistant manager be?"

He flashed an even row of gleaming teeth. "That would be my son, Trace, of course."

Of course. Who else would it be?

After dropping off the forms in the main office, I asked Sawyer, the twenty-something year old cook, where I could find the assistant manager and was kindly directed to the ladies washroom, where Trace was moonlighting as a plumber.

I walked in and found him spread out across the floor with his head under the sink and a wrench in his hand. It was a pretty good look for him, though I tried not to notice. He looked up at me and ticked his head once, as if to say, 'what do you want?' without actually saying the words.

"Look, if you don't want me here, just say the word and I'm gone," I said, crossing my arms. "I don't want this stupid job anyway. I'm just trying to keep my uncle off my back."

He sat up, wiping the thin veil of sweat from his forehead. I noticed his arms and neck had the same coating and was generously highlighting his muscles. Nice, defined muscles—

"It doesn't matter," he said, rising to his feet. He pulled up the edge of his shirt and wiped his face with it, revealing all sorts of hidden things like a ripped stomach and this v-shaped groove that started around his hips and moved all the way down, disappearing just below the hem of his jeans. "If it's not this, they'll just find something else."

It was all I could do to keep from reaching forward and tracing the deep ridges with my finger. I barely managed to tear my eyes away in time when his shirt came back down.

Now, what the heck was he going on about?

I looked at him with a blank stare.

"You can stay," he said finally, over-pronouncing each word as though I were hard of hearing.

It wasn't my ears I was having a hard time controlling.

"Right," I nodded rapidly, trying to erase the image of his bare abdomen from my mind like a real-life Etch A Sketch. "So, I guess I'll need some training?"

"And a uniform," he said, as he picked up his toolkit from the counter and walked out past me.

And maybe a bucket of ice.

I followed him back to the main office where he opened up a storage cabinet and then turned to me. His eyes surfed over my body. I crossed my arms over my chest, all modest, even though I had just assaulted him with my own eyes not two minutes ago.

"You look like a small," he said and then handed me a white T-shirt with the black logo on the upper-right corner.

I unfolded it and spread it across my chest, sizing it up. "It looks tight."

"It's supposed to be," he said wryly. "You can change in here. I'll wait for you outside."

As soon as the door shut, I pulled off my top and exchanged it for the too-small T-shirt. It *really* was tight, and didn't leave much of anything to the imagination. I wondered if I should insist on a medium as I eyed myself in the wall mirror.

I decided that I would, and pulled open the office door. Trace was leaning against the wall with his arms crossed, and his head cocked to the side.

His arresting blues lit up as he looked me over.

"I think I need a medium."

He slanted a smile. "I think so too."

I had anticipated spending the rest of the afternoon following Trace around and getting familiarized with my job, so I was rather surprised when he unexpectedly passed me off to Zane Brenner, the head bartender, instead. Apparently, Trace was less than willing to spend any time with me, training me or otherwise. In fact, he seemed to have a real aversion to it.

Luckily, Zane didn't seem to mind me, or the added task of having to show me the ins and outs while serving his own customers at the bar. Between his wry humor, and friendly nature, he was easily the most-likeable employee at All Saints.

The evening wore on quickly, and before I knew it, the place was filled up with customers, giving me ample opportunity to put my training into practice. I even got a chance to wait on a few tables by myself when the manager, April, and another waitress got held up with a shipment crisis at the back.

The job was easy enough and I got the hang of it fairly quickly, though my feet were singing an entirely different tune halfway through my shift.

Taylor and Ben showed up just after dinner as a fresh crowd of younger people began to arrive. It was Saturday night and All Saints appeared to be everyone's favorite place. Or maybe it was the only place in town, I still wasn't sure yet.

"So, do I get a 'friends and family' discount now that you're working here?" asked Taylor, fully amused with the revelation. She hopped up one of the bar stools.

"I don't need a discount," said Ben, without looking up from the menu he was browsing. "But I'll pay you an asinine amount of money if you can get us some beer in here."

"Let me think about that…um, no."

"Why not?" he laughed.

"I don't know, maybe because of this little thing called the law? Ever heard of it?" Apparently, I was really big on it.

"My father's a prosecutor," he said with a bratty smile. "Not only have I heard of it, I drink to it whenever I can."

I couldn't help but laugh at his backwards logic.

"Just ignore him," instructed Taylor. "He's inept."

"That's not what you were saying on the way over here," replied Ben as he rose from his seat and tweaked his eyebrows.

"You. Freaking. Wish."

Grinning wildly, he moved to poke her side, but she slapped his hand away before he could make contact. He didn't seem the least bit phased by it as he walked off to the restrooms, and even though she rolled her eyes at him, I definitely noticed her stare lingering a good while longer than it needed to.

When she turned back to me, her expression was weighty. "I was worried about you yesterday."

"Sorry about taking off like that," I said, tucking a loose curl behind my ear. "I had to get out of there."

"I don't blame you. Nikki was completely out of her mind. I still can't believe she did that," she said shaking her head. "It's too bad you didn't stick around though, Trace cut her down in front of everyone."

"He did?" My interest suddenly peeked.

"She deserved it too," she said unsympathetically. "I mean, who does that anyway?"

Psycho ex-girlfriends who forget to take their meds, that's who. "I just want to forget the whole thing." It happened, it sucked, and I've accepted it. I had no intention of reliving the events over and over again. I had enough real-life nightmares to contend with.

"I hear you, babe. So how's it been working with Trace anyway?" she asked. "Is it majorly awkward?"

"Not really," I shrugged. "I've hardly seen him tonight." That part was the truth. He had made himself incredibly scarce all evening, and I had the nagging suspicion I was the reason.

She laughed. "No kidding. That's what you get when daddy owns—" She stopped abruptly, softening her tone. "Hey, you!"

I turned around to see Trace walking up behind us.

"What's up, Taylor," he greeted her casually. "Where's Ben?"

"Manning his porcelain throne."

"Thanks for the visual," he said looking around, distracted. "What are you up to?" he asked her almost mechanically.

"Just talking shop with my girl," she smiled big at me and then back at him. "You came up a few times."

"Yeah?"

My eyes bulged. What the heck was she doing? The last thing I wanted was him thinking I cared enough to discuss him.

"Only good things," she added.

I turned away in an effort to hide my enflamed cheeks.

He shifted uncomfortably. "You should get back to work."

"You got it." I circled on the heel of my foot and was just about to high-tale it out of there when Taylor called out.

"Wait! I haven't ordered yet."

Oops. I turned back around embarrassed, pulling my pen and pad out from my black apron as I returned to the table.

"What can I get you?"

She grinned from ear to ear. She was seriously enjoying this way too much. "Let's go with Buffalo wings, and a pitcher of Root beer."

"Spicy or regular?"

"Spicy, of course." She gave me an open-mouth wink.

"Be right back with that."

"You're doing great," she cheered as I headed into the kitchen to place her order. "Keep up the great work!"

No doubt all of B.C. heard her on that last one.

By Eleven o'clock, the place was packed wall-to-wall. It looked like every soul in town had managed to find their way over to All Saints, and shockingly, no one seemed to mind the crammed personal quarters or the lack of quality oxygen. The live band was just starting in on their first set when the main lights dimmed down, and the dance floor filled up to capacity. Everyone appeared to have caught that Saturday night fever, and even I couldn't help but smile from the sidelines as I looked on with my serving tray tucked under my arm.

To my dismay, Nikki eventually showed up and spent the better part of the night determined to get back into Trace's good grace. I watched as she followed him around the place like a lost dog, hovering all around, nuzzling up to him, and batting her apologetic lashes that looked even faker than the synthetic hair extensions she had on her head.

As sickening as it was to watch, at least she was focused on him tonight, and not me.

Aside from that minor gripe, the job was going relatively well, and certainly a whole lot better than I had anticipated it would go. I even got into a decent rhythm of service and actually found myself enjoying the distraction, and even though I messed up an order that night, according to April, it was far better than the four she messed up on her first night.

I was on my way back to the kitchen to pick up that very order when a hefty man in his late twenties grabbed my arm and stopped me as I tried to pass by his table.

"Look it, Jasper, fresh meat." He was speaking to his lanky friend, but he kept his beady eyes on me.

"Can I get you something?" I said, roughly shaking my arm free from his sweaty palm.

"Sure. What are you selling?"

"Excuse me?" Everything about him screamed *creep*, from his crooked teeth to the dark glint in his narrow little eyes.

He laughed hoarsely. "You heard me, sugar, let's hear your specials," he said and stroked the top of my thigh.

I may have been new here, but I knew enough to know his hand didn't belong there.

"Get your hands off me," I said in my most aggressive voice, then took a nervous step back. I imagined I wasn't all that intimating to a man his size, but I would sure as hell still try.

"Take it easy," he said as he grabbed out at me again.

I smacked his hand away and swallowed hard as he rose up from his seat, belligerent in every way.

Crap. This was bad, really bad.

My mind raced as I anticipated what he was going to do next or how I was going to handle it, though none of it had a chance to come to fruition.

A dark figure appeared out of nowhere, abruptly pushing the aggressive man back into his chair. He was leaning down over him now with his face square up against his, and was saying something, though only loud enough for the two of them to hear.

I contemplated getting in closer to get a better view, or possibly running for cover somewhere out the back, but by the time the thought finished, the mystery man was already upright and taking a step back into view, adjusting the flaps of his black overcoat as though nothing had happened.

It was Dominic Huntington—unmistakably.

7. UP CLOSE AND IMPERSONAL

I watched in wonder as the formerly aggressive patron stood up from his chair and lowered his eyes to the ground, repentant, as though he had just sinned in the house of God and was begging for forgiveness. I couldn't believe what I was seeing, at what I had just witnessed. The stark change. It was surreal.

"I'm very s-sorry, miss. Please excuse my rude behavior this evening," he said, and then turned to Dominic for some sort of sign of approval.

Dominic gave him a slight nod and with that the man rushed out of the bar without even bothering to wait for his friend—Jasper, the lanky one—who got up shortly after, confusion draped over his face, and followed him out of the bar.

It was the darnedest thing.

I veered my eyes back to Dominic to thank him for stepping in like he had, though I immediately lost my train of thought as I took in the man before me.

He was even more stunning up close, dangerously so, with dark, penetrating eyes and smooth skin that seemed to glow in the otherwise unforgiving light. He smiled back at me; a sexy, crooked grin that conspired with the soft curves of his face to make every attribute a contrasting feat—alluring and menacing all at the same time.

"I-I—" I had apparently lost my ability to speak.

His lips curved up, pleased by this reaction. "I don't believe I've had the pleasure," he said and sat down at the now-empty table, his silky voice reverberating through my skin like the pulsation of my favorite song.

"Dominic Huntington." He held out his hand modestly, coaxing me to come closer to him.

I practically jumped at the chance to touch him. "Jemma Blackburn," I said, overly perky.

His hand was silky and soft, cool to the touch. I felt a strange sensation as soon as my hand touched his, almost as though my skin were numbing. I shook my head as if to chase away a spell and then remembered my manners.

"Thank you for that," I said motioning towards the exit. "I don't know what you told him, but—"

"It was nothing."

"No, really, thank you," I repeated meaningfully.

He gave a lazy smile. "It was my pleasure, Jemma."

My name had never sounded so appealing.

"To be truthful," he baited, his voice lower now. "I'm happy to have finally had the opportunity to meet you."

My eyebrows pulled together.

"You must know you're not particularly an easy person to get next to, Jemma."

I laughed outright. The idea that somebody that looked like him was having a hard time approaching somebody like me was downright amusing. "Yeah. *Right.*"

His eyes flared briefly, drawing attention to the thin scar that sliced through his right eyebrow. I wanted to reach out and touch it, comb my finger over it, know its story and burn it into my mind. But I fought back the urge.

"So, um, what can I get for you tonight?" I asked him, reigning myself in. "Anything you want. It's on me."

"Anything?" he challenged. His eyes darkened into the kind of stare I was always taught to be weary of. It made my legs want to run away and buckle all at the same time.

"Yes." The word sailed out way too easily. "No! I mean, yes, anything on the menu," I corrected, sans grace. "But if you want something from the bar, I'll have to call another waitress."

His lips pressed into a line. "That won't be necessary."

"Something to eat then?"

His mouth turned up again. "Later. Perhaps." His expression was amused, almost mocking.

Did I miss something? Was he laughing at me?

"Your bodyguard is watching," he said unexpectedly.

"My what?" I asked, and then followed his gaze over my right shoulder to Trace who was standing across the way from us looking wholly irritated. And of course, the never-too-far-away Nikki was right there beside him, watching him as he watched me. The whole thing made me want to hurl.

I turned back to Dominic who cocked his head, unaffected.

"If you're not going to order anything, I have to get back to work," I explained. "I don't want to get fired." And by the look on Trace's face, it was a definite possibility.

"I understand," he said, rising from his seat.

"Are you sure you don't want anything?"

He didn't answer, though he took a step towards me, and then sort of around me, brushing against me as he moved. I shadowed his turn as if I had been tied to him with a string.

"What time do you finish?" he asked, leaning into me in a way that jumbled all the thoughts in my mind.

"I-I—" I couldn't speak. I cleared my throat and tried again. "Two thirty. I finish at two thirty."

He offered another smile—a delicious crooked grin that

made the water pool inside my mouth—and then he walked away, leaving me standing in a puddle of my own drool.

It took me a minute to get myself together, to reel in the racing thoughts…like why he wanted to know what time I finished work at? Was he planning on meeting me? Was I supposed to wait for him? I had no idea what just happened, but I could feel my heart racing at the thought of seeing him again.

And why wouldn't I? He was gorgeous, and he definitely seemed interested in me. And after everything that happened to me this year, it felt like a damn good idea.

I took a deep breath and collected myself as best as I could. When I circled back around, I found Trace and Nikki—and now Taylor and the rest of the gang—staring at me in a sea of unhinged mouths and wide eyes.

There was no way I was walking into that pack of wolves. I turned on the balls of my feet and headed straight for the back-house where I would spend the rest of my shift counting down the minutes until closing time.

I managed to avoid Nikki, Trace, and even Taylor for most of the night, keeping them at bay by way of my increasingly convenient job. Everything was going well on that front until closing time reared its highly anticipated head. As soon as the place began to dwindle in bodies (and hiding places), it was clear my run had come to an end, no more so than when I came face to face with Taylor in the kitchen.

"Ok. Spill it," she said, cornering me at the sink as I brought in another load of dishes.

"I don't know what you mean."

"Dominic Huntington!" she shrieked, alerting everyone within a ten mile radius about our impending conversation.

I spun around to quiet her, pumping the air brakes. "There's nothing to say," I said, dousing her fire. "He helped me with a rude customer and I thanked him." I grabbed my bin and returned to the main hall, Taylor right in tow.

"Come on, what else?" she probed. "I know there's more."

"There isn't," I insisted as I picked up a litter of glasses from one of the party tables, though the truth was, I wasn't even sure of it myself. I definitely felt something. And he definitely asked about my work schedule, but what that meant—if anything—I had no idea.

"God, the way he was looking at you," she said as she leaned back against the table, her eyes sailing through the cosmos. "I wish you could have seen it from where I was standing."

"What do you mean?" I immediately halted, eating up every word by the spoonful. "How did it look?"

"Like he wanted to devour you," she giggled.

"Shut up," I said, though my face was screaming, tell me everything!

"So I guess you don't want to know about how he was eying you all night, or how he practically flew across the room when that guy grabbed you," she teased.

I rolled my eyes. I could hardly believe it.

"I swear," she said, noting my expression and then continued through laughter. "I've never seen anyone so eager to start a fight with a stranger!"

I laughed too but sobered quickly, remembering my fear. "Thank God he was here. That creep scared the hell out of me."

"Taylor," called Trace just then. "We're locking up."

"How are you getting home?" she asked me. "I'm riding with Hannah but I'm sure she wouldn't mind giving you a lift."

I shook my head. "It's cool. I have a ride." I think.

"Kay," she smiled big. "I'm out then. Call me tomorrow!"

I nodded that I would and watched her strut away, passing Trace on her way to the door. I moved to another table and had time to clear a few more glasses before he was by my side.

"Think you'll be back tomorrow?" he asked as he placed the chairs on top of the table I'd just wiped down.

"Bright and early…unless my uncle has a change of heart and decides that mooching off of him is a totally acceptable alternative."

"Great," he said, sort of under his breath.

"Is it?" I had to ask. He'd made it obvious that he didn't want me taking this job, or hanging around here for that matter. "I mean, is this going to be a problem?"

Maybe putting him on the spot like this might actually yield a straight response.

"You can probably head out now," he said without looking up as he lifted two more chairs. "They got this," he gestured to April, Zane, and Sawyer across the way. The other waitress, Paula Dawson, was already packing up her things.

"Are you sure? I don't mind."

He shook his head and picked up the bucket of dishes from my table. "It's covered."

I shrugged, "Nice." No sense in arguing there, I thought, and started moving before he changed his mind.

I felt him latch onto my arm as I passed him. My skin hummed in response to his touch.

"Do you have a ride?" he asked, holding me to his side as he peered down at me through his stirring eyes; deep soulful eyes that made me long to know the history behind them.

I nodded, struggling not to lose myself in the pools of liquid blue. "It's covered."

"Okay."

He didn't let go of my arm, or my gaze.

"Is that it?" I raised my eyebrow at him. I wasn't sure how much longer I could stand the heat without liquefying.

He looked down at his own hand still wrapped around my arm and quickly released it. "Yeah. That's it."

I felt a surge of vindication the moment I left All Saints and realized that Nikki was still outside with Morgan, probably waiting on Trace to finish work. This could have easily turned into a really ugly situation had I walked out of here with him. It was fast becoming obvious that the more I avoided Trace, the better off I would be. I just wasn't sure avoiding him was something I could actually do, or something I wanted to do, and I wasn't sure which one scared me more.

I searched the street for Dominic, not entirely sure if we had actually agreed to meet or not, and secretly found myself wishing that I would see him again tonight. That I could escape my own prison and delay the inevitable grief I always felt when I was by myself at night—even if only for a little while.

Sadly, it seemed my hopes had been dashed upon completing a thorough scan of the area and coming up empty of any impeccably handsome, luminary blonds. I pulled out my cell phone and crossed the street, heading down towards the main Boulevard as I keyed in the cab company's telephone number.

"Who are you calling?" asked a honeyed voice from above.

My heart jumped out of its cage as I looked up and saw Dominic walking on the cement ledge beside me. His black overcoat catching air as he walked the plank with feline precision.

My hand rushed up to tame my heart. "You scared me."

"Sorry," he said unceremoniously and leapt off the ledge. "You're early."

I flooded my sight with his profile as he continued to pace beside me. "They let me off early," I said, glancing over his shoulder at the unfamiliar grounds. "What were you doing?" I asked, straining my neck as I tried to see what was up there.

"It's a park," he leaned in and whispered, answering my query as though he could hear my thought. "I was taking a walk."

"At night?"

"Yes, at night. Don't you like the night, angel?"

"No, not really."

"Why not?"

One too many close encounters with the undead. Of course, there was no way I was opening that first-class ticket back to the nut house. "It's a long story."

"I have plenty of time," he said without looking.

"Well, maybe not a long story. More like an embarrassing one," I said and waived my hand dismissively, trying to seem detached and casual about it. "I'm just a little scared of the dark, that's all."

"Is that so?" He seemed amused by this.

"Yes, and I don't find it very funny. I mean, it's not like I sleep with a night light or anything, but I definitely try to avoid it if I can." And for the record, I wasn't opposed to a night light.

"Tell me, Jemma, what is it that you think is hiding out there in the dark?"

This was getting a little too close for comfort. "I don't know, the usual I guess…goblins and monsters and ghosts, oh my." I tried to laugh it out but it came out fake and pitchy.

His lips threatened a smile. "Well, you don't have to worry about that tonight. Not while you're with me."

"Is that right?" I said with a hint of ridicule. "Are you going to protect me from all the big, bad monsters?"

"Angel, I am the big, bad monster," he said grimly as he crossed his hands behind his back.

A cold chill traveled down my spine as I waited for a smirk or a wink, but neither came. I swallowed hard, suddenly very aware of how little I actually knew about Dominic. This man, as attractive as he was, could very well be some deranged serial killer just out on a midnight stroll, preying on his next victim. I mean, who takes walks at night anyway?

I could feel my heart pounding in my chest as the scenarios played out in my mind.

"Relax, Jemma," he said with a playful smirk on his lips. "You're making it far too easy for me."

Exhale.

I laughed nervously, trying to play it cool while feeling ten shades of ridiculous for allowing him to get the better of my fears so easily. Though who could blame me? After everything I've seen, there was just no telling anymore.

I forced a smile.

"Tell me about yourself, Jemma."

I shrugged. "There's not much to tell."

"Where are you from?"

"Lots of places," I said and then shrugged. "The last place I lived was Florida, but we moved around a lot before then so I guess I'm kind of a nomad. Wait—how did you know I wasn't from around here?" Hollow Hills wasn't a metropolis by any stretch of the imagination, but it wasn't that small.

"Word travels quick in these parts."

"Duly noted."

"Do you have any siblings?" he asked. If he was curious, his tone wasn't letting on.

"A sister."

"Older."

I nodded. "How did you know?"

He glanced down at me. "Lucky guess. And your parents?"

I could feel that suppressed sorrow thickening in the back of my throat as the memories flooded in.

"I don't remember my mother, but I was very close with my father before he died. It was unexpected—a heart attack," I lied, fumbling with my fingers as I relived the guilt of having to leave him behind. It was easier to tell that lie than the one listed on his autopsy report. "It's just me and my uncle now."

"I'm sorry to hear that," he said, bowing his head slightly.

"Thank you."

He crossed his hands behind his back again. "Your sister, she doesn't live with you and your uncle?"

I shook my head. "She moves around a lot."

"What sort of places?"

"All over really. Chicago, Portland, Toronto...she's even been to Dublin and she's not even Twenty-one yet."

"Impressive."

"I think so," I smiled proudly. I couldn't wait to graduate high school and hightail it into the world just like she did.

"Does she visit you often?"

"She tries to, but you know how it is."

"When was the last time you saw her?"

I thought back to the last time I'd seen my sister, when she came to visit me in the hospital and told me that I needed to start playing nice with the doctors if I ever wanted to get out of that place. Of course, I would be keeping that part to myself, for obvious reasons.

"It's been...a while. A few months."

He nodded without looking. "So that leaves you on your own."

"Yup. Just me and my uncle." Ugh, I said that part already.

"How about a boyfriend?" he asked.

I smiled, seeing an opening. "Thanks, but you're not my type," I quipped. I couldn't help myself.

Dead air. He wasn't even smiling.

My cheeks ignited. "I'm just kidding," I rushed to clarify. "It was a joke. I knew you weren't offering to be my boyfriend."

It seemed like a funny thing to say in the moment. He probably thinks I'm some high school twit now. Damn me for not having a better mouth filter on this thing.

"I knew it was a joke," he smiled lazily, and then craned his head in closer to me. "I'm just not sure I liked the part about not being your type."

"Oh." *Ohhhh.* Butterflies began waltzing in my belly as my lips moved again. "Well, that part was a joke, too." The words just sort of spilled out on their own.

He was grinning now, and God was he hot.

"W-what about you?" I stammered, feeling flustered and desperate to redirect the conversation. "What's your story? Do you have family here? A girlfriend?" I applauded myself silently for slipping that in.

"No family here. No girlfriend."

"Well, don't tell me everything all at once," I scoffed at his nondisclosure.

He smiled crookedly. "If you want to know something, you'll have to be more specific in your asking."

"Okay." I already had a question ready. "How old are you?"

His lips curled up. "Probably too old for you."

Probably. At least it wasn't a definitely.

"Your answers are still pretty vague," I noted.

"I never said they wouldn't be."

His eyes gleamed under the moonlight like two magnificent onyx stones—dark, mysterious, and beckoning. I looked away, afraid of what they were stirring up inside me.

"Everything okay?" he asked coyly. He seemed to be laughing at me again, like he knew he was having an effect on me.

"Yeah. Totally." I looked back up at my surroundings, suddenly noticing we had already reached the main boulevard and were about to take a turn down an unfamiliar road, though in all fairness, most of the roads were still unfamiliar to me at this point. "Are we walking all the way?"

"Yes. Is that a problem?" he asked, evaluating my face.

Well, let's see. Essentially, the Blackburn estate sat atop the undulating rises of Hollow Hills, overlooking much of the town below. It was a long way up the winding roads, especially on foot, and left us exposed and at the mercy of a wide number of possibilities (*night-walking* possibilities) so yes, it was definitely a problem for me.

Of course, I couldn't very well say that to him.

"Well, there's a lot of road to cover. I'm afraid my feet won't make it," I said instead, sounding incredibly lazy.

"It isn't very far if we take that short cut," he pointed. "We can go straight up through the wooded park and then cut through the cemetery—avoid all those side roads."

"The *cemetery*?" I stopped walking.

"Yes," he said, stopping with me. "Are you uncomfortable with cemeteries?"

"Um, yeah. Only entirely."

He examined me for a moment, grinning. "Because of the goblins and monsters, I presume?"

"No, actually. Because of the dead people."

He laughed as though I'd said something funny. "A taxi it is then," he winked and pulled out a cell phone from the inside of his overcoat pocket.

And not a moment too soon.

The taxi cab met us on desolate Edgewood Drive less than ten minutes later. Dominic insisted that he escort me all the way home even though he said he lived on the other side of town. I didn't argue and did my best to hide my delight as I climbed into the back of the cab with him. When we arrived at my place, Dominic told the taxi driver to keep the meter running as he slid out of the car, gallantly carrying my purse before extending his hand out to me.

I didn't hesitate to take it.

"Thanks again for your help tonight," I said as he walked me up to the iron gates where I entered the four-digit security code my uncle had drilled into memory. "I'm glad you were there." I shuddered to think what might have happened if he hadn't been at All Saints tonight to intervene on my behalf.

"As am I," he smiled and then crossed his hands behind his back. "I hope to be of assistance to you again. Soon."

I smiled at the undercurrent of his words. "I'm working again tomorrow night. There's a good chance I may need some assistance then if you're interested."

He dipped his head once. "I'll see what I can do."

There was a moment of awkwardness just then as I stood there idle, unsure of what the proper goodbye was supposed to be. A hand shake? A hug? My heart sped up. A kiss?

I chased the thought away and ended the night with a simple smile before starting up the driveway.

"Jemma," he called a few seconds later, his voice filling me up with exhilaration and causing my pulse to race.

He glided towards me, stopping just inches from where I stood. The anticipation overwhelming every cell in my body as I stood there, a captive member of his dark, entangling eyes.

This was it. He was going to make a move, I thought, bracing myself for a kiss.

"You forgot your purse," he said as he pushed something into the pit of my stomach.

"Huh?" I looked down and saw my handbag. "Oh...thanks?"

"You bet," he said, his lips coiled upwards as he took a step back, watching me with those eyes—those alluring, menacing eyes—and then stalked back to the taxicab.

I lingered for a moment, bemused at the exchange, before turning to make my trek up the long stretch of driveway, the sound of heavy steel gates creaking shut behind me.

That was...weird.

8. HEAD CASE

I woke up early the next morning, an elusive dream callously prying my eyes open before their time. I struggled to catch my breath as clips from my dream danced around my mind disjointedly, piecing themselves together in fragments.

The red sky was the first thing I remembered. It was the color of fresh blood. It poured over the desolate street, dusting everything in its crimson hue as I stood there alone, watching the strange firmament in wonder.

A figure moved in beside me. The midnight-black hair, the humming sensation in my body; I knew it was Trace even before I saw him. He took my hand in his and began talking to me—warning me about something that I inherently knew was important, but I couldn't hear any of the words. There was no sound, only visions of his lips moving. His dimples pressing in and out, reaffirming the severity of what he was trying to tell me.

"I can't hear what you're saying," I told him, shaking my head in frustration.

A raven called out above us, its voice echoing through the red sky before diving down to the ground beside me.

"Did you see that?" I asked Trace, but he was still staring forward, talking to himself in voiceless riddles.

I turned back to the raven and found Dominic kneeling in its place, the strange sky illuminating him in all the right ways. He stood up and reached out to me, stroking my cheek with the back of his fingers, letting me know everything was going to be okay. But I knew it was a lie.

"What's going on?" I asked them, but neither one responded. "Why won't anyone answer me?"

"This isn't their time," said a small voice from behind.

I turned towards the sound; a little boy no more than eight or nine years old. His dark hair was parted to the side and his eyes were a familiar shade of gray.

"What does that mean?" I asked him, bending down to meet him where he stood. "Whose time is it?"

"Yours."

I shook my head. "I don't understand."

"You have to go back. You have to make it right."

"Go back where? Make *what* right?"

"The answers you seek are right where you are," he said, pointing over my shoulder into the horizon.

I followed his gaze down the abandoned street. "There's nothing out there," I said, looking back at him. But he was already gone.

I turned back to Trace, easy as breathing. Something was always drawing me to him, magnetizing me in his direction. I wanted to be by his side, even in this strange dreamlike world. He reached for my hand and pulled me in close to him. His eyes speaking to me, telling me secrets I needed to know, but I couldn't make out any of their words.

"I don't like it here," I told him. "I want to go home."

He leaned in to me; to kiss me; to comfort me; and in my dream, I waited with bated breath for it, though our lips never connected. Instead, his lips moved down the base of my neck, caressing me as they glided over my hungry skin.

I closed my eyes briefly, indulging in his touch. When I opened them again, short blond curls filled my vision.

"This will only hurt a lifetime," said *Dominic* and then bit down into my neck.

The pain shot through my veins, burning as his poison consumed my being. He drank from me in unquenchable heaps, over and over again under the strange red sky.

And I didn't move a muscle to stop him.

It took me several minutes to steady my heart rate and breathe once I realized it was only a dream. I climbed out of my bed and tiptoed my way down the hall, intent on getting myself a glass of water to wash away the dream's bitter taste from my mouth. I wasn't sure what time my uncle woke up at so I was extra quiet when I rounded the corner, careful not to accidentally wake him up. I relaxed as soon as I neared his office and heard his voice looming from within.

"Jemma is my responsibility. I will decide what's best for her," I heard him say, and froze mid-step.

After a brief pause, he continued. "The problem is she's neither here nor there at this point. She's somewhere in-between. We can't go on this way, it's much too dangerous. The spell has to be broken."

The spell? What spell? What's too dangerous? What in the HELL was he talking about?

I took a step forward, greedily wanting a better view, better sound. The wood creaked monstrously beneath my foot giving me away as though the house were alive and openly playing for the other team.

Crap.

"Listen, we'll discuss this later at the meeting. Something's come up."

I took a series of track-star steps backwards towards my room and nearly somersaulted myself back into bed, pulling the covers up over my head and squeezing my eyes shut.

Several moments later, I heard my door creak open, followed by a brief stint of silence, before it closed shut again.

There wasn't a doubt in my mind that my uncle had just come in to see if I was awake. If I had been the culprit eavesdropping on his conversation, probably wondering how much I had heard.

Well, I heard enough.

I had no idea what was going on around here, or what he was talking about, but I had every intention of finding out.

I had an impossible time staying focused throughout the day. My mind, despite what I had been commanding it, continued to busy itself with the conversation I overheard this morning in my uncle's office as I struggled to make sense out of the senseless. After countless scenarios, I finally decided that I must have misunderstood what he had said, or the context in which it was said, because no other explanation seemed plausible. Jumping to paranoid conclusions was a surefire way to get myself admitted back to the hospital.

My thoughts quickly drifted to better things, like the conversation I had with Dominic last night—and our walk, and the shade of his eyes, and the fullness of his lips, and every other little distracting thing about him. It was absolute mutiny of the mind, and Dominic Huntington was reigning supremely.

After the big lunch rush, I was relieved to finally be able to sit down at the bar with Paula, the other full-time waitress, and have our first break of the day. We sat side by side eating our lunch as Zane balanced his cash register on the other side of the counter. Paula, with her dark blond hair pulled back into a proper and unassuming ponytail, seemed to be completely distracted with her own thoughts.

I needed to get us out of our heads.

"Is it always busy like this?" I asked no one in particular.

Paula shook her head.

"Not usually on Sundays." Zane responded without looking.

"Could have used an extra waiter," I noted quietly. "Where's Trace today anyway?" I asked and then nearly kicked myself for it.

"He doesn't work the lunch shift," said Zane, and then lifted one of his arched eyebrows. "Why? Did you miss him?"

Insta-defense set in. "No. I couldn't care less. I'm just curious about the work schedule, that's all."

Work schedule? That sounded lame, even to me.

"Sure," he said, not even bothering to hide his sarcasm. "Me thinks the girl doth protest too much."

I reverted to kindergarten coping skills and made a face.

"Do you like it so far?" asked Paula, her voice low and timid. "The job, I mean."

I nodded, picking up a stack of veggies with my fork. "Sure. It's alright. Not that I have anything to compare it to."

"Wait." Zane lifted his hand in the air dramatically. "Are you saying we popped your cherry here?" He leaned in closer, his skin a perfectly tanned gold.

I rolled my eyes at him. "Do you hear yourself? I refuse to dignify that with an answer."

"Dignify what with an answer?" asked Trace as he walked up from behind. His shirt was dotted with droplets of rain and clinging to his shoulders in an interesting way.

Not that I was staring. *Much.*

"Nothing," I said as I tried not to look when he slicked his hair back and leaned onto the counter beside me.

"Her cherry," blurted Zane. "We popped her cherry."

I turned pomegranate red.

"You what?" Trace looked over at me uneasily, his own cheeks slightly darker than before. "What's he talking about?"

"He's trying to be funny. *Trying* being the operative word," I explained and then quickly added, "It's my first job," as though that cleared up the whole thing.

It didn't.

Zane jumped in. "First job. Cherry. Virgin territory—"

Trace lifted his hand to stop him. "Thanks, I got it."

Awkward.

"Is April here yet?" asked Trace, undoubtedly needing to change the subject in a massive way.

"I think she's in the office," answered Paula.

"Thanks." He bounced his striking blues off of me once more and then took off for the back office.

I dropped my eyes to my plate. When I looked up again, Zane was grinning ear to ear.

"What?" I snapped, already defensive.

"What is that? What's going on there?" he said, ticking his head towards Trace. "I'm sensing a little *je ne sais quoi*."

"You're high on spray-tan fumes."

He smacked his lips. "Mm hmm."

"I'm meeting Dominic Huntington tonight," I blurted out, hoping that might quell his suspicions, and then cringed inwardly for trying so hard. Why did I even feel the need to defend myself?

Zane's eyes rounded out with delight at the revelation but quickly evaporated into something else as he eyed Paula. She flicked her salad back and forth with her fork, her expression obscured in thought, before she pushed the plate away.

"Excuse me," she said as she slipped off her stool and walked off towards the back. I could have sworn I saw a tear fashioning in the corner of her eye.

I looked at Zane. "Did I say something wrong?"

He leaned in across the bar as though there were prying ears all around us. "She used to go with him."

"Go with Dominic?" I recoiled. "Go with him where?"

His eyes peeked up at the ceiling. "*Go* with him," he repeated suggestively. "As in she used to *date* him." He shook his head in pity. "Poor girl had it bad, too."

I couldn't believe my ears. They were damn near on fire. How long did they date? Was it serious? Did they *sleep* together? I wasn't sure I wanted to hear any of it.

"What happened with them?" I asked, despite myself.

"He dogged her out, that's what. Dropped her like last season's Pradas."

"But I thought he just moved back here?" Maybe this was a mistake. Maybe he was talking about another Dominic Huntington. Okay so it wasn't likely, but it *was* possible.

"He did," he said as he pushed off the counter and returned to the cash register. "They moved fast."

"Oh." *Gross.*

I changed my mind. I didn't want to hear this anymore.

"My breaks over," I said as I grabbed our plates off the bar. "Later, Zane."

"Laters, Jem."

I rushed off to the back, putting as much distance between myself and that conversation as I physically could.

The hours passed by slightly disjointed, and for good reason. My head was sort of all over the place yet nowhere in particular. I felt tired, and under the weather, like *below sea level*, and while I initially just chalked it up to the surprise of finding out about Paula and Dominic, as time wore on, things seemed to go from bad to worse, and I quickly realized it had nothing to do with either one of them.

I was standing in the back storeroom looking for the paper napkins when it happened. It was as though a sudden surge of tiny needles began blitzing my skin and when I looked up around me, the entire room had become animated in an unnatural way, similar to what you'd see in the skewed mirrors of a Funhouse.

The melting walls and flashing black dots were the last thing I saw before I hit the ground.

In truth, it only felt like I was out for a split second, but I had no real way of knowing for sure. When I came to, I was face down on a cold tile with an open box of paper napkins scattered on the floor around me. The seconds felt like minutes, and it took forever for the room to slow its rotation long enough for me to regain my balance and stagger back into a seating position, my back planted firmly against the wall like an anchor.

Even still, my stomach wrenched and my head pounded harder than the bass line of a hundred tribal drums. I could feel my skin was clammy, and heated, crawling with uncomfortable, tingling sensations, and I knew I was far from out of the woods.

The door burst open as Trace came barreling through it, his usual controlled expression overtaken by concern.

"I'm fine," I said as he rushed over to me. My voice had surprised even me. It sounded far too shaky and weak to be mine.

"You don't look fine," he said as he bent down and scooped me up off the floor and into his arms.

I didn't have the strength to fight him off. I wasn't even sure I wanted to. Instead, I just wrapped my arm around his neck and resigned myself as he carried me out of the storeroom and into the private employee washroom.

"What happened? Did you black out?"

"I don't know," I said dimly as he placed me down onto the

chair. He grabbed a hand towel from the cupboard and turned on the facet, soaking it under the cold running water.

I could see his expression through the mirror, his face stirring with an array of emotions I couldn't quite decipher.

He returned to my side with the wet towel in his hand and bent down on the tiled floor before me. The fact that this was the second time that Trace Macarthur was kneeling down at my feet did not escape me.

"Are you okay?" he asked as he carefully wiped the sweat from my face. The cool wet cloth felt good against my skin.

"I think so," I sighed, letting my eyes close.

"Does anything hurt?"

I shrugged, looking down at my torso and limbs, twisting my left arm around, and then my right. Shit. Blood—*my* blood.

"Oh my God, I'm bleeding!" I said stupidly.

He cupped his hand around my arm and held it out, examining the wound with careful eyes. His skin was considerably hotter than mine—if that was even possible—and even though the added heat should have bothered me, it didn't.

"It's just a scrape, you'll survive," he said quietly. "I'll get a bandage."

"It all happened so fast," I noted, mostly to myself. "I guess I'm coming down with the flu or something."

He got up and tossed the towel into the sink. "Yeah, or something," he said, sounding frustrated.

I couldn't tell where the aggravation was coming from but it was making me feel uncomfortable, like I was some sort of burden to him. The whole idea seemed ridiculous since I never asked for his help to begin with. I contemplated saying something to that effect but decided against it being that he was my boss's son and all.

He opened up the bottom cabinet and pulled out a first aid kit and then returned to my side, pushing both his hands through his hair as he cleared the view in front of his eyes. His midnight black hair falling just short of his broad shoulders.

"Let me see your arm," he said without making eye contact. His thick lashes fanned out, shielding those incredible eyes.

I held out my arm to him and looked away for a distraction. I found one in the chair I was sitting on and began picking away at a loose piece of material as he cleaned and bandaged my wound.

Neither one of us filled the silence.

"It's probably that spell," he finally said in a barely-there voice. He was still kneeling on the floor in front of me, picking up the scattered first aid supplies.

My eyes reduced to slits. "What did you say?"

He raised his eyes to mine, unreadable in every way. "That fainting spell that's been going around," he clarified. "Maybe you should take the rest of the day off."

I shook my head. "I'm fine. I feel much better."

His mouth opened as though he were going to say something else, argue the point perhaps, but he just pressed his lips together and nodded instead.

After taking a few minutes to straighten myself out in the washroom, I headed back into the storeroom to pick up the napkins I'd gone in to get in the first place—before the room decided to go haywire on me. When I came back out, I found Trace in a heated discussion with his father at the foot end of the hall.

I could hardly make any of it out, though I could tell right away it wasn't a pleasant conversation. From Trace's rutted brows to his sharp hand gestures and quick body movements, everything about it screamed hostility. For a second, it looked like he might actually come to blows.

His father, on the other hand, was the polar opposite. His

stance was relaxed and his movements fluid and calming. It was clear he was trying to tame the beast—his loose cannon of a son—and by the looks of it, he wasn't doing a very good job.

I approached cautiously, like I was coming upon two animals in the wild, careful not to disturb them or make any sudden movements. That is, until I heard my name being spoken and then my back stiffened.

Why the heck were they talking about me?

What could they possibly be discussing about *me* that would have Trace so fired up? Was he angry that I fainted in the storeroom? Was he was worried that I'd become some kind of work liability? Something wasn't adding up. Trace didn't strike me as the type to worry about things like that. It had to be a mistake, I decided, though I continued moving forward slowly, absolutely intent on *accidentally* overhearing their conversation.

"Karl has the final decision," I heard Peter say, prompting me to move even faster now, to get as close as I could.

I made it all of three steps before Peter spotted me and quickly put the air brakes on in an effort to quiet his son. His resolve was nothing short of suspicious and only confirmed that they were *definitely* talking about me.

Trace glanced back, though his head barely turned halfway in my direction before he got the message and aborted the conversation, escaping into the main hall instead.

I couldn't shake the feeling that something was going on— here, at home, with my uncle—and I was over it. I was over the shady conversations, the secret phone calls, the cryptic explanations, the weird stares, all of it. They were hiding *something*, of this I was sure, and I was determined to figure out exactly what that was.

It was time to start tearing off the blinders.

9. REVELATIONS

The vast gray expanse was casting an abundance of misery all around us as the unrelenting rain hammered down onto the house, leaving no window untouched or ray of light obliterated. Mondays were painful—an unusual form of punishment where we were forced to pay restitution for all the horrible things we did on the weekend. Or so it goes. This particular one was already proving to be a colossal comedown before it even began.

My uncle sat in his usual chair reading the morning paper as I sloshed my cereal around feeling almost as disorderly on the inside as everything was outside. My mind was on spin-cycle.

Dominic never made it to All Saints last night, and even though there was a part of me that craved the very sight of him, I was relieved by his failure to show. I didn't necessarily want him seeing me in all my post-blackout glory, but more than that, I needed time to process everything, time to figure things out, and more importantly, time to map out my plan. *Operation-Tear-Off-The-Blinders* was in full effect, starting with my uncle dearest, and whatever the heck it was he was hiding.

I carried on with the rest of the morning like it was any other day, putting on an Oscar-worthy performance. I finished my breakfast, cleared the table, and got ready for school just as I normally would, though I made a special point to synchronize myself with my uncle so that we left the house at the same time.

He pulled away in his black sedan none the wiser, and I, as per usual, in the back of the town car. I waited for Henry to get us a safe distance from the house before crying out about a forgotten homework assignment that had to be turned in today.

We were back en route to the house in no time.

Once there, I told Henry that I would only be a couple of minutes and then took off straight for my uncle's office.

The rain hammered hard against the windows, pouring its dreary shades of gray into the large, dank office. I had no idea what I was looking for as I (carefully) ransacked his desk and drawers, doing my best not to displace anything or disturb the general layout of his workspace.

It only took a few failed tries before I found a manila folder with my name on it, hiding inside one of the bottom drawers of his desk under a stack of filed documents and loose work sheets. I opened it briefly, noting what looked like hospital records, and then slipped it into my backpack.

I moved to the sprawling glass bookcases that circled the entirety of the room and began skimming the hundreds of titles at random, looking for any suspicious objects or secret compartments that I could excavate for clues. I wasn't entirely sure what I was looking for, or even what I was expecting to find. The expectation was there though, evidenced by the savage turn my eyes had taken as they drank in every item, every sight and every corner, desperate to find something. Anything.

He had the oddest collections of books, I noted. Rows and rows of Bibles, eclectic editions I'd never heard of, encyclopedia-thick books on demons and *vampires* and other mythical creatures normal people didn't build libraries on.

What a strange coincidence it was that my uncle had an unbelievable collection of books on the very subject I was recently committed for. On the very creature my father was killed by.

Coincidence my—and then I saw them.

On the other side of the glass partition, in a special meshed enclosure, a series of leather-bound books that looked older and more valuable than all the other books combined.

The Origins of the Revenant Vampyre.

The gilded title leaped out at me.

I slid open the mesh door and slipped my hand into the cool, dry book-pen, carefully separating it from its siblings before wrapping it up in my work shirt and slipping it into my backpack.

Something told me I would find all the answers I needed right here in this room, in these books. The answers to questions I had yet to even form, and in that moment, like a dog with a bone, I vowed to come back again and again until I uncovered every last one of them.

I stalked the halls of Weston with even more anxiety than I had on my first day of school. I felt as though I were carrying a precious gem in my backpack, and just knowing it was in there made me hyper-vigilant about every single body around me, with my stomach doing roller-coaster dives every time an arm or shoulder accidentally brushed up against my body.

At lunch, Taylor was already waiting for me at my locker when I arrived carrying two semester's worth of catch-up homework. Her long blond hair was pulled to the side, and she was flirtatiously playing with one of her earrings while some tall, chestnut-haired, football-player-type wearing a lettered jersey hovered in the space beside her.

"Jemma," she called out to me, her eyes widening with excitement. "I want you to meet someone."

The football-player-type turned around at her announcement and drank me in with his desert-colored eyes.

"This is Caleb," she said, twitching her brows in a way that let me know he was worth knowing. "Caleb, this is Jemma. She just transferred here last week."

"Nice to meet you," I said shifting the weight of my books. I tried not to appear too antsy.

"Same," he said as he stepped forward and took the pile of books from my hands. "That's amazing."

"What is?" I asked, clearing a path to my locker. I twisted the dial on the lock back and forth until it clicked open.

"First time I've ever regretted missing school."

Mm-kay. Was that a line?

I looked back at him unsure. His expression seemed genial. If it was a line, he was definitely serious about it.

"Caleb here plays for the Weston Bulldogs. He's our star player," she beamed. "Best slap shot in the West Coast."

She must be referring to that last place hockey team she was bitching about earlier, but I didn't bother mentioning that part. I smiled back at her as though I cared.

"I was out half the season," he offered as though that might explain their current standings. "Shoulder injury."

"That's too bad."

"Yeah, but he's back now. Right, Cale?"

"You know it." His grin spread across his face, alive with the possibilities. "We're playing Easton next Friday. It's my first game back. I better see you both there."

"Are you kidding?" said Taylor, playfully pushing him. "We wouldn't miss that for anything." She was dead serious.

Personally, I could think of a few hundred other things I'd rather be doing on any given Friday night.

After a few more minutes of tantalizing hockey talk, I politely excused myself, letting Taylor know I had a catch-up assignment due and that I would be spending lunch in the library working on it. Luckily, she didn't offer to come with since she was obviously *normal* and not willing to spend her lunch break doing homework.

Once in the library by myself, I spotted a deserted table near the very back of the library, furthest from any prying eyes, and started in on the hospital records. I skimmed through the stack of files fairly quickly, only to realize there really wasn't anything new or useful in there—mostly just official records, some background information, and notes about things that I had discussed during my one-on-one sessions with my attending physician, Dr. Javier. All of which were *supposed* to be confidential and sealed. I didn't even want to start thinking about how my uncle got his hands on these.

I moved on to the book. On pins and needles, I carefully removed it from my bag and unwrapped my shirt from around it. It was definitely old. The leather binding alone was like nothing I had ever seen before, and the corner bosses and clasp definitely looked as though they were hand-crafted in a different era. I had to be extra cautious with it. The last thing I wanted to do was snag the cover or accidentally tear a freaking page out.

I wiped my palms against my skirt, said a little prayer, and cracked open the book.

The first detail that caught my attention was the paper. Or lack thereof. I didn't know what this thing was written on, but it definitely wasn't paper, that I knew for sure. Papyrus swiveled around my mind as a possibility but even that didn't seem to do the texture justice.

The second oddity was that the entire book appeared to be written by hand and had no copyright or author information anywhere in it. It looked a lot more like some old diary than it did an actual book. Then again, even diaries usually had a name scribbled somewhere on the jacket, didn't they?

My heart picked up as I peeled back the first page.

"Jemma Blackburn please report to the administration office. Jemma Blackburn," called a voice over the intercom.

Really though?

I shut the book and tucked it back into my schoolbag.

Taylor was already waiting for me outside the office when I turned the corner. "What's going on?" she asked, her eyebrows raised with curiosity.

I was about to ask her the same question. "No idea."

"I think your uncle's in there."

"Seriously?" I said and then peeked in through the window.

Yup. He was definitely in there. I couldn't help but think about the last time I was called into the office at school—six months ago when the men in white jackets came for me.

I pulled open the door and stepped inside. "Uncle Karl? What's going on?" I asked, already feeling queasy. "Is everything okay?"

"Jemma." He nodded his greeting. "You've been excused from your classes today. A family matter has come up." He motioned for the door. "Do you have all your things?"

I didn't move. "Did something happen? Is Tessa alright?"

"Yes, yes. Tessa is fine. Everyone is fine. Come on, let's get your things, and we'll continue this in the car."

I nodded and then followed him out, waving ominously at Taylor as she signaled for me to call her.

Outside, Henry was already parked and waiting for us at the front of the building as the rain continued to adorn itself to the world around us. My uncle and I both climbed into the back of the car, each taking a window seat.

He raised his hand to Henry who responded with a nod through the rear-view mirror and then raised the glass partition.

That can't be good.

"Hand it over please," he said as we pulled away from the school building, our conversation now in full privacy.

I looked down at his extended hand. "I don't know what—"

"I'm not in the mood, Jemma." He cut in before I could finish my lie.

I opened my backpack and handed him the folder.

He put it on his lap and then held his hand out again. "The other one," he said sternly.

It reminded me of my father's scolding voice—a voice I rarely used to hear but when I did, could reduce me to tears with just the sound of it.

I pulled out my faux-gift-wrap shirt and plucked the book from the center, handing it over begrudgingly.

"How did you know I had it?" I had to ask.

"Never mind that." He opened his briefcase and placed the book inside. "I think it's time we had ourselves a talk."

Perfect, just what I needed—a lecture from him on the finer points of why stealing is wrong. I should tell him to brush up on his lying speech as well because I'd been doing even more of that one lately.

"I'm sure by now you've already come to the realization that vampires aren't exactly a thing of fiction." He narrowed in his charcoal eyes for confirmation.

My mouth unhinged.

"I'll take that as a yes." He briefly turned his attention outside the window. "And I'm sure you overheard my conversation the other morning where your name was concerned, presumably prompting your sudden thirst for knowledge?" He looked over at me again.

I managed to wrangle out a nod this time.

"How far did you get with the book?"

"I read the cover," I said disappointedly—mostly in myself. If I had any real wherewithal, I would have read it during class.

"What's going on, Uncle Karl? What exactly do you know about vampires? And where did you get all those books? Are you some kind of vampire historian? Like a vampologist or something?" My eyes flared at the idea.

"Don't be ridiculous," he said and sharpened his stare. "There's a lot you don't know about the world we live in, Jemma. Things you won't ever read about in a textbook, or find in a library—not even in this *one* book," he said signaling to the leather-bound book inside his briefcase. "Knowledge is power, but it's also dangerous...in the wrong hands."

I turned my body towards him, intrigued.

"There are things out there," he said staring out the window as though said things were just outside the car, "that most people will never know about—can't know about. They will go an entire lifetime reading a different kind of history book, never knowing the full truth, and for that, they are blessed with the kind of blissful ignorance only a false sense of security can provide. You, my dear Jemma, no longer have that luxury for it was never intended to be yours to begin with."

"What are you talking about?" I recoiled. This conversation just took a strange, unexpected turn.

"I am talking about *your* truth, Jemma. About who you really are, and where you come from."

"I know exactly who *I* am and where *I* came from," I said, staving off the sudden trepidation that erupted inside. "This isn't about me. This is about vampires. Vampires who don't seem to be real to anyone but me and you and your creepy little books," I said flicking my hand in his direction.

"Indeed, it *is* about vampires," he conceded with a curt nod.

"That is where it all began, so that is where I will start."

A clap of thunder rumbled above us, pushing my erratic heartbeat further over the edge.

"Supernatural beings have existed since the dawn of time, Jemma. Angels, demons, the good and bad alike, all subsisting on the fringe of our reality. Every continent has its own version of the same tales and even though these written accounts can be found throughout the globe, it is important to understand that these beings are not of this world," he said, punctuating it with a sweeping hand gesture. "They're bleed-ins from other Realms that don't belong here, and so their time here has always been conditional—temporary. There is, however, one creature that defies this universal truth. One supernatural breed that is inherent to this world, and that breed is known as a *Revenant*."

"A Revenant? You're talking about vampires, right?" I asked, making the connection only because of the book title. It wasn't something you'd soon forget.

"Yes, Jemma, I'm talking about vampires, but more to the point, I am talking about a special breed of demon—a vampiric demon known as a Revenant. Unlike other demons, the very first Revenant rose from the ground right here on earth, over two thousand years ago in the Kingdom of Dacia—"

"The kingdom of *what*?" I heard myself interrupting, my eyebrows furrowed in bemusement. "Is this like a fairy-tale type of story?" It was a fair question, I thought.

"No, Jemma, this is not a fairy-tale type story," he said, frowning now. "Dacia was an ancient Kingdom that existed thousands of years ago. Today, that region is mostly known as Romania, all of which you can find in a *book*," he explained, exaggerating the word.

It sounded like a dig.

"The Kingdom, like most regions at that time was under constant attack by the Roman Empire. For a while, they had managed to stave off defeat, but with Dacia's diminished numbers and dwindling resources, they knew it would only be a matter of time before they would be conquered. Unwilling to surrender, King Decebalus ultimately took matters into his own hands, forever altering the course of humanity."

He paused and looked out the window, collecting his bearings. "What do you know of Nephilim?"

I shrugged. "Never heard of him."

"Not him, *them*," he corrected. "The Nephilim were said to be the offspring of humans and fallen Angels. Angels who rebelled against God and whose unsanctioned union with humans resulted in the creation of new bloodlines; beings that were neither Angel, nor human, but rather something in the middle."

"What do you mean something in the middle? Like a hybrid?"

"That's one way to look at it," he nodded. "Descendants who still carry that Nephilim blood today are known as *Anakim*—a rare people born with the strength of Angels and the Spirit of man. Earthly beings with otherworldly powers, if you will."

"O-kaaay," I said slowly, not quite sure how this fit in.

"It was one such bloodline—a faction of Anakim known for their magical delving and sordid affairs with the thralls of power—that were summoned by the King to come to Dacia's aid using their ethereal magic. The *Casters*, as they're better known today, knew full well that Dacia's greatest challenge was their army's lack of strength and numbers, and so they set out to create a spell that would essentially wake the dead, bringing them back to life stronger, faster, and more powerful than they ever could have been before, thus eradicating both pivotal problems in one impetuous move."

My eyes widened in horror as I knew where this was going.

"And sadly, it worked. The spell was cast, and the dead rose from the ground in droves. Only they didn't come back *right*. The newly reanimated were strong, yes, much stronger than their human counterparts, and they were virtually indestructible, but they had no interest in fighting a war, or heeding instructions, or doing any of the things they were brought back to do."

His eyes darkened into an eerie shade of smoke. "The only thing they wanted to do was feed, and the only thing that could satiate their appetites and sustain them, was blood."

"Holy crap. It's actually true."

"Language, Jemma."

"Sorry," I apologized, though I hardly thought a little curse word even remotely mattered at the base of what he had just recounted. And, plus, I wasn't crazy! "So these *witch* Angels or whatever—" I started clumsily.

"Casters," he corrected.

"Yeah—why didn't they just reverse the spell after they realized it wasn't working the way it was supposed to?"

"They certainly tried. Upon seeing their misstep, they immediately tried to rectify it with another spell that aimed to expel the reanimated ones from our world and send them back into the Hell from which they were believed to have come."

"So what happened?"

"Well, it didn't work," he said callously. "Undoing a spell is not a simple deed, Jemma. Once you create something, you have conjured a new reality. You cannot simply tap into a magical undo button. What you have created now exists, therefore you must work with that new reality, and it isn't always easy to do."

"Right. And since vampires are still around today, obviously they weren't able to do anything about it."

"Well, that's not entirely true. Most of the initial spells went awry in one way or another, though many of them are also responsible for the Revenant as we know them today."

"Is that supposed to be a good thing?" I snorted as flashes of my terrifying attack bouncing around in my consciousness.

"Well, yes. For one, they *can* be killed now. However difficult it may be, they're not indestructible the way *First Immortals* were. For another, they no longer have free reign over this realm as they once did, further hindering their survival."

"What does that mean, they don't have free reign?"

"Well, quite simply, they have restrictions now. Supernatural barriers that inhibit them. As long as they have these vulnerabilities, they can be exploited."

"Exploited how?" I asked and then said the first thing that came to mind. "Like with garlic and holy stuff?"

"Holy stu—good grief, Jemma." He did a double take as though I were the village idiot. "Apotropaic symbols can be useful in certain instances, though they should never be depended upon. There are many more layers to their evolution; crucial confines that shaped their very existence."

"Their susceptibility to wood, for example," he said, flicking down a finger, "could disable a Revenant instantly if driven through the heart, and their curse into darkness forced them to hunt only with the moon. They could no longer enter dwellings without a summon, which kept them out of homes and away from families. Even their inability to hold dominion over other supernaturals helped because it prevented them from exploiting powerful beings like the Anakim, and potentially achieving ultimate reign. All of these things were helpful in containing them, even getting an upper hand at times, though it certainly did not resolve the calamity."

Of course not. "So what did they do?"

"Well, they kept at it," he nodded. "And while they did eventually eradicate most of the *Firsts*, unfortunately, by that time it was simply too late. The ripple had begun. The reanimated had since infected hundreds of others, and it appeared that those who were infected directly had already become something different—something entirely separate and unaffected by the magic that had created their Makers."

He shook his head, ceded, as though he were somehow responsible. "And with that, a new breed was born, one that sat on the very crown of our Chain of Life, and sadly, there was nothing more the Casters or their magic could do. What was done, was done, and the rest is history. The Roman Empire eventually prevailed, and King Decebalus, unable to live with what he had done, killed himself shortly after."

"So that's it?" I snapped in disbelief. "Everyone just moved on, did nothing? Let the vampires continue multiplying freely?" I was unable to quell my anger. This was personal in so many ways.

"Certainly not," he said, looking outside the window as we made our way through the gates of the Blackburn Estate. "All things have their counterpart, Jemma, and evil is no exception. What nature cannot provide for, we create."

"Okay, good, so...what does that mean?" I asked as I picked up my schoolbag from the floor bed and waited for him to elaborate on his cryptic response.

"What it means, my dear, is that the rebellious Angels were not the only ones who fell."

10. THE SACRIFICE

I flopped down onto the leather chair in front of my uncle's desk as he returned the book to its rightful place and circled back around with another one in his hands, peeling back each page with the greatest of care. The book looked similar to the one I had *borrowed* earlier with the same gilded lettering and leather bound encasing, and was undoubtedly from the same collection.

"What is that?" I asked him, detonating the silence just as another crash of thunder rang out its reverberation around us.

The room was dim, cold, locked in the dreary atmosphere of the untold secrets it housed. It made me feel uneasy, like no matter how much I saw or heard here, I might still never find myself on the right side of the looking glass.

"The Powers," he started, taking a seat on the edge of the desk, "were *Warrior* Angels from the Second Sphere who controlled the borders between Heaven and Hell. Unlike lower ranking Angels who weaved in and out of our daily lives, Warrior Angels were of a higher ethereal caste, charged with governing the earth as a whole and protecting it against supernatural evil."

I nodded, craning my neck to get a look at the book title. The gold reflected oddly, obscuring the title and rendering it impossible for me to make out the letters.

"It's widely believed that no Warrior Angel has ever fallen from grace," he explained with detectable pride. "And by most accounts, that is as close to the truth as they will get. *We*, however, know different. We know that it was precisely their unwavering loyalty and sworn oath to protect this world that forced them to do what they did. In order to right the wrongs of the Casters and to stop the killings perpetrated by the Revenants, the Warrior Angels made the ultimate *sacrifice*."

He raised his eyebrow to me, prompting me to fill in the blank as though I should know this.

I didn't.

"They...killed themselves?" I asked, dragging out the words. Wait, that doesn't even make sense. How would that help anything?

"No, Jemma, they *Fell*," he said, nodding into the word. "They sacrificed their place in Paradise, and fell to Earth in order to create a new bloodline of Warrior Descendants who would be powerful enough to rival the Revenants, strong enough to slay them, and loyal enough to dedicate their lives to this mission," he explained, his dark eyes sharp and judicious. "It was from this blessed union of fallen Warrior Angel and spirited human, that the very first *Slayer* on Earth was born, giving rise to a legacy unlike any other. A legacy that has been protected throughout the ages by a secret order of Anakim."

He closed the book and placed it on the desk beside him. "That order is known as *The Order of the Rose*, and through its toil, Slayers continue to be born all over the world, some from bloodlines that go back thousands of years—sacred Warrior bloodlines that are carefully guarded and propagated to ensure the continuance of this lineage. So that the fight against evil can go on," he said with a rolling hand gesture. "So that Slayers can continue to be born and fulfill their destiny."

He narrowed his gaze to me and softened his voice. "You, my dear Jemma, are of this legacy."

My bottom lip dropped abruptly, engaging in a series of rises and falls as I tried to find some words—any words at all.

"I'm sorry, *what*?"

He reached forward and placed a steadying hand on my shoulder. "*You* are a Slayer, Jemma, a Warrior Descendant, and this is your birthright."

"What are you talking about?" I snapped, jumping up from the chair, causing it to sail backwards and screech across the hardwood floor. "Is this some kind of joke?"

"Of course not, I—"

"You're lying!" I snapped, cutting him off. "You're making this up! I don't know where you're getting this from, but you're mistaken. Or nuts. Or both." I couldn't keep a straight thought in my head. My eyes were wild with panic.

"I know this is a lot to take in, but I assure you, there is no mistake of your lineage. This is who you are."

"No." I shook my head. "It's not possible. If this were true, my father would have told me so. He wouldn't have lied to me. Not about something like this." My hands were trembling now.

"Thomas's omissions were meant to protect you. He wanted a different life for you, and for Tessa. A better life than the one your mother had."

My mother? I shook my head, unable to process any of this.

"He left Hollow Hills the week after Jacqueline left us," he said, his voice cracking on my mother's name. "He swore to keep all of this from you and Tessa, to protect you from the truth. You were only a child then, not even three. I thought it was his anguish speaking." He shook his head, visibly affected. "I thought he would come to his senses once he had time to mourn his loss. But he never came back. Not until Tessa."

"When she moved here," I remembered aloud.

The move happened right after Tessa's school placed her on academic probation. My father had been worried sick about her. About her future and the road she was headed down. In the end, they decided it was best if she went to live with my uncle. New town, new school, new rules. It was what she needed, he'd said.

Dammit, was any of that true?

"Tessa was *changing*," explained my uncle. "She was having the dreams, the visions, *sensing* the Revenants. It was much too dangerous to keep her in the dark. He had no choice but to send her back here where we could protect her—train her. And that is what we did. However, he refused to give you up, too. He said he still had a chance to *save* you, as he put it." He shook his head, clearly upset with his brother's decision. "It was then that he sought out the help of a Caster."

The conversation I overheard that morning came back to me. "To put a spell on me?" I asked, my throat burning from lack of moisture, my head spinning from lack of blood flow.

He nodded. "A Cloaking spell that would suppress your powers, keep them locked away. He'd hoped it would protect you."

I could certainly believe that part about my father. If any of this was true, I knew my father would do everything in his power to protect us, to give us the best life he could. And up until his death, he had done just that.

Which begged the question: "Why are you trying to break the spell if it's protecting me?"

"It's much too dangerous," he said as he motioned for me to sit down again.

I didn't hesitate as I was growing increasingly unsteady.

"Now that you've reached the age of maturity, I'm not sure the spell is strong enough anymore or the safe choice for you," he said, removing his glasses. "By suppressing your true nature, you're also suppressing your abilities...abilities that could mean the difference between life and death for you."

"What abilities?" I asked, my voice rasping.

He hesitated to answer the question. "Well, such as being able to *sense* a Revenant," he offered finally. "You must know that once a Revenant marks you, as a mere human, there's little you can do to deviate the attack. They are predators in every sense of the word. They will hunt you, drain you, and leave you for dead with no recollection of what transpired. There is no mercy there. No humanity whatsoever."

My mind flashed back to the attack eight months ago—the terrifying, relentless attack that still haunted my dreams at night—and I believed him.

"As a Slayer," he went on, "you have certain advantages over them, such as your ability to sense them. This allows you to track them and vanquish them before they even have a chance to mark you, virtually turning the hunters into the hunted."

Sense them? Track them? *Vanquish* them?

This man was off his freaking rocker. I had absolutely no desire to do any of that—none. There wasn't a single part of my being that was even remotely interested in getting involved in what he was going on about.

"No. That's not happening." I shook my head fully decided. "I don't want to sense them, or see them, or kill them, or know anything about them. I just want to make it through high school, graduate, maybe go on a road trip somewhere nice, and just—"

"Jemma," he interceded. "This is what you were born to do. This is your Calling."

"My Calling?" I repeated incredulously. "The hell it is."

A calling implies I have a choice, doesn't it? That I could answer the call, or not. That I have a choice in whether or not I accept this as my destiny? Well, I don't. I don't want anything to do with it. And I *don't* accept the call. Matter of fact, this line is no longer in service.

11. THINGS THAT GO BUMP

I called Tessa sixteen times that night, my hands trembling as I held the receiver and listened to it go straight to voicemail each and every time. I needed her to be here, to be my family, to be the one to tell me everything was going to be okay. But like usual, she wasn't here.

Nobody was.

I sat by myself on the floor, curled up in the cold shadowy corner of my lavish bedroom, when it finally occurred to me that nobody was coming for me. Nobody was going to make this go away. There would be no soft words of comfort from my mother, no protection from my father, no guidance from my sister.

It was just me, and *me* wasn't nearly enough right now.

A hot tear ran down my cheek as I gave up and left her a message. "You lied to me, Tess. You all lied to me."

I spent the next couple of days fully immersed in all things normal. I sat attentively in class (taking actual notes), going the extra mile at work, and even *really* listening when Taylor went on about the latest Weston Scandals—something I usually couldn't be bothered to care about. This week, I was all about it—all about everything—so long as it had nothing to do with Angels and Demons, or the like. Denial was funny that way.

For months, I wanted nothing more than for someone to believe me; to accept that I *had* been attacked by something that wasn't human—to tell me I wasn't crazy. I longed for the validation, for the answers. Well, I got my answers and I got my validation and they only made me long for the days when I was blissfully unaware of it all, proving the age-old adage that ignorance really was bliss. By the time Wednesday rolled around, I was praying for full-blown amnesia to strike.

First period History turned out to be a free-for-all the minute word came in that Mr. Bradley was out sick and that a substitute was on the way. It took Taylor all of thirty seconds to ditch her usual seat next to Nikki and grab an empty desk in front of me on the opposite side of the room.

Naturally, Ben pushed his desk in closer to us. It was like Taylor had some sort of gravitational pull on him.

"So Carly's having a house party next Saturday and everyone's going to be there," she said, her blue-gray eyes sparkling at the possibilities. "It's kind of a big deal."

"Tis the season," said Ben as he crossed his arms behind his head and leaned back in his chair.

"And what season would that be?" I asked, curious, but mostly just grateful for the much needed distraction.

"*Spring Fling*. It's like a month long event around here," sang Taylor. "There's house parties, carnivals, and of course, Spring Formal!" Her eyes nearly doubled in size. "You're going to love it. Make sure you can get Saturday off," she ordered.

I nodded that I would, already fairly certain I wasn't on the schedule next week-end anyway.

"Don't look now, but Nikki's throwing spears at your head again." Her lips barely moved when she said it.

I had no intentions of looking at Nikki, now or ever again.

"What's the bad blood with you two anyway?" asked Ben as though he had just noticed the tension, even though it was thick enough to slice with a machete.

"Isn't it obvious?" answered Taylor, undeterred by the fact that the question was directed at me. "There's only one Trace and two of them."

I rolled my eyes at her. "Way to fuel the fire."

"My bad," she laughed unrepentantly. "No one heard."

"So essentially, Nikki's tweaking out because our new little fish here," he said affectionately as he swooped his arm around my shoulder, "is swimming around in her pool?"

"Exactly."

"No, *not* exactly. I'm not swimming in anyone's pool, least of all Nikki's pool, nor do I have any intentions of getting in her pool." I struggled to keep my voice at a whisper. "This whole thing has just gotten completely out of hand."

"I think you two should mud-wrestle it out," said Ben, trying to make light out of the situation. "Winner keeps Trace."

I knocked his arm off my shoulder. "Pass."

"So what does Trace think about her anyway?" asked Taylor, leaning in closer to Ben. "He must have said something to you, you guys are like BFF."

"Contrary to what they keep telling you in *Cosmo Girl*," he said, shuffling forward in his chair. "We actually don't stay on the phone all night talking about our *feelings*."

"What?" she said, feigning shock. "What about the slumber parties? Don't tell me those are a lie too."

"Only one way to know for sure," he grinned. "Maybe you should come over tonight and find out."

"And do what? Stay up all night watching *The X Files* with you? No thanks, Skully," she scoffed, picking up her cell phone.

"Skully was the girl!" he said aghast. "And don't knock it 'til you try it."

I couldn't help but laugh. The way they went back and forth, it was like a ping-pong match—only interesting.

"Speaking of the unexplained," he said, changing the subject. "Did you guys see the paper this morning? They found another body out by the Falls. *Mutilated*, just like the last girl. They're talking serial killer."

"Shut up," cried Taylor, her phone frozen mid-air. "Who was the girl? Oh my God, Ben, did we know her?"

He shook his head. "They haven't released her name yet."

"How many girls have there been?" I asked, taken aback.

"This is the second."

I'm glad no one felt the need to mention this to me until now, being that I was new, *and* a girl. Was a small welcome basket with a news bulletin insert too much to ask?

A cold chill traveled up my spine as an unwanted thought crept into my mind. What if this was vampire-related? What if there were vampires right here in Hollow Hills? What if this thing mutilated that poor girl and was still out there, hunting for its next victim at this very moment?

Did vampires even do stuff like that—mutilate? Did they stalk their victims or were they randomly selected? I had no answers and felt completely sickened.

"You don't think it's related to Linley's death, do you?"

Ben shook his head. "They didn't say anything like that."

"Who's Linley?" I shared looks between the two.

"Trace's sister," answered Ben, somber.

My heart sank.

"But why would her death be related?" I asked thoughtlessly. I had always assumed her death was by natural causes. Some unfortunate, degenerative illness that took her away too soon.

Ben answered before I could take the question back. "Because she was murdered," he said, pained by the memory.

"Can we please talk about something else?" said Taylor, frowning. "*Anything* else. It's just too depressing."

The conversation quickly redirected to brighter topics like their week-end plans and upcoming parties, though my own mind stayed with Trace and his sister. I couldn't help but feel sorry for him; for his family to lose their daughter in such a horrible way.

My eyes ventured across the room as I tried to steal a quick glance at him. He was sitting sideways on his chair, his legs stretched out in front of him, tapping his thumb on the desk as Nikki went on about something he didn't seem vaguely interested in. As if sensing my stare, his cobalt eyes flickered up to greet me, catching my gaze and holding onto it without abandon.

I broke eye contact first, focusing my attention back in on Ben who was still rambling on beside me. When I looked back at him a few moments later, he was still staring at me with the same unreadable expression on his face:

Distant. Guarded. *Curious.*

His dimples pressed in and I swore I could see the semblance of a smile forming—a perfect, barely-there smile that caused my *already* erratic heart to jump a few more beats.

"There they go again," laughed Taylor, her voice jolting me out of...well, whatever the heck that was.

I gave her a warning look and put my head down on my desk. I didn't look back at him for the rest of the class.

Rainy weekday nights at All Saints were fast becoming my favorite shifts to work. The place was a desolate wasteland save for a couple of regulars watching the game up at the bar and a few familiar faces from Weston. It turned out Mr. Macarthur wasn't kidding when he said I'd be able to do my homework here, and that I wouldn't be the only one.

Taylor, Carly, and Hannah were all lined up in the banquet seat against the back wall. Their math books spread out in front of them like a tablecloth while Ben sat in the chair beside me; fidgeting, distracting me, and *not* doing his math homework.

"We need more popcorn, Jem," said Ben, shaking the wicker basket in my direction. His brown eyes glistening as he grinned.

I was just about to tell him that if he wanted some popcorn, he needed to get off his cushioned backside and get it himself. And then I remembered I worked here, and it was actually my job. I took the basket from him and went to refill it at the popcorn machine by the bar where Zane was spinning the rumor mill with an older blond woman I'd never seen before.

They were talking about the murdered girl in town, but I could only make out little pieces of it before my head jerked up at the sound of the entrance door crashing open.

Nikki drifted through the threshold with scowling Morgan in tow as thunderous flashes of lightning illuminated the pitch-black night behind them.

As if Nikki Parker didn't look scary enough before, now she had special effects.

I walked back to the table at a slightly more accelerated pace and dropped the basket in front of Ben just as Nikki and Morgan made a beeline for the table. By the time they started peeling off their soaking rain coats, I was already halfway to the *employees only* area.

Trace was leaning against the stainless steel counter talking with Sawyer when I walked into the kitchen.

"What's up?" he asked, noticing my frazzled expression.

"Nikki's here," I said simply as though that should clear up everything. "If anyone needs me, I'll be cleaning the washrooms."

His eyes widened.

Yeah, that's right. I'd rather scrub a toilet than be in the same room with Nikki Parker. And I wasn't even on washroom duty. I thought it said a lot, and in the moment, it definitely felt like the better choice, though nearly thirty miserable minutes later, I was silently vowing to never again make that idiotic mistake.

I knotted up the black plastic garbage bag and towed it down the hall to the back exit, pushing hard into the door with my shoulder before stepping out into the cool, quiet night. The crisp breeze danced around my skin as the sky adorned itself with flashes of light, boisterously threatening to pour over us again. And with the way I felt in that moment, I almost wished it would.

I dragged the garbage bag across the wet concrete over to the dumpster just a few feet away from the door and mindlessly threw back the lid. Unprepared to handle the stench of rained on garbage, I dropped the bag and covered my exposed orifices as the putrid smell assaulted my nose.

"Dammit!" I let out a string of curses into my hand as I staggered backwards, away from the foul odor.

In my rush to clear the area, I slammed back into something hard—unmoving. I turned around and immediately felt the blood drain from my face.

This was bad. *Really* bad.

And all I could do was stare at his fangs.

12. CRUEL INTENTIONS

I tried to scream out for help—God knows I tried—but it was like my voice had been ripped out of my throat by the bony claws of Fear itself, leaving me mute and defenseless.

I stammered backwards, instinctively putting as much distance between myself and this thing as I possibly could. His fangs were fully protracted, face shadowed by his hoodie, but I could see his black eyes and they were wild with a primordial hunger that made my stomach wrench. He rushed into me fast and aggressive, forcing me further back until I stumbled over the garbage bag and fell onto my backside, crashing headfirst into the dumpster behind me.

The full thralls of panic began to cut through as his shadow descended over me like a thick, dark cloud of poison that pulsed to destroy every living cell in my body. I let out a scream from the deepest part of me, and for a brief moment, could hear my own shrilling, desperate cry for help as though it belonged to someone else—just before it got swallowed up by a clash of thunder above.

I opened my mouth again to scream but instead tasted his brackish hand as he clamped it over my mouth and shoved me down hard, slamming my head against the cold, wet concrete. I barely had time to register the searing pain before he repeated the hit, this time causing my ears to ring out like a wailing police siren. I knew I wouldn't be able to withstand a third.

I thrashed my legs up and propelled my foot into his torso. Surprised, he staggered back a step though he was right back above me before I had a chance to make a move. His gangly fingers clawing their way to my mouth, to my neck, tugging away strands of hope each time they made contact with my skin.

I kicked at him again and again, fighting back tears as I tried to wrestle him off me, to knock him back long enough to make my escape, but he took each hit with a smile, demoralizing my every effort. I wasn't strong enough. My limbs were just too clumsy, too frantic, numbing from the panic. I was starting to shake, and I knew it would only be a matter of time before I froze up with fear.

And then my foot slipped.

One misstep was all it took before I felt his cold lengthy fingers wrap around my neck, squeezing my larynx as he pulled me up off the ground. I hurled my legs back and forth, wild and uncontrolled, fighting with every ounce of strength I had left to get him to loosen his grip around my windpipe.

"Feisty little bitch, are we?" he growled nauseatingly as he brought his other hand up and circled my throat with double the pressure. "Let's see how long that lasts."

The air ceased. I couldn't breathe!

I clawed at his hands with rabid fervor, digging my nails into his icy skin as I desperately fought for oxygen, for freedom, but it was futile. His hold was unrelenting, his lips upturned in glee. I was slowly suffocating to death and the sick bastard was enjoying every second of it.

My vision started to blur, darkness overwhelming the outer corners as though I were being sucked into a vortex. The realization set in that at any moment now, I was about to lose consciousness and become a comatose *un*happy meal.

It was in that moment that I felt something ignite in me. Something unfamiliar, something primal and desperate, and without any bearings, I did the only thing I knew how to do. I swung my foot all the way back, garnering the kind of momentum only desperation could muster and then blasted it forward, plunging my knee deep into his crotch.

His guttural cry wailed out around me as the death grip on my neck loosened without his permission. His knees buckled from the pain, forcing him into a slow descent towards the ground.

This was my opening. My one and only chance.

I threw him off me like a rancid, diseased carcass, and ran back to the exit door. Grabbing at the handle and tugging frenetically, I pounded on it, begging it for my escape—for my safety, but it denied me each time, refusing to budge even an inch. The stupid thing had locked from the inside and I was probably going to end up dead because of it.

I peered over my shoulder and saw him stammering back up to his feet again. Without thought, I raced off in the opposite direction, screaming out for help as another clap of thunder rolled out above us. I didn't have a chance to try again before I felt his merciless hand entwine itself in my hair and yank me back before throwing me down onto the unforgiving concrete. I hit the ground fast and hard, like I never stood a chance in hell of making it out of here alive.

Alone on the street in the dead pitch of night, I looked up into his ravenous black eyes and fought back the urge to spew as I realized I had only made this more exciting for him, aggravated his hunger for the carnage. He was the predator, and I, always the prey. No matter where I was or what I did, nothing could stop this horror movie from playing out its gruesome scenes.

This had been my fate all along.

I closed my eyes tight and sucked in a breath, too exhausted do anything else but shield my face with my quivering arms as he growled into the night and then dipped to the ground beside me. I couldn't believe this was going to happen. I couldn't believe this was how I was going to die.

Little flashes of my father began to pepper my mind, leaving tiny droplets of hope that maybe this wasn't so bad. Maybe now I'd be able to see him again and I wouldn't have to be alone anymore. We would be together again, safe and happy and away from all of this horror and bloodshed. Every flickering memory of him made it easier for me to resign myself.

"Ay!" I heard a man's voice shout out. It was sharp and edgy, vaguely familiar. "What do you think you're doing?"

I rolled my head back and saw Trace trudging towards us with a large, wooden baseball bat in his hand. He seemed taller in this light, stronger with that weapon. Better than any one person has ever looked before.

The vampire straightened out instantly. His palms were turned out to Trace as he backed away, moving deeper into the dark alley and inching further and further away from me. He didn't say a word as he retracted, though it seemed fairly obvious that he was afraid (or unwilling) to do this all over again with somebody else. Somebody his own size.

By the time Trace reached my side, the creature was already gone, having disappeared into the shadows from which he had come. Trace tried to take off after him, but stopped abruptly at the sound of my bloodcurdling scream that begged him not to leave me alone out there.

"Shit. Are you okay?" he asked, dropping the bat onto the ground as he crouched down beside me. The poignant sound of the wood clinking against the concrete echoed around us.

I sat up unsteadily, dazed, terrified, still shaking from the unquantifiable fear. I was fighting hard to hold back the geyser of tears that lurked just below the fragile surface.

"I'm fine," I lied. I was *so* not fine.

Trace clasped the top of my arm and helped me up to my feet. His warm hand lingered there, waiting to make sure I had my balance, and I let it, as I wasn't even sure of it myself.

Everything felt unreal, like I was having an out of body experience, like I wasn't even connected to myself anymore. Only to the memories of what happened, and to the part of me that was holding the visions together disjointedly. I stood there dumbfounded, my mind racing as I looked around, canvassing the street, the wet concrete, replaying the scene in my mind—the attack—and how close I had just brushed up against death.

I looked up at Trace who was staring down at me silently, his arresting blue eyes painting tracks all over my face.

I needed to get away from this place.

"Where are you going?" he asked brashly, pulling me back by my elbow as I tried to take off for the door.

"I'm going inside." My voice sounded hollow, distant.

"Inside?" He narrowed his eyes. "Don't you want to talk about this? About what just happened?" He ticked his head once towards the now-empty street. The one the vampire had disappeared into.

I wasn't sure how much of my hooded attacker Trace had actually seen, but at this point, it didn't even matter. The way I saw it, I had two options here: I could take the risk and find out—confide in him about what just happened to me, about what has been happening to me for months now. I could tell him all about the fang-bearing creature that just tried to kill me and all about the one before him, and maybe even about the sadistic fairytales my uncle's been churning, and then sit back and hope to God that he believed me and didn't think I was bat-shit crazy.

Or, I can skip that tired song and protect myself. Lie like my freedom depended on it.

"There's nothing to talk about," I said easily. "The guy was a freaking pervert. God only knows what he wanted to do to me. Honestly, I'd rather not talk about it."

I tried to leave, but he caught my arm again. "Jemma—"

"Trace, please. Let me go," I pleaded, trying to shake myself loose. "I don't want to talk about it. Don't *make* me talk about it." I could feel the strain in my eyes as I struggled to hold back the waterfall that ached to break free, threatening to unleash with it all the secrets I've been carrying inside.

He pumped his jaw several times as he exhaled long and hard through his nose, searing me with those hypnotic eyes.

"Fine." He let go of my arm.

I made it halfway to the door before stopping. When I spun back around, he was still standing there watching me, the wooden bat hanging loosely from his fingertips. His eyes were heavy with emotions I couldn't quite put together.

I held onto his gaze as I walked back over to him, and without thinking twice of it, draped my arms around his neck, pinning him inside a hug. I felt him stiffen beneath my embrace as though I'd just crossed over some invisible line. A line that was meant to keep us safely apart. But I didn't care. I had no intention of staying on my side anymore.

"Thank you," I whispered into his neck, my voice working hard not to crack. "You saved my life."

He seemed to hesitate at first, unsure of the connection, though after a few short beats, I felt his hand rise up along my side and gently glide across the small of my back until his arm was wrapped snugly around my waist. And he held me there against him, for a while, my skin humming under the warmth of his soothing touch.

After cleaning most of the dirt off myself, I swapped my ripped employee shirt for one of the clean spares in the office and returned to the main hall where Trace was waiting to take me home. On any other night, I would have vehemently refused his offer, especially with Nikki standing close enough to witness the gross-infraction, but tonight I didn't give a damn about it. Tonight, I didn't give a damn about her. I feared *them* more than I did her and nothing was going to make me step foot outside this building by myself.

I sauntered towards Trace who was at the bar going over something with Zane when I caught sight of Dominic walking in at the front. All of the light seemed to rush over to him as though it ached to be beside him as much as I did, and before I knew it, my still-shaky legs were detouring straight for him.

"Jemma." He said my name with all the right inflection as he took my hand into his and gently kissed the back of it.

My heart involuntarily thrummed twice its pace as a result of his lips making contact with my skin. For that small moment, I forgot everything else, and I liked him more because of it.

"H-Hey, hi," I said gracelessly.

A slow moving smile appeared. "I was hoping you'd be here."

"You were?" The words fell out of my mouth without any forethought. The kind of forethought that would tell you to stay calm and play it cool, like hot older guys were *always* hoping to run into you.

"Yes, I was," he smirked. "I was hoping I might take you out later. After work."

My insides lit up at the thought of it; at the very notion that he wanted to see me—was *hoping* for it even.

And then I snapped back to reality.

"What's the matter?" he asked. He must have remarked the change in my expression.

"I finished early. There was...an incident."

"Oh?" His dark eyes tapered. "What sort of incident?"

He reached out and moved a strand of hair away from my eyes. Such a simple gesture, yet it completely derailed my focus.

"I, um, I sort of had a run-in with this creep out back, a little while ago. Some deranged guy." *TMI, dammit.*

When I saw his eyes flare open, I quickly added, "I'm totally fine though, just a little shaken up."

"Are you hurt?" he asked and then grazed his hand over the side of my neck as though he were looking for a wound—a seriously specific wound.

My eyes thinned as I shook my head, "I'm fine."

"Come on then, I'll take you home."

"I already have a ride," I said, still searching his face for clues about what exactly he might know, if anything.

"I insist," he said, surrendering nothing.

Trace appeared beside me. "You ready to go?" He didn't bother acknowledging Dominic's presence.

"I'll be taking Jemma home tonight," said Dominic as he reached out and took my hand, gently pulling me closer to him.

Trace took my other hand and jerked me back beside him. "And who the hell are you supposed to be?"

I blinked into him.

What the hell was he doing? Didn't he know Dominic? Hadn't he told me to stay away from him not even a week ago? Why would he warn me about someone he's never even met before?

He must have been going off of hear-say, I decided. So apparently introductions were in order.

"Um, Trace, this is Dominic." I gestured over to him awkwardly and then went back the other way. "Dominic, this is Trace."

Neither one extended their hand.

"Right. So, anyway," I turned back to Trace. "You don't

need to drive me home after all. Dominic offered to take me." As much as I wanted to be around him—felt safer with him near me—the situation had not changed. Trace was unavailable. "It's probably for the best," I added, ticking my head towards the back where Nikki was sitting with the rest of our friends.

His jaw muscle tightened as his eyes moved from me to Dominic. "Excuse us." The words on their own were polite, but his tone was anything but. He pulled me over to the bar, away from Dominic, though he was still very much in earshot of us.

"I don't like this," he said, shaking his head. "I'd feel better if I took you home myself."

"I'll be fine with Dominic. Besides," I said, lowering my voice. "Nikki's sitting right there. I'm not about to piss her off on purpose."

He looked back at Dominic with disgust. "What do you even know about him?"

I shrugged. The truth was, I didn't know any more about Dominic than I did of Trace, or even Taylor for that matter, but that wasn't stopping me from talking to either of them. I was new in town, after all, it was to be expected.

"I think that's the purpose of getting to know someone," I pointed out. "So unless there's something specific you think I should know..." I gave him a couple seconds to answer. When he didn't, I went on, "I'm not going to have this pointless conversation again."

He exhaled loudly, jaw pumping again. "Give me your phone."

"My phone?"

"Yes your phone."

I took it out from my handbag and handed it over.

"If anything happens, or you need something..." He looked at me strangely. "A ride or *whatever*," he added, tapping the screen in rapid succession. "You have my number."

"Okay." I took the phone back apprehensively.

He looked over Dominic once more as though sending him some sort of silent warning and then nodded at me before walking off into the kitchen. I immediately saw Nikki jump up from my peripheral and take off running after him.

Just perfect.

She must have been gawking at us the entire time, and if she just witnessed him giving me his number, there was no doubt in my mind she was about to go tear him a new one. And, God only knows what she was going to have planned for me.

The night was still cloaked in a thin layer of dew when we left All Saints. The sky, a rich, dark indigo, was free of any blemishes and gleaming with a million little blinking lights of reassurance. Ironically, it was shaping up to be a picture-perfect night, despite everything that had transpired.

I followed Dominic alongside the building until he stopped unexpectedly in front of a Matte black Audi R8. He pulled something out of his pocket and pushed a button. The car responded on all fronts.

"What's this?" I asked him, surprised, my eyes darting back and forth between him and the wicked ride.

"This would be my car." His smile went up a notch as he moved to the passenger side and opened my door. "I thought it appropriate seeing as you don't enjoy walking very much."

"Walking *at night*," I quickly corrected, shrinking inward. I knew he would think I was lazy for protesting the walk home the other night.

"Isn't that what I said?" he grinned seductively, blurring out the rest of the world with that one little gesture.

I bit down a smile and climbed into the car.

The smell of expensive leather mingled in the air with Dominic's tantalizing cologne—a chocolaty musk—and enveloped me like a luxurious blanket. I barely had a chance to buckle myself in before we were zipping out of the parking lot and tearing down the blacktop road towards the main boulevard.

"So tell me more about this incident," he asked casually as though he were asking about the weather in passing.

I examined him as he drove.

"You seem to be quite incident-prone," he continued when I didn't answer. "I'm beginning to question your safety."

I too was beginning to question my safety. *Daily*.

"I'm fine." I forced a smile. "If it's any consolation, I plan on making use of that whole buddy system from here on out." That part was the truth. I had no intentions of going anywhere alone at night, ever again. The thought alone made me shudder.

He stole a glance before returning his eyes to road. "You don't have to pretend with me, Jemma."

"I don't know what you mean," I said, caught off guard.

"You put on a brave face, and a beautiful one at that," he said without averting his eyes from the road. "But I have a feeling you would not have left work in the middle of your shift had the incident been as uneventful as you would like me to believe it was."

"What makes you say that?"

"Just a hunch."

"You seem to have a lot of those."

A slow spreading grin appeared. "I'm very intuitive."

I couldn't help but smile. He was definitely charming. "Really, it was just a slow night," I explained, choosing my words carefully. "Plus, Paula the other waitress was there, and they really didn't need the both of us."

"I see." He shifted in his seat.

"You know her, right? Paula Dawson?" I asked, curious to see if he'd tell me the truth.

His cheek pulled up on one side. "I do."

"Didn't you guys date for a while?" I tried feigning nonchalance though my voice hitched up unnaturally at the tail end of the question.

"Yes, I enjoyed her company on a few occasions, though I'd hardly classify that as dating."

"Right. Okay." I was trying to be tactful with my inquisition, but the questions just seeped from my mouth like verbal diarrhea. "So...what would you classify it as then?"

"Inconsequential," he said without missing a beat.

Both his tone and demeanor were detached, unemotional even. I wasn't sure if that was a good thing or not. On the other hand, I had no reason to doubt that he was being anything but honest with me, however brutal that was for poor Paula.

I skimmed my neck with my fingertips as I thought it over and noted how incredibly sore I still was. I pulled down the sun visor and stole a peak in the mirror, quickly spotting the sickening color of purple my neck was taking on.

Perfect. How on earth was I going to explain this one away? I tripped and fell on a vampire?

And then it hit me. *That* was the reason Dominic looked at my neck...because it was bruising. Clearly that would have been the logical thing to assume since my neck had just been squeezed to the point of a near larynx dislocation. Jeez, what the heck did I think the reason was going to be anyway?

I closed the visor and relaxed into my seat a little.

"Everything okay?" he asked.

"Great," I lied. I needed to change the subject. "So, there's this party next Saturday," I heard myself say. "It's a house party for some Spring thing."

He flashed a crooked grin. "Spring Fling."

"Yeah, that's it."

"What of it, love?" He was smirking now.

I was hoping he wouldn't actually make me say the words but it appeared that he was enjoying watching me squirm way too much to save me from myself. "Well, being that I'm incident-prone and all," I said, using his word. "I was wondering if maybe, you know, you'd like to come along...with me?"

The minute the words relayed back to my ears, I winced at them, proving once more I was only a passenger in my own vessel. Desperation, fear, longing—they had all taken the driver's seat and were apparently asking guys out now. Who was I kidding? I'd probably ask out the entire hockey team if it meant I'd be safe from vampires. At least this option would allow me to spend more time with Dominic.

"Are you asking me out on a date?" He raised an eyebrow.

"No." I felt my cheeks warm. "I'm pretty sure I never said *date*, I mean...did I? I was just thinking we could—"

"We definitely could." He cut in with a smirk before I could further embarrass myself. "I'm looking forward to it, angel."

13. FRIDAY NIGHT LIES

The days following the attack blurred into one another like one long, tangled dream that obliterated any residual semblance of security I might have had left. I found myself hiding in an uncomplicated routine of sorts as I shuffled back and forth between work, school, and home. Long, dragging days broken up only by the finer moments when I'd get to see Dominic.

I had decided not to tell my uncle about the attack last week out of fear that he would use it as another excuse to push the whole Slayer *thing* down my throat. I had already told him emphatically that I had no intention of going down that road, and my feelings on that had not changed—attack, or no attack.

But it appeared that even adamant refusal was not enough to deter my uncle from his mission. Where other men might have laid the issue to rest, my uncle instead continued to offer his reassurance that I would have as much time as I needed to come to terms with all of this. As though *time* were the problem here. Clearly he was unable to cope with rejection.

Not only was he not dropping the subject of Bloodsuckers and Slayers, but as chance would have it, he was also after a little bit of my blood himself. It was all I could do to stop from leering at him like his neck had spewed two heads overnight when he sat across the table from me at breakfast and casually asked me to provide him with a sample of blood. So he could run some tests. Like it was a completely normal request.

When I asked him why, he hesitated to explain himself, and only stated that he wanted to be sure my bloodlines weren't damaged, and that I was in fact a *Slayer*.

"I don't understand," I said, feeling as though this was coming out of left field. "What about everything you told me last week—about the Angels, and us being Descendants of them? Was all of that a lie?"

I wasn't sure what I wanted the answer to be.

"Of course not."

"So why do you need to test my blood?"

"Because of the Cloaking Spell," he said, peeling off his glasses and setting them down on the table. "We need to run some tests to make sure nothing's been permanently altered before we even attempt to lift the Cloak. Should you allow us, of course."

"Altered? Is that even a possibility?" I asked, stupidly. If he wanted to test my blood to see if it had been altered, obviously, altering was a possibility.

His regretful eyes confirmed what I had already figured.

"Okay. So how long until we can actually undo the spell?"

"Well it's not quite that simple. As I explained before, spells cannot be undone."

"Then how are we going to remove the Cloak?"

"Our best recourse right now is to find the *talisman*. The Caster who created the Cloak most likely tied the spell to one. If the talisman is found and destroyed, then so is the spell."

"Oh." Interesting. "Like a magical kill switch?"

"Precisely."

Friday night, Taylor arrived at my house in her pristine-white convertible Beetle shortly after nightfall. Her wavy blond locks were pulled back in a neat ponytail, and she was sporting a denim mini with a black and purple letterman jacket. She could have easily stood in as one of the official Bulldog cheerleaders (or Ice Girls as they prefer to be called), and no one would have been the wiser.

We took our time heading across town. Perhaps a little too much because by the time we arrived, the school parking lot at Easton Prep looked like a patchwork quilt of shimmering metal. I'd never seen so many cars crammed together in one place before, except maybe at a concert once. Taylor didn't seem to bat a lash as she jumped in behind a stream of other cars that began parking in messy rows right there on the grass as though it were a perfectly appropriate alternative.

According to Taylor, the Weston Bulldogs and Easton Wildcats were longtime rivals, and so it really wasn't surprising that a game between the two would draw out this many people. Especially a game where the widely known star forward was making his first post-injury appearance back on the ice.

I followed Taylor into the arena as we made our way down the grandstands of what appeared to be the visitors side, and sat down in the lower mid-section next to Ben who had saved a couple of seats for us. Nikki, Morgan and Hannah were there too, though I noted it was Morgan who was sitting next to Trace, and not Nikki. Apparently, they were still on the outs since the incident at All Saints.

As per usual, Nikki didn't waste a chance to show her hatred for me with a flaming scowl as she barked out something along the lines of, "Who the *bleep* invited her?"

I resisted the urge to chuck my cell phone at her head though I could practically feel my palms itching for it. I turned to Taylor instead. "Where's Carly?" I asked upon noticing her absence from the group.

"On the ice," she ticked her chin to the rink where the Ice Girls were skating. "She's a Bulldog."

"We all are," leaned in Hannah. "But after Nikki got put on suspension, we decided to strike in support of her."

"Oh, that's..." *so freaking stupid.* "Nice."

Taylor gave me a crafty side look that let me know she wasn't part of that debacle. She rarely ever was.

"We're petitioning the administration for a hearing," continued Hannah. Her eyes glistened as she stared out onto the ice longingly. "Hopefully we can all be back out there soon."

Something told me she wouldn't be the one to make that call. In fact, something told me Hannah rarely ever made decisions about what she would or wouldn't be doing.

I offered a sympathetic smile and then focused back in on Carly and the other girls as they skated around the ice waving at the crowd in an effort to get them amped for the game.

Across the rink, the Wildcat Girls were getting ready to put on their own show in matching brown, white and orange outfits accompanied by their official mascot—some unfortunate guy dressed in an adult sized wildcat costume—also in coordinated school colors.

"There's Caleb!" squealed Taylor. Oddly enough, she really seemed to be into this. Or maybe she was into him. I wasn't sure yet.

"Where?" I asked, only mildly interested.

"Owens," she pointed to center ice. "Thirty-Six."

"Owens? Like, Carly Owens?"

"Yeah," she laughed. "They're twins. Didn't I mention that?"

"I don't think so." I hardly noticed a resemblance. Well, apart from the chestnut hair. And maybe the pouty lips.

She went on to wave at a dark-haired guy sitting a few rows below us. He was staring up at her adoringly.

"He's cute," I noted. Maybe he was one of *hers*.

"Dillon Walker. Biggest scumbag ever," she said as soon as he wasn't looking. "That's his pregnant girlfriend waddling up over there," she said pointing to an extremely pregnant sophomore girl. "And that's the skank he screws from Easton when his girlfriend's not around," she added, pointing to another scantily clad girl only a few seats away from him.

"Gross." Guys like that needed to come with warning labels.

The cool air bit against my skin as I focused back on the ice, waiting for the game to start. I tried not to notice the smokestacks that were bleeding from my nose every time I took a breath as it only forced me to pay greater attention to the profound level of freezing I was experiencing. It was becoming increasingly more difficult as each minute passed.

"Watch your mouth!" I heard someone yell.

The crowd to our right suddenly broke out into a scuffle, distracting me from my plight. Bodies from several rows jostled around as fists flew rapidly through the virgin air. I heard the girls screeching out in distress as the crowd collectively spread itself apart, distancing themselves from the commotion.

A few odd strays piled into the brawl, though after a few moments, we could see the Johnny-come-lately's were actually trying to break the fight apart, and not partake in it.

"What the hell happened?" I asked nobody specific.

"Trace got into it with two kids from Easton," answered Hannah who had somehow ended up behind Taylor and me.

I craned my neck to get a better look as the angry mob began settling down. I could see Trace shaking off a pair of (what looked like) friendly hands, as another man pulled the other two guys in the opposite direction. One of them was bleeding from his nose and walked away willingly though the other one was a lot less eager to leave. He turned around and grinned in our direction, proudly flashing the nasty cut above his right eye.

"Stupid boys," said Taylor as she tied her hair in a ponytail. "Can't live with them."

I waited for her to add the, *can't live without them* part, but she didn't.

I relaxed back into my place, bouncing a final glance down the line to Trace who also had his own little accolade settling in—a busted bottom lip, though not too bad for a two-on-one.

His piercing blue eyes locked in on me, hardening with what looked like anger, before averting back to the ice.

If I didn't know any better, I might have thought he just openly glared at me.

The night wasn't a total bust. After three intense periods of play, a decent intermission performance by both squads, and a stellar performance from the star-player himself, Weston took home the victory with a demoralizing 7-2 win over Easton. The stands roared with cheers as we rose in a standing ovation that I only participated in to get a better view of the nearest exit.

As soon as the arena started to clear out, we quickly swapped our seats for the parking lot where we hung around and waited for Carly and Caleb to round out the rest of the group. I sat on the hood of Taylor's beetle, listening as Ben went on about an after-party going on at some girl's house from Easton, and I could already tell Taylor was into it.

I immediately started devising a plan to get out of it.

Carly showed up shortly after still dressed in full cheer attire. After making a few rounds in the parking lot, she piled into Nikki's red jeep along with Morgan and Hannah and headed off to the Easton party together. And they weren't alone. More than half the cars had already cleared out.

"Who am I riding with?" asked Ben, looking directly at Taylor as he walked back over to us with Trace.

"Obviously with the person you came with, genius," replied

Taylor as she fetched her keys from her purse.

"Trace isn't going."

"Great," said Taylor, throwing her keys back in her purse. "I guess you're riding with us, which means we're stuck here waiting for Caleb." She wasn't happy, and she was about to get even more unhappy.

"Don't be mad," I said, turning to her with regret. "But I'm not going either. I promised my uncle I'd be home right after the game. He already texted me," I said holding up my phone. Both were lies. I was *so* going to hell.

"What? You can't be serious!" Taylor's bottom lip sulked out. "This totally sucks."

"I know, but I'll make it up to you tomorrow at Carly's party," I assured her, though I wasn't even sure I wanted to go to that one either. "We'll have a great time."

"We better," she warned, letting me know she wasn't going to be as forgiving with that one. Her smile quickly returned. "Alright, get in. Let's see if we can get you home before curfew without breaking any laws." The girl loved a challenge.

"Hold up," said Ben. "That doesn't make any sense. Trace should take Jemma home. He's already going that way."

I glanced over at Trace who looked annoyed with Ben's offer.

"You're going home anyway," said Ben, shrugging. "You can drop her off on your way home. That way the rest of us can go straight to the party." He nodded into it as if to persuade him.

Trace looked over at me, musing as he grazed his busted lip with the tip of his tongue. "Fine. Whatever."

"Done," said Ben, turning to Taylor. "Let's roll."

"Jemma?" she raised her brows, awaiting my approval.

"Yes. Go. Have fun! I'll be fine with Trace."

I think.

14. STRICTLY BUSINESS

The warm heat radiating from the vents felt like a godsend against my skin, which had all but anesthetized itself from the cold. Trace was leaning forward in his seat and checking his lip in the rear-view mirror, angling his face as he appraised the damage. I found myself watching him without meaning to, my eyes taking in the hard edges to his face, the deep indentations in his cheeks, the fullness of his heart-shaped lips...

It really wasn't hard to see why a girl might become slightly unhinged around him—*for* him.

"Does it hurt?" I asked, wincing as he patted the cut with his finger.

"Nah. I've had worse," he said and relaxed back in his seat.

I hadn't actually been alone with Trace since the *incident* last Wednesday. We carried on as if it never even happened, dutifully avoiding any real conversations and ensuring neither one of us had a chance to bring it up. It was just as well, I had no desire to talk about it anyway.

"You want my jacket?" he offered. He was looking outside the driver side window when he asked. "You're shaking."

I hadn't realized my shivering was that obvious, especially

since I hadn't seen him look at me once since we got into the car. "I'm okay, thanks."

He griped the steering wheel with one hand and threw the car in gear with the other, jolting me forward a little as he backed out of his parking spot.

"So what happened back there?" I asked out of curiosity and a newfound urge to make conversation with him.

"Back there?"

"The fight."

He shrugged, keeping his eyes on the road.

When he didn't offer anything up, I pressed on. "Did you know those guys?"

"Not really."

I looked him over. "Do you make habits out of fighting with people you don't know?"

"Do you make habits out of asking so many questions?" he responded crudely.

Alrighty then. I could totally take a hint.

"Sorry I asked," I said in the same tone and then twisted my body away from the sudden arctic chill that had nothing to do with the weather.

Neither one of us said another word until we hit Main Street ten minutes later. The entire street seemed eerily quiet, and sort of deserted as most of the shops had already closed up hours ago. Everyone who might be out on a Friday night was either still at the game, at an after-party, or on their way to one.

"Mind if we stop for food?" he asked, breaking the silence.

"You're the boss." I answered without looking.

He turned into the parking lot of the next burger place and pulled into the first spot before killing the engine. There was a grand total of two cars in the entire lot. I was surprised they stayed open for this kind of business, or lack thereof.

"What are you having?" he asked as he swung open his door.

"Nothing for me," I said as I glanced over my shoulder at the empty parking lot, scanning the barely lit street adjacent to the lot. The neighborhood looked questionable, at best.

Maybe it was the lack of street lights, or just my own paranoia, but waiting out here by myself suddenly didn't feel like an altogether great idea.

"I'm ordering you *something*," he persisted. "Might as well tell me what you like."

"Sure, that's fine." I wasn't paying attention anymore. I flung my passenger side door open and climbed out. "I'm coming inside with you."

I caught his stare over the roof of his car, his expression bewildered by my bizarro behavior, and then his eyes softened some, seemingly treated with a dose of understanding.

Once inside the restaurant, I made my way to a two-seater table by the window facing the parking lot and waited while Trace ordered his food. I felt safer having a panorama view of the area in case I needed to, I don't know, run for my life.

After a few minutes, Trace appeared with the food.

"I got you a cheeseburger and fries, and one of those strawberry shakes you order at lunch sometimes." He pushed the tray in front of me and sat down.

I stared back at him, surprised that he noticed what I ordered at lunch, especially since his eyes generally spent most of their time in another direction (that direction being *any* direction that wasn't mine). Or at least that's how it seemed.

He dropped his eyes and picked up his own cheeseburger, sinking his teeth in and biting off nearly a quarter of it.

"Thanks," I said, examining his ever-guarded expression. "How much do I owe you?"

He looked up from his dark lashes and shook his head.

I thanked him again and turned my attention back to the window, keeping care of my surroundings.

"How have you been?" he asked after a short pause. His voice was low, cautious. "Since the other night," he added unnecessarily. I already knew what we were talking about.

His eyes bounced around my face as though he were trying to gauge my answer before I gave it.

"Fine." I forced a smile.

"Did you talk to your uncle about what happened?" He picked up his burger without looking up this time.

I shook my head.

"Why not?" he asked, meeting my eyes again.

I felt his leg brush up against mine and nearly lost my train of thought. "I...I'd rather just forget the whole thing."

"That's pretty stupid," he said under his breath, though it was more than audible.

"*Excuse* me?"

Where the hell did he get off judging me? He had no idea what I'd been through. What I was *still* going through. I was barely hanging on as it was, coping the only way I knew how. Who was he to tell me that it was wrong?

A jeering rumble emitted from him. "It's wrong. And stupid. I don't really care how you justify it."

My head snapped up and locked in on his hooded eyes. Why did that sound like he just answered my thought?

He took a sip of his drink, and then sank back in his chair. His legs stretched out in front of him, coming out on either side of me—fencing me in.

"Pretending something didn't happen, doesn't make it go away. You get that right?"

"I'm not pretending it didn't happen." It came out far more defensive than I had intended it to.

"No?" He raised his brows. "What do you call it then?"

"I call it..." I didn't have an answer. "Just mind your own business and stay out of mine!"

"Believe me," he grumbled. "I'm trying."

"Try harder then. Shouldn't this already be like second nature to you by now?"

"What's that supposed to mean?" he asked, leaning in again.

I matched his advance. "It means, you should have plenty experience staying out of my life since you've pretty much treated me like I was the Plague ever since I moved here."

He raised his brows slightly. "Is that what you think?"

"Are you saying it's not true?"

His eyes flickered down to my mouth. Something flashed through them though it was gone before I could make it out.

"All I'm saying is, I think you should be prepared."

"Prepared for what?" I scoffed, though it lacked punch.

He seemed to be assessing me again, looking for unspecified particulars on my face, in my body language. "What do you think would have happened if I hadn't been there that night? If I didn't come out when I did?"

I felt a cold chill zip down my spine. I know exactly what would have happened if Trace hadn't been there to save me.

"Yeah, it's none of my business," he agreed, leaning back again. "But if I were you, I'd make sure I was ready for *next time.*"

"Next time?" I repeated incredulously. I hadn't exactly thought as far as *next time*, or what I might do if I came face to face with another one. I was still pretty swamped with trying to forget the last time. I crossed my arms in defiance. "I'm not planning on a next time."

He laughed grimly. "Life doesn't give a shit about your plans." There was real truculence there, dark undertones of anger, and pain, and regret. I couldn't help but wonder how much of this had to do with his sister—with her murder.

Even though what happened to his sister and what happened to me the other night were completely different and unrelated, I could see how *he* might equate the two. And I could certainly understand where he was coming from, and the point that he was trying to make, despite its crude delivery. We lived in a dangerous world, and the bottom line was that I needed to learn how to defend myself against predators—whether the human variety, or otherwise.

I nodded weakly, the only response I was willing to give.

He licked his lips and leaned back in his chair. "Like I said, none of my business."

15. FACE OFF

Dominic arrived at the house around a quarter past nine, dressed to kill in black slacks and a button-down dress shirt. He had a penchant for black clothing, it would seem, though I could hardly be persuaded to mind. It made his skin and hair absolutely glow in contrast, and when necessary, allowed me to easily coordinate my own outfit—dark jeans and a simple black lace camisole.

Like most of the privileged people from these parts, Caleb and Carly's house sat at the base of a cul-de-sac in a gated neighborhood not far from my uncle's house. The grand moonbeam-colored house was lit up with spotlights and was belting out music that reached far past the borders of their sprawling front yard. It was a packed house, evidenced by the circular driveway filled to the brim with cars that spilled out onto the surrounding street, forcing us to park several houses down.

An obscene ice sculpture greeted us on the front stoop.

"Is that a—"

"Indeed it is," answered Dominic as he ticked his chin to a sign that read, "Enter all ye who like to party."

There was no way Carly approved this. "How gross."

Dominic walked in ahead of me, towing me behind him as I acclimated to the change of scenery, to the watchful eyes. It was dark inside, heated, and loud, with people packed in at every corner—dancing, grinding, chatting in small groups, and throwing back questionable drinks from oversized, red plastic cups. One could easily be swallowed up by a crowd like this but Dominic glided through it with ease. It was like the parting of the seas the way people stepped out of his path; girls snapping their necks around to look at him, to devour him with their eyes as he passed. I wondered if he knew the effect he had on the opposite sex. The sheer desire he incited in them.

He had to know. Nobody could be *that* oblivious.

Taylor came sailing out of the kitchen as soon as she saw us round the corner, her golden hair bouncing freely around her back as a look of mischief danced across her face. I caught a glimpse of a few familiar faces over her shoulder, namely a disinterested Trace who was leaning back against a counter, his personal space completely swallowed up by a brunette in a skintight blue dress—undoubtedly Nikki.

"I'm so happy you're here!" she squealed, throwing her arms around my neck and bouncing us around like a jackrabbit.

She pulled back and eyed Dominic, grinning her approval.

"This is my friend Taylor," I bellowed over the music, making an official introduction.

He tipped his head to her, flashing one of his debonair smiles. "It's a pleasure to meet you, Taylor."

"God. You're like, smoking hot."

"Taylor!"

"What? He is!" she laughed. "And you smell to die for. Seriously, what cologne is that?"

I had to bite my lip to stop myself from laughing.

It seemed that with just a smile and a few blinks of his

smoldering eyes, Taylor had been reduced to a blushing heap of mush—fawning over everything from his scent, to his hair, to his car. Of course, Dominic didn't seem to mind it in the slightest, and may have even been enjoying it, so I just smiled along with them and let her rant go on uninterrupted. As entertaining as they were, it still wasn't very long before I found my own eyes drifting back towards the kitchen.

Back to Trace.

The conversation between us last night had gone from icy to nuclear and then back again in a matter of minutes, and left me agitated long after we left the restaurant. I couldn't figure out what it was about him that got under my skin so easily.

Maybe it was that ever-guarded exterior he wore like body armor, or the way he could validate or dismiss me with a minor shift of those piercing, reticent eyes. Or how he always seemed to be there at the most pivotal moments—like when I fainted at work, or when I was attacked behind All Saints. It was peculiar.

Everything I knew about him amounted to nothing and only left me with more questions. And a longing. A longing for answers, and for something else. Something I couldn't even name.

Trace looked up at me just then, meeting my prying eyes with his own blend of curiosity. The connection made my breath hitch, but I kept my eyes locked on him, and his on mine. There was something special about those eyes—

"Helloooo?" Taylor waved her hand in front of my face.

"Huh?" My cheeks heated up as I realized her and Dominic were both staring at me, waiting for me to answer a question I hadn't heard. "I'm sorry, what are we talking about?"

"We're inquiring about drinks," she laughed.

"What about them?"

"Whether you'd like one, love," Dominic whispered into my ear, his cologne filling up my space with its delicious scent.

I started to turn to face him and felt his lips graze against my cheek. I stopped before making the full rotation, knowing where his lips would end up if I completed it.

I nodded instead.

On our way to the kitchen, we landed in the middle of an argument between a red-headed sophomore and her boyfriend (who were both visibly upset and completely blocking the entry), arguing about whether she was flirting with some guy named Toby. Or Tony.

Judging by their slurred speech and glazed eyes, they were definitely drunk on a lot more than just love.

Taylor, never one to shy away from...well anything, was quick to wrap her arm around the feuding couple and offer mock consolation as she guided them out of the kitchen. I watched as she tactically inserted a freshman mediator into the car wreck of a scene and then slipped out unnoticed.

Clearly this wasn't her first drunken rodeo.

Seconds later, she was back in the kitchen introducing Dominic to the rest of the girls who promptly swarmed around him, cooing and pawing at him, and (most likely) unintentionally pushing me out of the circle. The whole thing was ridiculous.

I backed out and headed to the breakfast-table-turned-bar where I poured myself a glass of soda from the sidelines.

"Hey, Blackburn."

I jumped at the sound of his voice in my ear, nearly spilling my drink on myself in the process.

It was the hockey player slash party host.

"Hey, Caleb." I patted down my shirt to make sure I wasn't soaked in cola. "Great party."

"Glad you could make it." He smiled warmly and took a sip of his own drink. "Are you having a good time?"

"Yeah, definitely, it's amazing." *Amazing*? Okay, so I was

exaggerating a little. There was no law against it.

I put my cup down and refilled my drink.

"I saw you at the game yesterday," he said, bending forward slightly to catch my eye, his chestnut hair and high cheekbones highlighted under the dim overhead lights. "I wanted to talk to you after the game, but you left before I got a chance."

"Sorry, I had an early curfew—"

"Thanks for bringing the lady-bandit," interrupted Ben, appearing beside Caleb and I, visibly annoyed as he nudged his chin towards Dominic and his adoring fan-girls. "There's like fifteen girls around him."

"No there isn't." I stifled a laugh. "There's probably like five, six tops." It didn't matter either way, I was fairly certain that Ben was only concerned about *one* particular girl from the bunch anyway. Not that he'd admit it.

"You came with him?" asked Caleb, eying Dominic now.

"Yeah…I hope that's okay?" I suddenly felt weirded-out, like maybe it was inappropriate, or presumptuous, to invite him without clearing it with the hosts first.

"Sure, it's no problem," he said smiling. It seemed sincere.

I looked back at where Trace and Nikki had been standing and found the spot empty. He was gone. Both of them were. Probably together. I didn't want to care, but I kind of did.

I turned back to Dominic and found him still backed up against the wall, surrounded by my half-inebriated classmates. He looked over at me and twisted his lips into a smile. A fully kissable, dangerous smile.

He bent forward and whispered something to the girls and just like that, slipped through the pinning crowd and began walking back over to me, slowly, confidently, far more sure of himself than any other guy at this party.

"Have I told you how stunning you look tonight?" He punctuated his words with a gentle caress of my cheek.

I shook my head, biting my lower lip.

A look of torture took hold of his face when his eyes shifted down to my mouth. "Simply ravishing."

Funny, I was thinking the same thing about him. I could feel my heart rate climbing again.

He took a step forward, fully breaking the bounds of my personal space, and leaned in close to me like only he knew how to do. I was half expecting him to jam a purse or a cup into my belly when he said, "would you like to get out of here?"

Something in his eyes was tempting me—*daring* me, and I was nodding even before my brain had a chance to process the offer, or what exactly I might have been agreeing to.

"I just need to use the ladies room," I blurted out and then sashayed around him before he had a chance to respond. I snatched Taylor by the wrist on my way out of the kitchen.

"What's up, babe?" she asked as we pushed through the boiling crowd of people.

We needed a new plan for meeting up tonight being that I was supposed to be sleeping over at her house. And I needed a splash of cold water to help get my wits together.

"Bathroom?" I asked, and then followed her upstairs to the second floor washroom.

"Look who it is, Mor."

Nikki and Morgan were standing in front of the door with hands on their hips and scowls on their lips as soon as we rounded the corner. Somehow, it didn't feel like a coincidence.

"Excuse us," I said and tried to cut in between them.

"Actually, you're not excused," sneered Nikki as she stepped in front of me and blocked the door. "I think it's time the two of us had ourselves a little chat."

I crossed my arms protectively. I had no idea what she could possibly need to discuss with me (or whether or not she had any more liquor bombs planned) but I had the sneaking suspicion I wasn't getting out of here until I heard her out.

"Trace and I are getting back together," she blurted, smacking her scarlet lips together. "We were together last night. I just thought you should hear it from me first."

I held myself as taut as I could and tried not to give away any of the feelings rocketing through me just then—anger, annoyance, disappointment. *Jealousy*.

I was unsure how to process any of this, but the last thing I wanted to do was let Nikki know she was getting to me.

"That's really great for you," I offered, my voice noticeably on edge. "And you're telling me this because...?"

"Oh, you don't know?" she snorted. "You're even denser than you look, you know that?"

"Quit giving her a hard time, Nikki." Taylor squirmed her way in between us. "She's not after Trace, okay? She's here with Dominic Huntington so just back off."

"Did I ask for your opinion?" snapped Nikki as she shoved her back a step.

"Hey!" I flung my arm out in front of Taylor. "Leave her out of this," I warned, forming a barrier between the two of them.

"Look who's finally growing a backbone—how very stupid of you," snarled Nikki, insulting me and provoking me at the same time. "So tell me, Jemma, does Dominic know about your late night dates with Trace? Because I'm sure he'd be interested to hear all about them. I know *I* was."

"What late night date?" I could hear the hurt in Taylor's voice at the idea that I was keeping secrets from her.

"There was no late night date," I said definitively, my eyes never leaving Nikki. "And honestly, I don't think he would care. He doesn't strike me as the insecure-raging-bitch type."

Morgan's jaw nearly hit the floor.

Oh my God! Who gave my mouth permission to say that?

Nikki took a step into me. "What. Did. You. Just. Say?"

The house lights flickered on and off.

There must have been a storm coming in, though something about the air felt menacing, ominous, like a whispered warning, heeding me to back off. Playing with Nikki was like playing with fire, and I was bound to get burned.

I *so* didn't want to get burned.

I needed to diffuse this, and fast. "Look, I don't want to fight with you, Nikki. We obviously got off on the wrong foot—"

"Spare me the bullshit," she cut in, her lips in a frightening curl. "You pretty much sealed your fate the minute you moved here, and the way I see it, any girl with a death wish as big as yours is free game."

I staggered back a step, her strange threat having just sucker punched me in the gut.

"Whoa!" Taylor raised her arms in the air like a referee. "I think we need to calm down with the homicidal threats and take it down a few notches."

"She's right. C'mon Nikki, let's just go," said Morgan nervously, turning for the stairs.

Nikki didn't budge. "The best thing you can do, Jemma, is to stay the hell out of my way. You have no idea who you're dealing with and I promise you, you don't want to find out."

"Oh my God, we get it!" snapped Taylor. "You're the baddest bitch and Trace is yours. Message received."

"It better be. For Jemma's sake." She gave us the middle finger salute before turning on her heel and disappearing down the stairs with Morgan in tow.

I stood there motionless, caught somewhere between shock and anger. "What the *hell* is her problem?" How could someone have that much venomous hate for me without even knowing me?

"I know, right?" said Taylor, shaking her head incredulously.

"She's been on mean-girl steroids ever since you moved here. I've never seen her this bad."

"That doesn't make me feel any better."

"Sorry, babe," she laughed, though her smile was short-lived. "Look, I know it's not what you want to hear, but it's obvious she has it in for you and trying to be nice is only giving her more power. I think it's time to fight fire with fire and give her a little taste of her own medicine—hair remover in her shampoo maybe?" She ticked her brows mischievously.

She had a point—not about the hair remover, that was just insane—but about trying to be on good terms with Nikki. It was the equivalent of trying to put out a raging fire by asking it nicely. It was stupid, and pointless, and would only leave me with third degree burns in the end. Or worse.

Backing down from her time and time again only fueled her inferno and made her bolder and more powerful, and I refused to give her that kind of power over me. I was officially done taking shit from Nikki Parker.

I left the party with Dominic shortly after the altercation and drove out to Northern Peak, a lookout near the old Hollow Hills Cemetery. Though I was undoubtedly relieved to be away from Nikki and her madness, I wasn't particularly inspired by his choice of destinations. In fact, just hearing the word cemetery gave me the willies, though after a little coaxing and a promise that we'd only be *near* it, and not *in* it, I eventually agreed to go.

With the rain finally letting up, we parked at the back of the church and walked on foot the rest of the way. It was just a short march down the gravel path to a small clearing that overlooked the mainland. And he was right, the view was breathtaking. Glowing homes cascaded all the way down the hillside and met at the center of the expansive valley, peppering the town with a web of warm lights for miles in every direction. The bordering, phantom trees on the outskirts held it all together in total isolation, seemingly blacking out the rest of the world around us.

"It really is beautiful," I said in awe as we leaned against the dry stone wall and took in the haunting vista.

"It is," he agreed, gazing at me as he coiled a loose strand of my hair around his finger and then tucking it behind my ear. His touch sent a ripple down my back.

"Am I making you nervous?" he asked. His voice was like silk against hungry skin, smooth and seducing in every way.

Of course I was nervous. How could I not be with that voice in my ears, and those eyes on me, and that tugging smile on his lips? Everything about him stirred my insides.

"No," I lied, my heart hammering hard against its cage, threatening to betray my words.

He raised a skeptical brow and moved in closer as though he were challenging me to resist him. I already knew I'd lose that bet. I flattened my back against the stone wall, steadying myself so I didn't topple over from the sudden rush.

"Maybe a little," I admitted.

His mouth hinted at a smile as he studied my eyes with an intensity that made my cheeks warm. "You like me," he accused, seemingly amused by this.

"No I don't!" Something about the way he made the claim made me not want to give him the satisfaction.

He moved in closer until we were nearly touching and placed his arms on the stone wall on either side of me, leaning in. "Are you sure about that?" he asked, whispering into my ear.

I wasn't even sure of my name anymore.

His lips twisted into a satisfied grin. "That's what I thought," he said as his eyes drifted out over my head into the darkness behind me, before resting pensively on my face again. "Tell me,

Jemma, have you ever been kissed before?"

My heart was beating wildly now. If he could hear it, if he could feel it racing, he'd know the answer. But since he couldn't, I'd sooner die than admit I'd never been kissed.

"Tons of times," I said and then cringed at my own response.

"I think you're lying, angel."

I didn't look up when I answered, "Maybe a little."

His hands came up and moved through my hair, pushing the loose strands away from my face, and then slid back down the other way, over the apples of my cheeks. I shivered through each caress, sighing as he cupped my face in his hands.

"I'm going to kiss you now," he informed. "Is that okay?"

A strange noise bubbled out from my throat, some kind of inaudible mumble. I think it was a yes.

I looked up into his dark, smoldering eyes and inhaled sharply as his thumb skimmed the surface of my lips, studiously, tauntingly, before his own lips pressed down onto mine.

I felt the rush from his kiss soar through me like a missile, awakening every cell in my body with its searing emissions. His lips moved over mine hungrily, expertly, and I followed suit as the earth all-but stopped its rotation in honor of my very first kiss. My mind-numbing first kiss.

An entire lifetime came and went before his lips detached from mine and reemerged just below my ear as he strung an even row of kisses all the way down my neck, reaching my collarbone and working their way back up to the top, gently, slowly—deliciously slow.

And then came the pain.

The barrage of soft, velvety kisses ceased their torrent, and were replaced with a sharp ache at the hub of my neck. I winced from the pain and tried twisting away from it, but I was immovable. Something was hurting me, and worse, I couldn't break free from it.

And then, like a brutal flash of consciousness, the horrifying realization set in that it was *him*—Dominic.

He was biting me.

16. REALITY BITES

I could hear my own heartbeat pounding in my ears as Dominic Huntington locked me against his chest and growled into me, feeding on me freely and without my permission. I wanted to fight back, to hit him where it hurt and run, but I couldn't move. I couldn't do anything but whimper in his arms.

Something strange was happening to me.

An unmistakable feeling of lethargy washed over me, traveling through me—through my bloodstream, pacifying every cell in my body as it moved. And just like that, I was barely fit to stand upright anymore. My legs were weak beneath me, tingling like the rest of my body with synthetic sensations of solace, and serenity, and something else, something horrifying...

Pleasure.

It was *Dominic*. He was doing this to me—immobilizing me with his bite like the tainted venom of a pernicious snake, and all I could do was clasp onto him harder as hot tears burned disgraced tracks down the contours of my face.

The world was spiraling out of control around me, nauseating me with every rotation as an insidious, deafening, buzzing noise filled up the space in my head, drowning out all other sounds, including my own vitals. This was it. I was either going to black out from the blood loss, or worse, I was going to die because he wasn't going to stop.

My lids, too weighty for me to keep open anymore, slipped closed by their own accord, and my arms soon followed suit, dropping heavy to my sides. I was limp now, deadweight in his arms, and then suddenly, I was falling, crumbling to the ground.

Had he released me?

Or was I dead?

It took every bit of strength I had left to pry open my eyes from the noxious slumber and watch as a dark-haired stranger ripped Dominic away from me and hauled him off in a backwards bear hug.

"What have you done?" he hissed, throwing Dominic back several feet onto the ground.

The man stood glowing under the overhead spotlight. Tall and resolute, with strong, angled shoulders and the kind of warm, caring face you wanted to believe in, and for a moment, the way he looked at me, I thought maybe I had died and he was an Angel coming to collect my soul and carry me away to the hereafter.

Dominic's chilling laughter assaulted the air as he picked himself up from the ground and brushed the dirt off himself. "Hello to you, too, Gabriel. Is that any way to greet your only brother?" asked Dominic, grinning wildly as he stammered back a few steps, looking almost intoxicated.

His brother?

"You're a damned fool," replied Gabriel, his voice a quiet fury. "They're going to kill you for this, and you know what, Dominic? This time, I'm not going to stop them."

"It was worth it, brother. She tastes even better than she looks, if you can conceive of it," said Dominic, taking a predatory step towards me as though hungry for more.

Gabriel stepped in his path, keeping his back to me. I pulled my legs up closer to my chest and trembled violently. I wasn't sure if it was from the blood loss or fear. Probably both.

"Ever the martyr," laughed Dominic. "I suppose that means you're not interested in indulging in her then? I assure you, there's no better elixir than the blood of a *Slayer*."

I winced.

It made me sick to my stomach to realize he knew what I was all this time. That he was just playing with me—preying on me—waiting for the perfect moment to strike. But how? How had he been able to control himself all this time?

"We can always get rid of the *body* together," continued Dominic callously. "I'm sure it would make for a wonderful, brotherly bonding experience."

Gabriel's head spun around at the sound of my whimper. I hadn't even realized I was crying.

He started to move towards me but stopped abruptly, choosing instead to keep a safe distance between the two of us. "Are you okay?" he asked me, his voice soft but commanding, a flawless harmony that matched his face perfectly.

I wanted to answer him. I wanted to tell him how *not* okay I was, or lie for that matter and tell him that I was perfectly fine and just wanted to be on my merry way, but I couldn't say anything. I just sat there in a ball, frozen on the ground with my back against the stone wall, trying to stop my body from shaking.

"I'm not going to hurt you," he said, crouching down a few feet away from me. His short hair was longer in the front and covered his forehead and part of his eyebrows, and even though I couldn't make out the color of his eyes in the dark, I knew they were soft and I instantly felt safe gazing into them.

"He's telling you the truth, angel," said Dominic as he took another gut-churning step towards me. "You have nothing to worry about. He only kills our kind. Isn't that right, Gabriel?"

I didn't even attempt to understand what he was saying, I already knew not to trust a word of it. Everything he said sounded like a lie, a threat, and it turned my skin to ice.

"Can you stand?" asked Gabriel, ignoring him.

I wasn't sure. I'd been too petrified to move.

Gabriel nodded gently, encouraging me to try. I couldn't explain it but there was something about him that I wanted to trust. Something telling me I would be safe to try with him here. He had, after all, just saved my life.

Slowly, and with his protective eyes on me, I angled my legs to the side and reached for the wall behind me as I began trying to wrench myself up. Gabriel rose with me, mirroring my gradual pace as I tried to stand on shaky legs.

"Looks like I took a little too much," goaded Dominic. "Gluttony's always been a tough one for me."

The sound of his cackle, and the surge of blood rushing from my head to my legs, threw me into a tailspin and sent me tumbling forward through the air. I only felt the fall for a second before Gabriel's arms were around me, steadying me against his chest.

The last thing I remembered were those moss-colored eyes.

17. THE HUNTINGTON INQUIRY

I woke up alone in an unfamiliar room with a blinding headache and a raw throat that begged for liquids. The room was sizable, dated with ornately carved ceilings and Victorian furniture, and there was a quiet fire burning, coloring the room with a dancing pallet of gold and orange. I had no idea where I was, or how long I had been here, and with the curtains drawn as they were, I wasn't even sure if it was day or night anymore.

I let my legs drop over the daybed and tried to stand up, realizing fairly quickly that I was in no shape to attempt that twice. I sat back down and took in a few steadying breaths as I tried to piece together exactly what had happened to me.

As quickly as the picture appeared, so did the tremors and the petrifying fear I felt when Dominic fixed me to his body and nearly drained me to death. The surge of overwhelming emotions were telling me one thing—to get out of this place. The only problem was, I wasn't sure where 'this place' was.

Before I could chart my exit, the door creaked open and Gabriel appeared holding a glass in his hand. The sight of his face, and those kind, unearthly eyes, immediately helped quell some of the rising panic in me, though I couldn't help but wonder if his brother was also lurking somewhere nearby.

He took a few steps towards me, then stopped suddenly as though something had just stepped out in front of him. "May I?" he asked. He was *asking* my permission to approach me.

I nodded, but scooted back on the daybed just the same.

"How are you feeling?" he asked in a soothing voice as he pulled out a chair and sat down in front of me, holding out the glass of orange juice for me. "Are you dizzy or nauseated?"

I stared down at the juice, my throat burning for a taste of it like the arid desert ached for a touch of the rain, though I was unsure if I could trust him.

What if he drugged it? What if Dominic convinced him to "indulge" in me after all and they laced the juice with some kind of poison to knock me out? What if this whole thing was a trap?

But if that were the case, wouldn't they also be poisoning themselves if they then drank my blood?

"Would you prefer a bottle of water?" he asked, lowering the glass. I could only imagine what my face looked like as I debated whether or not I could take the drink.

This is ridiculous, I scolded myself. If he wanted to harm me, he would have done it while I was out cold and defenseless.

I shook my head and took the glass from him, nearly downing the entire contents in one swallow. "Thank you," I said, my voice still raspy from the drought. "How long have I been asleep?"

"A few hours. You look a lot better though," he remarked, examining my face. "Most of your color seems to have returned."

"I can't stop shaking."

"It's normal," he assured me, rising from his chair. He moved to the corner armoire and produced a quilt from it. "You lost quite a bit of blood, and you're probably still feeling the after-effects from the shock," he continued as he opened the quilt in front of me and then draped it around my shoulders before taking his seat again.

I tightened the blanket around myself. "Thank you for tonight…for being there. You saved my life."

"You should thank your sister. I was only doing what she asked me to do."

"My sister? You know Tessa?"

He tipped his head. "She asked me to look in on you while I was in town. I'm sorry I didn't get there sooner."

"You came soon enough," I remarked, afraid to think about what might have happened if he hadn't shown up at all.

"How much do you remember?" he asked, his tone contrite.

"Everything."

He looked saddened by this. I wasn't sure if his sympathy was for me, or for his brother.

"You must have questions."

That was the understatement of the year. "I don't even know where to start," I said through chattering teeth.

"Start wherever you're comfortable."

"I don't understand how this happened. All this time…He never tried to…I mean, the other ones, they always…" I shook my head, frustrated with my inability to formulate a sentence. "He just seemed so *human*."

"But he isn't. Neither of us are."

"So you're a…you're one too?" I drew myself further back away from him. I wanted no part of him.

"Yes. I am a Revenant."

"How is this possible then?" I asked shakily, referring to our face-to-face conversation. "Why aren't you trying to attack me like the other ones? You're not acting like a…"

"Like a monster? A predator?" His lips took a downturn.

"Well, yeah."

"I assure you, those urges are always there," he said, lowering his head. His dark hair sweeping over his soft, angelic eyes. "It's a part of who I am now, but I *can* control it."

This didn't make any sense. If there was one point my uncle drilled home harder than the rest, it was that Revenants did not control themselves. Ever. They had no semblance of humanity, they were predators created to kill. Was all of that a lie?

"Are you saying Revenants can control themselves?"

"No," he said sternly. "They cannot."

I felt my eyebrows furrow. "But you can?"

He nodded.

"Are you a different type of Revenant?"

"Not exactly," he replied cryptically, studying my reaction. "It's not what I am now that separates me from other Revenants. It's what I was before."

"What were you before?" I asked, beside myself with curiosity. I hadn't realized I'd been inching closer to him.

"A Descendant."

The room fell to silence as I sat back in my seat and let the weight of his words sink in.

"A Descendant," I repeated. It was neither a statement nor a question, but something in the middle.

He dipped his head.

"And that's why you're different?"

He nodded again. "The Revenant infection doesn't affect Descendants in the same way that it does a human being," he explained. "Mortals are fragile. Their souls are vulnerable. They're not built to withstand the reanimation process."

"You mean the coming back to life part?"

"Yes," he nodded once. "They come back warped— destabilized. They don't have any natural defenses against what's coming. Most of the time, it only takes a couple of days, sometimes just a few hours, before the infection takes over completely, overwriting their entire existence. Their humanity is always the first thing to go."

A wave of nausea washed through me.

"But Descendants are stronger, we're much more resilient," he explained. "While we can't stop the transformation, it doesn't overtake us the way it does a human. The vessel changes, some of the mechanics change, but we're still in control of the wheel."

"That doesn't sound like a vampire," I noted. "Maybe you're something else? Something new?" I was grasping at straws now.

"I knew my Maker. I am a Revenant," he said definitively.

"So you drink blood?" My voice cracked at the tail end of the question.

"I do—never human though, and only because I need it to survive." The sadness in his eyes was unmistakable. "My body will always react to the scent of blood, even in spite of me, but unlike other Revenants, I can decide whether or not to follow through with the urges—with the bloodlust," he explained, visibly torn by his reality. "That is the perpetual war inside of me. Between my mind and my body."

How could he live this way? How could anyone live this way? It was as though he were a conscious man trapped inside the body of a beast. It was the very definition of a living nightmare.

"What about Dominic?" I felt my throat constrict as my mind shifted to him. "If he can control this, why did he attack me?"

He paused before answering. "Because he *chose* to."

I didn't know how to absorb that.

"He wanted to know what you were—if you were a Slayer. There's been some debate about it..." His voice trailed off as though he were unsure of the terrain he was treading on.

"Because of the spell," I realized aloud.

He nodded.

Jeez, did everyone know about me?

"But that doesn't excuse what he did," he said, his tone

saturated with contempt for his brother. "There were other ways to find out. What Dominic did to you was a testament of what he really is. Of what he's *always* been."

"And what would that be, brother?" Dominic moved through the door so quickly, I barely registered the movement.

Gabriel sat back in his chair undaunted, his back to his brother and eyes on me. "I don't know, Dominic—a savage, cruel, disturbed, evil. Take your pick."

Dominic brought his hand up to his heart and mocked pain before turning his eyes to me. "Hello, angel." His lips twisted into a devious knot, sending a jolt of anxiety through my body.

"Back off, Dominic." Gabriel's facial expression darkened, his voice a low, threatening drawl.

"Relax, brother. I'm only here to answer her questions," he said as he sat down on another chair just a few feet away from me. "Wouldn't you like some answers?" he asked sweetly.

Deceivingly sweet.

I could hardly stand to look at his face anymore, and even though his very presence evoked tremors in me, I couldn't deny the fact that I did need answers from him. Who knew if I'd ever get another chance to ask my questions?

My heart rate picked up.

"You just need to say the word and I'll remove him," said Gabriel. His moss eyes were sharp, promising to hold fast to every word. I couldn't explain it, but somehow I felt safe being around Dominic when Gabriel was watching over me, like I knew I'd be protected from him—to the death.

I turned and faced Dominic, summoning every ounce of courage I had inside of me. It turned out there wasn't much in there. "You bit me to see if I was a—" I gulped hard as the ball in my throat threatened strangulation.

"A Slayer," answered Dominic, finishing my question. "Yes. Amongst other reasons." His impish smile made me queasy.

"Am I?"

His smile widened. "Why, yes, angel, you are."

"How do you know?"

"I tasted it," he said, wetting his lips. "Your blood is nothing like human blood, love. It's richer, sweeter, more potent, an all-encompassing magical rush." There was hunger and desire dancing all through his face now. "I imagine it is as close to Heaven as I'll ever be allowed to get."

My stomach twisted. "Were you trying to kill me?"

"No, but I suppose it was touch and go for a while there, wasn't it?" he chortled. "Normally, I don't have any trouble controlling myself, but with Slayers, well, you never know which way it'll go."

"So you knew there was a chance I was a Slayer, and you bit me anyway, knowing you couldn't control yourself if I was?"

"Do you really want me to answer that?"

I glanced over at Gabriel who was sat unflinching in his chair, watching me intently. He knew the answer, and so did I. Dominic Huntington was a *monster*.

"Did you know who I was from the beginning?" I had to know.

"I did."

I took in a breath. "Was that the only reason you…" I couldn't find the nerve to finish the question, and I hated myself for asking it.

"Was that the only reason I took an interest?"

I nodded.

"What other reason would there be?" His eyes were as menacing as black ice. I never knew eyes could be so cruel.

The lump in my throat tightened as tears of frustration began to pool in my eyes, blurring my vision.

How could I have been so stupid?

"Oh, I see," smiled Dominic, rising from his chair in one

fluid motion. "You want to know if I liked you? If I ever felt anything for you? If you were ever more than a pawn piece in my game of chess?" He was laughing now, mocking me, pouring pails of saline onto my already burning wounds.

I felt tears begin to trickle down my cheeks, and I slapped them away, angry that they'd fallen without my consent. I was hurt, and humiliated. And I'd heard enough.

"I want to go home," I said, my chin quivering as I fought to keep the tears at bay.

"Aw, don't be like that, angel. We're just getting started."

"Come on," said Gabriel as he rose to his feet and offered his hand. "I'll take you home."

The rustling silhouettes of trees bowed back and forth before us as they zipped in and out of view. There was something gripping about their sway, almost prophetic, like they knew the secrets of the world and rocked to the music of its lies.

"Can I ask you a question?" asked Gabriel, pulling me away from my private thoughts and back to the present drive.

"You just did," I pointed out.

He frowned at my petulance.

"Go ahead."

"Were you—" He paused to look at me, his expression pensive. "Were you in love with Dominic?"

The question caught me off guard. Not because of its delivery or implications, but because I wasn't even sure what the word meant outside of the familial sphere. I skimmed Gabriel's composed face as I repeated the question to myself:

Did I love Dominic?

"No," I shook my head. "I didn't know him enough to love him." It turned out I didn't know him at all.

"But you cared for him?"

"I thought I did," I said, feeling embarrassed by the

admission. "Pretty stupid, huh?"

"No." He answered without looking away from the road. "You had no way of knowing."

The kinder, more forgiving side of myself wanted to believe that, though the other side couldn't help but feel emotionally bruised by it, like I should have known better.

"What are you going to do about him?" he asked, gripping the steering wheel firmly. His all-business demeanor was even more rigid than before, if that was even possible.

"What do you mean?"

"Are you going to tell the *Council* about what happened?"

I heard my uncle mention the Council in passing—that they were the elected officials of The Order responsible for overseeing all matters regarding Descendants in everything from training, to tracking, to analyzing threats and assigning missions—though I had yet to meet with them personally.

"I don't know," I shrugged, examining his profile. "What would happen if I told?"

"He'd probably be sanctioned for death."

"He'd be *what*?" My eyes widened in horror.

"He would be killed, Jemma." He spoke without hesitation. "He's only been kept alive on the premise that he's a Descendant and can control himself, that he wouldn't be a threat to humans." He looked at me dryly. "Nearly killing one of their Slayers won't exactly speak to that. It's definite grounds for execution."

God knows I hated Dominic Huntington with the fiery force of an erupting volcano, and I wanted nothing more than to never lay eyes on his face again…but did I want him *dead* dead?

"I knew it would only be a matter of time," he continued, audibly detached. "And I've prepared myself for that."

"You've prepared yourself for his death?"

I couldn't help but feel sorry for him. Regardless of what I felt about Dominic, he was still *his* brother.

"I've prepared myself for what I'll have to do when that time comes," he clarified. "I vouched for him once before, and I knew the price I'd be paying if this turned out badly."

"I don't understand," I said, suddenly feeling as though we were having two separate conversations. "What price are *you* paying?"

He didn't look at me when he answered, "The price of having to carry out the sanction and right the wrong."

"Carry out the—wait, *what*? That's ridiculous," I said, shaking my head in disbelief. "They wouldn't make you *kill* your own brother." I heard myself laughing, like a nervous tick, though there was nothing funny about this.

He didn't respond.

"Would they?" I gulped down the mounting disgust. I couldn't even begin to imagine his position.

"I'm a Warrior Descendant, Jemma. My mother was a Slayer just like you," he nodded over to me, pride brimming from his eyes. "Even though I'm a Revenant now, my mission has not changed, nor has my loyalty to The Order. My duty, above all else, is to protect humanity and to follow the orders of those above me. That is what I was created to do."

I was taken aback by his unwavering commitment. Not even death could deter him. I'd never seen such a blatant display of devotion to anything other than oneself before.

It was rousing.

"I have no qualms about my obligations," he pushed on. "I knew what the consequences were when I asked for their mercy. I thought there might be hope for him—that he could be saved, but I was wrong. Dominic will never change. This is who he is."

"Why is he like this?" I wondered. "You seem so dedicated to all this Warrior Descendant stuff," I said, and remarked his frown at my too-casual choice of words. "Why isn't he?"

"For one, he *isn't* a Warrior Descendant," he said, glancing at me. "My father remarried shortly after my mother died. Dominic was from his second marriage."

"Oh. So you're half-brothers?" That explained why they seemed to have nothing in common, inside or out.

Gabriel nodded. "Dominic's a *Shifter*. His mother was a Descendant of *Guardian* Angels, same as my father was. He's entirely of that faction. A *Pureblood*."

"He's a Descendant of Guardian Angels?" I repeated aghast. "That seems so paradoxical."

"These aren't your textbook Angels, Jemma. Guardians are extremely powerful beings. They're known as the Defenders of Man because of their combat strengths and ability to shift into animal form in order to protect their *target*. They're strong and ruthless, and should never be taken lightly."

"Trust me," I scoffed. "I have no intentions of taking—" My head whipped back around. "Did you say shift into animal form?"

"Yes. Most Angels have the potential to transmogrify, but it's innate in all Guardians and their Descendants."

"So Guardian Descendants can like, shape-shift?" I asked, somewhat frightened by this revelation and its implications.

"Yes."

I swallowed hard. "Even Dominic?"

"Even Dominic," he nodded, stoic. "He can shift into any animal form, though he has to have taken the animal's life in order to transmogrify into it."

"That's really...disturbing," I said, thoroughly off-put by all of this new information. "I can't even imagine it."

"It's actually quite fascinating. The shift itself is—"

"That's okay," I interrupted, flinging my hand up in the air to stop him. "I wasn't asking for a demonstration or anything."

Gabriel nodded. "I forget how new all of this is for you. I

imagine it's a lot to take in all at once."

"You have no idea," I said, rubbing my temples. "I'm still trying to digest the part about being a Slayer, let alone Dominic being a Descendant of *Guardian Angels*."

"Don't be fooled by the names and titles," said Gabriel, remarking my expression. "They're all just different factions of Anakim depicting different lineages, and he may be a descendant of one, but he's still his own person with his own free will. We all are. Unfortunately, Dominic's free will has always gravitated to the darker side of things."

I could see that about him. "Was he always this way?"

"I can't remember a time when he wasn't."

"I'm sure that won't make it any easier for you..." *To kill him*, I thought, though I left that last part out.

"I suspect not." He turned to meet my gaze. "Does that mean you've made your decision?"

The answer seemed set in stone, like a heavy gavel anchoring me down under its uncomfortable weight.

Dominic *was* a monster. If I told the Council about what he had done to me—that he nearly killed me tonight—he would be put to death for it. And even though he hurt me, and I hated him, and he wasn't exactly human, and maybe even deserved to be punished for what he had done, somehow it just didn't feel right knowing that if I told, I'd be forcing the one person who saved my life to kill his own brother.

I could never do that. "I've decided not to say anything."

He blinked into me, surprised by my decision. "I'm not sure you understand the gravity of the situation," he objected. The truth was, I wasn't sure either. "I think you should discuss this with Tessa before—"

"No!" I shook my head decidedly. "I don't want her to know. I don't want anyone to know. It's only going to make things worse." *For me*, that is.

If Tessa found out about this, she would undoubtedly report back to my uncle and I didn't want to give him any more leverage over me than he already had. Nobody could know about this. I made a mistake, I'll admit that, but it's done and over with. I wasn't going to let it happen again.

"Promise me you won't say anything."

I could only imagine what he thought about me—about my decision to remain quiet. He probably thought I was being careless and stupid, or naïve about the danger Dominic posed.

Or maybe he was relieved by it.

Whatever it was, he wasn't saying. He simply nodded, and to my relief, let the subject drop by the wayside.

I turned my attention back to the bustling trees just outside my window and quietly prayed to myself that I would not go to my death regretting this decision.

18. BLINDSIDED

I lay on my back watching the moon radiate from my bedroom window for what felt like hours, trying to make sense out of everything that had transpired tonight. It seemed as though the levees of my subconscious had finally given out, forcing my mind to be flooded with a steady stream of everything I had been running from. Things that I'd been too afraid to look at—who I was, who I was supposed to be, what I was expected to do. What would become of the life I was desperately trying to hold onto? What would become of *me*?

The weight of each question resting heavy on my shoulders, and the consequences, insurmountable. I wasn't yet ready for it, for any of it—the truth, the future, the responsibility—but I also knew I couldn't stay where I was anymore either, because the only thing more dangerous than moving forward was standing still. And that was no longer an option for me.

So where did that leave me?

I knew I wasn't ready to be anyone's vampire-slaying human crusader, and truthfully, I wasn't sure I'd ever be ready for that. But I also didn't want to sit around here waiting to die. I was too young to die. I hadn't even lived yet.

I had a choice here. Not a good choice, but a choice nonetheless. I could hide myself from the world, cower away and do nothing, and hope to God that Dominic or someone like him didn't come along and find me again. Or I could become the person my uncle believes me to be and throw myself into the symbolical lions pit every day for the rest of my life. Either way, it felt like a lose-lose situation.

I racked my mind for a way out, for some kind of middle ground I was comfortable standing on. Not here nor there, but a safe place in the middle.

And therein lay my answer.

If I wanted to have a fighting chance, I'd have to go at least halfway into this. I had to make sure I was ready for him next time—like Trace had said. That I could defend myself. That I could fight back. That I could survive it. Because no matter how I looked at it, no matter how I tried to spin it, this was my reality now. It was life or death, fight or die—me or them.

And I chose me.

I woke up the next morning feeling surprisingly rested despite the all too familiar nightmare, and for the first time in a long time, I felt at peace with myself. There was a sweet release that came with making a decision, from resigning myself to a given path, and I couldn't help but indulge in its sap.

I inspected my neck thoroughly in in the bedroom mirror before making any attempts to leave my room and was surprised to find that the two puncture wounds above my right jugular had nearly healed overnight. There was definitely *something* at play here, something unearthly, and even though it was off-putting, I couldn't help but feel relieved because at least I wouldn't have to hide the marks under some ugly scarf at work today, or worry about trying to explain the telling wounds to my uncle.

I threw on my work uniform, stole one more glance in the mirror, and then hurried off to speak with Uncle Karl, who I found sitting at his desk in the office, shuffling through a stack of bills and other papers. He was surprised to see me; that much was evident on his face.

"I thought you were sleeping at Taylor Valentine's house?" he asked through creased brows.

I smiled at his use of her full name. "I decided to come home after the party. I kind of wanted to be in my own bed," I said, sitting down in the leather chair across from him.

"Is everything okay?" he asked, peeling away his reading glasses and setting them down on the desk, the concern billowing in over his eyes like a translucent film.

I took a nervous breath as I readied myself for the distorted version of the truth I was about to tell. "I was attacked by a Revenant last night after the party," I said, in an eerily calm manner. When I saw his eyes swell, I quickly added, "I'm fine though, I got away. Nothing happened." My tongue pelted out each lie as though it were an intrinsic weapon.

"For Pete's sake, Jemma. Why wasn't I told about this last night? We could have sent someone after them."

"I wasn't thinking about that," I said, shrugging my shoulder. "I just wanted to get back home."

He let out a displeased breath, though there seemed to be some understanding in his eyes.

The conversation was veering off course. I needed to get back to the point. "The thing is, I'm glad it happened, Uncle, because as scary as it was, it made me realize something."

He watched me curiously, uncertain of where I was going.

"It made me realize how much danger I'm actually in, and as long as I stay like *this*," I said, motioning to my pitiful self, "I'm just a sitting duck waiting for the next attack."

He sunk back into his chair and nodded solemnly as though

he'd already been grappling with this truth for a while now.

I, too, had been struggling with it...with the reality of who I was and of what I was supposed to do. Up until now, I hadn't been able to accept it as my truth—as *my* destiny, and even though I was still struggling to come to terms with it, the alternative was to stay in the dark; weak, unready, and vulnerable to predators like Dominic, and that was something I was no longer willing to do.

"I want you to break the spell," I said with conviction. If the spell was suppressing my abilities—preventing me from sensing Revenants—then I wanted no more part of it.

His eyes widened, pulling in the light from the room as a full-figured smile formed on his lips. "This is wonderful news, Jemma. I knew you would make the right decision—"

"I haven't made any decisions yet." I felt a mild tinge of guilt for not giving him the entire truth about what my true intentions were, but I batted it away. I had to stay focused on my new plan: *operation stay the hell alive.* "I'm going to take this day by day. Right now the only thing I know for sure is that I don't ever want to be in that position again, so I'd like to start training as soon as possible. If that's okay with you."

"Yes, of course. I fully support you in this." His eyes shifted away just then. There seemed to be something unsettling him. Something he wasn't saying.

It was making me uneasy. "What? What's wrong?"

"It's nothing for you to worry about," he said, doing his best to assure me. "I'm taking care of it."

I made a face letting him know I wasn't buying whatever it was he was trying to sell.

He brought his elbows up onto his desk and pressed his fingers together in a steeple. "We might have to delay your training for a little while," he finally said, his eyebrows pulled together in frustration. "We don't have a *Handler* ready for you just yet, however, the Council is working on remedying the situation. It's only a temporary setback."

"What's a Handler and why do I need one?" I asked, unsure of what that was and how big of a wedge it would throw in my plan.

"Of course, forgive me. I forget how little you know of the Order," he said, ill at ease. "Handlers are highly trained *Demibloods* that are part Slayer and part something else, usually a Caster or a Shifter."

That was just like Gabriel. His mother was a Slayer and his father was a Shifter, which would have made him a Demiblood. Or at least it did before he...changed.

"Their sole purpose," he continued, "is to train you and your *Keeper* and prepare you both for battle. As one. Together you will form a *Rig* and work for The Order. But without your Keeper on board, it's impossible to—"

"Why can't I just train alone?" I interrupted. I had no interest in hearing all the rules and useless protocol. That stuff was for the birds.

"Slayers very rarely work alone. It's far too dangerous," he explained. "Your Keeper is essentially your other half. They'll learn your every move, your every weakness, and they'll be there to protect your neck when it's on the line. It's a bond unlike any other." There was a strange twinkle in his eye that looked a lot like pride. "There is so much that goes into creating a powerful Rig, Jemma, but without the other half, it is virtually impossible to find a Handler willing to sign on."

"So, no Keeper means no Handler and no training."

"Precisely." His face hardened as he went on. "A Keeper must first Pledge himself to you, and unfortunately, yours is refusing to accept his responsibility."

My head recoiled. "What do you mean mine is refusing?"

He pressed his lips into a hard line, offering nothing.

"Who is it? Do I know him?" I pushed, crossing my arms as I tried *not* to feel offended by this news. I wanted to hear that this person was a stranger—someone I'd never met before, whose decision not to Pledge themselves to me (whatever the hell that meant) had nothing to do with *me*.

My uncle nodded that I knew him, affirming all my fears.

"Who is it?" I demanded.

He hesitated a moment before answering, probably looking for a way to soften the blow.

"It's Trace Macarthur," he finally said, shaking his head in disappointment—or abhorrence—I couldn't tell.

He immediately went into a monolog of sorts as he tried to downplay the whole thing, though I had already stopped listening to what he was saying. I was far too busy picking up my jaw and heart from the stinking floor.

By the time I arrived at All Saints, the hurt and shock I'd felt at the house was all but gone, having instead stewed itself into a sizzling fury that flamed my skin from the inside out. Of all the people my uncle could have named, Trace's name was the one that stung the most. Trace, with his condescending attitude and cold shoulders, and those stupid mesmerizing eyes.

I wanted it to be *anyone* but him.

I walked in and headed straight for the back area, bypassing all my coworkers as I combed every inch of the kitchen and office in search of him. When I didn't find him in his usual spots, I turned for the storeroom and nearly tore the door off its hinges as I stormed through the threshold.

Trace was kneeling down at the end of the room with a clipboard in his hand, taking inventory. He straightened out as soon he saw me, his eyebrows pulled together in bewilderment.

"You're a real jerk, you know that?" I yelled, glaring at him as I tried to catch my breath from the mad dash.

He raised his brows at me. "Good morning to you, too."

"You *knew* all this time and you didn't say anything?"

His demeanor instantly changed as the chain mail body armor shifted into place. He turned back to his inventory.

I moved closer to him, forcing him to look at me—to face me. "Don't you have anything to say for yourself?"

He tossed the clipboard onto the shelf and took a step back. "What do you want me to say, Jemma?"

There was something distracting about the way he said my name. It sounded really nice coming from his lips. Kind of soft.

I squared my shoulders, refusing to let it sidetrack me. "You can start by telling me why you lied to me."

"I didn't lie to you." His voice was deeper now, more purposeful.

"Like hell you didn't. You *knew* and you never said a word to me. What do you call that?" I didn't give him a chance to answer. "Did you know about Dominic, too?"

He lowered his head, his jaw muscles tightening. It was a clear yes—a pitiful one at that.

"And you didn't think to warn me?" I yelled, thrusting my open palms hard into his chest, though he barely moved an inch.

"What was I supposed to say?" he challenged. "'Hey, Jemma, I'm not sure if anyone mentioned it to you yet, but vampires are real and the only reason you're alive is to kill them. And by the way, your boyfriend's one too'," he said mockingly before turning serious again. "It wasn't *my* place, and besides, you would have never believed me."

"Yes, I would have."

"No," he insisted. "You wouldn't have."

"You don't know that! You don't know anything," I snapped, turning for the door.

"Really?" He snagged my elbow and pulled me back.

"Because I have this vague recollection of trying to talk to you about it *that* night," he said accusingly, his blue eyes glaring down at me. "Remember that? You refused to talk to me about it. What did you want me to do, hold you down and force you?"

I shook my arm loose though I didn't walk away this time.

I remembered the night of the attack vividly, and how unwilling I was to talk to him about what had happened. It was no secret that I'd grown incredibly good at pushing away the things I didn't want to face—things I wasn't *ready* to face—and as a result, I wound up ignorant to everything around me.

I had no one to blame for that but myself. But I was done living in the dark.

"Why won't you Pledge?" My voice was small, pleading.

He shook his head, his jaw clamped down hard to mark his resolve.

"They won't give me a Handler until you do."

"That's not my problem," he said icily.

I winced at his disregard and twisted for the door, afraid of what I might say or do next if I didn't walk away right that second.

I heard him cuss under his breath as he reached out and caught my arm again. "I'm sorry, that came out wrong."

"So you'll Pledge?"

"That's not what I meant."

"Well, then you can go to hell." I pulled my arm free and made a push for the door, refusing to look back even after he called out my name. The way I saw it, I was pretty much doomed—a dead girl walking. And Trace just loaded the gun.

I spent most of the day locked in a battle of patience with the clock, counting down the minutes until I could be free of this place—of Trace, and the constant reminder of a situation that appeared to be getting bleaker by the day. I felt hopeless, and restless, and angry that the seconds refused to tick by faster, like this day had been one big conspiracy, intended to drag out my misery to unfathomable proportions.

"Well? Let's hear it," said Zane when I sat down on one of the stools in front of his bar.

"Hear what?" I barely lifted my eyes.

"Whatever it is that has you in this funk."

"It's not a funk. And I don't want to talk about it," I said, picking apart a paper napkin.

"You know you can talk to me, right? I'm a bartender. This is pretty much what I do."

"I'll keep that in mind."

"You do that," he smiled, wiping down the counter in front of me. After a few wipes, he leaned in closer and whispered, "Who's the *T-D-H* at nine o'clock?"

My face contorted. "Huh?"

"Tall, dark and handsome—just walked in. He's staring right at you," he said, covertly ticking his head offside.

I peered over my shoulder to the door and saw Gabriel standing there by the threshold, not quite willing to come in all the way. He nodded to me, which I could only assume was his way of summoning me over.

"I'll be right back," I said and slipped off the stool.

"Famous last words."

I had no idea what Gabriel was doing here, but from the look on his face, I could tell it wasn't a casual call. Unfortunately, something inside of me was also speaking and it was telling me I didn't want to know, that I should turn around right now and put as much distance between the two of us as humanly possible. I guess old habits really do die hard.

"Can I talk you outside for a minute?" he asked, holding the door open for me.

I nodded wearily and stepped outside, inhaling sharply as the crisp night air collided with my exposed skin.

"Is everything okay?"

"Dominic was here tonight," he said matter-of-factly as he ushered me away from the front entrance.

I jerked at the mention of his name.

"He's gone," he assured. "Though not without difficulty." He looked down at something in his hand and then raised it up to me. A single, long-stem black rose stared back at me dauntingly.

"What the heck is that?"

"Compliments of Dominic," he said tartly. "He was pretty intent on giving it to you himself, though I insisted he not." He chucked the rose sideways, and not a moment too soon.

"I didn't know you were..." I trailed off, realizing Gabriel had been here this whole time, keeping watch. "Thank you."

"Don't thank me yet," he said, glancing over at the door and then back at me, his expression troubled. "He intends to talk to you and he'll try it again the first chance he gets."

I felt my heart rate accelerate; an automatic response to the thought of having to see Dominic again. "Talk to me about what?" I asked shakily. He had his fun—the game was over. What more could he possibly have left to say?

"I don't know, he didn't say."

I felt sick. I wasn't ready to see Dominic. It was too much, too soon. I was starting to shiver now, though I told myself it was from the cold air, and not from the fear.

"I think you should reconsider going to the Council," he said as he shrugged off his leather jacket and then wrapped it around my shoulders. "It may be the only way to protect yourself. You don't know the real Dominic—what he's capable of—especially when it comes to something he wants," he added, tucking his hands into his dark jeans.

He was only wearing a fitted, dark green T-shirt now, though he was clearly unaffected by the cold.

"And what is it that he wants exactly?" I asked, pushing my arms through the sleeves. It smelled of leather and mint.

"I'm not sure yet."

I swallowed hard. "But you think it involves me?"

He nodded, regretful.

The sudden rush of emotions caused me to stammer back, dizzy from the realization that this thing with Dominic wasn't over yet, that I wasn't free of him, or safe from him. I leaned back against the building and tried to steady my breathing.

"Are you alright?" he asked, taking a cautious step towards me. His concern felt genuine, like my safety and well-being mattered to him, which was strange because he didn't even know me up until yesterday.

"It's been a long day."

He gestured to my neck. "Do you mind if I take a look?"

I nodded that he could and then tried not to flinch when his cool fingers brushed my hair back to inspect the wound. "It's almost healed," I told him absentmindedly, looking up at the pitch sky, the stars, the moon—anything but his face.

"Yes, it looks much better," he agreed and took a step back, satisfied with his inspection. "There's a number of different enzymes in our bite, one of which has a fairly powerful healing agent," he explained, burying his hands again. "The mark should be gone by morning."

"Great," I mumbled. "It'll be good and fresh for Dominic when he comes back for seconds."

"You know what he is now. You don't have to let him near you again," he said, his green eyes gleaming in the dim light. "You can *stop* him from getting close enough."

"And how do you suggest I do that?"

"You're not as helpless as you think you are."

"You're right. I did take all those years of badminton in gym class. That's got to count for something, right?"

He wasn't amused. "I mean, you're stronger than you think you are. Your power is inside of you, you simply haven't tapped into it yet, but with a little training—"

"Training," I huffed bitterly. "That doesn't seem to be an option for me right now. I don't have a Keeper, which means no Handler is willing to take me on, which means I can't start training. So tell me again how I'm not helpless?"

"I'm sure the Council will find an alternate to stand-in and teach you some of the basics, at least until they can find a permanent solution. It isn't ideal, but it's not hopeless."

"Then why haven't they done it?"

He shook his head. "I'm not privy to all the details—"

"What about you?" I blurted out. "Weren't you a Handler before? Why can't you train me?"

"I don't think that's a very good—"

"Why not?" I interjected before he could finish turning me down. "You're a Revenant, and you're Dominic's brother. Who better to teach me than you?"

"I'm sure you'd be better suited with someone else."

"Please, Gabriel. I don't have anyone else," I pleaded, realizing I wasn't above resorting to tears.

His face softened, acquiescence looming on the edges. "I'm only going to be in town for a couple of weeks, at the most. I don't see what good it would do."

"A couple of weeks training is better than no weeks training, isn't it? Come on, Gabriel, you could help me if you wanted to. I know you can."

He ran his hand over the length of his face. "I suppose I could train with you while I'm in town, or at least until they find something permanent," he said and then held up his hand when I began to squeal. "Providing the Council approves it."

The way he said it led me to believe the chances of that happening weren't exactly in my favor.

"They'll approve it," I said boldly. "They have to." Because I wasn't going to give them a choice.

This was happening one way or another. Gabriel was my best chance at learning the skills I needed to keep myself alive. My only chance, really. It was him or nothing. If the Council couldn't see it my way, I would just have to find a way to make this happen without them.

19. TRAINING DAY

The rain battered the windshield as my uncle and I pulled up to *Temple* on the east side of town. The limestone structure was ornamented with rows of dimly lit windows, strange alabaster carvings, and a gated walkway that drew from the edge of the sidewalk all the way up to the bronze door.

"I don't understand why Gabriel and I can't just train at the house," I said defiantly as I looked through the blurring glass at the menacing building outside my window.

"Because that isn't the way we do things."

"What difference does it make to *them* if I—"

"Don't push your luck, Jemma." My uncle interjected before I could finish my argument. "It's a wonder the Council even approved this with the amount of opposition they had."

"Opposition?" I flinched back, surprised.

"Surely you can appreciate how unconventional this is." He looked at me expectantly. "The Order is built on tradition. Rites and Customs that have been adhered to for centuries, to advance us in our mission, and to protect us—our identities, our safety, our lineage. Anything that threatens to disrupt that security is naturally not going to be well-received."

"But this isn't even about that. This is about me." More to the point, this was about me staying alive, I thought, bitingly.

"Yes, it is about you. But it's also about Peter Macarthur. And Trace Macarthur," he said purposefully. "It's about order. There are other factors in this equation whether you are prepared to recognize them or not. I suggest you not tempt the fates any more than you already have."

I turned back to the building acridly, realizing where the core opposition had come from: from Trace's father, my boss. I wondered how close he had come to stopping this from happening. To stopping me from getting the training I desperately needed.

I couldn't help but wonder what other unknown *factors* might be out there, and just how many of those unknowns might wind up getting directly in my way again.

The lobby was quaint, circular in form, with glossy marble floors and cream colored walls. There was an empty reception desk at the front and a waiting area with red chairs and a glass coffee table at the center. Something about the room looked staged, as though it were all playing host to a sordid illusion.

The fortified doors on either side of the reception desk were unmarked, locked, and appeared to be leading to opposite sides of the building. I followed my uncle to the left door nearest the reception desk and watched as he swiped a plastic card through the security reader.

The light flashed green and the door unlocked, allowing us to pile into a small holding area where we waited in front of another armored door while the one behind us closed.

One could easily become incredibly claustrophobic in such a tight space, I thought, wiping my palms against my jeans. "Is it hot in here, or is it just me?"

Ignoring me, my uncle pushed his thumb into what looked

like a fingerprint identification machine, and then stood back as a woman's mechanical voice sounded over the speakers.

"Welcome, Karl Blackburn. Please enter your personal identification pass code."

He fingered six numbers into the keypad, and then waited for the light to flash green before turning the knob, giving us access into the cavernous building known as Temple.

"What was all that about?" I asked as we walked through the atrium. Guarding sphinxes and stone columns lined both sides.

"Precautions," he said simply. "This particular sector of the Order isn't open to the public, for obvious reasons. What goes on between these walls is one thing, the invaluable artifacts we safeguard here is another. We cannot allow just anyone to walk in."

"What sort of artifacts?" I asked as I blindly followed him through the large, double doors at the end of the atrium.

My head was still turned to him when he ticked his square chin forward, directing my attention into the room.

Two men stood together at the center of what looked like a large, empty assembly hall. The rectangular room had high ceilings, black and white tessellated flooring, and was flanked with theater-style seats on either side of the room. At the crown, a platform with seven leather chairs positioned at different intervals was regally presiding over the space.

I immediately recognized the man on the right as Gabriel. The other one was older, possibly in his late fifties, with hoary hair tapered around a smooth face, and he was wearing an all-black ankle length robe fashioned with silver buttons all the way down the front flap. It had the distinct look of a cassock though the wedding band on his finger made it apparent that he wasn't a member of the clergy.

"This is she?" asked the man as we approached them. He already had his hand extended to me when he asked the question.

"Yes, my youngest niece, Jemma."

I shook his hand and glanced over at Gabriel. He was standing quietly with his hands crossed in front of him and his head slightly lowered. He reminded me of a well-trained lackey.

"This is William Thompson," said my uncle, steering my attention back to the man. "He's our Council's Senior *Magister*."

That tidbit told me nothing.

"I'm quite pleased to finally meet you, Jemma," said William. "We're all incredibly fond of your sister and the work she's done. She's one of our brightest pupils."

My sister? I thought dimly.

Of course he knew Tessa. What was I thinking? She probably stood in this very spot, walked these very halls, trained in this very building. Strangely enough, the thought hadn't occurred to me until just then.

"Indeed, she is," agreed my uncle, the pride evident in his eyes whenever he spoke of Tessa. "Jemma has much to live up to, but let's not forget that she too is a Blackburn. I imagine she'll be a natural, just like her sister."

"Oh, I don't doubt it," agreed William, his smile reaching all the way up to his benevolent brown eyes.

Um, I do. I couldn't help but think of my past run-ins with vampires, particularly the last one with Dominic and how I'd only narrowly escaped with my life, thanks solely to Gabriel's aid. Nothing about that felt *natural* to me, certainly not the part where I almost got myself killed.

My eyes bounced to Gabriel who smiled back faintly— probably out of pity, because *he* knew the truth.

"You'll be in good hands with Gabriel," assured William, catching our exchange. "He's one of our finest Warriors, and truly an invaluable member of this Order."

"Thank you, Magister." Gabriel dipped his head in gratitude.

It was nice to know that not all Council members were against our pairing.

"Ah, Julian, right on time," smiled William.

I followed his eyes to a slender, dark haired man that had come up from behind us. He greeted William and my uncle but made no eye contact with me or Gabriel.

"Julian here is one of our top Sentinels," informed William. "He'll be overseeing your training with Gabriel."

"*Overseeing*?" I couldn't help but wonder what that meant. Was he going to be evaluating my performance and reporting back to the Council? Or was he there to spy on us because they didn't trust Gabriel to be alone with me?

"Think of him as a guard of sorts, for your protection. You won't even notice him there."

"Right." I eyed Julian suspiciously. *Spy it is.*

"Very good then," chimed my uncle after a brief repose of uncomfortable silence. "What do you say we leave them to it?"

"Certainly," agreed William and then turned to Gabriel with his hand extended. "She's in your hands now, Gabriel. Do right by her, and your brethren. I'll expect to hear an update on her progress by the end of the week."

"Of course." Gabriel shook his hand, and then my uncle's before leading us out of the room and back into the atrium.

I followed behind Gabriel and Julian as they led us through a slender corridor that connected to a large steel door on the opposite side of the atrium. We passed through the threshold in silence and descended a dark, winding staircase into the lower level of the building. The underground tunnels—built with a mixture of concrete, steel reinforcements, and fortified wood paneling—stretched deep into the underbelly of the cellar, and seemed to split off into several directions, each one peppered with doors at various points in the procession.

"What is this place?" I asked as we veered left down the first intersection. My voice sounded small here, distant, as though it had been insulated from itself.

"We call it the *Lab*. It houses our main training facilities and weaponry vaults." He stopped in front of a bolted door and pressed his finger into the reader.

I glanced up at Julian who stood beside me, towering over me by nearly a full foot. "I'm Jemma by the way," I said, extending my hand to him as I examined his features—dark eyes, strong Roman nose, goatee.

"I know who you are."

He peeked down at my hand but didn't bother taking it.

Okay then. Chatty *and* friendly. "Nice to meet you, too," I muttered to his back as he walked into the room ahead of us.

"After you," said Gabriel, holding the door open.

The room was extensive and surprisingly well lit in comparison to the dank hallway we had just come in from. The concrete floors were covered in blue sparring mats and the walls were railed with an impressive assortment of artillery and other oddly shaped weapons I couldn't name.

"What is all this stuff?" I asked, peering around the room.

"Just a few of the many weapons you'll eventually learn to use," said Gabriel, his demeanor all-business. He seemed perfectly at ease here as though he himself were a biological extension of the room.

I watched as he walked over to the bench lined up against the back wall and carefully removed his leather jacket. He placed it down on the bench and then moved to the matted area at the center of the room. Eyebrows furrowed, he crooked his finger and motioned for me to join him as Julian took his seat next to the door.

I dug my feet into the ground and crossed my arms. This

whole training-with-a-vampire-to-kill-vampires *thing* just got a little too real for me.

"Is there something wrong?"

"I just...I don't..." I shifted my weight around, trying to form a cohesive thought. "It's a lot to take," I finally said.

He stared at me expressionless.

"Being here, seeing all these weapons." I shook my head, feeling overwhelmed. "I don't know if I can do this."

His eyebrows rose.

"Figures," snorted Julian.

"What's that supposed to mean?"

He didn't bother looking up from his magazine.

"Never mind him," said Gabriel as he sauntered back over to where I stood. "Just focus on why we're here." He took me by the wrist and towed me to the mat. "We'll start slow. Just the basics," he added, carefully removing my zippered hoodie and tossing it onto the bench behind us.

I noticed he took great care not to touch my skin and wondered if it was for Julian's benefit, or his own.

"What are the basics?" I asked, rubbing my arms for warmth.

"Whatever it is you need to know to get to the next level. Right now, for *you*, the basics are defensive tactics."

I actually liked the sound of that.

"Once you're comfortable with your ability to self-defend," he said as he repositioned the mat, "you'll move on to other things like offensive striking, unarmed combat practice, assault drills, weapons training—" He stopped abruptly, remarking the horror in my eyes. "But for now, we'll just stick to the basics," he reiterated in a gentler tone.

I glanced down at my skinny jeans and camisole. "What about my clothes?" I had assumed tonight was going to be more of a *meet-and-greet* session and didn't really think to dress for an actual training session.

"They're fine," he said without looking. "You need to be able to do this in your everyday clothes."

"No one's going to care what you're wearing, kid," snipped Julian, his tone unmistakably mocking.

"No one was talking to you!" I snapped back. What the heck was this guy's problem anyway?

"That's right, I have a pulse. I'm not your type."

"Exactly." *Wait.* "What—?"

"That's enough, Julian." Gabriel put himself directly in front of me. "If you're unable, or unwilling to perform your duty, I'll be more than happy to have the Council reassign you."

"That won't be necessary," replied Julian, looking embarrassed now. He quickly shifted his attention back to his magazine and didn't say another word to either of us.

Gabriel turned back to me, his eyes doleful. "Come on," he said, ticking his head towards the mat.

The truth was, I still wanted to ram the magazine in Julian's big mouth but figured it would only make things worse for me. I tied my hair back into a ponytail and followed Gabriel instead. "So...where do we start?"

"We start by assessing what level you're at physically."

"That's easy. I'm the level right *before* beginner."

His mouth hitched up at the corner. "I was hoping for something a little more concrete."

"What did you have in mind?" I asked, uneasy.

"I was thinking we could simulate an attack."

I shook my head. "No. No way."

"Why not?"

"Because..." I wanted to tell him that I was too afraid, that I didn't want to be reminded of the way I felt that night, or the time before that—scared, powerless, weak—that it was already enough that I had to relive it every time I closed my eyes. But all I could manage to say was, "Just because."

He grimaced, examining me as though he might find the rest of my answer hidden somewhere on my face. "Look, I know this is difficult for you," he said after a thoughtful pause. "And I imagine you'd rather not be in that position again, but..."

No buts. I hate buts. "But what?"

"But it's going to happen again whether you want it to or not," he said candidly. "I'd rather it happen here first—with me, so that I can teach you how to take control of the situation and get out. That's all this exercise is about."

That didn't sound nearly as bad as what I'd envisioned in my mind. "So what your saying is, I won't be suffering any traumatic brain injury or blood loss tonight?"

"Of course not. I would never hurt you," he assured. A slow moving grin appeared. "In fact, I want *you* to do the hurting."

I couldn't help but smile at that.

"If you start to feel uncomfortable or it becomes too much for you, just say the word and we'll stop," he added, raising his hands in a solemn gesture. "You have my word."

I couldn't explain why, but I believed him. I *knew* he wouldn't hurt me. I knew he'd stop if I told him to. I knew I'd be safe as long as he was near me.

"Alright then, let's do this," I said, feeling a false sense of bravado wash over me. "Show me what you got."

His eyebrows shot up in surprise—or amusement—though I could tell from the shrewd way he began to circle around me that he meant business. Not wanting to feel like his prey, I mimicked his moves and circled right along with him as my heart rate nervously kicked into overdrive.

"I'm going to come at you from the back," he warned, his lips slightly turned up at the corners. No doubt he was in his element. "I want you to try to break out of my hold, okay?"

I didn't have a chance to respond. One minute we were circling face to face, and the next, he was behind me—one arm around my collarbone and the other one around my waist, pinning my arms to my side.

I gasped in surprise.

"Break out of my hold," he ordered when I did nothing but stand there frozen in his arms.

Ah, hell.

I immediately began pushing and squirming around in his arms, doing everything I knew of to try to free myself from his death grip, each time ending up with nothing to show for it but a bruised ego. Even when my squirms morphed into a full body buck, the only damage I managed to produce was self-inflicted pain from my own burning muscles.

"I can't," I cried out after a series of failed attempts. I was already winded and I hadn't even made a blot on his map.

He let go and spun me back around to face him.

"Well," he said, raking a hand through his dark hair. "I'm not going to lie. That was really bad."

"Gee, thanks," I replied sourly.

"Take a breath and try it again," he ordered and began another slow stalk around me, calculating his next move—my next move. There was something incredibly primal about it.

Distracted, I tripped over my foot and stumbled back a step. He shook his head and buried the smile.

In the span of time it took for me to look back up, he had already reached out and pulled my arm, spinning me to him and landing me with my back against his chest. His arms wrapped firmly around my torso once again locking my limbs to my body. There was something about the way he pounced with such speed and agility that seemed to leave me in a stationary stupor.

"Break out," he said into my ear when I didn't move.

I snapped out of my daze and began to squirm and buck again, digging deep for any semblance of strength I could find, but once again, all of my efforts came up short. No matter how hard I pushed, he remained immovable. It was like trying to lift a solid block of concrete off of me with a plastic kiddy shovel.

"Why are you doing *that*?"

"Doing what?"

"Wiggling," he said repugnantly. "Do you honestly think you can escape a Revenant by wiggling your way out?"

I stopped moving. "Well what do you suggest I do?"

"Use your strength to push out." He said it as though it were the simplest, most obvious thing to do. "You're a Slayer. You already have it inside of you."

"Then where is *it*?" I snapped back, annoyed. "Why isn't this working?"

He dropped his arms and took a step back. "My guess is it's probably the spell," he said, focusing in on me with a deeper intensity. "You need to understand the mechanics at play here, Jemma. Slayers are biologically built to kill Revenants. It's in your blood—right there in your DNA," he said, gently pushing his fingers into my clavicle.

I looked down distractedly and crossed my arms.

"Normally, you only need to be in the general vicinity of one to feel it," he went on. "That *feeling* is physiological, like a sensor or a switch that turns on the Warrior part of you—the part of you that isn't human, and that part takes over so you can do what you were created to do. That's where all your power and strength lies, but if that switch was never accessed before, then everything else that follows it remains dormant."

"So what you're saying is, my Slayer powers are sleeping?"

"For lack of a better term, yes. You have an entire part of you that's never been touched before." He started to circle me again.

"What's the point then?" I asked, my arms still crossed tightly across my chest. "As long as I'm still Cloaked, I have no chance of fighting you off, or any other Revenants for that matter. Not if my powers are dormant as you say."

"That may be true," he said, rounding out from behind.

"So what are we going to do?"

He tweaked his eyebrows. "We're going to *wake* them up."

20. FRIGHT NIGHT

After soaking in a hot bath for nearly an hour, I changed into my favorite camisole and fleece cutoffs and all-but crawled into my bed. My first training session with Gabriel was brutal and had me using muscles I didn't even know existed. Muscles that I knew I'd be paying dearly for tomorrow morning. Thankfully, I didn't have to worry about it for too long. Exhaustion took over and pushed everything else onto the back-burner as I effortlessly drifted to sleep.

However short-lived it was.

I wrenched upright in my bed sometime after midnight. I had been dreaming about *him* again—the blond hair and curls—though I didn't have a chance to experience the particular brand of terror those dreams usually caused. Something else had woken me. I remembered a knock and turned to stare at my bedroom door, still struggling to snap out of my slumber. Then, another knock, and I realized it was coming from the outside terrace.

I stumbled out of bed and walked to the door, cautiously pulling back the curtain to see who was out there. I was almost expecting it to be Dominic Huntington arriving straight out of my nightmares to torment me, and was equal parts surprised and relieved to find Trace standing there instead.

My eyes never left his as I pushed open the door. The cold air immediately rushed inside, twirling around my damp hair as it took up residency in my room, but I barely felt its chill. My skin was already warming from the inside out.

"What are you doing here?" I whispered, peering over his shoulder into the darkness. "How did you get up here?"

Even in the pitch of night, his eyes gleamed like two sapphires. "Can we talk?" he asked without answering my question.

I didn't see the point in reminding him that we weren't on speaking terms, or even asking if this could wait until tomorrow. The guy had just shimmied up my balcony in the middle of the night, and frankly, I wanted to know why.

I took a step back to let him inside doing my best not to notice when his arm brushed up against me as he passed. Or that he smelled really, *really* good. I flicked on the desk lamp and stalked back to my bed, taking a seat on the edge of it as I waited for him to say something.

Trace stayed by the door, leaning against it as his eyes moved curiously around my room taking in the sights. I tried to read his face for any hints as to what this late-night visit was about, or what kind of mood he was in, but as per usual, his expression gave nothing away.

His eyes settled on me just then and I watched as they moved down the length of my body and then back up the other way before shifting away. If I didn't know any better (which I did), I would have thought he just checked me out.

"So, um, what did you want to talk to me about?" I asked, still feeling the heat from his stare embedded in my cheeks.

"I heard you started training today."

"And you rushed over to congratulate me?"

"No." He seemed to be studying me. "So it's true then? You're training with Gabriel?"

I nodded and watched as he pushed up from the door and took a few steps in, circling around the edge of my desk.

"You know he's a *Rev*, right?"

"A what?"

"A Revenant—a vampire," he said distractedly, looking down at something on my desk.

"Yeah, I got the memo this time."

"I'm just making sure." His eyes met mine again briefly. "I wouldn't want you accusing me of being a jerk or anything."

"I'm sure there'll be plenty more opportunities for that."

His dimples pressed in, making it look like he was fighting back a smile, though it never made it to the surface. "So that's it then? You're really doing this?"

I wasn't sure if he was referring to my training with Gabriel, or the whole Slayer thing in general. My answer was the same either way. "What choice do I have?"

"Aren't you protected?" he asked, leaning back against the desk now. His arms were crossed over his chest and his sweatshirt was pushed up to his elbows, highlighting his brawny forearms. "Like with a Cloaking spell or something?" he continued when I failed to produce words.

I nodded, clearing my throat. "They're trying to break it. My uncle said it's too dangerous to stay this way—that the spell won't hold." I couldn't find the courage to tell him that I'd agreed to break it for reasons completely unrelated. That I wasn't out to save anyone's skin but my own. "Why do you care anyway?"

"I don't care," he answered coolly. "I just wanted to hear it from you."

"And why is that?"

His dark lashes swooped down. "So that when I told you to

187

stay away from me," he said, looking back up. "I'd mean it."

"You want me to stay away from you?" I blinked into him, unsure that I'd heard him right.

He clenched his jaw and gave a slight nod.

"Why? Because I'm training with Gabriel?" I sounded like a child getting reprimanded unfairly.

"That's part of it."

"And the other part?" I stood up from the bed, wanting to keep the uncomfortable feelings from rising to the surface. "What exactly was it that made you feel so compelled to ban me from your life that you had to run over here in the middle of the night to do it? Do you really hate me that much?"

"I don't hate you," he said gruffly and then lowered his voice. "I just don't want you in my life."

I wasn't sure what was worse; the fact that he didn't want me in his life, or that it was hurting me so much to hear it.

"You need to tell my father you're quitting All Saints," he went on as though he hadn't just sliced me open with his words. "The sooner you do it, the better."

"I don't *need* to do anything," I snapped back, angry at his audacity. "Where do you get off coming here and demanding I quit my job?"

"That's not what I'm doing."

"Isn't it?" I didn't understand what this was about or why it even mattered to him if I stuck around at All Saints or not. There had to be more to this. Something or *someone* else behind it. "Is this about Nikki?"

"Nikki?" His tone matched the confusion in his eyes.

"Because you're back together?"

"I'm not back together with Nikki," he said wryly.

Something akin to relief coursed through my body just then, surprising me by its presence.

Why did I even care if he was with Nikki or not? Did I

dislike *her* so much that it gave me joy knowing she didn't have him? It had to be that, I decided, because I wasn't ready to entertain the alternatives.

"So if this isn't about Nikki, why are you pushing me to quit?" I asked, still trying to make sense out of this.

He shrugged lazily. "I just figured you would, now that you know the truth."

"What does that have to do with anything?"

He arched his brow at me—a silent jab. "You didn't think it was a coincidence that we ended up going to the same school and working at the same job, did you?"

"What are you saying?"

"Do I have to spell it out for you?"

"No, you jerk, but you *could* stop talking in riddles."

He lifted off the desk and took a couple of steps towards me. "I'm saying that it was a setup," he said huskily, closing the distance between us. "To get us together—"

"Together?"

"—But since we all know that's not going to happen," he continued, his eyes flicking down to my parted lips. "There's really no need for you to be working there anymore, is there?"

My heart was pounding hard against my rib cage, though I had no idea why. There was something about the way he looked down at my mouth that made my pulse go mad.

I took a step back as I tried to get my wits together. There were too many emotions surging, too many questions.

"I don't understand. Why would they want to" —I paused, wetting my lips— "get us together?"

"Use your imagination," he said, cocking his head to the side.

When my cheeks flushed red, he narrowed his eyes and shook his head as though he knew where my mind had gone.

"They were trying to manipulate the situation to get to me, so that I'd cave and resume my duties as a Keeper."

"Using me as the bait?"

"Something like that."

I choked out a laugh. Hopefully they had a backup plan.

"So when you say 'resume your duties', does that mean you're not working for the Order anymore?" I asked, trying to digest this new piece of information. At least this would explain why he had been refusing to train with me. "Can you even do that—*quit*?"

"I guess you could say I excommunicated myself."

My eyes widened. "Why?"

A pained expression crossed his face but he buried it just as quick as it appeared. "The 'why' is complicated."

"When did this happen?" I pushed, hungry to know more.

"Three months ago, right after my sister—" He stopped short as though he couldn't bear to say the words out loud.

A heaviness washed over me. "Was she the reason you quit?"

"No, but it made leaving easier. Look, I didn't come here to talk about Linley—" His marshaled expression cracked at the mere mention of her name. He squared his shoulders as though digging deep for strength.

"I'm sorry," I whispered, reaching out to console him.

The urge to comfort him was curiously overwhelming, but he stepped away from me before I could touch him, taking a seat on the edge of my bed instead. He was drawing a clear line in the sand and every inch of my body was painfully aware of it.

"I didn't mean to—"

"It's alright," he said in a tone that made me believe it was anything but. "Forget it."

There was something about the way he reflected back to me that chipped away at my protective wall. It was like looking into a mirror and seeing the person I was when I'd first lost my father. Closed off, harrowed, unwilling to let myself feel the pain. In a lot of ways, I was still that person.

"It's hard for me too, you know."

"What is?"

"Talking about him…my dad."

He didn't answer.

Neither one of us filled the silence, the room suddenly heavy from the strain of our combined loss. I wished I could know what he was thinking; what was going on behind that thick, impenetrable facade of his. Did he think I couldn't understand his pain—his grief—because my sister was alive and well? Or did he not trust me enough to confide in me?

"She would have been twenty next month," he said after a long pause. His eyes were painted in sadness, shades of despair so agonizing that it hurt just to look into them. "I still pick up the phone to call her sometimes, like she's still here."

I stepped towards him but stopped, weary of the line.

"How screwed up is that?" He looked up at me expectantly, his voice full of vulnerability. This was a different side of him, a side I'd never seen. It seemed completely incongruent with the hard exterior I had grown accustomed to.

"It's not screwed up…it happens to me, too."

"You're just saying that." Disbelief stained his tone, though there was something else hiding in there, something that sounded a lot like *hope*.

"It's the truth," I insisted, watching his expression soften. "Like right before I open my eyes in the morning, my dad is still alive, and I swear everything is right in the world."

His eyes stayed on me as I moved to take the seat beside him. I could almost feel the grief radiating off of him. Or maybe it was my own grief, I wasn't entirely sure anymore.

"But then I wake up and remember that he's gone and he isn't coming back, and all the pain and guilt comes rushing back to me."

I could tell he knew what that felt like by the way he lowered his head, and in some strange way, it made me feel connected to him. Less alone.

"Most of the time I feel like I'm just waiting. Waiting for him to come home, waiting for it to stop hurting, waiting for it to be okay to live without him again, but it's like it never happens." I pressed my lips together and dropped my eyes, feeling overexposed. "Sorry, I'm totally rambling and I'm not even helping."

"I like when you ramble."

My head popped back up, surprised by the softness in his words. He seemed distracted and unaware of the comment.

"What if it doesn't happen?" he asked without meeting my eyes. His body was facing forward, concentrated on some unknown marker. "What if it never stops hurting?"

"I don't know," I shook my head. "I try not to let myself think that way. I have to believe it'll get better."

"And if it doesn't? Do you think you could live with the pain for the rest of your life?"

"I guess I would have to."

"What if you had another choice? What if you could change the past?" His voice was low, controlled. "Would you do it?"

"Like if I had my own time machine?" I resisted the urge to laugh considering the gravity of it.

"Something like that."

I didn't have to think about it. I knew without a doubt that if I could go back in time and change things—warn him about what was coming—I would do it. "In a heartbeat."

"Even if it goes against the rules? Even if other people get *hurt* because of it? Would you still do it?"

"I-I don't know. Why are you asking me this?" I suddenly felt suffocated under the weight of the conversation.

"It's just a hypothetical," he said curtly. "Would you do it?" His eyes met mine, stirring me with their depth.

Would I sacrifice innocent people so that I could have my father back? I felt the shame before I gave my answer. "I would give anything to have him back," I admitted, dropping my head.

I wasn't sure what that said about me but I imagined it wasn't anything great.

He pushed his knee up against mine.

"I would too," he said in a gentle voice that made me warm. "There's nothing I wouldn't do for someone I loved."

His words felt intimate, sacred, like I shouldn't have been allowed to hear them. It made me wonder what it would feel like to be loved in that way by someone...

To be loved in that way *by him.*

He pulled his leg away from me, steering me back from my errant thoughts. "It's getting late." His eyes were pinned on the door. "I should probably go, let you get back to sleep."

I nodded and then rose with him even though I wasn't sure how I would ever get back to sleep after everything that had been said tonight. My mind was still reeling from the eddy of emotions circling inside of me and showed no signs of slowing down. I had to get some of it off my chest before he left.

"About what you said earlier tonight," I began cautiously, following him to the balcony door. He turned to face me, his eyes distracting me with their intensity. "I just want you to know that I respect your decision not to be a part of this *thing* anymore, whatever your reasons are. And I'll keep my distance if that's what you want." I nodded into it, affirming it as my truth. "But I'm not going to quit my job at All Saints. I just thought you should know that."

I braced myself for his reaction.

"Okay." He answered too easily, almost as though he had been expecting my refusal all along.

"*Really?* That's it?"

"Things would have been a lot easier if you never moved

here," he muttered and then stepped out onto the terrace, his dark hair blending into the night.

"Well, I'm sorry your life is worse now that I'm in it," I called out after him. "If it makes you feel any better, I wish I never moved here, too."

He stopped abruptly as though I had just flung an insult at his back. Heart pumping, I felt my temperature spike with anticipation when he turned around and walked back over to me, stopping just inches from where I stood in the doorway.

"I don't," he whispered, leaning in. His face was so close to mine that I could feel his breath on my lips. "I said my life would have been easier, not better."

"Oh." My voice was a murmur, barely audible had it not been for his close proximity. "So then, um, are you saying that you're...I mean, are you happy that..." *Jeez, Jemma, speak much?*

His dimples pressed in, a prelude to his barely there smile. "Yeah, something like that." He pushed off the door-frame and walked away without saying another word.

Before I could formulate a guess as to how he was going to get off the balcony, he'd already cleared the railing and launched himself over the ledge in one fluid movement. It was completely elegant, and reckless, and stupid. Not to mention, impossible to land.

In a state of panic, I ran to the railing and peered over the edge, praying I wouldn't find him splayed out all over the concrete below like tattered road kill. But what I found was even more disturbing. I found absolutely nothing. *Zilch. Nada.* No sign of him whatsoever.

It was as though Trace Macarthur had just jumped off my balcony and vanished into thin air.

21. CHEMISTRY

I had two missed calls from my sister when I walked into school the next morning, already frazzled. I had yet to take any of her calls since I left her that message over two weeks ago, and with good reason. I was angry with her for lying to me, for hiding the truth from me for all these years. And it didn't matter that I knew I'd forgive her (eventually), right now I was still mad as hell and I wasn't ready to let any of it go.

Not to mention, there were slightly more pressing matters to contend with, like training with vampires and ex-Keepers who appeared to vanish into thin air.

"Whoa!" cried Benjamin, grabbing my shoulders to steady me after he blew out of the main office, nearly running me over in the process. "I just saved you from a serious face-plant right there. You owe me big time."

"I think you almost just *caused* my serious face-plant so I'm not sure that qualifies as an actual save."

"You say tomato," he laughed, walking backwards down the hall. "I say you owe me."

"Hey, Ben, hang on a sec." I took a few rushed steps to catch up with him and then lowered my voice. "Have you seen Trace this morning? I need him." I paused to cringe at the playback. "I mean, I need to *find* him. Is he here today?"

His dark blond brows shot up. "Freudian slip?"

"No. Lack of sleep slip. I mean, it's a lack of sleep—there's no slip." I broke eye contact and adjusted my schoolbag awkwardly. "So? Have you seen him?"

"Yeah he's around here somewhere. Probably at his locker checking his pretty self out in the mirror again," he grinned, running his palm over his buzzed hair.

"So he's really here? Like, you've actually seen him?"

"Yes, I've actually seen him," he repeated mockingly, though his smile quickly dissipated once he noticed my expression. "Are you feeling alright, Jem? You look a little pale."

"What? No. Yeah, I'm totally fine." I tried to laugh it off but it came out unnatural and pitchy. "I lent him my chemistry book yesterday. I'm just trying to get it back before class."

That sounded completely legit. But then why didn't he look convinced? *Shoot.* Did Trace even take chemistry?

"Jemma!" Saved by the freaking bell.

I turned around to see Taylor coming up behind us carrying a bucket of soapy water. I was happy to see her up until I caught wind of the troubled look on her face, and then not so much.

She shook her head. "Just don't freak out, okay?"

"Wow, Tay. Way to stay calm. I think you missed your calling as a crisis counselor."

"Shut up, Benjamin!"

"What's going on?" I asked her, already worried.

"It's not that bad." She grabbed my wrist and started towing me down the hall, the bucket hanging rigidly from her other hand. "We can totally clean it. And hardly anyone saw it. It'll be like it was never even there to begin with."

Okay, now I was freaking out. "What are you talking about?"

She didn't answer until we rounded the corner, only adding

to the dramatics of it all. She stopped in the middle of the hall and pinned her eyes on the target.

I followed her gaze...to my locker.

The letters S-L-U-T were painted across it in big, black marker for *all* to see. And *all* were definitely seeing. Dozens of other students were walking by, pointing and snickering, obviously chomping at the bit for the chance to spread this newly acquired piece of intel all over the school.

False intel.

Not that it mattered though. The truth seldom ever did in the face of a juicy lie.

"It's not that bad," she said, her tone lacking conviction.

"Really? How can it be any worse?"

Ben stalked up to the locker and began rubbing his finger over the marker in an attempt to erase it, or merge with it, I couldn't tell. "It can always be worse," he said without turning back. "It's permanent marker."

I groaned.

Taylor tightened her arm around my shoulder as we stood side by side, staring at my locker like a scene from some tragic car wreck—a car wreck that was my life.

"Morning, ladies." Caleb appeared smiling next to us, along with a far less chipper Trace. "Why are you all...*oh*." He dropped off as soon as my vandalized locker registered. "Damn."

"I know, right?" Taylor was taking it pretty bad. She picked up the bucket and moved it to the base of my locker.

"Any idea who did it?" asked Trace, his eyebrows furrowed.

"I'll give you one hint," said Taylor ringing out the excess water from the rag. "Her name starts with Nikki Parker."

"Nikki?" His tone was dripping with skepticism as though he couldn't even fathom Nikki doing something like this. What planet was he living on anyway?

I rolled my eyes at him.

Even though I had no proof that she did this, I was willing to bet more than a pretty penny that she absolutely *could* do something like this and most likely did. If not her, then who? I couldn't think of a single person who had it in for me even half as much as Nikki did on a good day. Clearly, the girl had issues. That much had already been established.

"It's not coming off," cried Taylor, throwing the rag back into the bucket just as the first bell wailed around us.

"I'll take care of it," said Caleb, reaching for the bucket.

"And what exactly are you going to do? Wave your magic wand around and make it disappear? It's permanent marker, Cale."

Caleb looked at Ben strangely before answering her. "I have a special cleaner in my locker. Industrial strength. It should get rid of it, no problem."

Taylor started saying something back to him but I'd already turned my attention to Trace who was watching from the sidelines. I had some unfinished business to settle with him.

"Can I talk to you for a minute...alone?"

Everyone piped down, their eyes suddenly heavy on us.

"...so that you can give me back the history book I lent you yesterday," I added choppily.

"Chemistry."

I turned to Ben with doe-in-the-headlight eyes. "Huh?"

He was grinning. "Don't you mean your chemistry book?"

Dang it. "Right. Chemistry. That's what I meant."

I grabbed Trace by his sleeve and shuffled us away from their accusing eyes before any other comments could be made. He looked down at me with questioning eyebrows though he didn't say anything as I towed him along.

"Here's the thing," I said as soon as we were in front of his locker and out of earshot. "I know we're supposed to be staying out of each other's business and all, but you have to admit it's kind of hard to do when you throw yourself off my second-story balcony in the middle of the night and then disappear without a trace."

His dimples ignited. He was laughing at my unintended pun.

"You know what I mean." The second bell rang, but I hardly cared. "First I thought you were dead, then I thought I was losing my mind and just imagined the whole night, like it was all part of some convoluted fantasy I was having." I flattened my back against the locker next to his, exhausted by the incessant questioning of my own sanity.

"Fantasy, eh?"

My cheeks warmed at the sound of his husky voice. What the heck was wrong with me? *Stay focused, dammit.* "Just tell me I didn't imagine it."

"You didn't imagine it." He shut his locker door.

"How did you do it?"

He thought about it for a moment and then stepped out in front of me so that we were standing face to face. Everyone around us faded into the background as he leaned his body into mine and rested his forearm against the locker beside my ear, like he was going to lean in and whisper something, only his lips never made it to my ear.

"You want a play-by-play?" he asked, his molten eyes never leaving mine.

Whoa, gummy legs. I grabbed the locker behind me to brace myself. "I-I want to know what you are."

"What I am is late for class."

"That's not what I…" I trailed off when his eyes dropped down to my mouth, sending whatever was left of my concentration to hell. I finished off the sentence with an inaudible squeak.

A *freaking* squeak.

"Sorry, I didn't catch that," he said as he pushed off the

locker and started down the hall.

I let the air expunge from my lungs as I tried to bury the electric charge racing through my body just then. Fortunately for me, it simmered right down the second I noticed Taylor and the others were still standing by my locker, gawking at us with various degrees of astonishment on their faces.

Well, that's just perfect, and I forgot the dang book too. I darted off to catch up with him before he reached them.

"I need your chemistry book," I whispered, anxious and still visibly flustered by our exchange. "I told them you borrowed it. They'll know I was lying if I show up empty handed."

"That's too bad," he whispered back, a smile tugging at the corner of his lips. "Because I don't take chemistry."

Taylor was already waiting for me at my locker when I got there at lunch. I still hadn't been able to figure out how she consistently managed to get out of class ahead of everyone else and was just about to ask her to spill her trade secrets when I noticed my locker behind her.

"How did you do it?" I asked excitedly, giddy at the sight of my slander-free locker.

"Wasn't me, babe," she said, glancing back at the empty canvas. "It must have been Caleb."

It looked great, good as new. You couldn't even tell anything had been written there before. I wondered when he had the time to do it. He must have come between classes.

"I bet Nikki was all torn up to see it gone."

I laughed. "You still think she did it?"

"Well, let's see," she said, pressing her pink fingernail to her lips. "Was it mean, vindictive and catty? Check, check, check. Sounds like Nikki to me."

I shook my head knowing she was probably right.

"Anyway, enough about Nikki. We can plot her takedown

later," she said, re-applying her lip-gloss sans mirror. "We have more important matters to discuss right now."

"Such as?" I stuffed my books back into my locker.

"Such as you and Trace—" She held up her hand to silence me when I began to protest. "And don't even try to deny it, I have *eyes*. I could practically see the fireworks shooting out of your head this morning. I want to know what's going on with you two and don't spare any of the dirty details!" Her eyes were twinkling like two brilliant slate-blue stars.

"There's nothing going on. We're barely even friends."

"Come on, I've seen the way you guys look at each other. You don't look at someone that way and feel nothing."

My cheeks flushed. "I don't look at him in any kind of way."

"Um, yeah you do," she said emphatically. "And he looks at you the same way. At first I thought it was just some kind of forbidden fruit thing, but I'm starting to think there's more to it. It's like there's this pull between the two of you, but you're both too stubborn to admit that you're into each other. It's kind of delicious to watch."

"I'm not into him," I lied, knowing the truth was slightly more complicated than that. "I mean, obviously, I find him good looking, he's a good looking guy—"

"He's an Adonis."

"—But there's more to liking someone than just being attracted to them, isn't there? And none of that even matters if the feelings aren't mutual, and I happen to know for a fact that he doesn't like me, nor does he want anything to do with me. He said so himself."

"You're probably right," she said, though I knew it was a loaded statement. "I'm sure that's the reason he got into it with those two guys from Easton that night at the game...you know, because he doesn't like you." She tweaked her eyebrows the way she does when she's spilling a secret. "I know when I don't like someone, I definitely make it a point to defend their honor whenever I can," she added, every word rich with sarcasm.

Defend their honor? I shut my locker door and turned to face her. "What are you talking about?"

"I'm talking about Trace beating up those guys from Easton because of some inappropriate comments they supposedly made about you," she squawked, beaming as she let the cat out of the bag. "Inappropriate *sexual* comments."

"What?" My eyes grew wild. "There's no way that's true."

"Oh it's true!" she insisted. "You can lie to yourself all you want but boys don't beat up other boys over girls they *don't* like. It's like, sacrilegious."

"I don't know where you're getting this from but I don't believe it for a minute."

I couldn't believe it. It just didn't make sense.

Okay, sure, I was willing to admit Trace and I shared a few bond-worthy moments, some prolonged stares, maybe even some kind of hormone-induced attraction that sometimes got the better of me, but that's where it ended. Trace did not *like* me. He was unavailable, complicated, and up until yesterday, I was pretty sure he hated me.

"Ask Benjamin if you don't believe me. He's the one who told me the whole story this morning. He wouldn't lie."

"What story?" asked a familiar voice.

Taylor screamed at the sight of Trace. Like an actual balls out scream. My eyes swelled to the size of two Ping-Pong balls as I shot her a way-to-go look.

"Oh, hey, Trace. Uh..." She let out a phony laugh soaked in tension. "You should seriously think about wearing a cow bell or something, you scared the bejeezus out of me! So who's hungry? I know I am," she announced, backing away, still laughing, and then bolted for the cafeteria.

Smooth, Taylor. Really freaking smooth.

"What was that about?" asked Trace, looking down at me, his eyebrows pulled in suspicion.

I shrugged, backing up a step. "She gets a little high-strung if she goes without food for too long. It's like a low blood sugar thing." I had no idea what I was talking about.

"Okay." I wasn't sure if he bought it or just didn't care either way. It looked like he wanted to say something else but decided against it. He dropped his eyes and turned to leave.

"Where are you going?" I asked. "Cafeteria's this way."

"I know." His dimples made a minor appearance.

"Aren't you coming?"

"Not today." I could hear him fidgeting with his car keys.

"You're not eating lunch?" It came out a tad over dramatic, like the way you might respond if he had just declared he was an alien who didn't need oxygen. Like, *what do you mean you don't breathe air?*

I couldn't help but notice he looked a little on edge too—nervous even. But nervous about what?

I took a step towards him, my curiosity getting the better of me. "Are you going off school grounds to eat?"

He shook his head and threw a quick glance over his shoulder. "I just have this thing to do," he answered without actually answering the question. He was definitely hiding something. "I'll catch up with you guys later."

"What thing?" I probed, following him down the hall now. "Is this like that thing you did last night?"

"I don't know what you're talking about," he said over his shoulder. "Just drop it." His tone was sharp—a definite warning.

"I'm talking about the aerial disappearing act you—"

He was in my face before I could finish the sentence, leaving only a whisper of air between us. His jaw set in an angry line and his eyes tapered, letting me know I'd pushed it too far. He was just about to say something when we both caught sight of a freshman girl walking by us, watching us curiously.

He cupped his hand around my elbow and pulled me into a nearby empty classroom, slamming the door shut behind us.

"What do you think you're doing?" he growled, closing the distance between us. "You can't talk like that around here."

I took a step back and bumped into a desk. "I didn't see her. I thought we were alone," I said as I crossed and then uncrossed my arms like a nervous tick. "I wasn't thinking."

"Obviously."

My eyes narrowed. "This is all your fault anyway. If you would have just answered my question this morning, I wouldn't have had to ask it again."

"Did that look like the time or place to you?"

"Then when is? My bedroom in the middle of the night?" I wasn't sure why but my cheeks flushed just then.

He let out a tired breath and glanced down at his silver watch before meeting my eyes again. "Alright, fine. What do you want to know?"

"Huh?" I hadn't expected him to concede.

"You have sixty seconds, make it count."

My mind went blank.

I must have rehearsed a hundred and one different questions since the day I met him and suddenly, when it counted, I couldn't think of a single one to ask. This was my one chance and I was about to blow it.

And then it happened. In a haze of panic, I blurted out the one thing I *really* didn't want to talk about. "Did you beat up those guys from Easton because of me?"

His head jerked back as if stunned by the question. And he wasn't the only one. Of all the questions I could have asked him, *this* is what I went with? What the heck was I thinking? I wholly blamed Taylor for this—for putting it in my head to begin with.

"Is that what you think?" he asked in a mocking tone, though the way he crossed his arms over his chest told me he wasn't as relaxed as he wanted me to believe.

"That's not an answer," I pointed out.

"No, I didn't beat up anyone over you." He flexed his jaw muscle and then muttered, "Not really."

My eyebrows shot up. "*Not really?*"

"I just didn't like the way they were talking, that's all."

"The way they were talking about *me?*"

"They might have mentioned you. I don't remember."

He could plead the fifth all he wanted, I wasn't buying his nonchalance or sudden amnesia for a minute. "Right, well, you might want to be more careful next time. You're giving people the wrong impression."

He took a step towards me, his shoes clipping the tips of mine. "And what impression would that be?"

"You know, the impression that you...like...someone."

"You think I like *you?*" He placed his hands on the desk behind me and leaned in closer, barricading me inside the space.

A surge of heat rushed through me. "I didn't say that."

"Then what are you saying?"

What am I saying? "I'm saying that *other* people might get the wrong impression, you know, other people that aren't me." Other people like Taylor, I thought, though I refused to throw her under the bus to prove my point. "*I* personally couldn't care less whether you like me or not." Okay, so that wasn't entirely the truth but surprisingly, my voice didn't falter when I said it.

His eyes drifted down to my lips. "I don't like you."

"Good," I said, flustered. "I don't like you either."

"Good." His cobalt eyes—hooded by thick, dark lashes— were still staring down at my mouth.

I suddenly felt lightheaded, like my knees might give out at any moment. The way he was looking at me, at my lips, like he wanted to kiss me. It was making my head spin.

"Stop that."

His eyes climbed back up to mine. "Stop what?"

The door crashed open behind us. "Dammit, Trace, I've been waiting outside for you since the bell!"

I couldn't see who the voice belonged to but she sounded really familiar. And annoyed.

"I'll be right there, give me a minute," answered Trace without stepping away from me or taking his eyes off me.

"Fine! Hurry up. I mean it."

Unable to resist, I peered over his shoulder just in time to catch a glimpse of Morgan's red hair leaving the classroom.

Wait, *Morgan*? What the heck was he doing with Morgan? And how did she know we were in here?

He was still staring at me when I turned back to him.

"Where are you going with Morgan?"

"Time's up," he said, ignoring my question. He pulled his hands off the desk and stepped back, taking all the heat with him. I instantly felt the loss.

"I still have questions."

"I told you to make it count." He crossed his arms though his mouth hinted at a smile.

"Can we meet up later?"

He stared back at me strangely.

It was hard to decipher what was flickering through his eyes though I was already preparing myself for a battle, certain that he was going to turn me down. And then, just like that, his expression changed—relaxed. "Okay."

"Okay?" I nearly fell off the desk. "Really?"

"After school…if you want."

"I want." *I definitely want.*

22. THIRD WHEEL

My heart picked up its thrum as soon as I spotted Trace standing by his locker after school. This type of reaction was happening more and more lately, like I'd developed some sort of heart arrhythmia every time I got too close to him. Or him to me. I told myself they were just palpitations, like a stress response, probably caused by my aversion to his mood swings.

"Ready to go?" I asked.

His Adam's apple bobbed as he swallowed hard. "About that," he said, staring into his locker. "I don't think—"

"Don't even try to get out of it. You said we could talk. We're talking." I wasn't about to make this an option for him.

He didn't answer.

"That is, unless you want me following you around school every day asking you questions?" I shrugged innocently. "Who knows, maybe that's exactly what you want."

He shot me an irritated look like he knew what I was up to. "I'll meet you in the parking lot in five."

"Great," I faked a smile. "See you then."

I decided to detour through the athletics complex on my way

to the parking lot so that I could thank Caleb in person for helping me out with the locker situation. I knew that he had off-ice hockey training after school so I figured the fitness center was the best place to start looking.

"Are you lost or something?" asked a tall senior with short brown hair and matching eyes. He walked up from behind me and was carrying a hand towel slung over his shoulder.

"I'm looking for Caleb Owens," I said as I peeked inside the fitness center, hoping to spot him training with the rest of his team. They seemed to be in the middle of some sort of group discussion.

"I think he's still in the locker room." He gestured over his shoulder and smiled. "I can go get him for you."

"That's alright, thanks. I'll just wait for him over there," I said, and ambled off in the direction of the changing rooms. I mean really, how long could it take for a guy to change his clothes?

I leaned my back against the wall, fully intent on waiting for him outside in the hallway. That is, until I heard the muffled whispers of two distinct voices coming from the other side of the door—a male and female. Voices that I was almost certain belonged to Caleb and *Nikki*.

Truthfully, it was none of my business why Caleb and Nikki were hanging out together in the boy's locker room, and I should have turned around and booked it, but somehow, I just couldn't get my feet to obey. Maybe she was talking about me, or plotting her next assault against me, all of which were perfectly valid reasons why I had the right to know what was going on behind that door.

At least that's what I kept telling myself when I cracked open the door and peered in through the slit.

It took every ounce of restraint I had not to burst out screaming as I watched Nikki fist her hands into Caleb's shirt and push him back against the locker door like some rabid dog in heat before sealing her mouth against his in a kiss. And not just any kiss, a hands-all-over-your-body-tongue-in-each-other's-mouth kiss that made me want to wash my eyes out with bleach.

What the hell. *Nikki and Caleb*? How? When? I couldn't think of a single time I saw them talking to each other, let alone give out signals that they were into each other. And what about Trace? How could she be *that* crazy possessive about him one minute and then be out here making out with his friend the next?

Something about this smelled foul—and it wasn't just the stink coming out of the boy's locker room. I shut the door and made a run for the parking lot.

I wasn't sure whether I was going to tell Trace about what I'd just witnessed in the changing rooms. According to him, he wasn't even with Nikki anymore, so did he still have the right to know about her after-school extracurricular activities with Caleb? And if so, was it my place to say something?

Confused, and kind of grossed out, I headed across the student parking lot to meet up with Trace. I found him leaning against the side of his car, talking with Ben. Both were still wearing their school uniforms—minus their ties and blazers. I was actually relieved to see Ben there, for about a second, because at least I could postpone the Nikki thing.

"Nice of you to show up," said Ben with a Cheshire grin plastered across his face.

"Funny, I was going to say the same thing to you," I shot back, adjusting my schoolbag. "I didn't know you were coming."

"Yeah, neither did I." His grin deepened as if he had a secret. "Believe me, Jem, chaperoning the two of you isn't my idea of a good time either."

"Chaperoning us?" I looked over at Trace who was now glaring murderously at Ben.

Was this his idea of a joke?

As much as I liked Ben, there was no way we would be able to talk openly if he was tagging along with us the entire time. Had Trace even considered that in his idiotic rush to make sure we weren't alone—which is *so* obviously what he was trying to do.

"At first I was like, nope, ain't gonna happen," continued Ben, shaking his head. "But when he told me you knew, that he already spoke to you, there was no way I was missing my chance."

"Your chance to what?" If this was about ragging on me about Trace or those two guys from Easton, or the chemistry book thing from this morning, I was turning around and walking home.

"To hear the truth," he answered simply. "Straight from the source."

"The truth?" What the heck was he talking about?

"You should hear some of the stuff they've been saying about you. It's hard to tell the truth from the rumors."

"Rumors? What rumors? There's rumors about me?"

"Crazy rumors. You riding shotgun or what?" he asked as he threw his schoolbag into the backseat and stood in front of the open passenger door, waiting.

There was no point in sitting next to Trace now. Besides, I was almost positive I wouldn't have been able to resist smacking him in the head at that close range.

"Go ahead." I pulled the front seat forward and climbed into the back feeling frustrated and confused.

Trace slid into the driver's seat without saying anything and adjusted his rear-view mirror until our eyes met. I rolled my eyes at him and then sunk back in my seat, ignoring the prickling sparks I was feeling all over my body.

I was *really* starting to hate those sparks.

23. RIDING IN CARS WITH BOYS

"So these rumors," I asked Ben as we pulled out of the parking lot. "Do I even want to know what you're talking about? Because if this is about Nikki, I'd rather not know."

Ben turned to Trace, his eyebrows furrowed as if he were asking him a silent question.

"She doesn't know about you," said Trace.

"What do you mean she doesn't know?" Ben seemed shocked by this revelation. "But you said—"

"I said she knew who she was. I didn't say she knew anything about you or the others."

The *others*?

"So what then? They're just giving her bits and pieces?"

"How should I know?" snapped Trace. "I'm not her Keeper."

"What are you two talking about?" I cut in, my nerves bordering on the edge of panic. "What don't I know about you?"

Ben swiveled around in his seat to face me, a comical grin spreading across his face. "That I'm Anakim too—a Shifter."

"You're…Oh." My eyes widened as I took in this new piece of information. *Ben was a Shifter.* My heart rate picked up.

Ben was a Shifter—the same faction as Dominic.

His smile faded. "Do you even know what that is?"

As if I could forget. "Yeah, a Guardian Descendant who can shape-shift," I said and then shook my head. "I'm just a little surprised. I thought you were, you know, regular."

Trace and Ben burst out in laughter.

"What exactly is *regular?*" asked Ben. His back was leaning against the front dashboard—which was both illegal and incredibly dangerous.

"I don't know, like *not* Anakim," I said dimly. "Can you not sit like that?"

"I believe the word you're looking for is *human.*"

"Right." Ben wasn't human. No big deal.

I flinched at the sudden realization that if he wasn't human then neither was I. I didn't fit into that category anymore either. I was something else now...something that wasn't altogether sitting too well.

"Are you okay?" asked Trace through the mirror.

I nodded, pushing the uncomfortable feelings down. "I guess it just feels strange to think of it that way."

"It's because you grew up human," explained Ben. "I'd probably be tripping too if someone showed up tomorrow and told me I wasn't Anakim, that I was like a Martian or something."

"A Martian? Seriously?" Trace shook his head.

"At least it's an upgrade," continued Ben, ignoring Trace's scorn. "Just think of how much worse you would have felt if they told you you're the offspring of a demon, or worse, a Revenant."

"And to think, all this time I've been feeling like my entire life has been a lie, and really, what I should have been thinking was, well at least I'm not a demon. Thanks for putting it into perspective for me."

"Hey, no problem, that's what I'm here for," grinned Ben. "I'm like a walking silver lining."

"More like a walking punch line," said Trace, jabbing him in the arm. He was noticeably more at ease—both of them were actually—almost as though they could finally relax a little now that their guards were down. It was nice.

"So why am I only finding out about you now?" I asked, sharing looks between the two. "Why have you been keeping yourselves a secret from me?" It would have been nice to know that I wasn't the only freak in town.

"We weren't the secret," said Ben. "You were."

"How was *I* the secret? Everyone and their grandmother knows who I am and what happened to me."

At least that's how it seemed.

"We knew you were Cloaked and had no idea you were Anakim, but they didn't tell us anything after that. Only that we should treat you like any other mortal," he shrugged like it was a run-of-the-mill situation. "And when you never showed up at Temple, we just assumed they were keeping you that way. Some people said it was because you weren't really a Slayer—that you didn't have the *Mark*—but I'm not the kind of guy that listens to rumors." He winked. "Well, most of the time anyway."

"What Mark?"

"The Mark of the Anakim," he said, flexing his hand. "It's the white rune at the center of your palm. It sort of works like a fingerprint, except that it identifies your bloodline."

I looked at my palm. There were several curved lines, none of which seemed out of the ordinary. "I don't see anything."

"Here, let me see." He moved closer to me, grabbing the headrest for support as he took my hand into his free one. "Mmmm, soft skin," he remarked as he examined my open palm.

"Thank you, because this isn't awkward enough."

His eyebrows furrowed. "That's weird," he said, turning to Trace. "She doesn't have the Mark."

"What does that mean?" I asked, pulling my hand back protectively and then re-examining it myself.

At this point, I was fairly certain about my lineage. Between what my uncle had told me and what I learned through Dominic's taste test, I was pretty sure I was a Slayer. So where the heck was my Mark?

"I don't know," said Trace, his eyes meeting mine in the mirror. "It probably has something to do with the spell. I'm guessing it'll appear once they remove the Cloak."

"They haven't done that yet?" asked Ben, surprised. "Is that why I've never seen you at Temple? Training and whatnot?"

"I train." My tone was unnecessarily defensive. "I train in the evenings with Gabriel. I just started."

"Why are you training at night?"

"She has to," said Trace before I could answer. His eyes met mine in the mirror again, his gaze intense. "Because of her schedule with school and work."

That was weird. Why did Trace just hide the fact that I *had* to train at night because Gabriel was a Revenant? Was that supposed to be a secret?

"That's cool, makes sense," said Ben, and then straightened. "So do the others know? Don't tell me I'm the last one to know because I swear, I'm gonna be so—"

"Nobody knows, just Morgan."

"You expect me to believe Morgan knows and *didn't* tell Nikki?" Ben laughed. "Man, you know nothing about girls."

"Wait a freaking minute!" It was my turn to hug the headrest. "What do you mean Morgan knows? Is she Anakim too?"

"Yup. Both of 'em are," answered Ben. A devilish grin appearing on his lips. "Nikki's a bitch, I mean witch—"

"Caster," corrected Trace.

"And Morgan's a *Seer*."

"A Seer?" I balked. "A Seer of what?"

"Of the future, of Souls, stuff like that."

"Like a psychic medium?"

"Basically. If you want to use human lingo," he said, twisting his face in disapproval. "Seers are Descendants of *Messenger* Angels so they're all about their premonitions and connecting with the *Spirit Realm*. She's good too. Scary good."

I wasn't sure how I felt about this. For sure it was freaky, though at this point, everything I learned about the Anakim was freaky so that didn't really leave me anywhere new.

A thought occurred to me. "What about Taylor? Is she Anakim too?" Words couldn't describe how much I wanted this to be.

"Nope, she's a mortal," answered Ben. There was a vacant undertone in his voice, a subtle masking of what I could only imagine was his inner discontent. "Hannah is too, but Caleb and Carly are Casters like Nikki. They're just not as powerful as her."

Oh, good. So in other words, Nikki—who despises me with every fiber of her being—was not only a witch, but she also happened to be a powerful one. That was precisely the thing I wanted to hear.

My head was still spinning when we pulled into the parking lot of Starry Beach, the lakeside park that was playing host to the upcoming Spring Carnival. The overcast draped over the grounds like a bad omen, diluting all the would-be vibrant colors and replacing it with soulless shades of gray.

I peered up at the sky, worried it might rain on us at any moment as we made our way over to a picnic bench away from the crowd of workers setting up the fair rides. Ben hopped up onto the table and patted the seat next to him.

"Are you okay?" asked Trace, his eyes raking me over as he sat down on a picnic bench across from us.

"Not really, but I will be." As soon as I stop free-falling through the rabbit hole and figure out which way is up again. "Do Taylor and Hannah know?" I wondered, examining my palm again.

"No." Ben and Trace answered in unison.

"Humans don't know about us," said Ben. "No exceptions."

"Why not? I mean, we're not evil, right? We do good. If it were me, I think I'd feel safer knowing there were people out there protecting us from all the bad shit in the world."

"You'd think that, wouldn't you? But no, that's not the way it is. Humans are a skittish people, Jem, and fear can make them do crazy things especially when it comes to their fear of the unknown. Just look at their history books."

Witch hunts and vampire hysteria came to mind.

"Can you just imagine the chaos," he challenged, "If people knew what was out there? No one would want to leave their house. Forget about work, and lattes, and paying your taxes. It would be a stockpiling-supplies, shoot-your-neighbor-cause-he's-walking-funny, every-man-for-himself kind of world. Trust me, you don't want to live in that world."

He had a point. Humans didn't exactly have a great track record when it came to dealing with the supernatural. "But you guys hang out with Taylor and Hannah every day. You obviously don't mind taking some risk."

"We normally keep a safe distance," explained Trace. "You know, together but separate."

"So what changed that?"

"Carly happened," said Ben.

I vaguely remembered Taylor mentioning how she and Hannah used to be a lot closer last year before Carly moved here and started hanging out with them.

"So Carly brought them into the group. Why isn't she concerned about getting close with humans?"

"Because she's way too consumed by her human-envy to see anything clearly ninety percent of the time."

"What do you mean *human envy*?"

"Don't listen to him, he's an idiot," answered Trace. "She doesn't have human envy. She just wants a normal life."

I couldn't tell if it was understanding or pity in his tone.

"I keep telling her it's overrated, but you know how girls are," said Ben, leaning back on his elbows now.

I shot him a surly look. "No. Why don't you enlighten me?"

He put his hands up defensively, declining the invitation.

"So Carly, Caleb and Nikki are Casters. Morgan's a Seer and Ben's a Shifter." I turned back to Trace. "That leaves you."

He blinked languidly.

"Trace is what we call a *Reaper*," said Ben.

"A Reaper?" I kept my eyes on Trace. "What is that?"

"It's pretty sick," answered Ben, walking over to where Trace was sitting. "Reapers are Descendants of *Transport* Angels, you know the Angels responsible for collecting the Fallen and shuttling Souls between Realms."

No, not really, but okay. I glanced back at Trace who was watching me carefully as if to measure my reaction.

"Demibloods like Trace have a pretty good grasp on moving between time and space, I'll give him that much," said Ben, taking a jab at him. "But Purebloods take it to a whole other level. They move back and forth on the *Timeline* the way we walk in and out of rooms. Needless to say, they're kept under lock and key by the Council and rarely ever mingle with us common folk." His tone let me know he was annoyed by the segregation.

My mind snagged on the part about Trace being able to

move between time and space. "Is that what you did on my balcony last night? Move between time and space?"

"Just space," replied Trace. "It's called teleporting."

"Freaky shit, right?" Ben hopped up beside Trace so that they were sitting shoulder to shoulder. "First time I saw him port, I nearly pissed myself."

That makes two of us.

"And the moving between *time* part? We're talking about time travelling, right?" The intimate conversation we had in my bedroom about changing the past immediately came back to me, but I didn't want to bring up the details in front of Ben.

Trace confirmed it with a nod.

I needed time to process the ramifications of what this time travelling thing meant. It was just too much—too big of a deal—to digest in one hazy afternoon.

My curiosity about him, however, begged for me to find out what else he could do. I wondered if he responsible for the warm current I felt every time he touched me? Or if he had some sort of hypnotizing gift? Or mind reading ability? Too embarrassed to ask him outright, I went with the safer question:

"Do you have any other *abilities?*"

"He can read your thoughts," answered Ben.

"Only if I'm touching you."

My eyes swelled. "That day in the restaurant—you heard me." *And in my bedroom.*

He nodded again.

I felt the crushing blow of panic set in as a dozen questions filtered in all at once. What else had he heard? How many times had we touched? Could he hear me now? *Hello?* I immediately started cursing at him in my mind.

"You're freaking out, aren't you?"

"No," I lied, swallowing hard. "I'm just taking it all in."

And I was, though I suspected it would be a while before I

would be square again.

I spent the rest of the week shuffling between school, work, and training with Gabriel, and as a result, the week had flown right by. By Friday night, I was exhausted, and admittedly a little green in the eyes since everyone I knew was out having a great time, doing normal teenage stuff—partying, unwinding, hanging out—and getting ready for the carnival this week-end.

Everyone, that is, except me.

I was stuck in the secret underground training facilities of some ancient building having to learn self-defense tactics and kill strikes like my life depended on it—because it actually did. It wasn't really the stuff dreams were made of, and would have been a total nightmare if it wasn't for my skilled, easy on the eyes instructor who made it slightly more bearable for me.

"Now drop your chin as far as you can," ordered Gabriel. His arm was coiled around my neck and his other hand was on my waist, confining me against him. "You want to take the pressure off your neck and shift it to your chin. Good, just like that."

As soon as I had the brunt of his arm off my windpipe and could breathe again, I maneuvered us into what I liked to call the *stop, drop and roll back*, which basically consisted of, well, dropping to the ground and rolling back.

And for the first time since I started training with him, I actually executed the move flawlessly, having dropped us to the ground and then rolled myself back over my would-be assailant to gain the upper position over him. I even fake-staked him with my fist for good measure.

"How do you like me now?" I sassed, feeling all smug.

His lips curled into a smile as he stared back up at me from the ground. "There may be hope for you after all, Jemma."

"Thanks...I think?"

He rose quickly to his feet, the movement registering only as a blur. "And had you not just driven your imaginary stake through my left lung, it would have been an impressive kill," he added, straightening out the creases on his black T-shirt.

"Come again?"

"The heart would be about here," he said pointing to the *center* of his chest. "Between your left and right lung."

"Oh. Right. I knew that."

"Let's just hope you strike better than you lie," he said with just a hint of ridicule as he moved to reposition the mat.

"I wasn't lying. I just forgot...that...I...didn't...know...that piece of information. There's a difference, you know."

Smooth, Jemma. Talk about a face-palm moment.

Julian and Gabriel both stared at me like I had three eyes.

"What? There *is* a difference," I insisted. It was too late to quit now.

Gabriel looked like he was going to say something, maybe impart some more wisdom on me, but decided against it. "I think we're about done for the night. Get some rest. We'll continue this tomorrow evening."

"Actually, I can't tomorrow," I said following him over to the back bench while Julian gathered his things. "I'm busy."

"You're not scheduled to work. I already checked." He didn't look up at me as put on his shoes.

"It's not that. I'm going to the carnival tomorrow. I promised my friends."

He straightened out and faced me. "I don't think that's a very good idea. You're not ready."

"I'm not ready for the carnival?"

"You're not ready to be exposed to potential danger."

I swallowed the sudden ball of nerves that had formed in the back of my throat. "And when you say potential danger," I began, lowering my voice so that Julian couldn't hear us. "You mean Dominic, right? Are you saying he's going to be there?"

"It's always a possibility."

"Great. So how much longer am I supposed to hide away from the rest of the world?"

"You shouldn't look at it that way," he said as he started for the door. "You need to train. That should come first."

I sighed and followed him out into the corridor, leaving Julian to lock up behind us. The truth was, I was really looking forward to this day off, to getting a break from work and training and vampires, and well, reality. And I promised Taylor I would be there. I didn't want to let her down. Not *again*. There had to be a way to make this work.

"Couldn't we start training earlier tomorrow, like at sundown? That way we could finish early and I'd have enough time to do both." It seemed like a fair compromise.

"I suppose we could do that though I'm not sure I feel comfortable with you going to the carnival by yourself."

"I wouldn't be," I piped up quickly. "I'll be with friends."

He didn't seem comforted by this.

"Of course, you could always come with me," I added with an innocent smile. "And then you wouldn't have to worry about it at all." Not that that was very likely. Gabriel didn't have an off switch and was always worrying about one thing or another.

He arched his brow as if to express the same sentiment.

"So?" I pushed, drunk on the fumes of my own exhaustion. "What do you say? Is it a date?"

He gave me another disapproving look and then finally conceded with a nod. That was all the response I needed.

It was on like Donkey Kong.

24. THE CARNIVAL

The scent of buttered popcorn and cotton candy mingled in the air like a childhood relic, filling me with a heavy dose of nostalgia. It made me long for a simpler time. A time when I was expected to be nothing more than my father's daughter. When I was still allowed to be *just* a kid. Looking back on it now, it seemed like such a long time ago—a lifetime ago.

I buttoned up my jean jacket as Gabriel and I headed towards Starry Beach to meet up with Taylor. The boardwalk was breathing life, lit up with game booths and fair rides as far as the eye could see. Gabriel's eyes scanned the grounds like a soldier doing reconnaissance, weary of everyone and everything around us. I told him to relax (twice already since we arrived) though it was like trying to tell a bird not to fly.

It didn't take us long to find Taylor and the others huddled together in a messy circle over by the Ring Toss game. Everyone was accounted for, including Nikki who had her arm twisted around Trace's bicep.

The sight of them together like that sickened me; mostly because of the strange urge it incited in me that made me want to run over there and rip her away from him like a bad dream.

"Are you alright?" asked Gabriel under his breath. He must have noticed the rigid turn my walk had taken.

"Perfectly," I lied, though it was drowned out by Taylor shouting my name as she left Carly's side and rushed over to greet us.

"I'm so happy you came!" She threw her arms around my neck and waltzed us into that jackrabbit dance again. And by us, I mean her. I just sort of got dragged along for the ride.

Gabriel's cell phone rang, breaking up the moment.

"I have to take this," he said and then ticked his chin towards my friends—his way of telling me to wait for him in a crowd. After all, there's safety in numbers, though he'd probably think twice about the crowd he was sending me into if he knew anything about *witchy* Nikki Parker.

Taylor laced her arm through mine as we meandered back towards the Ring Toss game in no particular hurry. Her eyes blazing with anticipation and delight.

"Oh. My. God!" She tugged my arm playfully. "*Gabriel* Huntington? What the heck happened to Dominic?"

Crap. What was I supposed to tell her? He turned out to be a vampire and attacked me in the middle of a make-out session? Right. That should go over well.

"It just didn't work out," I shrugged, aiming for vague.

"Oh." She blinked at me, the disappointment filtering in over her eyes. "When did this happen?"

I could tell she was hurt that I hadn't confided in her about the "breakup" sooner. She took things like that pretty serious.

"Last week," I mumbled. "I was going to tell you. I wanted to. I just…I wasn't ready to talk about it yet."

"Gosh, Jemma, you sure do move fast," heckled Nikki. "What is that, like a brother a month you're averaging? You may want to think about a bigger city. I don't think this town has enough guys to hold a girl like you over." Her hyena cackle rattled my ears. "I hear New York is beautiful this time of year."

Morgan and Hannah snickered in unison like an exclamation mark to her public lashing.

If the urge to knock her over wasn't strong before, it was damn near uncontrollable now. "Are *you* really one to talk?" I shot back before thinking good of it. It felt like the rage was manifesting itself in my face, burning up my cheeks and firing off my mouth like a weapon of mass destruction.

She unlatched herself from Trace and swarmed over to me in a cloud of her over-the-top designer perfume. "And what pray tell is that supposed to mean?"

"What does it mean?" I repeated with my own brand of sardonic disdain. "I think you know exactly what it means," I said and glanced over her shoulder at Trace.

He buried his hands in his pocket and pumped his jaw muscle, entirely unaware of what was going on, or of what was coming. I couldn't help but feel sorry for him. He really didn't deserve to be thrust into the middle of this.

Even though I wanted nothing more than to call Nikki out on her two-timing ways (especially after everything she'd done to me), I wasn't sure I could do it if that meant hurting Trace in the process. I couldn't do that to him, not like this. Not in front of all these people.

I turned to Taylor hoping she had some sort of viable exit strategy ready, but she just stared back at me dazed and confused like she didn't know where any of that had come from, or where I was trying to go with it.

"If you have something to say, you better just go ahead and spit it out," snapped Nikki, her brow arched high and mighty.

"Forget it," I finally mumbled, dejected. It had to be one of the most anticlimactic moments of my life.

"Forget it?" she parroted, laughing. "Seriously, I can't believe I ever wasted a second worrying about you. It's like you're completely clueless."

I bit down my anger and tried to steady my voice before answering, "Well let's just hope for your sake that's true."

"For my sake?"

"Yeah, I mean, hypothetically, how bad would it be if it turned out I wasn't as clueless as you thought I was? That I actually knew a few things and was just waiting for the perfect moment to drop them on you?"

"Oh my God, drop them!" cheered Taylor beside me.

Nikki narrowed her eyes as though she were summing me up, wondering what information I could possibly have on her and why in the world I wasn't outing her with it.

"Is everything alright here?" asked Gabriel, appearing on my free side. His timing was kismet—every time.

I nodded, "Everything's fine."

Nikki's scarlet lips twisted into a smile as she drank in Gabriel from head to toe, who in turn, proceeded to ignore her completely and perform a quick crowd-sweep instead. I felt my own grin deepen with satisfaction as hers faded out. She turned on her heel and walked back over to Trace who was talking privately with Ben.

I noticed he was holding fast to his promise to stay away from me, physically, though his eyes were a different story.

"I think you need to kiss," said Taylor.

My head snapped back to her, eyes gaping.

"The kissing booth," she clarified. "Nothing cleanses the pallet like a good make-out session, and it just so happens that you're signed up as an official Kisser."

"I'm *what?*" I laughed, because it was *that* absurd.

"I signed you up," she beamed, her eyes drifting casually between Gabriel and me. "Well, both of us actually. And Carly."

"Well, you can just un-sign us up because there's no way I'm kissing strangers in a kissing booth after getting called a—" I broke off, preferring not to rehash the sordid details of my scarlet letter in front of Gabriel. "I'm not doing it."

"Come on, it'll be fun, and besides, it's for charity. And it's tradition. And it's for charity!" she repeated sans eloquence.

"I'll tell you what," I smiled and shoved my hand into my pocket, wrangling out a twenty dollar bill. "Here's a twenty. Let's not and say we did."

She shook her head decidedly. "I'm not reneging on tradition, and you shouldn't either. Do you really want the ghosts of carnival's past haunting you until graduation?" The glimmer in her eyes told me this had nothing to do with spooks and everything to do with kissing hot senior boys.

"I'll take my chances."

She turned to Gabriel, eyelashes fluttering in full-flirt-mode. "How about you? Care to volunteer those fine lips in the name of charity?"

"Taylor!" There had to be laws against this sort of thing.

Gabriel cleared his throat, looking wholly uncomfortable.

"Alright, never mind," she said with a sad frown that almost made me reconsider. *Almost.* "I can totally take a hint."

That had yet to be proven.

"Meet back up in thirty?" she asked, hopeful. "Those bumper cars have our names written all over them."

"You got it." I gave her a quick hug and then hauled Gabriel off by his jacket before she had a chance to change her mind.

A medley of animated songs and sound bites filled the airwaves as Gabriel and I traipsed through the crowd of carnival goers, side by side. The moon hung low in the distance, plumes of mist slithering over its crest like a band of wandering ghosts. Otherworldly in every way.

"Are you going to tell me what that was about back there?" asked Gabriel. I could feel his eyes boring into me.

"What? With Taylor?" I shrugged. "She can be a little pushy sometimes, but it's harmless. You'll get used to her."

"No, not her. The other one."

"Nikki." I shuddered for dramatic effect.

"There was a lot of tension." He placed his hand at the small of my back and steered us around a pack of idle bystanders.

"I guess you could call it tension. Personally, I think pure unadulterated hatred is much more fitting." I met his solemn eyes and smiled. "It's been like that since the first day I met her. At first I thought it was just some territorial thing over Trace, but now...I don't know," I said, flashing back to her tryst with Caleb. "I'm not sure what it's about."

"He was supposed to be your Keeper, wasn't he?"

"Yeah. *Supposed to* being the operative words."

"And she's also Anakim."

I looked up at him. "Are you going somewhere with this?"

"There's a very unique bond between a Slayer and her Keeper," he explained, his voice low. "She may have felt threatened by your arrival."

"Okay," I nodded. I could've accepted that. "Except that Trace left the Order months before I got here. He had no intention of being my Keeper, then or now, and she knew that."

He considered it. "Then what do you think it stems from?"

"Your guess is as good as mine." The cool air pressed against my cheeks as a sinister feeling washed over me. "All I know is, I don't trust her. Something about her gives me the creeps. And you know she's a Caster, right?"

He nodded, unmoved.

"I still don't know what that even means. Am I supposed to be scared of her? Can she actually hurt me? Half the time I'm sitting there wondering if she's going to turn me into a freaking toad. It's no way to live."

His lips curved into a smile. "She can't turn you into a toad," he assured. "The amount of power needed to do something like that would probably kill her."

"Well, she looks at me like she's contemplating it."

His grin deepened.

"So what exactly *can* she do?" I asked, turning serious.

"It depends, really, on her bloodline and how well she's honed her Craft," he said, his eyes scanning the area again. "Most Casters her age already have a fairly good grasp on controlling the elements and manipulating energy, though I wouldn't put it to the test anytime soon. It's best if you just try to avoid any conflict with her. Besides, you have more important things to concern yourself with."

"Believe me, you're preaching to the choir. I don't want any more trouble than I already have. Problem is, trouble seems to find me even when I'm running away from it."

"I've noticed," he said grimly.

"Sometimes it feels like the more I wish for peace and quiet in my life, the more chaotic my life becomes." I laughed a little though I didn't feel it in my heart. "Guess I should probably stop wishing for that then, huh?"

He didn't answer. Something in his weary eyes told me he'd given up on wishing a long time ago. Like he had seen and done too much to ever go back to that childlike state of wishing. Somewhere in the back of my mind, I wondered if my own eyes would end up looking that way someday. If I, too, would outgrow my wishes. The thought of it depressed me.

"Look at us, this is supposed to be our night off and what are we doing? We're talking shop." I shook my head, disappointed.

"What would you rather we do?"

"I don't know, anything but this," I said as I scanned the area and spotted the Ferris wheel at the end of the boardwalk. "There! I want to go on that!" I pointed, desperate to salvage whatever was left of my night off. Of my youth.

"The Ferris wheel?" He faltered slightly.

"Don't tell me you're scared?" I goaded.

"Of course not."

"Then come on!" I laughed, grabbing onto his lapel as I dragged him clear across the boardwalk.

We took our place at the end of the line and peered up at the massive roulette. Each of its carriages illuminated in bright neon colors, dangling weightlessly above us. My stomach bottomed out—in a good way—just looking up at it.

"Shoot, we need tickets to get on," I realized as we progressed further into the line. I pointed at the admission sign beside the ride operator.

Gabriel glanced over his shoulder and then ticked his head. "There's a ticket booth right over there."

"Hold on," I said, grabbing his arm as he began to lead us out of the line. "One of us should hold our place."

He looked back at the booth apprehensively as though it were miles away from where we were standing. "I'll get the tickets," he offered and then grimaced. "Stay where I can see you."

I gave him a little salute and continued following the line, keeping a close watch on him as he crossed over to the Ticket Booth. He walked just the way you'd expect him to walk—controlled, determined, militant. There was nothing casual about it.

The line started to move again, quicker now, and within a couple of minutes, I found myself near the front of it. I looked back at Gabriel who was still stuck behind the same group of people since the last time I checked and decided to let the couple behind me pass. And then another one.

When I faced forward again, I noticed that the Ferris wheel operator (a young man with dark blond hair and a really bad complexion) wasn't alone anymore. There was a man in a baseball cap and black coat standing with him, leaning forward with his back to us and whispering something privately. The tour operator looked up at him wide-eyed but otherwise expressionless and then nodded slowly. Something about it seemed...unnatural.

Before I could make anything of it, the man in the baseball cap turned around and faced me. His eyes were still shadowed by the hat but there was a wayward grin playing across his mouth. A mouth that I was familiar with. A mouth that I had both fantasized about and feared in equal parts.

"Hello, angel," he smiled, tossing his hat away as he gave light to the face from my nightmares. "I've missed you."

25. SECRETS

Watching Dominic move across the platform felt surreal. It was as though someone had knocked all the air out of my lungs—out of the world—and snatched away my ability to perform even the most basic human functions, like breathing or thinking or moving. All I could do was stare at him, paralyzed by the fear that had cemented my feet to the ground.

My mouth dropped open to gasp for air, to scream.

"Now, now, angel. Be a good girl," he warned sweetly, pressing his finger against my lips to silence me. "You wouldn't want any of these people to get hurt, now would you?"

My eyes flickered briefly to the happy, unsuspecting people around me, wondering what exactly he might do to them. Was he really capable of hurting them? Was I willing to take that risk? I shook my head. Or at least I *think* I did.

"Come on," he said, leading me to the waiting carriage. "We're going to take a little ride on the Ferris wheel," he announced and then sat down at the far end, pulling me into the seat beside him. I didn't even put up a fight, too afraid that he would follow through on his threat.

My eyes darted back around to the ticket booth, searching

for Gabriel as though he were my one and only hope. I watched as he tore through the crowd, racing to make it back to me in time—to save me—but it was too late. The Ferris wheel was already moving, lifting us up higher and higher off the ground.

The crushing look on Gabriel's face sent a rip through my heart as he watched us ascend further out of his reach. A look that only exemplified itself when Dominic leaned over the seat and waved down at him gloatingly.

"You look ravishing tonight," said Dominic when he finally righted himself. He swung his arm around the back of the carriage and coiled his lips in a pleased smile.

Ravishing how? Like a steak?

The terror permeated my blood as I ran through all the definitions of *ravishing* in my head. I tried to convince myself that if he wanted to attack me—to feed on me again—he would have tried to take me to another place, a private location with no witnesses. That had to count for something, right? *Right?*

"Did you miss me, angel?"

I forced myself to look at him. "I can't say that I did."

"Really?" His eyebrows pulled into a point as he relaxed back into his seat, wetting his lips. "Then I haven't been starring in your dreams every night since our kiss?"

I scoffed at his selective memory of that night. "Only if you count my nightmares."

His laughter bubbled out, short and sweet. "As long as I'm haunting you, I suppose I don't mind the means." There was something truly terrifying about the way his baby-faced features nearly canceled out every sinister word he uttered.

"What do you want from me, Dominic?" My voice spiked unnaturally. "Haven't you had enough fun?"

"There's no such thing."

"Are you going to try to kill me again?"

He clicked his tongue as though insulted. "Now where's the

fun in that? I have far bigger plans for you, love, none of which involve your death." His grin widened. "Certainly not in the immediate future."

An icy chill clawed its way down my back. "What plans?" I asked, choosing to ignore the latter part of his statement since my heart was already thwacking hard against my chest.

"Patience, angel. Don't you like surprises?"

"No," I said with absolute certainty. "I don't."

His eyes shifted briefly to the crowd below. "Let's just say you're going to help me get something."

I swallowed hard. "Does this something have a name?"

"How do you name the unnamable?" His cheek hitched up in a jeering way. "I couldn't possibly."

"How am I supposed to help you get it if I don't know what it is?" I asked, wanting to keep him good and talking.

"That's the thing about vengeance, love. It has a way of working itself into the equation." He reached forward and took a strand of my hair into his hands, twisting it gently around his index finger. "I only have to sit back and let its wrath light the way."

"So this is about getting revenge on someone?" I scoffed, swatting his hand away from my hair. "Revenge on who?"

"Careful now," he warned, though I wasn't sure if he was referring to my probing question or the fact that I just swatted him away like a bothersome fly.

"I'm sorry," I said, doing my best to sound it. "I'm just trying to understand what you want from me...so I can help you." I forced myself to smile at him.

"You wish to help me?" he smiled back, sliding in closer. His eyes were glazed with a familiar look of want.

A look of *hunger*.

"Not like that!" I dug myself deeper into the corner of the carriage, wishing I could disappear into the metal. "I swear to

God, Dominic, if you try to bite me again I'm going to hurt you," I warned. I had nothing to back it up with but he didn't need to know that.

"If I bite you again, you're going to enjoy every second of it," he said and raised his hand to my cheek, gently caressing it with the back of his knuckles.

His cold touch sent a lingering shiver down my arms, a shiver that I was horrified to find wasn't completely revolting.

"See how nice that feels?" he whispered.

I could feel my mouth losing moisture by the second. I swallowed hard, trying to loosen the knot in my throat.

"You shouldn't fight it, angel. I'm a part of you now. Your skin hungers for my touch even when your mind tells it not to."

I shook my head. I didn't want to listen to this—to hear it. Somewhere deep inside, I knew there was truth to what he was saying. I knew his bite had done something to me that night— changed something—and the thought of it petrified me.

The breeze picked up and ruffled my hair as the Ferris wheel came to another stop, holding us atop the world as though we had orbited into a different plane of existence.

"Why are you bringing me into this?" I asked, trying to take control of the conversation again, redirect it back to neutral grounds—back to his plans. "I'm not even from here. I don't know anyone you know."

"That's not entirely true."

"Well, except for Gabriel." A surge of panic pierced through the good vibrations. "Is this about *Gabriel*?"

He pulled his hand away and casually sank back into his seat, and for the faintest of seconds, I felt the nick of guilt because I actually missed it.

"I won't help you hurt him."

He examined me with curious eyes. "And why is that?"

"Because he's my friend," I answered indignantly.

"Your *friend*?" he repeated, testing the word out in his mouth, swirling it around with his tongue. "So then he told you the truth? About how he came to be?" His smirk told me he already knew the answer. When I didn't respond, he laughed and said, "I didn't think so."

"I never asked him to."

"Then ask him, love. See if he opens up the vault." He took up with my hair again. "I bet he won't. I bet he'll put her first. He always does."

"Put who first?"

"Tessa, of course."

"*Tessa*? What does my sister have to do with this?"

"See now, if Gabriel was a real *friend*, he would have told you all of this already." His mouth curved into a sly grin. "He wouldn't have left you out here in the dark, angel, especially when there's so much danger waiting for you here."

"You're just trying to scare me," I said, doing my best to steady my voice though I was far too unsure of what the hell was going on to accomplish the feat.

"Maybe." He caressed my cheek again. "But I'm telling you the truth. He'll always protect her, and her little secrets too, even if that means putting you in danger."

I glanced down at Gabriel who was watching the wheel make its way back around, his arms crossed rigidly across his chest. Gabriel who had done nothing but help me since the day I met him. I had no reason not to trust him.

Dominic on the other hand...

"I don't believe you," I said, facing him again. "You're just trying to turn me against him. It won't work."

"Ask him to tell you about how he met her," he dared. "And when he refuses, you are more than welcome to come and find me, and I will tell you everything you want to know."

"Why don't you just tell me now?"

His smile deepened as though my question brought him much joy. "It would be my pleasure to tell you now."

"Okay..." I waited.

He leaned forward briefly. "For a kiss."

I didn't even have to think about it. "Forget it! I'd rather melt my lips off with acid."

His laughter rang out melodically as the giant wheel of horrors gradually crawled to a stop.

From my peripheral, I spotted Gabriel pushing through the crowd of people waiting to get on as he made his way over to the loading ramp to meet me. I threw a pleading glance back at Dominic, praying he'd let me get off this thing without incident.

He nodded as if to answer my silent plea. "I'll be seeing you," he sang playfully, chilling my blood with his song.

I turned back to Gabriel who was holding his hand out like a life preserver, his eyes gleaming an apologetic shade of olive green. I grabbed it with all my heart and nearly somersaulted myself off the ride.

"Did he hurt you?" he asked with an exasperated look.

I shook my head, "I'm fine. Let's just go."

He put his hand on my back and funneled me past him where I began to move towards the exit, thinking he was right there behind me. It was only when I heard the gasps in the crowd that I turned around and found him plucking Dominic off the cart by his shirt and slamming him into one of the metal railings.

Dominic's maniacal laughter pierced the air as Gabriel yanked him off the rail and rammed him into another one on the opposing side. The structure trembled under the impact.

"Stop it!" I yelled, running back over to them, terrified that the whole thing would come tumbling down on us.

"You'd be wise to listen to her," said Dominic, his eyes wide with merriment over Gabriel's total loss of control. "You're causing quite a scene here, brother."

Gabriel halted, his cautious eyes peering over his shoulder at the crowd that had amassed around us. He let go of Dominic abruptly as though scorched by the contact. "This isn't over," he said, shoving his finger into his brother's chest.

Dominic's lips twisted in an evil curl, welcoming the challenge. It was the look of a lunatic—a madman.

"Come on, Gabriel," I said, tugging at his arm desperately. "Let's go." The sooner we got out of here, the sooner I could crawl under a rock and hide.

Gabriel took a step back, his livid expression softening some and making it easier for me to drum up the courage to pull him away from the scene. To my relief, he didn't resist and followed quietly as I led him down the ramp, away from Dominic and the hungry crowd of people looking for a show.

"Nice job, skank." Nikki's faux smile greeted me as soon as my feet hit the pavement. Morgan and Hannah hung on either side of her like a bad accessory. "It takes a special brand of slut to get in between two brothers," she spat out venomously.

I wanted to shout in her face that what happened back there had nothing to do with me, and that in fact, I was nothing more than a spectator in some long-time-coming revenge plot between the two of them and my *sister* over something that apparently happened long before I even got here, and that frankly, I didn't have the slightest idea what was going on!

My mouth flopped open as I tried to edit the sentiment into something a little more condensed and less revealing, but was pulled away by Gabriel before I could get any words out.

"Thanks a lot," I said as I fell into step with him. "You didn't even give me a chance to defend myself!"

"You don't need to defend yourself to her," he said plainly. "We have more important things to contend with."

"Starting with how you know my sister?" I yanked him back by his elbow, forcing him to face me. "You never did tell me how you two met."

"What happened up there?" He ticked his head to the Ferris wheel like an accusation. "What did he say to you?"

When I didn't answer, he folded his arms across his chest. "This is important, Jemma. I need to know what he said."

"He told me I was going to help him," I said, trailing a group of kids as they passed around us to get to the *Duck Pond* game. "Something about revenge...or vengeance? He didn't exactly outline his plan for me, but he did mention you and Tessa."

He looked tense though not surprised.

"He also said you're keeping secrets from me." I watched his expression harden. "Things about you and Tessa and the past. Things he thinks I should know about. Is he telling the truth, Gabriel? Are you hiding stuff from me?"

"It's not as simple as that, Jemma."

"Yes, it is. You're either lying to me or you're not."

"Of course there are things you don't know. A lot has happened over the years, but those things aren't only mine to share."

"What does that mean?"

"It means you have to talk to your sister."

"So basically what you're saying is, you can't answer any of my questions because of Tessa."

Isn't that precisely what Dominic said? That Gabriel was covering up for her. That he would always put her first. Maybe Dominic was capable of telling the truth after all.

"She's only trying to protect you, Jemma, and this is the only way she knows how to do it. You may not always understand what she does, but she has your best interest at heart."

"I don't need her to protect me. Not if that means being lied to all the time. I deserve to know the truth. Whether or not you and my sister want to admit it, I'm already involved in this. Dominic involved me."

He knew I was right—I could see it in his eyes. I also saw that it didn't matter one bit. His loyalty was to her and it was clear that he was going to continue protecting her...but for what reason? What could Tessa possibly have done that was so bad that she couldn't even tell her own sister? Tessa who'd always done everything perfect and right since the day she was born.

It was becoming painfully obvious that if I was expecting the two of them to tell me the truth, I'd probably be waiting around until the end of days.

"Dominic offered to tell me everything." I put it out there mercilessly, hoping it would raise the stakes a little. It scared me to think that I'd be desperate enough to take him up on his offer, that I was even considering it.

"You can't trust him."

"I know," I agreed, meeting his somber eyes. "But I don't know if I can trust you either."

And that scared me even more.

26. BREAKING BREAD

A light drizzle peppered the windshield as Gabriel and I turned onto the main thoroughfare after leaving the carnival. We hadn't said a word to each other since we left the boardwalk and that was perfectly fine with me. I had no desire to hear another word from him unless that word was birthed from the truth.

I reached forward and turned up the volume to an ear-bending level to drive home the point.

He tipped forward and turned it back down. I could feel his eyes appraising me as though he were trying to decipher a puzzle. "You're angry with me."

"I'm surprised you were able to figure that out without Tessa's direction."

"That's not fair."

"Neither is being lied to all the time," I shot back, watching plumes of fog spiral in and out of view outside my window. "I trusted you, Gabriel. You were the only one I trusted and now I don't know if I can believe a single word you say."

"I'm sorry you feel that way."

"If you were sorry, you'd tell me the truth. I don't know anything about you; how you *changed*, if you *chose* it, how long you've been this way. I don't even know how old you are! How do you think that makes me feel?"

A heavy silence pressed down on us as the windshield wipers swooshed back and forth methodically.

"You need to eat," he said without looking.

"I don't need to eat. I need to hear the truth!"

"I'm a Revenant."

"I'm aware of that."

He looked down at my stomach, his eyes mapping my torso. I reflexively covered up, hugging my abdomen with both arms.

"I can hear your stomach," he said, bringing his eyes back up to mine. "You're hungry. You need to eat something."

He heard my stomach noises? *How freaking embarrassing.*

Before I could confirm or deny the fact, he had already made the decision and was pulling into the parking lot of an old diner that overlooked the highway.

Might as well, I figured. I was two stomach growls away from starvation anyway.

The old diner was lit up like a Christmas tree—if your Christmas tree was decorated with white florescent sky lights, a neon blue *open* sign that flickered something terrible, and the kind of red banquet seats that made you wish you carried protective eye-wear on you. The only saving grace was that it looked to be about as lively as a morgue at midnight, which at least meant we could talk freely and not have to worry about slipping up in front of nosy patrons.

We walked to the back of the diner and sat down opposite each other in a booth by the window. A young, busty blond in her mid-twenties rushed out of the back-house wearing a fitted yellow uniform that looked as though it had just rode into town straight out of the fifties.

"Can I get you guys a drink to start with?" she asked, smiling as she dropped a set of menus on the ivory table.

"I'll have a Coke." I turned to Gabriel who was sitting perfectly straight in his seat, both hands planted on his lap. It was almost unnerving how *proper* he was.

"Just water, please."

"No problem. I'll be right back with those," she smiled and walked off.

"Four years."

I looked up at him and blinked. "Four years *what?*"

"I've been a Revenant for four years," he said calmly. "I was twenty-one when I *turned*, and that was four years ago."

"Four years. That's it? I thought you'd be something more dramatic. You know, like a century or two."

"Sorry to disappoint," he said evenly. His eyes seared into mine, waiting for another question.

I was happy to oblige. "Did you choose it?"

"I would never choose this," he said, every word slicked with repugnance.

"How did it happen?"

The waitress cut through with our drinks and placed them down on the table in front of us.

"Are you ready to order?" she asked, oblivious to the epic conversation she'd just interrupted.

I realized I hadn't even looked at the menu. Unwilling to suffer the extra wait, I went with the tried and true. "Cheeseburger and fries."

"Perfect." She jotted down my order on her pad and turned to Gabriel. "And for you?"

"Nothing for me, thank you."

"You sure?" she asked, tilting her head to the side as she smiled at him. It seemed like a flirty gesture.

He nodded, resolute and unaware of it.

"Okay. Well, if you change your mind, just give me a shout," she said, pointing to the nameplate on her bust that read *Lana*.

I waited for her to disappear behind the counter again.

"Will you tell me how it happened?"

He ran a hand over his face and nodded. I guess I finally wore him down enough to spill the goods.

"It happened four years ago," he began, glancing out the window as though the pictures were replaying for him in the distance. "I came home after being out of town on assignment and found my brother entertaining Revenants in our living room. True Revenants, not Descendants like us."

My eyes widened.

"Seeing them there in my home, *invited*, where my family lived..." I could see the fury settling in over him like an old familiar friend. "I did the only thing I knew how to do. What I'd always been trained to do. I *reacted*."

"Meaning you vanquished them?"

"Without question." He glanced out the window again, his eyes sweeping the parking lot carefully. "Later when the dust settled, so to speak, I'd learnt that Dominic had been involved with one of the female Revenants from the coven," he said turning back to me. "And that he fancied himself in love with her."

"Are you saying Dominic was in love with a Revenant when he was still Anakim?" I had no idea why I was so surprised, this sounded exactly like something he would do.

He nodded, his expression undisturbed. "Dominic has always taken pleasure in breaking the rules. He's always gravitated to the dark side but nothing like what he became after that day. It was as though something in him had switched off. He vowed revenge on me for what I'd done, though as it turned out there wouldn't be much time for retribution since ironically, both Dominic and I were fated to die anyway. Or so we were told."

"What you mean *fated* to die?"

"On the *Paradigm*," he answered plainly. "The grand scheme of things—of all things. There is much we can manipulate in this world, things we can prevent or alter, though death is not one of them. It's a Cardinal Law. If you're ordained to die—if it's your time to go—Death will come for you until the debt is paid and the balance is restored."

I felt a prickling chill slide down my back. There was something about the way he described death, like it was a living breathing entity, and it made my skin crawl.

"Dominic, being the nonconformist that he was, refused to accept this fate and instead chose to spend every waking moment he had left looking for some kind of loophole—a way to cheat death. And indeed, he found it."

"By Turning," I realized aloud.

He tipped his head once. "You must *die* in order to become a Revenant, thus satisfying the Paradigm, which in turn left him free to reanimate without any consequences—cosmically speaking." His moss-green eyes gleamed as he stared back at me from across the table. "And through that discovery, he'd also found the perfect way to make me pay for what I'd done. By turning me into the very thing I hated most. The thing I was raised to hunt and kill."

I couldn't believe what I was hearing. "*He* did this to you? He's the reason you're a Revenant."

"And I've had to carry that guilt with me ever since. For both of us. For my family."

"Why would you feel guilty?" I asked, confused by his admission. "He's the one who did this, not you."

"Yes, but he did it because of me," he said blinking slowly. "If I hadn't vanquished them...if I would've heard him out first, found another way, none of this would have happened—"

"You don't know that for sure," I interrupted, shaking my head. "And besides, you can't make people do things that aren't already in them to do, Gabriel. You taught me that, remember?"

He looked up at me, his expression somewhat surprised.

The waitress returned to our table with my order and placed the plate down in front of me. "*Bon Apetit.*"

"Thank you." I skimmed a French fry off the top.

"Have you changed your mind?" she smiled at Gabriel, wiping off the area in front of him with her dishrag. "A lot of people get an appetite after smelling the food."

I tried not to laugh.

"No, I'm fine. Thank you."

"Another glass of water maybe?"

He shook his head. She hadn't noticed his glass was still full. Or that mine was almost empty.

"Could I get another coke?" I asked, shaking my glass.

"Sure thing. I'll be right back with that."

"So, how does my sister factor into all this?" I asked when she was gone.

"I think I should let Tessa tell you that part herself. It isn't my place to speak for her," he said, pushing his untouched glass of water to the side.

"Okay, fair enough." I took a mega bite of my burger and smiled as the flavor exploded on my tongue. "How about your father? Is he still around?" I asked through a mouthful of food.

His taut expression tightened. "He's alive, however, he's chosen not to be a part of our lives anymore."

"Why not?"

"Jemma." He regarded me as though I'd lost my mind. "Dominic and I are Revenants. The Huntington bloodline has ended because of us. We've disgraced our family—our lineage, our entire race. How could he not renounce us?"

"But the Council…you still work for them, and the Magister said you were one of their best—"

"That may very well be, but it doesn't change what we are. I can still work for the Order, though I will never be anything more than a foot soldier to them, and I'm okay with that. Had this happened even a decade ago, I would not have been allowed to live, let alone step foot inside Temple, regardless of whether I was a danger to them or not."

"What changed their minds?"

"I suppose the realization that Turned Anakim could be of use to them since our bloodlust can be controlled. We are strong, nearly indestructible, and most importantly, *expendable*. As long as we operate in the shadows and do as we're told, we are permitted to exist."

"That's horrible."

"Perhaps," he agreed, though not wholeheartedly. "But I understand their reasoning. They don't want other Anakim seeing this as an acceptable alternative though I don't see how any Anakim worth their Mark would ever choose this. It's a disgrace; the lowest form of existence."

The hatred he felt for Revenants was palpable. He was raised to hate them, to hunt their breed and kill them without so much as a second thought, and now he was one of them. I could only imagine the mental anguish this caused him. My heart ached for him in ways I couldn't even articulate.

"Here's your coke," said the waitress as she set it down in front of me and then sped off to answer a ringing phone. I barely noticed her that time.

"Well, I think he's missing out," I said, taking a sip of my drink. "Your father, that is. My life's only gotten better since you came into it, and I can't imagine anyone feeling differently about you. It's his loss."

Gabriel smiled back at me. It wasn't a toothy grin by any stretch of the imagination, though for Gabriel's standards, it might as well been a full Cheshire smile. And that was enough.

We chatted quietly for the rest of my meal, mostly keeping to lighter subject matters until it was time to pay the bill. I still had a lot of questions though for now I was satisfied in what I'd learnt. The most important thing was that I felt I could trust him again. Paradigms and Fated deaths would have to be revisited again some other day when my brain wasn't completely fried and overloaded.

"By the way," I said as we stood up from the table to leave, my curiosity getting the better of me. "How did you know you and Dominic were fated to die anyway?"

Gabriel paused. Something about the look on his face made me hesitant to stick around for the answer. "A Time Keeper," he said finally. "From the future."

27. EXCAVATION

The rain came down like liquid ash, dusting the world in its wet gossamer as I made my way into All Saints the next morning. Trace and Paula were already setting up and didn't seem in the least bit fazed by the constant rainfall. I, on the other hand, couldn't remember the last time I'd seen the sun and was growing increasingly vexed by it.

I'm sure it didn't help that I hardly got any sleep last night. After Gabriel dropped me off, I'd spent the better part of the night tossing and turning, musing over the potential ways my sister factored into everything Gabriel had told me. I wanted to know her secrets; all of them.

I couldn't help but think she was connected to the mysterious Time Keeper from the future. Whatever it was she was hiding, I wasn't about to just let it go. This was more than a few skeletons in her closet. This was a bone yard's worth of skeletons. A bone yard that I'd been dragged into on more than one occasion and I was determined to find out why, even if that meant I would have to unearth every last rickety bone myself.

By the time the lunch rush was over, I settled down at one of the back tables and busied myself with a list of all the possible people this mystery Keeper could be, though the names seemed to be few and far between. At the top of the list was Trace—the only Reaper I actually knew...

And then there was Linley.

For one, she was a trained Keeper, and Trace's sister, so I knew she had the same abilities as he did, which meant she too could travel freely between space and time. Not to mention she was also the same age as my sister and could very well have been friends with her.

The more I thought about it, the more all signs pointed to Linley as *the* Keeper. But why did Gabriel say she was from the future? Had she traveled back in time to warn them about their impending death? And why? What was so special about Dominic and Gabriel's death that she felt the need to save them, especially if our deaths are supposed to be fated—inevitable?

More importantly, I couldn't help but wonder what this all meant for the rest of us, and for the loved ones we'd already lost. Loved ones like my father. Could they too be saved?

"Is there any particular reason why you've been staring at that wall for the last ten minutes?" interrupted Trace as he sat down in the banquet seat across from me.

"Is there any particular reason you've been watching me stare at it?" I countered, dodging his question as I tucked the list inside my book.

His lip twitched as though it wanted to sprout a smile. "What are you working on?" he asked, ticking his chin.

I lifted up the novel so he could read the cover.

I was supposed to be working on my *Lord of The Flies* essay for English, but I couldn't seem to get my brain to shift into homework-mode. Somehow, it just didn't seem as important as all the other things going on in my life as of late.

"It doesn't look like you're getting a lot done."

"Looks can be deceiving. You of all people should know

that." In fact, everyone in this town seemed to be perfectly versed in the comings and goings of deception.

"I guess I had that coming."

I turned my attention back to my essay. "What do you want anyway? I know you didn't come over here to talk to me about my homework." I looked back up at him in time to catch his dimples ignite—no smile.

"The work schedule for next week." He placed a sheet of paper on the table and slid it over to me. "I put you on the day shift for spring break. Is that alright with you?"

"It's fine, thanks," I said, slipping the schedule into my messenger bag. At least I'd have my evenings off. Gabriel was kind of a stickler when it came to my designated training hours.

"I also took you off the schedule this Friday," he added, glancing down at my open binder. "It's Spring Formal."

"Yeah, I know." *As if I could forget.* "It's pretty much all Taylor can talk about these days," I said, less than excited.

"I guess you don't like dances?"

"Not by Taylor's standards. She already has everything planned out right down to the color of eye shadow she's wearing. I feel like there's something wrong with me because I couldn't care less if I went wearing a potato sack."

Trace leaned back in the seat and laughed. A real guttural laugh that upon hearing it, made me realize how much I enjoyed the sound of it. "I bet you'd still look beautiful," he offered, carefully appraising me now.

I felt my cheeks warm as his words registered. Unsure of how to react to them, I began busily flipping through my novel in an effort to appear unaffected.

My to-do-list floated out from within the pages.

"I shouldn't have said that." His voice was low, regretful. He caught the list and skated it back over to me. "I'll see you later," he mumbled, rising from his seat.

"Hold on a sec," I said, grabbing his wrist as he tried to pass by me. "I need to talk to you about something."

I figured this was as good a time as any to start my excavation. I waited for him to settle back in his seat before continuing. "I was hoping you could explain some things to me, you know, about Keepers." I folded the piece of paper in half and stuffed it into my back pocket.

"What do you want to know?"

I wanted to know everything, like what their powers were used for and how they factored into vanquishing demons. But most of all, I needed to know under what circumstances a Keeper might travel to the past in order to save someone's life, and if this could be done for other people—other people like my dad.

But I had to be discreet about it.

"I don't understand why Time Keepers are used to hunt demons," I began, careful with my words. "Is it just because of your *porting* ability, or is there another reason?"

"There's lots of reasons." His dimples flashed briefly.

"Like what? The other day, Ben said you could move between time and space, but I don't see how traveling to the past fits in with any of this."

"It doesn't. Not really," he shrugged. "They don't like us messing with that anyway. We mostly just *port* or *realm jump*."

"Realm jump?"

"Yeah, to get to the other worlds—as part of the *Covenant*."

I think I was getting more confused as this conversation went on, which was *so* not the purpose of this inquisition.

"They told you about the Covenant, right? The peace treaty."

I shook my head. "There's a peace treaty? With who? The Revenants?" This seemed like a great thing. Why hadn't anyone bothered mentioning it to me? If we had a peace treaty going on with the demons, what the heck did they need us for?

"No. Between the Anakim and the Angel race."

My face blanched.

"Look, maybe you should talk to your uncle about this," he said, leaning forward to examine me as though I might keel over at any moment.

"No, I'm fine. I can handle it. Please, just tell me what this coven thing is. I need to know."

"The Covenant," he corrected as he sank back into his seat and shrugged. "The story goes that back in the day when the Angels first came down to earth, there were some problems within the ranks, you know, some of the Watchers who were supposed to be looking out for mortals were...well, helping themselves to them."

"Helping themselves?"

He cleared his throat. "Mating."

"Mating. Right." I could feel my cheeks blushing. "Which, um, resulted in the Nephilim—our earlier ancestors," I quickly added, remembering what my uncle had said about the Fallen.

"Exactly." He cracked a half smile. "In the early days, the Angels made no distinction between any of them. They hunted them all equally—the Fallen, the Nephilim, and eventually even the Anakim even though their only crime was being the Descendants of a hybrid race," he explained, tracing the frost down the front of my glass. "Anyway, a lot of blood was spilled on both sides."

I felt a shiver run down my spine.

"Cut to a few hundred years later, leaders from both sides had finally had enough of the bloodshed so they came together and drafted a peace treaty that promised armistice amongst the races. Basically, they'd stop hunting us as long as we agreed to stay hidden from mortals and helped the Angels vanquish demons—from this world and *beyond*. Neither side has broken the Covenant since."

This world *and beyond*?

"So what you're saying is, as a Keeper you can like, take me to another *world*?" There's no way I heard that right.

"I can take you to many worlds." His crystalline blue eyes burned into me, sending my heart into a chaotic tailspin.

I took a sip of my water, hoping the icy liquid would quell my racing heart and keep me focused. "And you can take me to another time, too? Like another era—say, I don't know, the 1920s?" *Or Florida, eight months ago.*

"I can, but I won't." He was still staring at me with a stirring intensity. "That kind of thing has to be approved by the Council."

"But you no longer work for the Council," I reminded him, doubtful that he was actually concerned with their rules.

"True," he said, raising his chin slightly, proud of his defiance. "But *you* do."

Crap.

"Besides, they check us twice a month whether we're with the Order or not. If I get caught traveling, I could end up Bound and I can't have that."

"What do you mean they *check* you?"

"Traveling leaves temporary traces on our skin, kind of like a cosmic time-stamp." He clenched his fist shut. "Because of that, Reapers have to check-in with 'the powers that be' every other week so they can make sure we haven't gone anywhere without their authorization."

Dammit.

Everything in me felt as though it were sinking. I let myself believe (even if for only the faintest of seconds) that somehow, someway, I would be able to go back and see my father again—maybe even save him. The vessel for this unfathomable act sat right before me, tempting and daunting with the face of an angel, and all I could do was look at it, but never have it.

"Come on," he said, cocking his head to the side. "Don't look at me like that. You wanna get me Bound?"

I shook my head, trying to hold back my tears. "I just wanted to see him again. One last time."

"It never works out that way. You'll always want to go back."

"How do you know if you've never gone?" I challenged.

He didn't respond though something in his eyes was telling me that he knew it well, and from firsthand experience.

"You've done it, haven't you? How did you get around the check-in?" I asked without waiting for the confirmation. "Is there a way to do it, like some kind of loophole?"

He looked back at me as a quiet war waged in his eyes, the deep blue's churning up dangerous winds that promised oblivion to anyone who dared enter, and suddenly I wanted to do nothing else but dance in the eye of the storm.

He let out a long and depleted breath, "There's always loopholes, Jemma. Always."

28. ENCOUNTERS OF THE WORST KIND

"Feel like doing a mall crawl tomorrow?" asked Taylor first thing Monday morning as I unpacked my books in front of my locker. "We can pick out your dress for the dance."

"I can't. I have detention."

"For what?"

"For being tardy. *Thrice*. Mr. Gillman's words, not mine."

She nodded knowingly. "I had him last semester...major anal retentiveness. What about after detention?"

I shook my head. "I have to fill in for Paula tomorrow. She has a doctor's appointment or something, and then I'm meeting up with Gabriel."

"Gabriel, huh? Oh la la," she gushed, making kissing noises. "That's incredibly mature. And super attractive."

"I know, right?" She batted her eyelashes at me. "So is he taking you to the dance Friday night?"

Just the thought of Gabriel being forced to attend some high school dance was enough to induce a fit of laughter.

"I think he's a little old for that," I reminded her, although in actuality, I wasn't sure if he was twenty-one, twenty-five, or four? "Besides, we're just friends. I'm sure he has much better things to do on a Friday night than take me to a high school dance."

"So you're going stag?" she asked and then nodded over to someone behind me.

"Yeah, I guess so," I said, turning to follow her gaze. "I'm not even sure I want to—"

"Hey, Blackburn," smiled Caleb, the apparent target. He looked dapper as usual, in a frat-boy sort of way.

"Hi, Caleb."

"Well, I gotta go. I'll catch you two after class," smiled Taylor before jetting off down the hall in typical Taylor fashion; bubbly and forever up to no good.

I closed my locker and started towards my first period *chem* class. Caleb followed.

"So, a little birdie told me you don't have a date for the dance this Friday."

I shook my head. *Freaking Taylor.*

"I was thinking maybe we could go together."

I stopped walking and turned to face him. "Isn't there someone you'd rather go with? I mean, we barely even know each other," I pointed out.

"Are you saying you don't want to go with me?" There was an ample amount of hurt and surprise in his expression, like he honest-to-God never heard the word 'no' before.

"I just thought that maybe there was someone else, you know, someone you *like*…more than friends." It took everything in me not to blurt out Nikki's name right there in the hallway, in the middle of all the morning chaos.

"Nope. Can't think of anyone," he smiled.

Either he was in serious denial or he was the world's greatest liar. Neither one sounded like an appealing trait.

"We can just go as friends if you want. I'd be okay with that," he added with a modest shrug.

I considered it.

Maybe this would give me a chance to get to know the real Caleb Owens. Maybe even probe him for information about Nikki and find out once and for all what was really going on between the two of them. I could do that. I could *totally* be persuasive when I needed to. *Sort of.* How hard could it be?

"Sure, I'd love to go with you."

Gabriel was already waiting for me in the parking lot of All Saints after my shift ended later that day. As per our usual routine, we were supposed to be heading over to Temple, though those plans were promptly nixed when he informed me that our training session had been canceled due to an emergency Faction meeting. One that required the entire building to be sealed off and secured.

"Is that something they usually do?" I wondered as we pulled out of the parking lot in his black SUV.

"It's not uncommon to secure the building, especially with so many leaders present."

Interesting. I wondered if my uncle was included in that roster. "So what's this meeting about anyway?"

"I'm not sure," he said without deviating his eyes from the road. "I wasn't given any details."

"Can we attend?"

"Council members and Elders only."

"Oh, good, more rules and secrets." Because I didn't have enough of those in my life. It was like a sickness in this town.

"I'm not allowed to attend either." He offered it as solace, but it didn't make me feel any better. "If you're up for it, I know another place we can train tonight," he said, bouncing a quick glance at me. "It's not ideal but we wouldn't be bothered."

I'd rather go stake out this meeting but apparently that option wasn't on the table. On second thought, "What if we blow off the rest of the night and catch up on our sleep instead?"

"Jemma."

"What? Not all of us are frozen in time." I flipped down the sun-visor to inspect the dark circles under my eyes. "Some of us actually need to rest."

"Not as much as you need to train. What are you going to do the next time you encounter a Revenant? Are you confident in your abilities to defeat them—to vanquish them?"

"Vanquish them?" I looked him over as though he were the most absurd man on the planet. "The only thing I plan on doing is running as fast as I can, unless I somehow get captured, in which case my new plan is to kick ass until I get free, and then run as fast as I can." There was no two ways about it. I was a girl with a plan, and I was sticking to it come hell or high water. *Or vampires.*

He scoffed without looking. "That's a horrible plan."

"It sure beats getting killed though."

He shook his head, but he didn't argue the point. We continued the rest of the drive in silence.

It wasn't until a little while later that I realized we'd somehow ventured into one of the shiftier neighborhoods outside of Hollow. Between the broken streetlights and boarded up buildings, I had already decided this was exactly the sort of place I didn't want to visit on any day of the week. Least of all, after dusk.

"Where are we going exactly?" I asked, locking my passenger side door. "This neighborhood is giving me the creeps."

"We're going to my place."

"Your place?" *Had he lost his damn mind?* "Um, you live on the other side of town...you know, on the nice side."

"That's my family home," he corrected, regarding me cautiously as though I might snap at any moment. "I don't live there. I have a small apartment up the street."

"So what you're saying is, you actually pay money to live around here?" I was completely flabbergasted by this revelation.

The smallest impression of a smile appeared. "It's a small price to pay for obscurity."

We entered his apartment building through an unhinged side door and took the stairs up all the way to the third floor. The hallway was dank with mangy carpets and flickering lights that faded in and out like some cautionary tale I didn't want to know. Sounds infiltrated the hallway at every turn—a baby crying, a shouting couple, police sirens in the distance—all attesting to the unsavory living conditions of life on this side of the tracks.

I latched onto the back of Gabriel's leather jacket and scooted in closer as we made our way down the hall of horrors, stopping only when we reached the last apartment on the left.

He unlocked the door and held it open for me. "After you," he nodded, clearing the path.

I swallowed hard and stepped into the darkened apartment, my anticipation reaching its peak. Gabriel followed in behind me and flipped on the lights before double-bolting the front door.

I turned slowly, peering into the skeletal apartment as I tried to reconcile myself to the fact that Gabriel lived here. That he spent his days and nights here, all alone in this tiny apartment in the middle of hell. It was downright depressing.

There wasn't much to his place—a small kitchenette on the left with no appliances except for a mini fridge and stove, and a bare-boned living room on the right that housed a black leather futon and small wooden coffee table. It was a far cry from the lavish family home I'd woken up in the first night we met.

"So this is where you live," I said, doing a listless spin.

He moved in from behind me and placed his hand on the

curve of my back, guiding me into the living room. "Yes, this is where I stay when I'm in town, which isn't very often. Kitchen, living room, bedroom, bathroom," he said, ending with a gesture directed at the two closed doors on the far right of the room.

"So why didn't you take me here *that* night?" I wondered.

"You needed first aid, food and water, and blankets amongst other things." He directed me to a seat on the futon. "All of which were things I did not have here."

I sat down and looked up at him with skepticism. "You're telling me you don't have food or blankets here?"

"What purpose would I have with any of those things?" he challenged, pulling up another chair next to me.

"Right. Sorry." Nice one, Jemma.

"It's perfectly alright," he said, brushing off my faux-pas.

"So what happens when you bring a date home? Don't they find it weird that you don't have like, basic amenities? Or do you only date girls that are, um...the same as you?"

"He doesn't date at all," answered a familiar voice.

I turned abruptly, startled by the unexpected voice, and found my sister standing in the threshold of Gabriel's bedroom door like a passing specter from some alternate reality. It had been so long since I'd seen her in the flesh, I almost didn't recognize her. I almost didn't trust my eyes.

"Tessa?"

"I hope I'm not interrupting anything."

"When did you...I mean, where did you...?" I shook my head unable to string a cohesive set of words together.

We had spent so many months apart. What could I possibly say to her that would solidify all the thoughts and emotions running through my mind in this moment?

"You cut your hair," I said stupidly, not moving from the couch. An elementary observation about her hair ought to do it.

She nodded unceremoniously, tucking a strand of her chin length jet-black hair behind her ear.

I took in the rest of her features—her heart shaped face, her round cheek bones and ash gray eyes, and of course, that alabaster skin that could make a porcelain doll jealous. It was all there. Everything was exactly the same, but somehow different. More defined—ripened, weary. She carried the expression of a girl who had lived one too many nights in the desecrated shadows.

"What are you doing here?" Gabriel's voice startled me. He was standing now, staring at her with a foreign intensity I couldn't quite decode. "I thought you were on assignment."

"I was—I *am*. I don't have much time. I came to see Jemma," she said, turning to me. "I came to give you something."

"Okay," I nodded wearily, still in a state of disbelief. "Like a present or something?" She *had*, after all, missed my birthday being that I was in the hospital, but was this really the time or place?

She held out her fist in response and opened her palm. A long ruby red crystal fell from the center, dangling weightlessly from the silver chain wrapped around her finger.

Gabriel's eyes swelled in horror as he watched the necklace rock back and forth in the air like a pendulum.

"The Blood of Isis."

29. THE IMMORTAL AMULET

"The blood of *who*?" I asked, feeling the thickness in the air press down on me like a cold, wet blanket.

I could almost swear I saw Gabriel take a step back from the corner of my eye. Like he was physically afraid to be near the necklace. Whatever it was, it had him shaking and suddenly I wasn't so sure I wanted to be around to find out.

And for sure I wasn't putting the thing on.

"That's not possible," said Gabriel, still stunned by the sight of it. "It has to be a fake."

"I promise you, it's *very* real." Tessa circled the room in haste, closing the blinds and making sure all locks were secured. When she was done, she sat down on the coffee table opposite me. Our knees just inches apart for the first time in a very long time.

"Has the Council confirmed its authenticity?"

"No." She answered without looking at him.

"Then how do you know it's not a fake?"

"I just do, now will you please sit down," she ordered cutting him a hard look. "I don't have a lot of time."

Gabriel lowered himself into the arm chair.

Her gaze softened as she took him in. "You said she was in danger and this is the only way I know how to protect her. Nobody can know about this—especially not the Council. Not yet anyway. I need to know that I count on you."

"You know you can." He said it sure as fact.

She refocused her sullen grays back on me. "I need you to put this on, Jemma, and I need you to promise me you won't take it off until I tell you it's safe to do so. Do you understand?" She held the necklace out to me like some morbid offering.

"I'm not putting anything on until you tell me what's going on. What the heck is that?" I eyed the necklace accusingly.

She rolled the ruby red pendant between her ashen fingers. "*This* is the Blood of Isis. Better known as the Immortal Amulet."

"Okay...and why is Gabriel so afraid of it?"

"I'm not afraid. I was caught off guard."

"Because it's a very powerful amulet, Jemma, believed to have been used in the First Rising Spell. The one that created the original Revenants."

My head ticked back a notch. "And why would I want to put that thing around my neck?"

"Because, apart from its necromancy capabilities, the Immortal Amulet is one of the most powerful Protective Hedges known in our world."

I turned back to Gabriel. "Necromancy?"

"The act of conjuring the dead—one of the forbidden arts."

The room suddenly felt as though it were tilting. My sister was actually trying to strap me into some dead-raising necklace and worse, she was acting like it was just another day at the office. And *I* was the one they institutionalized.

"Look at me," ordered Tessa, taking my chin in her hand. "You couldn't conjure the dead if you tried doing it on purpose. You have nothing to be afraid of."

I wasn't sure if I should be offended by that.

"The only thing you need to know is that its Power of Protection ensures the wearer of the necklace is granted immunity from all perils; mortal or supernatural."

"What does that mean? Speak English, Tess!"

"It means you'll be indestructible as long as you wear it."

Indestructible? "*Wait*, really?" I felt a wild, uncontrollable smile tugging at the corner of my lips. The truth was, that didn't sound half-freaking-bad.

"Yes, really," she said, raising the necklace and then carefully lassoing it around my neck. "As long as you have this on, no one can bring harm to you, but you're not to remove it under any circumstances—not even in the shower. Is that understood?"

I nodded, picking up the amulet as I examined it with a curious eye. There was something incredibly hypnotic about it. Something about the way it caught the light and reflected back to me, letting me know I was in the presence of a great Power.

"This doesn't mean you can start being careless now. If you find yourself in danger, avoid a confrontation at all costs—run if you have to. Especially if that situation involves Dominic Huntington. Is that clear?"

Good thing I already had the running thing down pat.

"Do you really think he'll do something to me?" I asked, bouncing glances between the two of them. "I mean, he had his chance to make a move and he didn't. He seemed a lot more interested in getting even with the two of you..."

"That's what I'm afraid of," said Tessa, her raspy voice low and forlorn. "The only way he can hurt me is by hurting the people I love. He's done it before. You don't know him. You don't know the things he's capable of doing, even to his own family."

"I do know! I know what he did to Gabriel." I wanted her to know that I wasn't that naive. That I had picked up a few details along the way and was still standing on my own two feet. *More or less.*

"You told her?" I couldn't tell if her glare was rooted in anger or just shock that he had the audacity to flout her.

"Not everything. I told her how I turned. I had no choice, she needed to know the truth about Dominic." His voice was surprisingly firm on the point. "I left you out of it. I thought she should hear that part from you."

"Well, then." She turned back to me, steely eyed. "It looks like you don't even know the half of it."

And that's exactly what I was afraid of.

30. BEDTIME STORIES

The rain gathered traction as it batted down over Hollow Hills and all of its collared inhabitants without the slightest regard for our well-being. I sat on the couch, face to face with my sister, waiting for her to fill in the holes to a story that has been chock-full of them since the very beginning. Outside, the wind howled viciously, loud as an army of disembodied ghosts convening on the other side of the glass, crying out to us for sanctuary, for reprieve.

"I'm not perfect," started Tessa. "I've made a lot of mistakes in my life, mistakes that I'm still paying for today, and I accept that." She lifted her chin as if to illustrate her valor. "Even still, I always hoped I'd never have to have this conversation with you. That you'd never be in a position where you *needed* to know any of it, but I guess that's not possible anymore. I don't know how else to keep you safe now."

She hadn't even revealed anything and already I had the overbearing urge to run for the door.

"Two years ago, I made a decision to do something I knew was wrong in order to help a friend." Her eyes bore into me with a grounding intensity. "To help my Keeper."

"Are we talking about Linley Macarthur?" I turned to Gabriel as the house lights flickered aggressively. "Was she the Keeper from the future?" The one from his story.

Gabriel nodded.

"I knew it." It came out smug.

"She was more than just my Keeper—she was a sister to me."

I was surprised to hear so much emotion in Tessa's voice, a voice that had always been so cool, calm, and collected under even the most intense fires. Sometimes irritatingly so.

"It all started senior year, the night we went to Easton's Fall Festival. Linley thought it would be fun to get a tarot reading from some Gypsy hack running one of those fortune-telling booths," she said with a dismissive hand gesture. "Turned out she wasn't a hack after all. Probably had some Seer blood in her," she added, almost as an afterthought.

A riotous round of thunder rang out around us, jolting me with its reverberations.

"She read Linley, told her things about her family that no one else knew. Things about who she was. That she was gifted—different from the others. Everything she said was spot on and Linley was loving every second of it. We both were." Tessa's eyes slid over to Gabriel before boomeranging back. "That is, up until she drew the Death card."

"The *Death* card?" I spoke in whispers, frightened to my core at the prospect of such a thing existing. I didn't want to know, and yet I couldn't stop myself from digging deeper. "What is that? What does it mean?"

"It means she prophesized Linley's death. She knew something was coming, something horrible and unnatural." Tessa's distant eyes traveled over my shoulder, imaging it, reliving the scene in her mind. "The next day, Linley went to see the Council and told them about what happened. She demanded one of the Elders read her to disprove the prediction.

She demanded it even though deep down she knew it was true."

"And did they?" I swallowed hard. "Confirm it, I mean."

She gave a morose nod. "Nothing was ever the same after that night. Over the next few months, Linley became completely obsessed with it—with her future—with changing it."

"But I thought you couldn't stop Death? I thought it was like, ordained?" I didn't mean for it to ring out so lax.

"It is. Death is the one appointment we all have to keep no matter who you are or where you come from. Linley knew that better than anyone, but she also wasn't the type of girl to give up on what she wanted—even if it went against the very laws of nature—and what she wanted more than anything else at that moment was to find a way to come back."

"What do you mean come back?" I blurted out, somewhat taken back by this. I was under the impression she wanted to stop her death, not return from it. "So Linley wanted to be a Revenant?"

"No."

"Then what? I didn't know there was another option."

"There wasn't. Well, not a feasible one anyway, and that was exactly the problem," explained Tessa. "She knew her family would disown her if she willingly accepted Revenant blood into her body, and since family meant everything to her, there was no way she could go down that road. She needed another way and she vowed not to stop until she found it. She was incredibly stubborn that way."

"Did she ever find anything?" I wondered, overcome by my own disturbing curiosity.

"Depends on who you ask." Tessa's disparaged expression made it clear where she stood on the matter. "She became fixated on the idea of recreating the necromancy spell, the one that created the First Revenants, and using a variation of it on herself."

"But isn't that the spell that turned them all into evil, bloodthirsty killers to begin with?"

"She was convinced that if she made some key changes to the original spell, substituted the demon blood with the blood of a higher being, she could come back proper."

"Is that even possible?" I asked, turning to Gabriel as though he were the expert on all things resurrection.

"I suppose everything's possible, but..." He shook his head.

"It's unlikely," said Tessa. "Before she could even consider testing her theory, she needed to get her hands on the spell's incantation which can only be found within the codex of the Original *Scribes*, and of course, the Immortal Amulet used in the First Rising Spell. The Scribes were scattered all over the world, guarded and nearly impossible to come by, and there were even fewer pieces of the Amulet. It was mission impossible, but odds like that never stopped Linley."

She sounded kind of kick ass.

"Anyhow, after some digging around, she found out that our Order had been in possession of a copy of the Scribes, and that the Huntington Sentinels had been charged with their safekeeping. Unfortunately, she also discovered that they perished in a fire two years prior—a fatal fire that destroyed the Scribes and *killed* both the Huntington brothers...Gabriel and Dominic."

My mouth fell open. "*What?*" I turned to Gabriel, slack-jawed. "You and Dominic died in a fire?"

His dark hair grazed over his eyes as he dipped his head. "That's what I've been told, though I have no recollection of that particular expanse in time."

"Because we changed it," explained Tessa, tucking a strand of hair behind her ear. "We went back and changed what happened. We warned Gabriel, we stopped the fire, we stopped all of it. But it wasn't supposed to be that way. We weren't supposed to change anything. When we got back, the other reality had already been erased—gone to everyone but Linley and me. It was as though it never even happened and *fixing* it was a lot easier said than done. Gabriel was alive because of what we—"

"But he was meant to die." My voice was abnormally pitchy. "He didn't want this, he didn't want to be a Revenant!" How could she not go back and fix her mistake? How could she allow Dominic to impose this eternal life-sentence on Gabriel?

Tessa steeled her gaze. "We don't always get what we want, Jemma. That's life, whether you like it or not." Her iciness reverberated in the room.

"So you didn't even try?" I asked, tremulous. I didn't want to believe that. I didn't want to believe that my sister would just leave Gabriel to live out his life as the thing he hated most in the world. All because of her own bad decisions.

"Of course we tried." She seemed annoyed by my questions. "We went back as soon as we realized what was going on—that Dominic had Turned—but by then it was already too late. He had his own plans and he made sure we couldn't get in his way."

"I don't understand."

"There was nothing she could do," offered Gabriel in her defense. "Dominic was using a *Binding Sprite* to ensure no one could travel back to that point in time and alter any of the events that had transpired. Tessa and Linley tried, but they couldn't get through the protective barrier. No one could."

It was clear he wasn't harboring any blame or resentment towards them. So why was *I* getting so worked up about it? And what the heck was a Binding Sprite?

"We couldn't go to anyone for help," continued Tessa. "Our Laws are clear and we violated nearly every one of them in the worst possible way. We were between a rock and a hard place. What Linley and I did..." She rattled her head. "Linley would have been Bound—maybe worse, and God only knows what the Council would have done to me for leading the charge."

My thoughts briefly flashed back to Trace and his distress over the possibility of being Bound by the Council. Whatever that meant for them, it clearly wasn't something they could live with.

"So what ended up happening with the Scribes?" I asked after a short reprise. "Did Linley ever get them or was it all for nothing?" I couldn't fathom the desperation needed to pull off something like this in the first place let alone what it would feel like to come up empty handed.

"They weren't there," she answered dryly. "Linley found the vault empty. They must have been moved before we got there, but we had no way of knowing for sure. Besides, I had more pressing matters to contend with at that point."

I furrowed my brows, wondering what could have been more important than the Scribes they went back in time to get.

"As in the coven of Revenants in the living room," she clarified, reading the confusion in my expression.

"Right. Dominic's girlfriend." I'd almost forgotten.

"His *girlfriend*?" scoffed Tessa. "She was a Revenant, just like the others. Nothing more."

"So you're the one who vanquished her," I said, having just realized it myself. "You vanquished Dominic's girlfriend and Gabriel backed you up, right? That's why Dominic hates you. That's why he said all those things about you."

She nodded unceremoniously. "And I'd do it again without question."

"And the Amulet? Who'd you have to kill to get that one?" The second the words left my mouth, I wished I could rewind time and stop them from ever seeing the light of day. Her expression alone was enough to make me want to throw myself to the gallows.

"How easy it is for you to judge me from your sheltered existence," spat Tessa. "I could fill a stadium with the amount of blood I've had to spill, and you know what, little sis? Soon your hands are going to be just as bloodied as mine."

"Tessa." Gabriel reached out to calm her, but she smacked his hand away. "Don't do this."

"Don't tell me what to do," she warned, her eyes a deadly shade of gray. "I've spent the last three months on the run trying to keep this Amulet safe, and I risked it all to come here, for Jemma—"

"Three months?" Gabriel stood up suddenly. "You've had the Amulet in your possession for *three* months?"

"More or less," she said, dusting her hands across her jeans. "Does it really matter how long I've had it?" There was a slight edge to her voice now. It was clear his question was making her defensive.

"Why didn't you come to me?"

"Why do you think? Jesus, Gabriel. I had men coming at me from every direction—men who would happily slaughter their entire family to get their hands on the Amulet. I couldn't take the risk. You would have done the same thing."

Gabriel sharpened his stare. "Whose men?"

"That doesn't matter right now—"

"WHOSE MEN?" he boomed.

I straightened my back as though standing at attention. I never heard his voice sound so vociferous, so commanding. I didn't know how else to react to it.

Tessa speared him with contempt. "Engel."

"Dammit." Gabriel pinched his eyes shut and stalked off towards the kitchen.

"Who's Engel?" I asked, my throat drier than a bag of cotton balls.

"Engel is my problem, I'm taking care of him." Tessa stood

up and took a few steps towards Gabriel. "Look, I have a plan. He's been on my tail for weeks now and he hasn't caught me yet. I have him exactly where I want him. If you just—"

"And where is that?" interrupted Gabriel. He stood in the kitchen with his hands flat against the counter. "We're talking about *Engel*, Tessa. Four generations of Slayers have tried and failed to vanquish him. Does that even register with you?"

"Tried and *failed*?" I recoiled, trepidation filling every cell in my body. My sister was going up against a vampire that four generations of Slayers have tried and failed to vanquish and she thought I was the one that needed the Protective Hedge?

What in the actual hell! I reached up and pulled the Amulet off from around my neck.

"What the hell are you doing?" snapped Tessa, spotting me from the corner of her eye. "Didn't I just tell you not to take that necklace off until I tell you to? What part of that didn't you understand?"

I shook my head. "There's no way I'm wearing this when *Engle the Slayer killer* is after you!" I waved the necklace in her direction. "You need this more than I do. I can handle Dominic."

"You couldn't handle a goddamn handlebar let alone Dominic Huntington." There wasn't a thread of humor in her words. "I have enough going on without the added distraction of having to worry about whether you're safe, too."

I hadn't considered that. But still—

"Put the necklace back on *now*. I'm not going to ask you again, so help me God." The homicidal twitch in her left eye really drove home the point.

I slipped the necklace back on and cowered into my seat before she could say another word to me.

She turned her attention back to Gabriel, cornering him in the kitchen. "I need you in on this with me." Her voice was low, stringently even. "This is our chance, Gabriel. Our one shot."

He shook his head. "It's *suicide.*"

"Not if we go in it together," she insisted.

He still looked unsure.

"We're holding all the cards right now. He's been tracking me for weeks for a reason. He's scared to make a move. All we have to do is make it first."

"Get him before he gets you," he noted, crossing his arms.

"Exactly. He'll never see it coming." Her mouth took on a diabolical curl. "I'll lead him to an isolated location outside of town, make him think he's got me cornered and that I'm out there all alone. He won't be able to resist. He'll show himself and we'll be waiting to take him out when he does."

Gabriel considered it. "That could work."

"It *will* work. It has to." She took a step closer to him and raised her hand as though she were going to touch him but then decided against it. "I'm tired of running, Gabriel. This is my chance, my way out, but I need you. I need you in on this with me. Will you do it? Will you help me?"

"Yes." He answered without the slightest hesitation or concern for his own well-being. "Whatever you need. Whatever you want. I'll do it."

31. DETAINED

"You're late, Miss Blackburn," croaked Mr. Gillman as I strolled into detention Tuesday afternoon. "Surely you appreciate the irony given your current circumstance."

I glanced up at the wall clock. "Sorry," I muttered, sitting down in the first seat by the door.

"As I was communicating erstwhile your interruption," continued Mr. Gillman. "I have a prior engagement that requires my immediate attention, however, I will return periodically to check in on you. I expect silence in my absence and will not hesitate to further extend your punishment should any of you feel the need to leave the room without permission." He picked up his briefcase and gave one final look around the near-empty room. "Questions?"

I shook my head and watched as he whisked out of the room, slamming the door shut behind him.

Curious, I glanced over my shoulder to get a better look at my cellmates and immediately spotted Trace in the back corner of the room. Our eyes met briefly, once again igniting those irritating butterflies in my abdomen. I straightened out, opting to lay my head on my desk and indulge in some much needed

R&R rather than contend with the pesky swarm in my belly.

Less than a minute later, I heard a chair pull out behind me followed by a gentle poke on the back of my shoulder. I held my breath as I twisted around and found Trace sitting in the desk behind me. His dimples pressed in on both sides, though there was no real smile accompanying them.

"Hey," he said, sounding weary.

"Look at you, breaking all your own rules again."

The edge of his mouth curved up slightly.

It was no secret that Trace wanted to spend as little time with me as possible for reasons that were still unclear to me. The funny thing is, between work, school, our circle of friends, and the fact that he was increasingly finding reasons to come talk to me, we probably spent more time together than anyone else in our group.

"What are you in here for?" he asked, tapping his thumb against the desk as he openly examined me.

"Oh, you know, the usual. Started a gang, beat up a few kids from Easton. You?"

"Same."

I laughed, thinking it probably wasn't that far from the truth.

He shifted his attention to the other two guys sitting in detention with us. The dark-haired one was scribbling something down in his notebook, possibly sketching, and the other one had his earphones on and was bobbing his head back and forth listening to his music.

"Heard you're going to the dance with Caleb." His voice was quiet now, almost as though he were working hard to subdue it.

"As friends," I clarified. I wasn't sure why I felt the need to specify that part.

He leaned in towards me. "Does he know that?"

"Of course he does."

His eyebrows dipped with doubt.

"I mean, I *think* he does. Why? Did he say something?"

"Not really." He pushed back in his chair, rocking on its hind legs. "He just likes to get under my skin."

"Under *your* skin?"

"Yeah."

"Meaning?" There was a strange undertone I couldn't ignore. It sounded a lot like jealousy.

"Nothing. Forget it." He shrugged it off but I couldn't help but notice the tension in his jaw.

"O-kay." I dropped it, sensing he wasn't going to elaborate. Plus, I had more important things to ask him. "So, um, who are you going to the dance with?" I asked choppily. My attempt at sounding casual was a miserable failure.

"I'm not."

"You're not going?"

"Nope." He cocked his head to the side and watched me.

"Why not? I mean, isn't this thing supposed to be sort of a big deal around here?"

"You're spending too much time with Taylor."

I laughed outright because that was exactly who I'd gotten my intel from. Serves me right.

"Besides," he continued, glancing down at my lips. "The girl I wanted to take is already going with someone else."

My insides pinched.

Even though my instincts were to assume he was referring to Nikki, I couldn't stop myself from replaying all the things Taylor said to me the other day. That he looked at me in a special way; that he liked me. I felt the knots in my stomach tighten as my silent hope ignited.

"That's too bad."

His eyes flickered down to my mouth again, this time lingering on them as though he were trying to memorize their shape. "It's probably for the best."

"Yeah." My voice was a disappointed whisper. "Probably."

He dragged his eyes back up to mine. "I've been thinking about that *trip* we talked about the other day."

Trip? What trip?

"I decided to take you."

My eyes swelled. Oh my God, he was talking about time traveling—to see my *dad*. "But what about the um...obstacles?"

"I've got it covered."

"And the...risks?"

"I've weighed them out."

"Are you for real?"

His magnetic dimples flashed as he nodded.

"When?"

"I was thinking Friday night," he said, working his jaw.

I shot him an irritated look. "Very funny. Friday night is the dance."

He leaned in close again, this time throwing off my concentration with the comely scent of his cologne. "I know."

"Why Friday?"

"Why not Friday?"

"Are you trying to stop me from going to the dance with Caleb?" I asked, only half-serious.

"Maybe," he said, still leaning in close to me. "Or maybe I'm just available that night." He licked his lips like an invitation.

I pulled back, not wanting to lose complete focus. *Again.* "Is that really the only time we can do this?"

Wait a minute. Why was I arguing? This was a once in a lifetime opportunity to see my father again. Who cares about the stupid dance? Crap. *Taylor cares*, I reminded myself. I didn't know how well she was going to take it when I told her—

"How about tomorrow?" he asked, letting me off the hook before I could concede. I couldn't help but notice the discontent in his expression. Or was it sadness?

I didn't have time to decode it.

"Tomorrow's good," I nodded. I couldn't believe this was going to happen. I was going to see my dad again! What would I say to him? What would I wear? The excitement sizzled through every cell in my being. "Tomorrow's perfect."

The school parking lot looked eerily empty—deserted, grayed out from the overcast of swollen clouds. The wind picked up speed as I scanned the lot for Henry, whom I was sure I'd mentioned my after school detention to, but there was no sign of him anywhere. The only cars left were Trace's blue Mustang on the far left, and an old rusty van about twenty feet out.

Weird, I thought, as I searched my bag for my cell phone.

"Hey, excuse me, miss." A young woman with pixie blond hair hopped out of the van and started towards me. "We're kind of lost," she laughed, scratching the side of her face as she bounced a quick glance at the parked van. "Do you think you could point us in the right direction?"

I adjusted my schoolbag. "It depends where you're trying to go. I'm still kind of new in town myself."

"We're trying to get to this place called, uh—" She turned back to the van. "Babe, what's it called again?"

A dark haired man with a serious five o'clock shadow slithered from around the side of the van. "Place is called All Saints," he answered, taking a drag of his cigarette. It sounded as though he had some kind of accent. Or throat cancer.

"You're pretty far," I noted. "You'll need to get back on the throughway and head east towards town."

"Is that right?" She scratched her neck again and leaned in closer. Her blotchy skin looked as though it could use a generous helping of foundation. "You mind jotting it down for us on our map over there? Bobby's not too good with directions."

I looked back at *Bobby* who offered a slight smile.

Something about them seemed...off. I couldn't put my finger on it. "Sure, I guess," I said without moving. "But I should probably go get my friend. He's lived here much longer than me and can probably give you better directions."

"You wouldn't mind? That would really help us out."

"It's no problem," I smiled and stepped back. Giving them one final look over, I turned and headed back towards the student entrance. Something inside me was telling me to make a run for it but I chose to ignore it, fearful of what I would look like to them if I did.

Besides, it was daytime. They obviously weren't Revenants so what was I so worried about anyway?

Before I could answer myself, I felt something crash against the back of my head, knocking me to the ground on all fours. A strange taste entered the back of my throat—metallic in nature—nauseating me with its flavor. Stunned, I rolled onto my backside and looked up at the woman as she tossed a fat rock to the side. *What the hell just happened?* Did she hit me with that? I felt disoriented, tired, like I could sleep for a hundred years and still never be rested enough.

She bent over me, snatching my arms up with her wet, clammy hands. "Grab her legs," she yelled, and Bobby did.

Suddenly I was suspended in the air being carried away towards the van. *The van.* Oh God, they were going to throw me in there. Kidnap me; hurt me; do heaven knows what to me.

I started kicking and thrashing my legs, bucking relentlessly until they could no longer contain my body. Bobby dropped my legs first and ran back to the van as I fought to free my hands. He reemerged from the side door yielding something, but it was only when he stepped out of the shadows that I caught sight of the knife.

"Help!" My frenetic scream exploded in the air like a

gunshot. "Someone, please help me!"

"Don't just stand there," yelled the blond, struggling to maintain control. "Help me get her in the van, you idiot!"

Bobby ran back to us at full speed, his eyes wild with intention. "Get up!" he ordered, pointing the knife at me.

As soon as he was close enough, I slammed my foot into his knee cap, eliciting a loud pop that caused him to stagger back from the impact. He cursed out in pain, and for the slimmest of seconds, I felt the fervor of hope burn through me at the possibility of having broken his knee, but the lunatic never went down. Was he even *human*?

He thrust the knife at me again, this time aiming for the side of my leg, but he failed to stick the landing. I kicked the knife out of his hands as the blond snatched up my arms again and began dragging me across the concrete.

"Let me go!" I screamed, trying to free myself from her grasp as my back scraped against the rocky terrain. "HELP!"

"Knock her out, Bobby! Shut her the hell up!"

I kicked my legs out as soon as he came near me, this time aiming for the other knee.

"You want me to cut you, bitch? I'll cut you," he warned, flailing the blade in my direction. And then suddenly, he was gone, soaring backwards through the air like a bag of trash.

I looked up and found Trace standing in his place, sublime fury infiltrating every curve of his spectacular face. In an instant, he was perched over me like the statue of an Adonis, freeing me from Blondie as he sent her sailing several feet across the parking lot. But there was no time to thank him, to pray at his alter. Within seconds, she was back on her feet, coming at us again.

"Trace, behind you!" I warned as I watched Bobby rush him from the other side, his knife outstretched.

Trace turned at the last moment and grunted as Bobby made contact with his torso. I couldn't tell if he'd been punched or stabbed. Panicked, I began crawling towards him but was yanked back by my hair before I could reach them.

Blondie had but one goal and that was to drag me back to that van, with or without Bobby's help. Fingers entwined in my hair, she dragged me mercilessly as I kicked the air in vain.

"Get off me, you psycho!" I roared through furious tears. All I wanted to do was claw her eyes out with my bare hands. And in that moment, I was sure I could do it if given the chance.

"You're only making this worse for yourself," she snarled, ripping at my hair as she dragged me without mercy.

I felt a swell of fire tear through my body. It was fear and rage and panic merging into one big melting pot that had finally hit its boiling point.

I reached back for her arm and used it as a crutch to pull myself back up to my feet. Her hands came out at me again, flailing and desperate, but they never made contact with my body. I was in control now and I wasn't even sure how I was doing it. With one stabbing look in her hollow eyes, I swung my fist into her face, hitting her square in the jaw. Before her eyes could steady themselves or register the impact, I swung again, knocking her out cold in one final strike.

I wasn't sure how I'd managed to do it but I felt powerful in that moment, proud even.

Adrenalin coursing through me, I spun around and spotted Trace and Bobby still warring several feet away. Blood stains dotted both their shirts, but I couldn't tell whose blood it was. Panic over took me at the thought of it being Trace's, of him being hurt because of me—to save me.

Without thinking, I catapulted myself onto Bobby's back and began pounding the side of his head with my fist. It was exactly the momentum Trace needed to gain the upper hand. In the blink of an eye, he had snatched the knife from Bobby and turned his weapon against him. But Bobby wasn't giving up that easy.

He dipped me sideways just far enough so I'd loosen my grip on him and then launched me off his back.

I hit the concrete and bounced.

Within seconds, Trace and Bobby were back in position, ramming into each other again like two raging bulls. Their fists flying through the air, erupting against bone and muscle. I couldn't bear to sit back and watch, to risk *his* safety.

I stammered back to my feet and rushed Bobby again, this time tearing and clawing away at his face, at his eyes, doing whatever I had to do to win this fight. To end it. But I didn't have enough strength left inside me to make any kind of dent. He bent forward and tossed me off his back again, landing me hard against Trace's body. Both of us went down in a tangle of limbs.

"Stay down," he ordered, rolling me off his person before jumping back up to his feet.

Winded, I tried to get back up too but didn't fair nearly as well as Trace did. I was just too tired, too dizzy. Everything was spinning out of control again.

I heard grunting and brash words, though they sounded as though they were coming from a distance—from some far away, long-since forgotten space in time.

And then blackness.

"Jemma? Jemma, open your eyes."

I blinked several times before focusing in on the most stunning blue eyes I'd ever seen—pristine blue eyes ringed in rich, dark sapphires. Only one man could boast such beauty, such perfection. Somewhere in the hazy recess of my mind, I knew I could spend forever looking in those eyes and still never tire of their resplendent beauty.

"Are you okay?"

"What happened?" I asked, noting the thick gray clouds blooming behind Trace's head. A part of me hoped, prayed, that it was all just a bad dream. But I knew better.

"We have to go—*now*. Can you walk?"

I held onto his arm as he pulled me up off the floor and immediately spotted the unconscious blond.

"Where's the other one?" I looked around and found Bobby splayed out on the concrete, not too far from where we'd been fighting. He was down and bloodied, but still alive.

"We need to get out of here before they wake up. My car's over there," said Trace, ticking his head at his parked Mustang.

"Shouldn't we call someone? The police or something?" I asked, confused. I wasn't sure what the protocol was here.

"For what? They can't help us." He stepped forward and snaked my hand into his, the urgency evident in his eyes. "We're on our own, Jemma."

I tossed one more glance in Blondie and Bobby's direction and gave in, knowing he was right. "Okay. Let's go."

I followed dizzily as he led us fast across the parking lot towards his car. Tiny droplets of rain began falling over us, baptizing us with their touch as a mass of angry skies spread out above like a necrotic carpet.

"Drive," he said, tossing me the keys.

"I can't! I don't know how to drive stick. I don't even have my license!" My voice was several octaves too high.

"Shit." He bent forward slightly, clutching his side in pain. There was blood all over the place. *His* blood.

"Oh my God, you're hurt!"

"Give me the keys," he ordered, holding up a bloodied hand.

I tossed them back and climbed into the passenger seat.

Within seconds, we were tearing down the back roads heading fast towards the woodlands. This wasn't the way back to town, I knew that, but I didn't say anything. I trusted him to get us to safety. Wherever that may be.

I looked down at his side and cringed. His crisp white shirt was saturated with crimson blood stains.

"You're bleeding out," I rasped through burgeoning tears.

"It's just a cut," he said as he put pressure on the wound in-between shifting gears. He turned off the main road and began crisscrossing through trees and brushes as we made our way deeper into the forest.

"I'm so sorry," I cried, shaking my head as I tried to make sense out of what just happened.

"Why? You didn't do it."

"But it happened because of me. You were just trying to help me and now you're hurt. Because of me!" I was practically hysterical and it really wasn't helping the situation.

"I'm fine, just calm down," he said, as though it were even remotely a possibility.

"I don't even know who they were…or *what* they were." I flashed back to my bone crushing blow to his knee and cringed. "Were they even human?"

"Yeah, they were human," he said. "More or less."

My eyes narrowed. "What kind of answer is that?"

"They're *Runners*, Jemma. Bottom-feeders under the control of Revenants. Half the time they're so doped up they don't even know their own names." His face twisted in agony as he glanced down at his wound.

My bottom lip dropped. "So you're saying they're humans sent by somebody…by a Revenant? That they're under their *influence*?"

"Exactly."

"But who? Who would do this?"

"I don't know," he shook his head and looked at me, worry etched in his eyes. "Have you made any enemies lately?"

I could think of half a dozen people off the top of my head.

Nikki and her minions, Dominic, my attacker from All Saints, Engel...my list of enemies was growing bigger by the day.

"It could be anyone," I said, swallowing the lump in my throat. "God, I'm not safe no matter where I go, am I?"

"We're Anakim," he blinked tiredly. "We're never safe."

His words thrummed in my ears like a gong. "What do you think they wanted?"

"I thought that was pretty obvious." He pumped his jaw muscle without looking at me. "They wanted *you*."

"For what?"

He shook his head. "It looked like they were trying to bring you somewhere...probably back to the Rev that gave the order," he said, slowing down to park behind a throng of evergreens.

"Is there any way we can find out who's behind this?"

"It's going to be hard."

"But not impossible?" I asked, watching him pull the keys from the ignition. "Is there someone you can call, like a contact or something? Or should we go to the Council? Do you think they can help us with this, or is it better to just—"

"You ask too many questions, anyone ever tell you that?" He flung the driver's side door open and climbed out of the car without answering any of them.

I scanned my surroundings trying to figure out where we were but saw nothing telling. There was nothing but trees and shrubs and dirt for miles in every direction.

Trace appeared on the passenger side and pulled open the door, holding out his hand. I looked down at it, questioning it as though it could speak to me. As though it had the answers I sought in this foreign world.

"You can trust me," he said, inching it closer.

I placed my hand into his and climbed out of the car.

32. TRANSFERENCE

"Where are we going?" I asked as Trace led me further away from the car and deeper into the dew-kissed forest.

"We can't go back to town right now. They know who you are. They'll know how to find you." He stopped in a small clearing and turned around to face me. A canopy of plush green leaves blanketed the two of us like a beautiful quilt. "We need to go somewhere safe until we figure this thing out."

"Where did you have in mind?" I asked, crossing my arms. He better not be thinking about camping out here.

"My father's cabin up north." He looked at me with calming eyes. "No one knows about it. It's completely off the grid."

"But the car—" I began, thumbing in the direction of where we'd come from but stopped short when he started grinning.

"We won't need it," he said. Before I could ask another one of my daft question, he quickly added, "We're using another mode of transportation."

"Oh. Right…that *porting* thing you do."

"Yeah, that porting thing I do." He took a purposeful step towards me, breaking into my personal space.

"What are you doing?"

He uncrossed my arms and gently began pulling me towards him. "Your body needs to be touching mine for this to work."

"Oh, so we...okay." My heart sped up feverishly.

I let him pull me in closer until I was pushed up flush against his body. Careful not to graze the injured area, I circled my arms around his waist and breathed in his intoxicating scent as he slid his own arms around my back, sending my body into a near-state of rapture.

He cleared his throat. When I looked up at him, I could see he was fighting back a smile.

"What?"

"Nothing," he said, shaking his head.

Was he laughing at me again?

"I want you to take a few deep breaths, okay? You're going to feel cold for a bit, but it's normal. Don't be scared."

Before I could ask any more questions, I felt his body temperature (and my own) drop abruptly, jolting me upright. I tightened my hold on him as the forest began blackening out around us. The freezing air licking at my skin as the world I thought I knew ceased to exist.

In an instant, my mind was spinning out. Or maybe it was us that was spinning—falling, folding upon ourselves in a stateless state, and then suddenly we were solidifying again, the world slowly taking up its form around us. Except the picture was different now. Gone was the forest and its pine-green beauty, and in its place was a darkened living room inside a strange log cabin I'd never been to before. And the cold. The cold was near arctic. I began shivering wildly, still holding onto Trace as he held on to me.

The room solidified with colors, each detail falling into place, almost as though its molecules were being put back together again one by one. Or maybe it was our own molecules. And then, just like that, our body temperature rose, buzzing, climbing back up to a normal level. Well, as normal as it could be while standing this close to Trace Macarthur.

I stepped back and looked up at him in awe. "Oh, my God."

He tried to laugh but winced again as he clutched onto his side in obvious pain. "I'm okay," he assured upon seeing my worried expression.

"No you're not. You should have taken us to a hospital!" I reached forward to touch him.

He caught my wrist mid-air. "There's a first aid kit in the bathroom. First door down the hall."

I pulled my hand back and followed his instructions. When I came back into the living room, he was already sitting on the wooden coffee table unbuttoning his shirt. Unprepared, I froze mid-step in the entrance at the sight of his peeking flesh.

He looked up and quirked an eyebrow. "You okay?"

"What? Yeah. Totally." My cheeks flushed. *Get it together, Jemma.* "I'm fine."

I stepped in the room and handed him the first aid kit. Not wanting to get caught staring again, I busied myself looking around the room, pretending to be interested in the decor. The antlers above the stone fireplace only mildly held my interest.

"Can you help me get this off?" He motioned to his injury as proof that he needed my assistance disrobing.

I nodded coolly though I could feel the heat surging through me when I knelt down on the area rug before him. Without making any eye contact, I carefully took the collar of his shirt and began sliding it off his shoulder, then down his arm—his taut, muscular, beautiful arm. To my relief, the sleeve came off easily, exposing the entire half of his body.

I looked up at him and caught him watching me.

My heart thumped at asinine levels as I reached up and took the other side of his shirt, gently sliding it over his shoulder. Careful not to scrape it against his injury, I slipped my thumb under the fabric and let my finger graze against his skin as I dragged the shirt down his arm. His skin was as warm as a fever and ignited my blood like a fire storm.

I peered back up at him in a daze and noted that his eyes had closed again. Even in this sorry state of pain, he was the picture of otherworldly perfection.

"I can hear you," he whispered. His eyes flicked open and sang with regret.

"Huh?"

He gestured to my hand that was still touching his skin. "I try not to listen in—I prefer not to, but..." he shrugged as though it were beyond his control.

Oh crap. My cheeks felt volcanic, like at any moment they would burst into flames. *Say something, Jemma!* "I was just thinking that you, you know, still looked *decent* despite what happened to you tonight."

He arched a brow at me.

"Just shut up," I warned, even though he hadn't said anything. If he knew what was good for him, he'd leave it at that. "How well can you hear me anyway?" I wondered if it would be inappropriate to demand we test this thing out.

"Well enough." He looked down to examine his wound.

The bleeding had slowed considerably but there was a gaping wound that looked as though it would need a few stitches. I tossed his shirt on the armchair and tried to move around him to take a seat on the couch. Far away. Where there would be no more skin-to-skin contact.

He grabbed my wrist. "Where are you going? I need you to do this for me." He motioned to his injury again.

"Do *what* for you?" I recoiled.

"Stitch me up."

"Are you insane? I can't *stitch* you up."

"Yeah, you can." There wasn't the slightest hint of reluctance in his voice. "It's just like sewing."

"And what makes you think I know how to sew?"

His dimples flashed on both sides. "Wishful thinking."

I looked down at his sultry eyes, and those perfect lips, and that chiseled jaw from the gods, and prayed for the strength not to throw myself at this man like some unworthy peasant.

"Sit," he whispered, pulling me to the floor again.

"I don't have a steady hand."

"I can't do this on myself."

"I'm going to butcher you—turn you into Frankenstein!" A hot one for sure, but a Frankenstein nonetheless.

"I'll walk you through it. You'll be fine." He bent forward to pick up the first aid kit from the floor and let out an audible grunt.

I couldn't stand seeing him in pain like this.

"You need painkillers," I said, taking the first aid kit from him. I cracked it open and searched through its contents for the contraband. "Here, take these," I ordered, handing him a packet of over-the-counter painkillers.

He tossed two in his mouth and swallowed sans water.

Without waiting for his prompt, I pulled out some gauze and a bottle of antiseptic and started cleaning the area around the wound until I had a clear view of the puncture. I may have been a novice at stitching flesh together but I certainly knew how to clean out a wound. And it *definitely* needed stitches.

"Lean back," I told him, standing on my knees now. "We can't close the wound until we flush it out or it'll get infected." Of that I was sure.

He slid back onto his elbows, exposing his washboard abdomen and causing my core body temperature to rise even higher than it already was. I bet they outlawed bodies like his in certain parts of the world. I bet it was downright illegal. And for good reason, too. I was a hop and skip away from going into cardiac arrest.

Leaning over him, I poured the antiseptic liquid into the wound until I felt (in all my infinite medical wisdom) that it was sterile enough to be sealed. "I think that should do it," I mumbled, trying to keep my eyes from roaming.

"Thanks." He offered a bleak smile and straightened out.

When he pulled out the needle and a spool of string that bore an alarming resemblance to a fishing line, I decided that it was the perfect time to distract myself with a phone call. I grabbed my phone and checked for service.

"What are you doing?" he asked, looping the string through the needle head with ease. It was obvious he'd done this before. With his short fuse and propensity to brawl, he probably stitched himself up every other day.

"I'm calling Gabriel to let him know where we are. Maybe he can help us—"

"No way," he said, taking the phone from me quick as a thief. "How do we know he wasn't the one who sent the Runners?"

"Are you high?" I snatched the phone back. "Gabriel would never do that. Ever. He's a good guy."

"He's a Rev—"

"You don't know him!" I snapped, cutting him off. "He would never do anything to hurt me. It's not him, Trace. Trust me."

He stared back at me, his sublime blue eyes taking me in.

"Besides, I think I know who's behind this," I added, fingering the Amulet under my shirt. "But I need to speak to Gabriel first. He needs to know what's going on."

"Fine," he said, though the tension in his jaw never gave.

My phone call with Gabriel was short and to the point. Even though he presented his usual calm and reassuring facade on the exterior, I could hear the anxiety undertones in his voice. We were both thinking the same thing: that this was probably related to Engel and the Amulet. So what now? Unfortunately, there wasn't anything he could do until sundown, for obvious reasons, so I was ordered to stay with Trace until he got there and not to answer the door to anyone but him.

As if I'd planned on doing otherwise, I thought, hanging up the phone and turning my attention back to the beautiful boy sitting before me.

This was going to be a long day.

After a brief crash course in sutures that didn't cover nearly as much as I would have liked it to, Trace handed me the sterilized needle and cocked an eyebrow. "Are you ready to do this?" he asked, knowing full well I wasn't.

My hand shook. "This isn't going to be pretty."

"That's okay," he smirked. His dimples flashing as though they were winking at me. "I'm pretty enough."

That he is, I thought, biting down the words. Sucking in a deep breath, I pinched the wound shut with my thumb and forefinger before driving the needle into his flesh.

"Gah!" I squealed as hair-raising tingles zipped down my spine. I think I felt the entry more than he did.

"You're doing fine," he said, trying to reassure me. He was the one getting his skin sewn together by a high school student and he was trying to keep *me* calm. Figures.

"The calmer you are, the better it is for me," he answered.

Startled momentarily, my eyes shifted to our connected body parts as realization set in. "You know, this reading my mind thing is going to take some getting used to."

He shrugged. "I don't mind working on it with you."

Private one-on-one sessions with him flashed through my mind, making me blush. I thought I saw him smiling from the corner of my eye but I was too mortified to look up and confirm it.

"Does it ever bother you?" I wondered, curious to know more about his ability. "Hearing other people's thoughts?"

"Sometimes," he admitted. "I hated being touched as a kid. I didn't know how to block it out."

I couldn't imagine being constantly bombarded with other people's mundane thoughts and noises every time I made contact with someone. "It must be horrible."

"It's not all bad." He shrugged it off. "It has its advantages, too."

"Like what?"

He let his seductive gaze pour over me, slow like molasses. "Use your imagination."

I pulled my hand back just as my mind derailed. I didn't want him to know what I was thinking, and I sure as hell couldn't focus when he looked at me that way.

His eyebrows rose.

"Stop it."

"I'm not doing anything," he laughed coyly.

"You're distracting me and if you don't stop it and let me concentrate, I'm going to end up sewing your belly button shut!"

The hint of a smile graced his face as he looked down at me, seemingly fascinated.

"No more messing around!" I ordered.

He nodded solemnly as though he had every intention of obeying my orders. After a brief pause, he craned his head to me, filling up the air with his all-consuming presence. "You know, you're nothing like what I expected."

"What were you expecting?"

"I don't know," he said, wetting his lips. "Something else. You're...*different*."

Different? I narrowed my eyes. "What do you mean *I'm*

different?"

He seemed amused by my outrage.

"You're the one who's different from one day to the next!" I shot back unable to hide my indignity. Frankly, it was a little hard to take coming from *him*. I'd yet to meet a moodier guy than Trace Macarthur.

The whites of his eyes flashed. "I meant it as a compliment."

"Oh." My cheeks reddened. "So did I."

"No, you didn't."

"I just meant that you're difficult to read sometimes. Some days it seems like you don't want anything to do with me, or at least that's what you tell me. And then other times, I think…I don't know, something else. It's hard to keep up."

He lowered his head. "I know."

"So why are you like this with me?" I pushed, unsatisfied with his response. "Why do you talk to me and sit next to me and offer to take me to see my dad after you made it clear that you wanted nothing to do with me?"

"Can't people change their minds?"

"I guess they can," I shrugged, struggling to keep my hands from shaking as I needled another stitch into his side. "It just seemed like there was something more behind it."

"There was."

"And now?" I looked up at him wanting to read him like a book; to know him and all of his secrets.

"And now I'm having a hard time remembering what it was." There was something incredibly moving about the way he looked at me, about the way he let me see him—*really* see him. Even if it was only for a moment.

"So then…" I paused, swallowing the mounting butterflies. "What does this mean exactly?"

"Does it have to *mean* anything? Can't I just sit next to you if I want to sit next to you?" He reached forward and gently moved a strand of hair away from my eyes.

My heart pounded in my chest as I tried not to get lost in those spellbinding pools of blue.

"Am I distracting you again?" he smiled.

Unable to deny it out loud and keep a straight face, I rolled my eyes at him in an effort to appear flippant. I heard him chuckle softly, but I didn't meet his eyes this time.

"So how about you tell me who you think is behind this? Would be nice to know why I took a knife to the stomach."

"I'm not sure," I started, unsure of where to go with it.

"But you have a theory." It wasn't a question.

"I think it might have to do with my sister, Tessa."

His eyebrows furrowed as he watched me—studied me. "What makes you think that?"

"She's in trouble," I explained, eyes lowered. "I can't tell you much about it because I don't really know the details myself. Just that there's these Revs after her, dangerous ones, and since we met up last night, I just thought it might be related—"

"Tessa was in town?" he cut in, his interest peaked.

"Yeah, not for long though. She came to see me—to warn me about what was going on."

He nodded, taking it in. "So you're thinking these Rev's followed her last night and saw you with her? That they're trying to use you to get to her now?"

"Maybe." I tried to read his expression, but he gave nothing away. "What do you think?"

"I don't know," he shrugged. "Rev's don't usually go through all this trouble. They must really want something from her."

I swallowed hard, afraid to think of what they would do to me if they found out *I* was the one who had the Amulet now and not her. I was way out of my league with this—

"The Amulet?" Trace's dark brows pulled together as he covered my hand with his, stopping my movements. "What do you mean you have the Amulet?"

Shit. I yanked my hand back. "Dammit, Trace!"

"Jemma—"

"You have no right to eavesdrop on my private thoughts!" I shouted, fumbling to come up with a plausible diversion. "You're...you're misconstruing everything I'm thinking!"

"I'm not misconstruing anything," he asserted. "I heard you, Jemma. You said you had the Amulet. What Amulet? The one my sister was looking for? The Immortal Amulet?"

Double shit. I had no idea what to do or how to answer him. Tessa didn't prepare me for this. She didn't tell me what to do if I accidentally blew my cover telepathically announcing my possession of the Amulet to someone who could read minds. She just didn't prepare me for any of this!

God, it was all her fault!

"Answer me!"

"Look," I said, deciding to do the only thing I knew how to do—lie. "I don't know anything about a *moral* Amulet, so whatever you think you heard, you're wrong."

"You're lying." His eyes burned holes into my soul. "You're lying to me and you're not even doing a good job of it."

"You're the liar! You're the one who lied about everything, about who you were, about—"

"Don't try to turn this around on me." He tipped forward, his stance both authoritative and intimidating all at once. "Linley died for that Amulet. Do you have any idea what she went through trying to get it?" His eyes glistened with a blinding rage. "What I went through trying to find it for her?"

"I..." I dropped my eyes. I couldn't bear to look at him like this, to face him and lie to him again. I felt as though my heart were splintering into a million little pieces.

"Look at me, Jemma."

"No." I shook my head. "I don't want to lie to you, Trace."

"Then don't."

I pressed my lips together, forcing the silence.

"Alright." He leaned back, the body armor that had begun to dissolve seemed as though it were shifting back into place, closing him off from the rest of the world again—from me. "Just tell me one thing then," he said, defeated. "Was it the Council? Were they the ones who gave you the Amulet?"

I didn't know what to do. If I answered his question, I would be admitting to him that I did in fact have the Amulet. Then again, he pretty much already knew that.

"Please, Jemma." A tired breath escaped, jagged and slow. "I need to know if they gave you the Amulet."

"Why does that matter?" I wondered, buying myself time.

"Because it does," he said, heated. "It matters if they knew where it was and lied to me about it...if they knew all along and let my sister die anyway. It matters to *me*."

Suddenly it made sense why he left the Order. Why he had such animosity towards them. He *blamed* them. He thought they knew how to save Linley and refused to do it. That they fed her to the Revs without so much as a second thought.

I shook my head in response.

"No it didn't come from them or no you won't answer me?" The muscles in his jaw popped as he watched me squirm under his penetrating stare.

He looked so angry with me, so disappointed. It was damn near intolerable. After everything we'd gone through, after all the times he came to my rescue, I couldn't bear to sit here and lie to him. Not about this. Not about something this important to him.

"The Council doesn't know anything about it," I said, meeting his disparaged eyes. "They weren't the ones who gave it to me. Tessa was."

33. ATONEMENT

Silence wrapped itself around us like the familiar embrace of an old friend. Neither one of us spoke, though in the dim light of the cabin, I thought I saw something telling flicker through his eyes. Something vulnerable—grateful—and I found myself wanting to reach forward to touch him. To swipe away the ebony strand of hair from his eyes. But I didn't dare move.

He broke the ice first. "Do you think you can finish this for me?" He motioned to his partial stitches.

I nodded and scooted in closer.

"Are you wearing it now?" he asked when I started up again, his baritone voice barely above a whisper. "Is that why you don't have a scratch on you?"

"Tessa said it has some sort of protective power."

"How long?"

I wasn't sure if he wanted to know how long I've been wearing it or how long my sister's had it—

"Both," he answered before I could ask the question aloud.

"Less than a day for me. Three months for Tessa."

I went on to tell him about Engel and his men; about how Tessa's been on the run from them for the last few months and wanted out of whatever mess she was in. He listened intently as I relayed what little information I had and filled him in on Tessa and Gabriel's plan.

"And what about you?" he asked casually. "Where are you going to be when this ambush goes down?"

"As far away as possible," I said, finishing up the last stitch.

"Good," he answered absentmindedly.

"Good?"

"You have no business being there. You're not even almost ready for that."

"How would you know?" I fired back. He was right, but that was beside the point. "When was the last time you saw me train? That's right, *never*. And wasn't I holding my own today? Didn't I knock out Blondie all by myself?"

"Yeah you did." He smirked as though he were enjoying the memory. "But they were Runners, Jemma. There's a difference."

"Whatever. Fine." I couldn't argue the point. "It's not like I want to run off and battle a bunch of vampires anyway. Home is exactly where I want to be when all of this goes down." I only wished Tessa and Gabriel could be there, too. That we all could be safe from the darkness that haunted us like a plague.

"No desire to battle vampires?" His tone was marred in disbelief. "That's a joke, right? Because you won't have much of a choice once they break the spell."

"What do you mean?"

"You're not the only one that can't sense them. They can't sense you either. It's a two way street. Once you remove the Cloak, they'll be drawn to you again. You'll be fighting them whether you want to or not." He stared at me intensely before his expression softened with what looked like pity. "They didn't tell you that part, did they?"

There was that feeling of dread again. "No, they didn't." I definitely would have remembered hearing something like that.

"Why am I not surprised," muttered Trace.

I couldn't help but wonder what this all meant for me. Would they be able to sense me the same way I was going to sense them? And what did he mean when he said they'd be drawn to me? Would there be a pull? A connection? Would they seek me out in a crowd of people?

"It's not too late you know."

"To do what?" I asked rhetorically. "Keep the only defense I have against them suppressed? I'm not even sure that's a possibility anymore," I sighed, frustrated by my lack of information and control over the situation. "And besides, where would that leave me? If I break the spell, at least I'll see them coming, right? I'll have a fighting chance."

And more importantly, I'll know who to stay away from and which direction to run. It was the lesser of two evils and we both knew it, but then why was he looking at me that way? Like it mattered to him. Like *I* mattered to him.

"What's it to you anyway?" I challenged. "If I didn't know any better, I might actually think you cared about me." It was only when I said the words aloud that I realized I wanted them to be true. I wanted him to care about me *that* way.

The muscles in his jaw started working again. "It's a good thing you know better then," he said without meeting my eyes.

Yeah, good thing, I sighed. At least he stopped acting like I was the Black Plague. It was a step in the right direction.

I opened the first aid kit and pulled out some antibiotic ointment and non-stick bandages to dress the stitches with. "So? How do they look?"

He tilted his head to the side and examined my work. "Not bad actually," he remarked, genuine surprise in his tone. "Looks like the scar won't be that bad either."

"It's kind of cool if you think about it."

"What is?"

"You know, that you'll always have something to remember me by every time you look down at it."

Something in his expression changed—darkened.

"You know, in case you forget me when I'm gone," I added, kicking the joke like a dead horse.

"I wouldn't forget you," he said under his breath.

"Because of all the grief I've caused you." No doubt.

"No." His jaw set in a hard line. "Because you're not really the kind of girl a guy can forget, Jemma."

I wasn't entirely sure what he meant by that, but it did strange fuzzy things to my insides.

After finishing up his bandages, Trace put his shirt back on and headed outside to check the area and make sure nothing was out of the ordinary, though he seemed fairly certain we'd be safe here. At least for now. While he was gone, I pulled out my cell phone and checked for service again in the hopes that I could reach Henry and find out exactly what happened to him today. Unfortunately, my bars kept flicking in and out every twenty seconds making the task a lot harder than need be.

"Who are you calling now?" asked Trace when he returned a few minutes later. He looked annoyed as he locked the door behind him and began closing all the curtains.

The room darkened with each swoosh.

"I'm trying to reach Henry," I said, my eyes following him around the room. "He was supposed to pick me up after detention but he never showed up. Don't you think that's weird?"

"That's my fault," he said and then flopped down on the sofa beside me, draping his arm around the back. "I saw him waiting for you after school and told him I'd give you a lift."

I stared at him, surprised that he volunteered himself.

"I was going that way anyway," he muttered with a tinge of

defensiveness.

"Thanks, I guess. What about work? Aren't they going to be worried that we didn't show up?"

"I took care of it already." His hard eyes moved to me, softening as he looked me over. "Are you hungry? Do you want something to eat or drink?"

I shook my head. "I don't think I could handle any food right now. My stomach's still in knots," I said, hugging my arms for warmth. I swear it felt as though I'd developed a permanent case of the chills ever since I moved to this godforsaken town.

He pulled the throw blanket from the armrest and tossed it over to me.

I thanked him and spread the blanket around myself. "You want to share?" I asked, offering him a corner.

He shook his head and sunk deeper into the couch. His eyes quickly slid shut as though he were trying to shut out the world around him. As though they were the gatekeepers to a place he didn't want me entering.

Seconds turned to minutes.

I really didn't want to watch him sleep and yet I couldn't look away. He looked so peaceful like this. Vulnerable. Not at all like the powerful, guarded being I knew him to be. The kind of being who could make dreams come true and open up doors to worlds I never even knew existed. Like this, he was just another boy. Just a beautiful sleeping boy.

"What?" He quirked an eye open, catching me.

"Nothing," I shook my head nervously, hoping he didn't suspect I'd been watching him this whole time. I pulled my knees up to my chest. "I was just thinking."

"About?" Both his eyes were open now, studying me like a treasure map.

"About tomorrow." I shrugged because it wasn't a *complete* lie. "You're still taking me to see my dad, right? You didn't change your mind or anything?"

"Why would I change my mind?"

"I don't know…with everything that's happened today, I was worried you'd think it wasn't the right time."

"Actually, we'll probably be safer in the *past*."

His strange words resonated as reality set in.

The past was going to come alive tomorrow. It would no longer be just a string of fleeting thoughts and movie reels buried in my gallows of my subconscious. It was a place I could go to. A place I could sink my feet into. A physical reality he was going to make happen for me. I was excited and petrified all at the same time.

"How will it feel seeing him again?" I wondered, knowing he'd been in my shoes before and could provide insight.

"Bittersweet." His eyes met mine in the dark.

"Bittersweet," I repeated, trying to accost myself to it, to wrap my mind around the sentiment.

He must have noticed the strange expression on my face because he reached over and took my hand into his.

"Don't worry," he whispered, lacing our fingers together. "It'll be okay."

And in that moment, I really believed him.

34. UNEXPECTED DEVELOPMENT

I awoke sometime later in Trace's arms. Warm, humming arms that wrapped around my shoulders like a lullaby. I was amazed at how good they felt there. Like they belonged there. Like we were always meant to be this way—or had been this way before—me and him, two hearts beating as one.

"Sleep well?" he asked, voice strained.

How did he know I was up? *Oh, gawd*, had he heard my rambling thoughts again? Panicked, I immediately tried to pull myself away from him.

He tightened his hold on me, keeping me pressed against him. "Careful," he warned. "I'm injured, remember?" I could hear the smile in his words.

"Sorry," I frowned, peering up at him under my lashes. "I don't know how I got over here."

"I guess you just liked it better on this side." The deep whisper of his voice sent a molten shiver down my back.

This was bad. *Must. Detach. Now.*

"I hope I didn't make you uncomfortable," I said, stumbling to find a safe spot to place my hand for liftoff support. "I'm pretty much delirious from the moment I wake up until I have a

306

shot of caffeine or something so, you know, anything I say or *think* until that point should really just be ignored." I settled for his thigh and gently pushed myself off of his taut (though surprisingly comfortable) body.

His cheek hitched up on one side, revealing his dimple.

"Did Gabriel call?" I asked, discreetly smoothing out my disheveled hair as I tried to change the subject. This was beyond embarrassing.

He pursed his lips, rocking his head side to side.

"What time is it anyway?" I'd noted the sun had already set and figured Gabriel was probably on his way, but I wanted to be sure. The truth was, I wasn't sure how much longer I could take being alone with Trace like this. Apparently I couldn't keep myself off of him. Even in my sleep.

"Almost ten," he said, spreading his arm against the back of the couch as he kicked out his legs in front of him. There was something wildly enticing about the way his body untwined.

"Great," I croaked, hugging myself as I glanced around the room looking for something to distract my eyes with. Coming up empty, I turned back to Trace and found his eyes were still on me, watching me thoughtfully. The butterflies ignited again. "So how about that math test?" I asked out of nowhere.

He cracked a smile but didn't bother entertaining my idiotic attempt at a conversation. Thank God because I really didn't want to talk about math, or tests, or anything school-related for that matter. What I really wanted to do was—

Bang. Bang. Bang.

A series of hard knocks erupted at the front door causing me to catapult myself off the couch as if I'd been caught doing something naughty. Trace, obviously amused by this, made no attempt to stifle his laughter, even as I speared him with contempt all the way to the front entrance.

He peeked through the window before unlocking the door.

"It's our friendly neighborhood vampire," he informed and then swung the front door open in a gust.

Gabriel stood on the other side of the threshold wearing his black leather jacket and a worried expression. He looked as though he was working hard to hold it all together.

"Are you alright?" he asked, tipping his head as if to scan my face for injuries or signs of distress.

I stepped outside and gave him a quick hug. "I'm fine. Thank you for coming." I pulled back and motioned for him to come in.

"I can't," he said, shaking his head as he glanced over my shoulder to Trace. "He needs to invite me in."

I turned to Trace expectantly, but he just stood there, stone-faced with his arms crossed over his chest.

"Trace!"

It felt like an eternity before he spoke.

"Come in," he finally said, though it sounded a lot more like a dare than a welcome.

Two wax candles burned leisurely on the coffee table as the three of us convened in the living room. Gabriel sat firm on the armchair while Trace and I took our previous spots on the sofa with a bundled blanket sandwiched between us, courtesy of me. There was a stretch of awkward silence before Gabriel took the lead and began compiling information about what had gone down today. Unfortunately, we were nowhere closer to figuring out who was behind the attack though Engel and his men were definitely at the top of everyone's suspect list.

"So if he's behind this, what's the plan now that they've made Jemma?" asked Trace.

"Tessa reached out to them already," answered Gabriel. "She let them know she's interested in dealing. That should put them back on track for now. The next step is to track her tails and see how many men are on her."

"So they still think Tessa has the Amulet?" verified Trace.

"They have no reason not to," answered Gabriel. "The focus is back on her, which is what we want. As long as they believe Tessa's interested in making a deal with them, it should give them enough incentive to back off of Jemma."

"*Should*?" Trace and I repeated at the same time.

He nodded, regretful. "There's no way to know what their next move will be, but at least we know what they're after. It's easier to control the outcome this way. Until this thing is over, you're simply going to have to lay low for a while," he said, his eyes regretful. "I know this isn't what you want, but that means certain conditions for you, Jemma."

"Like what?" I gulped.

"Curfew. School and back. And never alone. I'll stand watch throughout the night and maybe Trace can keep an eye out during the day when I can't be there. Tessa was adamant about this, and I must say, I fully agree with her."

My head was spinning. I needed permanent chaperones now? And Trace of all people? He didn't want to get close to me, and he sure as hell didn't want to be involved in vampire business.

"Trace can't do it," I said shaking my head. "Maybe we can ask Julian or one of Tessa's—"

"I'll do it," said Trace, speaking over me. His eyes locked in on mine. They looked so determined—almost feral. "I won't let her out of my sight."

A slash of heat tore through my body.

"Then it's settled," nodded Gabriel, content.

"Great," agreed Trace.

Apparently, I was the only who thought this had all kinds of bad written all over it.

35. BACK TO THE PAST

Trace was outside my house early the next morning under the pretense of driving me to school. It was only after I climbed into his Mustang that he informed me we were actually ditching school and going to his house instead.

I made zero protests.

The rain came down like axes, making it hard to see anything, though I immediately recognized the gated community as Caleb and Carly's and was surprised to find that Trace lived just a few houses down from them. Where the Owens' house was all glass and pallor, Trace's house was the polar opposite; a stunning dark-stone mansion with wood finishing and a decadent porch that wrapped around the house like a ribbon.

Inside, the foyer opened to a vaulted living Room with high beamed ceilings and limestone floors that stretched to what seemed like the ends of the earth. As breathtaking as it was, the chill was unmistakable. The house felt empty—jarringly so. Not of furniture but of something else; of family, of life. I couldn't quite put my finger on it.

We left our shoes in the mudroom and went up to the

second floor where Trace ushered us into his bedroom. With my back pasted against the door, I scanned the expansive room, taking in the mahogany furniture, the blue walls, the large double bed to the right and matching navy comforter. I noticed a small desk on the adjacent wall-unit and couldn't help but smile to myself as I tried to imagine Trace sitting there doing his Math homework.

Everything seemed nice, and tidy, and smelled *good*; the remnants of a spicy cologne I already knew and loved.

"You can come in all the way," he said, pulling out the desk chair like a ligneous invitation. "I don't bite."

"I know that." My heart was beating so fast I thought I might pass out if I got any closer to him. "So what's the plan for today?" I asked instead, still not budging from the door.

His dimples flickered as he pressed his lips together. He moved to the edge of his bed and slumped down onto it. "I take you to go see your dad. That is what you want, isn't it?"

"Yes, that's what I want." *Desperately.*

"Okay." His eyes traveled down the length of my body. "Did you bring a change of clothes or were you planning on seeing him in your Weston uniform?"

"I have other clothes in my bag," I croaked, my throat already dry as chalk. I hated the way he disrupted my normal bodily functions without even trying.

His eyes climbed back up in no hurry. "You can change in here," he said and then instantly appeared in front of me, making my heart flutter. Flattening his palm against the door, he leaned into me, reaching. His mouth hovering around my ear, my neck, dizzying me with its nearness.

Every cell in my body stilled. I was afraid to move or speak or God forbid inhale his heavenly scent and truly lose all control over my limbs.

He turned the door knob and tugged the door open behind

me, causing me to lurch forward into him. Thigh to thigh, you couldn't slide a piece of paper between us, we were that close. And holy smokes, I needed an icepack.

He looked down at me for what felt like an eternity, his jaw hard at work as our nearness charged the air around us. I could feel my body humming—vibrating from the heat of his body pressed up against mine. His head tilted towards me, inching closer as though he were going to kiss me, and I held my breath, curious to know if his lips felt as soft as they looked.

He stopped abruptly and steeled his gaze. Before I could assemble another thought, his arm dropped from the door, freeing me from his cage. It was over before it even began.

I slid away gingerly and watched as he exited the room in silence.

Needing a moment to catch my breath, I staggered to the chair and sat down. I couldn't figure out how he caused my entire body to go haywire with nothing more than his proximity. I swore to myself that the next time he broke into my personal space like that, or played those damn hot-and-cold games with me, I would give him a real piece of my mind. Or something. Who did he think he was anyway?

I quickly changed into a pair of skinny jeans and my favorite V-neck tee before letting him back into his room. My arms were crossed and my guard was up. Though, they both faltered as soon as I noted the unnerving look on his face.

"There's a couple of things we need to talk about before we do this," he said as he walked over to his dresser. He picked up his silver watch and swapped it with the one he was wearing.

I sat back down in the chair and rubbed my palms against my jeans. "Let's hear it."

"There's a reason the Council doesn't let us travel back without their consent," he said, taking a seat on his bed just across the way from me. He leaned forward on his elbows. "The temptation to change things can be...overwhelming.'"

I could understand that—heck, it was one of the reasons I wanted to go back—but I stayed silent, hands folded in my lap like a good little girl.

"The problem is that even the smallest change can open up a *Ripple*." He gave me a meaningful look. "And believe me when I say, you don't want that to happen."

"Why not?" I wasn't even sure what it was.

He paused before answering. "Say you go back to the day your father died and you decide to warn him about what's going to happen—"

Sounded like a perfect plan.

"—you'd inadvertently be setting off a *butterfly effect*. Chances are he'll accept that Death is coming regardless of your warning because he's Anakim, but before he goes, maybe this time he prepares his final wishes for you. Maybe he decides that you should go stay with a distant cousin or an old friend. Maybe you never end up coming to Hollow Hills and you never meet me—we never make the trip. How do you then get back to the present now that you've erased it?" His eyes were sharp, focused. "That's a Ripple. Even a small Ripple could destroy everything."

I swallowed the lump in my throat.

"I need to hear you promise me you won't do anything stupid. That you'll leave the past exactly as you found it because as far as your dad's concerned, it's just another day. Can you handle that?"

I didn't know if I could do it. I didn't know if I'd be strong enough to see my father and not warn him about the attack—about what was going to happen.

"Jemma?"

I had no other options. My hands were tied. "I promise," I said, tasting the bitterness the words left in my mouth.

He rose from the bed and walked over to me. "If it's too

much for you, you don't have to talk to him. We can keep our distance." He held out his hand and I took it easily. "I'll still take you to see him."

"I need to be able to talk to him...to *hug* him." My eyes welled up at the thought of being able to feel my father's embrace again after so many months. Something I never even allowed myself to dream of.

"I understand." He reached out and tucked a strand of hair behind my ear, his thumb grazing my cheek as he wiped away a lone tear that had fallen.

The gesture made my knees and heart tremble.

"When you're ready to go, just start thinking about the day you want to go back to," he instructed, soothing me with the deep whisper of his voice.

"Any day I want?"

"Any day." His dimples pressed in as he hedged a smile. "Just make sure it's not too far in the past if you plan on talking to him. And make sure the *Jemma* from the past isn't around either," he added, deepening his smile as though he would have enjoyed the doppelganger run-in.

"Got it." I rubbed my palms against my jeans. "And then what happens?"

"And then I put my arms around you and read your thoughts. I need to *see* the place in order to get us there so I'll have to lift the memories from your mind."

"Okay."

He took my hand and pulled me in closer to him.

As soon as his arms were wrapped around me, I shut my eyes and began sifting through my memories, searching for a good day to revisit—the perfect day—and settled on the morning of my dad's very last birthday. I remembered it as if it were yesterday. Our house, the molten sun shining, the bear hug I gave him before leaving to catch my bus. Every moment was still vivid in my mind, and it was Trace's for the taking.

The cold quickly flooded my body like an arctic blast, and with that, we were in Hollow Hills no more.

36. SUNNY SIDE UP

The scorching sun kissed my skin like a long-lost love. I'd forgotten how good it could feel. How medicinal its warmth could be. I wanted to stay in this moment forever; let the heat encase my body like a tomb. But alas, I had miles to go.

"Where exactly are we?" asked Trace, peering down the length of the street as we stepped out from behind the hedges.

Apparently, getting us there didn't necessarily mean he knew where *there* was.

"This is my old street. Well, my old bus stop to be exact." We both looked up at the stop sign in unison as though it were some fascinating museum artifact.

"And that's my house." I ticked my head to the modest cream colored Mediterranean house adorned in tall palmetto trees at the end of the street.

"Have you figured out what our story's going to be?" asked Trace as we started down the street side by side. It felt like an impromptu quiz the way he pressed me for an answer.

I thought about it for a moment. "I'll tell him you're new in the neighborhood and that today's your first day at Cape High." I paused as I reran the story in my mind. "And that we missed the bus," I added, remembering that this would be the second time he was seeing me this morning.

"Not bad," remarked Trace, his dimples pressing in modestly, beckoning me. "I'm impressed."

He was impressed that I lie well? I shook my head, "you would be."

"What's that supposed to mean?" His eyes looked like two dazzling orbs in this sunlight.

"You know, just that you look like the kind of guy that would be impressed by something like that."

He looked intrigued. "And what kind of guy is that?"

I shrugged as though I hadn't given it much thought. "The kind of guy that has a lot of secrets. The kind that dates girls like Nikki Parker and answers questions with questions. The evasive kind." I wanted to add 'the hot brooding kind' to the list but figured it was best to leave that one out.

He tipped his head in a nod, soaking it in. "You think you have me all figured out, don't you?"

I couldn't hold back my laughter. "Not even a bit."

By the time we turned up my driveway, my heart had all but climbed up into the back of my throat, threatening a complete system failure. I was going to see my dad again. Right here. Right now. After all this time and a *funeral*. I had no idea what was in store for me but I refused to let my fear of the unknown stop me. I drew in a lungful of air and pushed open the door.

The familiar sights and aromas assaulted my senses as I walked into the house. It felt peculiar being here after so much time away. Even though everything was the same and I was more than nostalgic for it, somehow, I'd become a stranger to the house. Like I didn't quite fit here anymore.

Apparently, I didn't fit in *anywhere* anymore.

"Jemma? Is that you?" called my father from the kitchen. The sound of his voice hit me like a lightning bolt.

I staggered back, shaking my head. I wasn't sure I'd be able to set my eyes on him without breaking down.

Trace slinked our hands together. "You can do this," he whispered, rubbing soothing circles on the back of my hand with his thumb. "Just breathe. *I got you.*"

My insides pinched at his words. I couldn't figure out how he was able to transmit exactly what I needed to push forward, but he did, and I liked him more for it.

I walked into the kitchen and found my father sitting at the table with a cup of coffee cradled between his hands. The sun dusted his features, giving him that same ethereal look I often imagined him with nowadays. It took every ounce of strength I had to resist the urge to run over to him and crawl into his lap like I did when I was a kid. When I didn't know any better and thought there'd never come a day when I wouldn't have my father.

"Who do we have here?" he asked, furrowing his dark brows similar to the way my uncle did when he was talking *Rev* business. It was unnerving how much they looked alike.

I couldn't stop staring. "This is Trace. He just moved here. We missed the bus." Frankly, I couldn't have done a poorer job lying if I tried doing it on purpose.

"Nice to meet you," jumped in Trace, extending his hand to my father. The sight of them shaking hands made my heart swell.

"Likewise," said my father. His dark eyes bounced between the two of us before settling back on me. "Are you okay, Jems? You're looking a little—"

"Yeah, I'm totally fine." I stood there looking anything but. I needed to get a major grip.

"Alright." He nodded in a circular motion, not quite believing it but unwilling to press the issue. "Let me grab my keys. I'll give you two a ride to school."

"It's okay, Dad. You don't need to do that. We're catching the next bus," I lied, easy as breathing.

He looked rather confused by my decline. I guess that made sense considering I wasn't exactly one to turn down rides at that particular point in my life. You might have even said I was allergic to public transportation.

"Trace is new, remember? He needs to learn the route," I added, hoping it sounded plausible enough. I felt bad lying to him like this but I guess it was for his own good.

"Alright, fair enough. You might as well sit down then," he said, motioning to the table, grinning copiously. "Looks like you have time for that breakfast after all." He winked at me before bending down to pillage the fridge, and I nearly broke down in complete hysterics. I never in a million dreams thought I'd get another chance to have breakfast with my dad.

I remembered asking him for a rain check this very morning all those months ago, assuming there would be a lifetime of *tomorrows* to have breakfast with him. The younger *Jemma* had far more important things to do—like meeting Jake Miller at the bleachers before class. Everyone said he was going to ask me to the dance and I couldn't think of a single more important place to be at the time. How utterly stupid I was.

If only I knew. I'd take it *all* back, trade a hundred dances and first kisses for this one breakfast with my dad.

And now, thanks to Trace, I wouldn't have to do any of that. He made the impossible possible by giving me a chance to right my wrong and rewrite the past.

I sat down at the table and watched as Trace interacted with my father while he whipped up a batch of his famous pesto scrambled eggs and bacon. I'd never seen Trace so loquacious before. It was kind of endearing to see, and the fact that it was with my dad made it that much more special.

As they carried on about junior hockey and classic cars, I found myself studying my dad; his voice, his mannerisms, the lines in his face. I needed to remember it, all of it, and brand those memories into the forevermore of my mind.

"Jemma here is on the varsity cheer squad," said my dad as he set down a plate in front of me. "She's the only sophomore on the team." He sounded so proud of me when he spoke. I never noticed that about him before.

"Is that right?" Trace's eyebrows shot up with interest. He was eating up every word of it. Probably picturing me in my cheer uniform this very second.

I rolled my eyes at him.

"I got lucky with this one," continued my dad. "Never gave me any problems. She's a good kid. A little high in the maintenance department, but a good one just the same."

Was he trying to make me sob? I wasn't sure how much longer I could keep it together. Sucking in a lungful of air, I bore down into my scrambled eggs and blinked back the budding tears as Trace and my father went on with their near perfect, off-the-cuff conversation. It was far too easy to fall in line with the normalcy of it all. I would feel the loss later, of this I was sure, but for now, all was right in the world.

The morning passed like falling water, evading me with every drop. It didn't matter how bad I wanted to reach out and trap it—freeze it—keep the water at a standstill. It was impermanent, another fleeting moment that would soon be over. I ate my breakfast in a daze, hardly saying a word all morning which was very unlike me, especially back then. But I couldn't help it. I just wanted to hear my dad speak. I wanted to hear him complain about the stifling humidity and rave about his super bowl predictions. Every word he uttered seemed so important, so utterly crucial to my survival. I only wished I could stay here and listen to him speak forever.

Once everyone had finished their breakfast, I cleared the dishes from the table and loaded the dishwasher for what felt like the last time. The sun was shining through the window, though it didn't feel right on my skin anymore. Inside I felt as gray and unsettled as the Hollow Hills firmament. The storm clouds had already gathered in my heart, knowing I was going to have to say goodbye to everything all over again.

I looked back at my dad and straightened my shoulders as I prepared myself to leave him. *This would not be goodbye*, I decided. I refused to say those words to him. I refused to let him go. I would find a way back to him, and maybe, just maybe, I'd even find a way to save him.

"I'll see you later, Daddy." I nestled into his arms and breathed in his familiar scent, hoping I could take it back with me as a keepsake. "I love you to the moon and back."

He squeezed me tight as he dropped a kiss on the top of my head. "And I love you more than all the stars in the sky."

I quickly detached from him and bounced out the door, hurrying off so he wouldn't see my face soaked with the tears I could no longer contain. Trace said his goodbyes on his own and then jogged to catch up with me as I made my way down the street, back to the bus stop from which we had sprung.

"Are you okay?" he asked upon reaching me. His deep voice was rich with concern.

I wiped under my eyes and pulled in a deep breath. "No, but I will be," I nodded, doing my best to put on a brave face. "That was a lot harder than I thought it would be."

His face looked pained. "I'm sorry, I should have known—"

"Don't apologize," I interrupted, stopping abruptly to face him. "What you did for me today..." I shook my head. Words couldn't express what those moments meant to me. What they did for my shattered heart. "I'll never *ever* forget it."

A humble smile graced his face and I could see he was pleased. He was happy that *I* was happy, and it melted my heart. Overcome with emotion, I pushed up on my toes and leaned into him, bouncing a kiss off his cheek. He didn't move an inch—not forward nor backward—not even after I pulled away.

"What was that for?" he asked, his jaw muscle ticking.

For being there for me when I needed him. For putting himself at risk time and time again. For taking me to see my dad even though he didn't have to do it. Regardless of what he may have *said* in the past, he's been there for me more times than I can count and I was eternally grateful to him.

"Just for...everything," I answered, silently vowing that I would one day find a way to repay him.

His dimples pressed in as a small smile formed on his lips. "You ready to go *home*?"

I sighed, not entirely sure where that was anymore. "As ready as I'll ever be."

37. CONTACT

Hollow Hills greeted us with its elegiac song. Water trickled down the window like tears, welcoming us back to a melancholy world that never rested. It was already late afternoon by the time we returned, which had surprised me. Apparently, time moved a lot quicker here...or perhaps it moved slower for us in the past? I wasn't yet sure how that worked.

Trace and I spent the next couple of hours alone in his bedroom where we sat on the floor with our backs against the bed and the music humming in the background. We talked about everything and nothing; killing time as it were, and for the most part, we kept things light and easy, and we were both content with that. That is, until I unwittingly asked about his mother.

I wanted to know what time she would be home and hoped to pass it off as a minor curiosity, but the truth was, I was afraid I'd wind up face-to-face with her having to explain what I was doing in her son's bedroom, unsupervised. Mothers always made me incredibly uneasy. I didn't know how to interact with them—probably because I never really had one.

Trace swallowed hard and lowered his eyes.

"Did I say something wrong?" I asked, confused by his response. However backhanded my intentions, it was an innocent enough question.

"No, you didn't say anything wrong." He looked up at his iPod deck and listened for a few beats. "My mom's not well," he finally said, turning back to me with guarded eyes. "After Linley died, she had a hard time coping with everything."

He went on to tell me about the breakdown his mother suffered after his sister's death. Though he didn't offer too many specifics regarding what that entailed, I could tell it was something that weighed heavily on him.

"She's been in an institution for the last few weeks," he revealed, growing more sullen with every admission. "My father said it was for her own good, but I know he just got sick of dealing with her. Out of sight, out of mind."

My heart sank.

"I try to go visit her every day before school but it's hard seeing her that way." He looked up at me and shook his head, possibly mistaking my silence for fear. "She's not crazy. She's just heartbroken." His eyes were gleaming in the dim light, deepening the shades of blue.

"I know," I said, covering his hand with mine. I didn't know what else to say to him.

"You don't have to say anything," he answered softly and then turned his hand around so that his palm was flat against my own. His eyes never strayed from mine as he laced our fingers together, causing my heart to drum even faster. "I didn't tell you about her to get anything back from you."

But how could I not give him something back? After everything he'd done for me, the least I could offer was my friendship, my compassion. Maybe even the gift of knowing he wasn't alone. That I'd traveled down a similar road to his mother and came out of it okay, even if it was under different circumstances. Sometimes all we needed was a shoulder to lean on, or in some cases, a hand to hold.

I looked down at our entangled fingers. "I watched my father die eight months ago at the hands of a Rev. I watched him give up his own life so that I could get away, and I've had to live with that ever since. I pretty much lost it after that and wound up getting committed." I glanced up at him, gauging his reaction before saying anything else. "I was out of it for a long time. The more I resisted, the more they drugged me into oblivion. So much so that I actually started to believe that maybe I *did* imagine the whole thing. Maybe I *was* crazy."

He cleared his throat as though he were going to say something but decided against it. The gesture made me hesitate, like maybe I was doing that rambling thing again and revealed a little more than he was ready to hear.

"The point is that I came out of it okay, and your mother will too. When she's ready to cope with the world again, she will. She just needs time." I squeezed his hand reassuringly.

He stared back at me without speaking.

I couldn't tell what he was thinking from his ever-reticent countenance, and I wished—not for the first time—that I could read his thoughts the way he could read mine.

"No, you don't. Trust me."

"That bad?"

He didn't answer.

"Are you freaked out?" I asked, biting my lip nervously.

"Why would I be freaked out?"

"Because of what I told you," I shrugged, afraid to ask him what he thought of me now. "I don't want you to look at me differently now that you know." I dropped my gaze knowing I couldn't bear it if this changed things between us. Especially now that we were in a good place.

He shook my hand a little as if to call back my attention.

"You really don't remember, do you?"

That wasn't the answer I was expecting. I looked up at him and found him studying me curiously. "Remember what?"

"The first time we met."

"In History class?" I remembered it vividly but what did that have to do with anything?

"That wasn't the first time." He licked his lips, still watching me with that guarded expression. "I was the one who took Tessa to see you...at the hospital."

"Oh." *Oh. My. God.* I pulled my hand away.

He saw me while I was in the hospital? While I was sedated and blitzed out of my mind, ranting and raving about vampire attacks and who knows what else? How could I not remember this? How could I not remember *him*?

I felt naked, overexposed. "How many times did you...?"

"A few."

"Can you be a little more specific?" I could feel my ears buzzing with heat though I wasn't sure if it was from embarrassment or my mounting anger. "Did I speak to you? I mean, did I even know you were there or were you just observing me from a distance like some kind of caged animal at the zoo?"

"Jemma." My name passed softly through his lips as he tried to reach for my hand again, but I pulled it away. "It isn't what you think."

"You don't *know* what I think." I jumped up to my feet, overcome by the urge to move around. To jog. To run away. "How could you not tell me about this?"

"Because I thought you knew." He was in front of me before I could blink, rerouting all my attention back to him. "Look, I'm sorry you don't remember but it's not like any of this was a secret. I took Tess to see you because she asked me to. And yeah, I saw you a couple of times, because I was there with her," he added, his voice calm and sensible. "I wasn't peeping through your window or hiding under your bed."

Okay, fine, so he kind of had a point. I suppose it wasn't his fault I didn't remember or was too drugged to know the difference. And here I was thinking I'd gotten a fresh start in a new town where no one knew anything about me. He knew me. He knew from the moment I laid eyes on him that day in History class. He knew me even before then.

Maybe that was the pull I felt for him. Maybe my subconscious self remembered him all along and was just waiting for the rest of me to catch up.

And then something painful occurred to me. "Is that the reason you wanted to stay away from me?" I sat down on the edge of his bed and looked up at him, petrified to my core of what he would say next.

"Jemma." He shook his head, a silent plea for me not to go there. The fear in his eyes alone made it impossible for me to refrain. I had to pry deeper. I needed to know the truth.

"That's it, isn't it? That's the reason you wanted to stay away from me, isn't it? Because I'm a total head case, right? Whatever, it's totally fine, Trace. I just wish you would have told me the truth from the beginning. I would have understood. I would have accepted it." While my words were full of certainty and courage, my eyes were stinging with tears I knew he could see. How idiotic I must have looked.

He let out an angry curse as he pushed both hands through his hair and sat down beside me. "I never *wanted* to stay away from you," he said, closing his eyes as though the weight of his words—of his secrets—were too much for him to bear. His thick dark lashes fanned over his eyes like a shield, distracting me with their splendor. "You don't know what you've done to me, Jemma. What you *do* to me."

My insides knotted as his weary eyes met mine.

"From the first time I saw you, all I wanted to do was be near you. To get as close to you as I possibly could."

Suddenly, I was very aware of our proximity—of how close we were sitting. And the bed we were sitting on. And the way his knee was pressed up next to mine. And my breathing. Oh God, my breathing.

"I've always wanted you, Jemma." His deep voice thrummed through my body and sent a delicious tingle down my arms. "In spite of everything, I wanted you."

"Well you had a funny way of showing it," I murmured, breathless and dizzy from his confession. A confession that I had secretly longed to hear since the day I met him.

"I don't want to stay away from you anymore. I'm tired of fighting it." His fingers brushed against my cheek softly, feeling my skin, testing my response. "I don't want to live in the past anymore, and I'm sick of worrying about the future. None of it is worth it if I can't have this." There was something hidden in his words. Something he wasn't saying, or was saying, but I couldn't concentrate when he looked at my lips that way. Like he wanted to taste them.

He leaned in closer—close enough that I could feel his warm breath feather across my lips. "And you want to know something else?"

I nodded, barely able to focus through the haze that had infiltrated my mind.

His mouth moved to my ear, drowning me in his heat. "I know you feel the same way about me."

My breath hitched.

"I know you're going to *love* me someday."

My inclination was to deny it and pull away from him but my body wasn't having any part of it. I swayed towards him like a wanderer to its Northern Star, feeling lost and found all in the same breath. Every cell in my being was electrified under his touch, craving him like the analeptic I never knew I needed.

His lips grazed a track along my jawline as his hands weaved their way into the crux of my hair. Grasping the nape of my neck, he guided me to him, pulling me in until our noses touched, until our breath was mixing together in a tonic of heated euphoria. So close and yet I wanted to be closer still.

"Trace..."

His lips brushed against mine in response and I nearly toppled over from the brief contact.

My hands rushed up for support, gripping his arms as I tried to steady myself from the hint of a kiss I was now starving for. A flood of emotions scrolled through his eyes, ensnaring me in their mystery until I could take no more. There was no more denying what I wanted...what I needed.

Kiss me.

His lips crashed down onto mine in a heated rush and I welcomed them, basking in the slow burning charge. My hands moved again, reaching higher this time, wrapping themselves around the back of his neck and clutching. Pulling. Fisting themselves in his hair and then moving down the cambers of his shoulders. A low growl escaped the back of his throat as his kisses grew more urgent, each one stirring me with their velvety caress. Every fiber of my being wanted this—wanted him, and it charged me to know he felt the same way.

His hands slid down over my curves, gripping my waist and pushing me further back onto his bed before his mouth found mine again. We collapsed together, our bodies adhered to each other in a way that would have you believe we were born this way. That we were always meant to be this way. He hovered over me like a dazzling apparition, the manifestation of my past, present, and future all wrapped up in one divinely sculpted Adonis. And I, evermore his willing worshiper.

He deepened the kiss, parting my lips as he touched his

tongue to mine. Fireworks ignited all around me, inside me, crackling on the surface of my skin like a live wire. I clutched onto him harder, savoring the sweet taste of his mouth and the feel of his full lips against my own. I never knew lips could feel this good—could taste this good. I couldn't get enough of them. Of him. I was consumed, hypnotized in every sense of the word.

I could stay like this forever.

"So could I," he whispered back huskily.

He brushed his lips against mine and pulled back, propping himself up on his elbow above me.

"Why are we stopping?" I asked, still trying to catch my breath as I stared up at his perfectly shaped mouth, voracious for more of its elixir. "What's wrong?"

"Nothing's wrong," he smiled, his dimples igniting on either side as he looked down at me in a novel way—a tender way. "I just want to look at you for a minute," he murmured, his finger tracing a line over the bridge of my nose and down to my swollen lips.

Even after all this time, I still couldn't look at him without blushing, yet I couldn't bring myself to turn away from him either. I was a fiend, addicted to the way he looked at me. To the way he made me feel when he watched me with those glacial eyes. I could spend a lifetime under his spell and it would still never be enough. He was utterly and completely spellbinding.

"You more," he whispered and then dropped a soft kiss on the tip of my nose.

I couldn't help but smile at him. At his sweetness.

"I mean it," he said and then moved his jaw along my cheek, scorching me as he breathed in the scent of my hair. The look on his face was of pure ecstasy and it made me feel good knowing I did that to him. "I've never seen anything more beautiful. You make my heart do crazy things."

The butterflies began waltzing in my belly again, this time to the sweet melody of his words. Words that were meant for me.

I weaved my fingers into his hair and kissed him again, biting and teasing his lips until he gave in and came back down to me. Back to our seismic kisses that moved us through the span of ten thousand perfect lifetimes.

Minutes turned to hours, and hours ceased to exist altogether. It was heaven like this with Trace and I never wanted to come back down.

38. HOLLOW EVE

I woke up the next morning to another dull, overcast sky. A thin veil of fog hovered over the grounds like a ghastly parade of misplaced souls, each one waiting to have their day. Trace was already waiting outside for me by the time I came downstairs which lit up my uncle like the fourth of July. It was as though he had a vested interest in my friendship with Trace—kind of like the interest Trace's father had shown. There seemed to be something more to it. Something else going on. Whatever it was, it only further invoked my suspicions about the two of them and their strange meddling ways.

"Are you going to Spring Fling together?" asked my uncle as I laced up my converse sneakers at the front door. The fact that he knew the dance by name even though I hadn't mentioned it to him was unsettling.

"I don't think Trace is going."

"That's unfortunate."

Tell me about it, I thought. What I'd give to see him all gussied up in a nice suit.

"I take it you're still attending in spite of his absence?"

"Yeah. I'm going with some friends actually. It's no big deal."

Please let this be the end of it. I so did not want to have this conversation with my uncle right now. Or ever.

"I see," he nodded, tucking his newspaper under his arm as he interrogated me with his eyes. "Anyone I know?"

"The usual…Taylor, Carly, *Caleb*. Like I said, no big deal." I picked up my bag and smiled. "I better get going, I'm going to be late for school," I added, tossing my schoolbag over my shoulder and hurrying out the door before he had a chance to ask another question.

Trace's eyes stayed pinned on me as I walked around the car to the passenger side where he leaned over and opened the door for me. I climbed in and waved goodbye to my nosy uncle as we backed out of the driveway in silence.

In my rush to get ready on time and avoid my uncle's third degree this morning, I'd failed to prepare myself for the possibility that things might be weird between me and Trace after spending the better part of yesterday performing mouth to mouth resuscitations on each other. We hadn't exactly discussed what any of it meant for us or how things might change.

Even after Gabriel picked me up and took me back home— back to reality—I still hadn't had a chance to process any of the potential repercussions. I already had too much on my mind, like my father and how I was going to save him, Tessa and Gabriel and the impending duel they would soon be facing, and Dominic and his obscure threats that I knew not to take lightly. There was so much to worry about and all I wanted to do was shut it all off and have one night of peaceful rest.

Of course, Gabriel wasn't any help in that regard; he was the embodiment of apprehension. He'd spent the entire night on my balcony, pacing and keeping watch like an armed prison guard ready to shoot anyone who dared cross the boundary. As much as I appreciated him being here, his presence was more of a reminder that I wasn't safe. That trouble was on the horizon.

No matter how I tried to spin it, that feeling of imminent doom still wafted in my abdomen like a virus unwilling to retract its claws. Engel, Dominic, and even Nikki; they were all a part of my interminable affliction. The question was, which one of them would be my end?

"I spoke with Gabriel this morning," said Trace matter-of-factly as we turned onto the main throughway. Plumes of ground fog drifted alongside us like our own personal escorts. "He said everything went okay last night."

"Yeah."

He waited for me to elaborate.

"I woke up *alive* so...victory, right?" I shook my head at my own comment. Why did I say such idiotic things when I was nervous? Mouth filter. Get one. Seriously.

"Right." He paused momentarily, his eyes watching me with great interest. "I guess it beats waking up dead."

"I'd say so." I sunk deeper in my seat.

"Right."

Clearly we'd left planet earth and entered some kind of weird morning-after-the-kiss dimension.

"Jemma—" My phone beeped, interrupting him.

"Sorry," I said, glancing down to read the message. It was a text from Caleb:

Morning, beautiful. What color is your dress? I'm picking up your corsage today.

"Crap."

"What's wrong?" asked Trace, his soulful eyes trailing from me to my phone.

"I don't have a dress for the dance." I pressed out an awkward smile. "I was supposed to go shopping with Taylor yesterday, but I...got *distracted*." With his mouth, that is. I glanced out the passenger window to hide the fact that my cheeks were picking up color.

"What about that potato sack idea?"

I turned back to him, smiling. "If I don't figure something out soon, it might have to come to that."

"Or you can always just skip the dance," he offered, though it sounded a lot more like a plea than it did a suggestion. "Stay with me instead."

My heart fluttered and then took off into overdrive. "I can't. I have to go. I already told Caleb I would go with him. And I promised Taylor."

A stretch of silence passed between us before he spoke again. "Is that the only reason you want to go?" he asked, his jaw working overtime.

"What other reason would there be?"

"I could think of a couple."

"Such as?" I searched his face for clarity.

His jaw muscles were still pumping hard.

"Whatever it is you need to say, I wish you'd just come out and say it."

He didn't miss a beat. "Do you like him?"

"Caleb?"

"Yeah, Caleb," he replied in a tone that bore a striking resemblance to jealousy. It was obvious the question had been eating at him for some time now.

"No, I don't like him." I answered easily because it was the truth. "Not in that way." *I like you*, I wanted to say, but I didn't have the courage to say it out loud.

His dimples pressed in content, though they vanished just as soon as Caleb's next message chimed in. We rode the rest of the way in silence with him staring out at the road, and me wishing I could grow any semblance of a backbone.

The dark silhouette of Weston Academy towered over us as we pulled into the student parking lot. There was only a few minutes to spare before the bell, evidenced by half the student body making a unified dash for the doors. I knew I should have been running right along with them—caring like they did, but I just couldn't seem to make my legs get on board.

"Thanks for the ride," I said as we walked towards the side entrance together.

He tipped his head in response.

My attention shifted briefly to a dark raven calling out in the distance. I watched as it rose up over the building and then disappeared behind a hem of evergreens.

"So how are we going to do this whole chaperoning thing?" I wondered, hanging back at the door. It wasn't quite the question I wanted to ask him, but it was a start. "Are we just walking in there together like it's nothing?"

"It *is* nothing. I'm a friend walking another friend to her class." His detached tone struck a sour chord with me.

"Right." I stepped out of the way as a straggling mob of juniors shuffled past us.

Trace stepped back with me, closing the gap between us. "That's not how I meant it."

"Then how did you mean it?"

"As far as everyone else is concerned, I'm just a friend walking a friend to class."

I looked up at him, instantly melting in the fervor that were his eyes. "And as far as we're concerned?"

"As far as we're concerned...I'm something more," he said carefully, testing out the words. "If you want me to be."

"I do." I flushed at how fast the words sped out of me.

A small smile formed on his perfect lips, and suddenly, all I could think about was how good his mouth felt against mine yesterday, and how natural kissing him had been. Like we were put on this earth for the sole purpose of kissing each other.

I was so caught up in his lips that I completely missed the

words that were coming out of them. I looked up at him and found him waiting for an answer to a question I hadn't heard.

"Huh?" I shook my head dimly.

His smile deepened, setting off his perfect dimples as his gaze traveled over my shoulder, gauging our surroundings—probably looking for witnesses. When his eyes met mine again, he didn't bother repeating the question. Instead, he slinked his arm around my waist and pulled me into him possessively.

"What are you...?"

My voice dropped off as his lips connected with mine, setting off a familiar blast of want that tore through my body like an inferno and weakened my knees like a malady. He kissed me with passion, with hunger, and I returned the gift two-fold, burying my hands into his hair and pulling him in even closer than he was.

The side door clicked open, startling our lips apart. Without forethought, I slammed my hands into his chest and pushed, sending him sailing a good two feet away.

"There you are!" squealed Taylor. She stepped out from behind the door and joined us in an awkward triangle. "What's going on? Why are you guys out here?" Her eyes sparkled as she reached her own conclusion. "Ooh! Are we ditching?"

I exhaled a sigh of relief. She hadn't seen anything.

"We were just about to go in," said Trace, licking his lips in a slow and deliberate manner.

It completely threw me off.

"You're lucky you don't have Gillman. He would have nailed you both to the cross. It's like he gets off on ruining our lives. And F-Y-I," she said, swinging her attention to me, "I have the perfect dress picked out for you for the dance."

"You picked out a dress for me?" I couldn't help but smile at her.

"No, I picked out the *perfect* dress for you," she grinned, placing a hand on her hip. "You didn't leave me much choice since you bailed on our shopping date. You really need to get your priorities straight, you know that?"

If only she knew, I thought, as I pulled her into a hug. "Thanks, Tay. I owe you."

"Anything for my *bestie*."

My warm fuzzy feelings were quickly extinguished when Nikki appeared at the door. Her hair was twisted up in a messy bun and she had a pencil sticking out of it as though she were some model student, ready to solve math problems on demand.

She greeted us with a sneer. "I hate to break up this little special-needs party, but Mr. Bradley wants you to get your raggedy butts to class a-sap," announced Nikki, obviously pleased with her paraphrasing skills. "That is, if you're done groping each other."

"Ha. Ha." Taylor rolled her eyes at her and headed inside. Trace followed close behind with me on the tail end.

Nikki reached out and grabbed my arm, holding me back.

"I may have underestimated you," she whispered, only loud enough for the two of us to hear. "But I won't make that mistake again."

She let go of my arm and walked away, leaving me standing outside alone with no inkling about what she was referring to. Trace reappeared, holding open the door for me.

"You coming?" he asked.

I nodded, glancing up at the mammoth building as I made my way over to him, noting the long row of windows on the top floor where our History class was. A class in which I had a perfect view of. A thick block of ice formed in the pit of my belly as realization set in.

She'd seen us.

39. THE DANCE

Spring Fling arrived with little more than a whimper. At least it did for me. I couldn't get a hold of Tessa, which wasn't altogether that unusual under normal circumstances, but with everything we were facing, it only served as fuel for my already out-of-control anxiety. How was I supposed to get excited about the dance when the people I loved most in the world were in danger? How could I not panic when I knew our lives were hanging in the balance? That *any* day could be *the* day?

Stop it! Tessa's fine—everything's fine, I told myself as I dialed her number again. But with every ring that went unanswered, the apprehension gnawed deeper at my insides.

"Would you please hang up the phone and try on your dress?" nagged Taylor, oblivious to it all. She was standing in front of my vanity mirror, holding the dress she picked out for me; a stunning red gown with a sweetheart neckline and mermaid skirt.

It really was the *perfect* dress.

I held up my "just a minute" finger and waited for the phone to go to voice mail before giving in to her badgering. It's not like I had any more wiggle room. We had less than fifteen minutes before the limo arrived to pick us up.

Lucky for me, my hair and makeup were already done courtesy of Taylor who had booked the two of us an after-school appointment at a swanky salon just off of Main Street. It was the first time I had my makeup done professionally, and even though I felt like a cake getting a layer of icing applied to my face, I had to admit, the finished result was pretty nice.

"This dress is going to look killer with that Smokey Eye," said Taylor as she helped me step into the dress and then zipped up the back for me. "And red's his favorite color, too."

I turned to the mirror to catch a glimpse of the finished product. "Wow, look at us, Tay."

We were a sight to be seen. My curve-hugging red dress, her flowing royal-blue one; my smoldering makeup, hers shimmering.

"We're freaking goddesses," smiled Taylor, and for faintest of seconds, I actually felt like one.

Gabriel arrived several minutes ahead of the limo that Caleb and Carly's dad had arranged for us. I was beyond surprised to see Trace with him, looking devastatingly handsome in a black and white tux. So handsome in fact that I almost didn't notice Gabriel's lack of formal attire. *Almost.*

"What's going on?" I asked as the two of them simultaneously took me in from top to bottom and then back up again.

"Wow," said Trace, his eyes filled with hunger.

Gabriel cleared his throat. "Trace is stepping in tonight," he informed. "I'm tracking."

I could feel the excitement bubbling inside me at the prospect of spending the evening with Trace. The sentiment, however, was short lived as suspicion set in. "Why tonight?" I wondered, peeling my eyes away from Trace who was starting a fire in me with just his stare. "You're not planning anything, are you? You'd tell me if something was going down, right? I have the right to know, Gabriel. I'm in this—"

"Nothing is going on. It's simply a good opportunity. You'll be safe amongst friends and faculty, and with Trace," he added, nodding over to him. There was no falter in his words.

I had no reason to doubt him.

"Okay," I agreed, feeling the turn of events had finally swayed in my favor. I smiled over at Trace and then said my goodbyes to Gabriel as the Limo pulled up to the house.

Spring Fling was being held in a ritzy Hotel Ballroom on the outer edge of Hollow Hills. Strobe lights crisscrossed each other high in the sky as rows of limousines and other overpriced cars made their way up to the entrance. Weston Academy's finest were out in droves, decked out in lavish gowns and expensive tuxedo's that cost more than most people made in a month.

The air was thick with fog and the moon hung low above us, oversized and blurring at the edges with the haze that covered this town like a dirty secret. Somehow it felt right. Like I belonged here amongst the torrid chaos and fog. Like this was exactly where I was always meant to be.

"Trace! Over here!" squealed a familiar voice as we made our way inside the lavish ballroom. Nikki stood at the center of her two minions wearing a gold sequin dress, with matching stiletto shoes. It killed me to admit it but she looked great.

Trace walked over to greet her as the rest of us moved to find our table at the far end of the dance floor. Caleb, who looked quite handsome in his black tuxedo jacket, moved ahead of me and pulled out my chair before taking the seat beside me.

"You look great," he said, tipping into me. "I didn't get a chance to tell you earlier with everyone around."

"Thank you," I smiled and took a sip from my water glass as

I glanced around the ballroom, taking it all in.

The room hummed under the soft purple light, its gilded ceilings crowned in decadent crystal chandeliers that sparkled brilliantly above us. Everything was draped in white, right down to the white peony centerpieces and floor-to-ceiling curtains.

"Care to dance?"

I glanced out at the barren dance floor that took up nearly half the ballroom and cringed. "No one's dancing."

"We can easily fix that," he smiled.

"Maybe later, but thanks." The last thing I wanted was a room full of eyes on us. Besides, I was here with him for a reason: to find out what's going on between him and Nikki.

Trace pulled out the empty chair on the other side of me and sat down. To my dismay, Nikki quickly followed, filling up the seat next to him as though she were his date.

Come to think of it, maybe she was. Maybe they decided to go together at the last minute. As friends. *Or friends with benefits*. The thought of it made me queasy.

Taylor and Carly sat down beside Caleb accompanied by their dates, senior twin brothers Aiden and Finn Gallagher, with Ben and his date taking up the remaining two chairs. Morgan and Hannah were at another table with their own dates. Frankly, I was surprised they were allowed to leave Nikki's side at all.

"Do you want something from the bar?" asked Caleb. "A Coke or something?"

"A coke would be great."

"I'll come with you," sang Nikki as she stood up from her chair and adjusted her dress. "I need to powder my nose."

"Sure thing," smiled Caleb. He offered his arm and the two of them strolled off across the dance floor.

I watched with suspicion as Nikki leaned into him and whispered something private in his ear. Caleb nodded in return, never missing a step as they continued on side by side.

"What's up with those two?" I asked, turning to Trace.

His eyes and attention were both fixed on me. "What two?"

"Nikki and Caleb."

He shrugged unaffected.

"Doesn't it bother you that your date just walked off with another guy?" I was trying to get to the bottom of this whole Nikki and Caleb thing—not to mention this whole Nikki and Trace thing. You know, two birds, one stone.

"No, it doesn't," he said calmly. "And she's not my date." He paused for a minute and then leaned in closer. "Does it bother *you* that *your* date just walked off with another girl?"

"I can't say that it does," I answered honestly, smiling as my eyes lifted to meet his. "I'm pretty content right where I am."

"I'm pretty content with where you are too."

I gave him a playful shove but he caught my hand mid-air and held it, lacing our fingers together as though we were each other's missing piece. My skin hummed under his touch.

"People can see us," I reminded him, despite myself.

"Let them." His dimples graced me with their presence as his eyes glided over me, taking in the sights. "I've already used up all the restraint I had sixty seconds after you opened the door."

His confession lit up my insides like a fireworks show.

"Do you think your date would mind if I stole a dance?"

"You know him better than I do."

He stared ahead as if to ponder the question and then leaned into me again. "I'm pretty sure he would."

"That's too bad," I said, disappointed.

"Only for him," he smiled and then rose from his chair, offering his hand.

40. CENTER STAGE

The soft amethyst lights danced over Trace's form—playing with the blue in his eyes, the contours of his face—solidifying the fact that he was an angelic being, in every way. He stood facing me in the middle of the empty dance floor, taking me in as though I were made entirely of magic.

"Can I have this dance?" he asked, pulling me into him until we were standing heart to heart.

I wanted to tell him he could. That he could have *this* dance and *all* the dances after that, but all I could muster up was a meager nod. He smiled down at me in a tender way and then began moving, swaying us to the sound of the music as the crowd in the room slowly melted away. It was just me and him again—Jemma and Trace. Just the way I liked it.

"I have a secret to tell you," he announced, his warm breath tickling my ear as I pulled in his spellbinding scent.

"Is it bad?"

"Depends who you ask, I guess."

"Tell me."

A bashful look of want swept across his face, endearing and charming all at the same time. "I think I'm falling in love with you."

I stared up at him dumfounded.

"No. That's not right." He shook his head. "I *know* I am."

There was a tsunami of emotion washing through me, every wave threatening to pull me under. I didn't know what to say, what to do. "I-I..."

"You don't have to say anything. I just want you to know how I feel." He needled me with his eyes again. "No matter what happens, always remember that."

A heaviness pressed in on me. "Why do I suddenly feel like you're saying goodbye?"

"I'm not saying goodbye," he said, though it lacked conviction. "I'll never say goodbye to you."

There was a light tap on my shoulder and then a voice. "Mind if I cut in?"

I turned to see Hannah standing behind me with a lopsided grin on her lips. I couldn't decide whether this was the worst possible timing or the best.

"Oh, um, okay. Yeah. I guess so," I said reluctantly, stepping back from Trace.

"Jemma." Trace tried to hold onto my hand.

"Find me later," I said, pulling my hand free. I needed a minute to get my thoughts together, to process what he had said.

I hurried off to the ladies room, leaving Trace and Hannah behind on the dance-floor.

I hardly recognized the girl reflecting back to me in the mirror. The hair, the makeup, the ball gown; it was all so beautiful, so glamorous, and yet inside I felt the same. Scared. Confused. Unsure of myself and everything around me. I turned on the faucet and cupped my hands under the running water. I wanted to splash my cheeks with it; to drown in it; to wash this foreign girl away from my sight.

If only it were that easy, I thought, letting the water pour out from my hands before turning off the faucet.

"Speaking of the little she-devil," said an irritatingly familiar voice as I reached for the paper towel to dry my hands. "Here she is now."

Nikki and Morgan were standing by the door gawking at me, bony shoulder to bony shoulder. Even though Morgan was a good three inches shorter than Nikki, her five inch heels gave her the edge she needed to make the cut.

Wanting to avoid yet another confrontation with them, I tried to bolt for the door but Nikki had already locked it behind her and was walking over to me, slow and steady, like a hungry snake on the hunt.

"What exactly do you think you're doing out there?" she asked, venom oozing from her accusatory words.

"Can you be more specific?" My patience with her was wearing thin.

"With Trace. I saw you."

"So?" Trace had made it clear that there was nothing between the two of them. Her days of claiming him were over.

"Are you trying to kill him or are you really that dumb?"

"What the hell are you talking about?"

"Don't act like you don't know."

"I'm not acting," I snapped back. "I have no idea what you're talking about."

"She doesn't know," said Morgan suddenly. It was more than just giving me the benefit of the doubt. She *knew* it, sure as fact. "He hasn't told her."

"What is he thinking?"

"You know what he's thinking," answered Morgan, regretful.

Nikki's eyes snapped back to me as if she were just seeing me—really seeing me—for the first time. The way she stared at me startled me. For the first time since I met her, her hard, icy facade had faltered. There was something else in her eyes. Fear, pain, worry? I couldn't quite pinpoint it but it was making me uneasy.

"I won't let his happen," she said, a vow of truth that only she understood. "If he won't stop it, *I* will."

"Stop *what*? Can someone please tell me what's going on?" I said, my words crackling as they surfaced.

"Morgan, tell her what you saw."

"I can't," said Morgan as she turned to fluff her red curls in the mirror beside us. "It's not my future to share."

"I swear to the heavens," snapped Nikki, her fists balled up at her sides. "If you don't tell her right now I will tear this building down, brick by goddamn brick!"

The bathroom lights flickered violently as she spoke. It was almost like her emotions—her fear, or rage, or whatever it was going on inside of her—were manifesting themselves in the electricity around us.

"TELL HER!"

"Alright, alright, just calm down!" shrieked Morgan, pulling her back a step. "You're gonna to fry us all, for God's sake."

"I have perfect control over my ability," retorted Nikki.

"So you say," scoffed Morgan, "but I happen to remember a backyard bonfire incident that—"

"Can both of you just shut up and tell me what's going on?" I said, breaking up their little tiff. "What did you see?"

Morgan shook her head, a subconscious gesture that instantly told me it was going to be bad.

"Look, I didn't ask for any of this. It's not like I have control over what I get to see. Sometimes it's good, sometimes it's bad, but it's not like I can do anything about it."

"I understand," I nodded, digging deep for patience.

"I promised him I wouldn't share what I saw with anyone,

but I don't know what else to do, you know? He's my friend, too, and what he's doing is just plain wrong. I can't stand by and watch him throw his life away. I have to believe that I had the vision for a reason, to like, save him."

"Save him from what? What was the vision?" It came out loud and frantic, like a child lost in the woods, calling out for its parents. I hardly identified the sound as my own.

"Oh, for crying out loud," said Nikki, shoving Morgan out of her way. "He's going to get himself killed! For *you*—because of *you*—to save *you*! Do you understand what I'm saying?"

"You're lying!" My immediate instinct was to reject it. To reject these foul words that were nothing more than the desperate attempts of a desperate girl trying to hold on to a guy that no longer loved her.

"I'm not lying," she said, her expression overcome with despair. "I wish to God that I was."

I shook my head hard as though trying to shake the conversation loose from my mind.

"Just ask him. He'll tell you the truth if you ask him." Water pooled in her aquamarine eyes.

The veracity hit me like a gunshot, making me feel sick to my stomach. She wasn't lying. Every cell in my body knew it. She was telling the truth and she was petrified to her core of it.

Trace was going to die.

Because of me.

41. PARTY CRASHER

It took me a while to get myself together enough to leave the washroom. Trace was waiting for me outside the door when I walked out behind Nikki and Morgan. The concern in his eyes only made it harder for me to look at him. To face him. I was angry with him for not telling me the truth about the vision—the real reason he had been keeping his distance from me when I first moved here. He knew getting close to me would eventually kill him and he did it anyway. My anger ebbed as a flood of other emotions cannonballed through me.

"Are you okay?" he asked me as the three of us circled around him. His hand came out towards me, a sympathetic gesture, but I twisted away from his reach.

"I'm fine." I couldn't find the warmth in my voice anymore. I was already building a wall around myself, laying out the bricks in a frenzy, only this time, it wasn't to protect myself from the outside. It was to keep the outside—to keep Trace—from getting in.

Morgan stepped into Trace's line of vision. "Can I talk to you for a minute?"

He tried looking around her. "Jemma—"

"It's important," she pushed.

With his shoulders back, he nodded and then followed her over to the main bar that was already swarming with students and faculty alike. His eyes grazed over me as she spoke to him, letting me know I was the topic of their discussion. I wondered if she was alerting him to the fact that I knew the truth. That I finally knew his secret. I couldn't help but wonder what he was thinking at that very moment. Would he be willing to accept the inevitable heartbreak that would come when I told him I could no longer see him?

"You need to stop this thing with him before it's too late," said Nikki, watching Trace from a distance like an implacable lioness stalking her prey.

"How am I supposed to do that?" I could feel a heavy thickness settling into the back of my throat. "What am I supposed to say to him?"

"Figure it out, or I'll figure it out for you." Her words were meant as a threat and she wasn't even trying to hide it. "I won't let him die, not for anyone, and certainly not for *you*. You're not even worth the gum under his shoes."

"And you are?" I shot back, angered by her constant barrage of biting comments.

"I guess we'll just have to wait and see," she answered, her tone a sadistic song of secrecy.

God, I hated that tone. I hated everything about her.

She turned on her heel and started off towards Morgan and Trace but paused suddenly, mid-strut. "Oh. I almost forgot," she said, spinning behind an umbrella of long, ebony locks. "Taylor's outside looking for you. It sounded important."

"Okay." She totally didn't have to relay that message to me. Maybe she was turning over a new leaf. "Thank you."

Her lips curled up on one side. "You're so very unwelcome."

Okay then. Maybe not.

I made my way to the front of the Hotel and exited through the double glass doors. I spotted Taylor right away; under the veranda, chatting privately with Hannah and a senior guy whose name I couldn't remember.

"Hey, is everything okay?" I asked Taylor as I approached the three of them. "Nikki said you were looking for me."

"Walk with me?" There was something odd about her tone though I couldn't quite put my finger on it. It definitely lacked that distinct bubbly pitch that was all Taylor.

I examined her face as the two of us made our way down the pathway towards the parking lot. Her expression was vague and unreadable, hollow even. "Is everything okay?" I repeated, feeling the chill in my bones deepen.

"I've never felt better."

"Are you sure? You seem a little...off." There was no nice way of putting it.

"I just don't want you to be upset with me."

"Why would I be upset?" I tried slowing her down but she squirmed out of my grip. "Tay, talk to me."

"He's waiting for me. I can't be late."

"Who's waiting for you? Your date?" I couldn't remember her date's name for the life of me, and I felt horrible about it. Shows what kind of friend I've been lately.

"No, not him."

"Then who?" My insides gnawed at me, begging me to turn around. Something wasn't right. I could feel it, and her failure to respond was only making the feeling worse. "We should go back. We're missing the party," I reminded her, as though I actually cared about the stupid dance.

"It doesn't matter. I *have* to meet him."

I flinched at her aberrant disregard of something she had raved about incessantly for the last few weeks. The dance mattered—it mattered to *her*, and up until a few minutes ago, it was the only thing that mattered to her.

"I'm going back inside, I don't feel good," I baited, hoping my announcement would sway her from going forward. "Can you come with me? I need to get some water and sit down for a bit. I'm sure your friend won't mind if you meet him a little later." Once I've had time to gather plenty of reinforcements and figure out what the hell was wrong with her.

"I have to see him. He's waiting for me." She marched on without even so much as a glance in my direction. This wasn't Taylor. Not *my* Taylor. It was as though some alien had invaded her body and taken over her mind.

Before I could say another word (or drag her back inside by her hair) she came to a sudden stop between two parked limousines. Maybe she'd finally came to her senses, I hoped, though her failure to turn around wasn't very reassuring.

"Okay, so...what are we doing exactly?" I glanced around the empty parking lot and waited for her to say something that would explain her odd behavior. When she didn't, I leaned in and waved my hand in front of her face in a bid to get her attention. "Hello? Is anyone home?"

The limousine door suddenly sprung open. Startled, I jumped back and then gasped as Dominic slithered out from the back of the glossy black car. He was wearing a tailored suit and a condescending grin that told me in no uncertain terms that he was behind this somehow. His skin seemed to glow under the frosted moon, casting an angelic reverence over him, though I knew there was nothing holy about him.

"You look exquisite, angel." He took a step towards me but I quickly moved back. He didn't even acknowledge Taylor's presence even though she didn't break eye contact with him once.

"What are you doing here?" I didn't give him a chance to

answer. "We're leaving. Taylor, come on!" I tried tugging on her arm but she refused to budge. It was as though she were under some kind of spell. "What did you do to her?" I accused.

"I can't help it if she desires my company."

"Like hell she does."

With his eyes still leveled on me, he raised his forearm to Taylor and flashed a wicked grin as she wrapped her hands around his bicep, latching onto him as though he were her life line.

"You're not going anywhere with her."

His smile deepened. "Oh, but I am. Of course, you're more than welcome to join us. I'd actually prefer it if you did."

I scoffed at his absurdity. "I'm not going anywhere with you." That much I knew for sure.

"Suit yourself." He ushered Taylor back to the limo and helped her inside before climbing in himself.

"Taylor! What are you doing?" I yelled over to her, frantic now. "Get out of the car. RIGHT NOW! You don't know what you're doing. He's dangerous—"

"You're wasting your breath, love." He knew it, and somewhere deep inside, I did too. He slammed the door shut and rolled down the window. "She won't be changing her mind about joining me. I promise you."

It was clear Taylor was under some kind of spell and was going, with or without me. She had no idea what she was doing, no control whatsoever. I couldn't let her leave with him knowing what he was. Knowing the kind of monster he could be. She was my best-friend and that meant everything to me.

Without giving myself any more time to think about it, I walked over to the car and pulled the door open. "Push over."

"Gladly." A twisted smile spread across his face letting me know this had been his plan all along. He slid over just enough so that our bodies would still be flesh up against each other.

"Where are we going?" I asked as I tried to carve more room for myself by way of my elbow.

"I have something special planned."

"I'm sure you do, you sick son of—"

"Ah, ah, ah, angel. You don't want that beautiful mouth of yours getting you into trouble again, now do you?" His hand came up as though he were going to caress my face.

"Don't you dare touch me!" I warned, twisting away from his reach.

Curls of fog wafted in and out of view as the limousine veered down the throughway in a hurry. I didn't know where we were going but I knew it wasn't anywhere good.

"I swear to God, if you hurt one hair on her head, I will make it my life's mission to kill you. *Slowly.*"

A quiet groan rumbled at the back of his throat. "I think I'm rather enjoying this new side of you. Very feisty." He was discernibly enthralled. "Of course, I've never been one to desire the damsels in distress. I've never quite understood their appeal."

"I don't give a damn what you desire!" I snapped, already angry and on edge. "I care about my friend and keeping her away from sickos like you, so just spare me the details."

His smile morphed into a full blown laugh. "I sure hope this one turns out to be worth it in the end."

"And what's that supposed to mean?"

His lips curled into a satisfied grin. "Well, you don't seem to have very good taste in companions, now do you? Perhaps a little too trusting with your heart?"

"Better than having no heart at all."

"That almost hurt," he smirked, shifting in his seat. "You'd be surprised how liberating it is to only care for yourself."

"How very progressive of you." I couldn't even fathom being that cold-hearted. That empty. "What about your family? Your friends? Don't any of them matter to you?"

"I pay them no mind therefore none of them matter."

"What a sad way to live."

"Not it the least. Consider the alternative—you yourself are a prime example," he said in a mocking tone. "How well has your heart served you thus far?"

I didn't answer. Even if I had a good enough response, I wouldn't share it with him. He didn't deserve it. I would never share another part of myself with him again.

"Your silence speaks volumes."

"So do your condescending assumptions." I picked up my vibrating phone and stole a quick glance at the text message from Gabriel:

We lost Engel. Dominic is missing. Get home ASAP.

A day late and a dollar short. Story of my life.

Dominic snatched my phone from my hands. "I guess we'll just have to see how far that heart of yours takes you—how much you can truly endure. I think you know as much as I do that this is only the beginning for you."

A sickened feeling flooded my insides.

All I wanted to do was get away from Dominic Huntington and all of his thinly veiled threats and manipulations. But I had no way to escape, and nowhere to run to. I was stuck here, at the mercy of whatever vile thing he had planned for me, and all I could do was continue to trudge forward *knowing* in the very pit of my soul that something horrible was about to come my way.

42. THE AWFUL TRUTH

The moonlight silvered the abandoned church, making it appear bigger than it was. From the limousine window, I noted the endless rows of boarded up windows peppering the front of the run-down structure as it cast its depraved shadow over us. It was a side of the Hollow Hills Cemetery I'd only heard of but never actually seen before, and didn't look particularly safe for human occupation.

"Shall we, ladies?"

Taylor exited the limousine without even batting an eyelash. She was completely out of her mind and it was hardly her fault, but that didn't stop me from wanting to wring her pretty little neck. And I totally intended to...if we ever got out of this thing alive.

"Come on, angel," said Dominic when I didn't move from my seat. "You know very well you aren't going to let her go off without you."

He was right. I was here for one reason; to protect Taylor from Dominic, and the only way I could do that was by ignoring every fiber in my body as it screamed for me to save myself and run. I climbed out of the limo, my fists balled up at my sides as I tried to resist the urge to attack him right then and there. What good would it do? He was stronger than me— faster. And I had Taylor to carry. Fighting him would prove futile. I needed another way. I needed to outsmart him somehow.

But first I needed to figure out what he had planned.

"So is this the part where you pretend to be all nice and *human* and then attack us when we least expect it?" I wanted to sound flippant, unafraid of what would come next. All the while, my hands were trembling and the air around me seemed to be thinning, making it harder and harder for me to fill my lungs.

"No, love. We already played that game." He turned to me with a smirk as we walked through the cemetery gates and trudged towards the old, condemned church. "I'm sure you remember it quite well," he said, holding the door open for us.

It was sickening the way he took pleasure in other people's pain. "You're depraved."

"Indeed, I am," he agreed easily. "And I have no qualms about it." He stopped in the middle of the room and glanced around as though searching for something he'd misplaced.

I shuddered as my eyes moved around the empty space. The altar and church pews were missing, and whatever else remained was either damaged by the rain or covered in black soot, the remnants of a fire that took out the church and half the surrounding cemetery decades ago. Through the shattered windows, I could see the leftover tombstones leering over at us like a corps of spectators, fog swirling around their feet, beckoning us to join them in their final dance.

I shuddered again as the hairs on my body stood tall. "All this because someone dusted your vampire plaything."

His face hardened. "Watch it, angel."

I perked up inside knowing I'd hit a nerve. "Well, it's true, isn't it? You're mad at the world because she's gone and there's nothing you can do about it, so you use that as an excuse to wreak havoc on everything and everyone around you."

Anger flooded his expression.

"It's pathetic if you ask me."

"No one asked you." The ice in his voice was unmistakable.

"No one ever does," I mumbled bitterly. Avoiding eye contact, I tightened my arms across my chest and rubbed them for warmth. "So what's your plan anyway? To lure my sister and Gabriel here so that you can annoy them with your revenge games?" I needed to keep pushing his buttons.

He clamped a hand around Taylor's wrist and began towing her away. She followed clumsily behind him.

"They aren't going to come," I baited, following him through the dank room. "They have better things to do than play your little high school games."

"Good." A dark grin spread over his face. "What I have planned neither requires them nor concerns them."

Okay, now I was confused. I thought this was about getting revenge on Tessa and Gabriel for vanquishing the Rev he loved. If it wasn't about that, then what the heck were we doing here?

He came to a stop in front of what looked like an old ministry room. The walls were slick with mold and the stain-glass windows were fogged with a thick veneer of ash and grime. "Do not leave this room," said Dominic as he shoved Taylor through the threshold and closed the door behind her.

"You're not leaving her in there!" I tried to get around him but he quickly put his arm out and blocked my path.

"Believe me, angel, she's far safer in there then she would be out here with us. Now walk," he ordered. "We have business to tend to."

I felt a cold rush zip down my spine but I knew he was right. At least she'd be out of his reach. And besides, with his mind control, she was a total liability at this point.

"Fine. Anywhere in particular?" I asked, working hard to keep the fear from showing up in my voice.

"Right there," he ticked his chin to a lone chair placed near the front of the room. "Sit."

"I don't *do* commands."

"And I don't do petulant children."

"Well, I don't do—"

"Sit. Down. Now."

I flopped down onto the chair with my arms crossed over my chest as I waited for him to make his big reveal.

The only way I could even begin to think of a way out of here was if I knew what I was doing here in the first place. Unfortunately, Dominic seemed intent on keeping a tight lid on everything and it was starting to get on my nerves.

"Any day now," I said when he didn't say anything.

Dominic dropped his hands on the armrests and leaned into me. "You have quite a mouth on you, angel. You ought to learn when to shut it as you're making it far too tempting for me to do it for you."

I swallowed hard, my bravado dissipating into dust.

"That's better," he said with a stony smile before straightening out. He looked down at me again; his eyes sharp as knives, expression hard and chiseled to the bone. "You truly are an infuriating creature."

I wanted to tell him the feeling was more than mutual but pressed my lips together instead, afraid of what else would come bubbling out if I didn't.

"As much as I long to purge you, I find myself equally desiring to possess you—to *break* you in and own you."

Purge me? Own me? My mind flatlined. I didn't know which part of that to process first.

"I may have underestimated the degree of distraction you

would pose," he went on, undaunted. "It's not something I'm prepared to deal with."

"What are you talking about? Are you threatening me?"

A crooked half-grin flashed. "It just means you should tread lightly."

"Or what?"

"You have something I want," he explained, ignoring my question as he walked around my chair with his hands crossed behind his back. "And I intend to have it."

"*Me*? I thought this was about Tessa and Gabriel?"

He laughed dryly. "Your first mistake was assuming you understood my motives. My reasons for returning here had nothing to do with my past paramours or my desire for revenge. Both pale in comparison to what I truly desire." His eyebrows ticked with a brand of arrogant mischief that was uniquely his.

"Then what is it you *desire*?" I was almost too afraid to ask, but I had to know.

"Power." He smiled at my confusion. "Which leads me to your second mistake."

"And that is?"

"Coming here."

The danger hit me like a freight train. With terror permeating inside me, I jumped up from my chair and tried to make a run for the door but he quickly snagged my waist and pulled me hard into his chest.

"Let me go!" I yelled as I fought to break free.

"Sit down, angel. We're not done," he said, pressing his mouth to my ear. "That is, unless you'd like me to mail you your friend's heart in a box tomorrow morning."

My stomach retched. God, what had I done? What had I gotten myself into?

"The Amulet, love." He spun me around and pushed me back into my chair. "You have it. And I want it."

"What Amulet? I don't know what you're talking about," I lied, doing my best to appear confused—innocent.

"I'm going to say it one more time, and then I'm going to bring your friend out here and drain a pint of her blood every time you answer incorrectly." His steely eyes were darker than night. "The Amulet. Now."

My heart pounded hard in my chest as I struggled to form a cohesive thought. I didn't know what to say—what to do. I knew he couldn't hurt me as long as I was wearing the necklace; my sister made sure of the fact. But what about Taylor? What would stop him from draining her to death?

"Dominic, please—"

"I warned you, angel." He was at the door within seconds, pulling Taylor out from her makeshift prison. He lugged her back to me by her arm, his expression unmoved—unflinching. In an instant, he was before me, crooking her head to the side. His long, pointed fangs piercing through his wicked grin.

"Hold it," shouted a familiar voice.

I turned to see Trace standing at the doorway still wearing his perfectly tailored tuxedo and a matching frown. He looked calm and in control as he strode over to us.

"Let her go."

"That's not going to happen, Romeo." Dominic seemed amused by the interruption, excited even. It was almost as though he preferred doing this in front of an audience. "I'm leaving here with the Amulet one way or another. This one's pulse, on the other hand, is optional."

"You're bluffing," baited Trace.

"Care to test that theory? I've already orchestrated two attacks. Albeit failed attacks." He narrowed his eyes accusingly to Trace. "I'm sure you remember. You were there."

It was Dominic all along. He was the one who sent the Rev and those demonic Runners after me. He was heartless; soulless.

He would take Taylor's life and wouldn't think twice of it, and Trace would be next. Morgan's premonition made that clear.

"You shouldn't have come here," I said, trying to hide the fear emanating from my voice. How could he be so stupid? How could he put his life at risk like this? It only brought him closer to destiny; closer to his gruesome end.

"I had to." His expression was one of powerless defeat. "I wouldn't be able to live with myself if he hurt you."

Dominic laughed, an evil grin curling across his lips. "You're a little late, Romeo. We've already sailed that boat weeks ago. Though, if my memory serves me right, there was a lot more pleasure involved than pain."

"What are you talking about?" Trace's eyes reduced to slits as realization set in. "You bit her? He bit you? When—" He didn't bother waiting for a confirmation. He charged into Dominic like a missile, knocking him off his feet and landing several paces back.

"Trace! Don't!"

I tried to stop him—tried to jolt him out of his rage-fueled onslaught, but it was too late. They were already entangled in a web of fists and hate-filled expletives. Trace was playing right into the vision and there was nothing I could do to stop him.

Fists pounded against bone, and flesh tore open, spewing blood all over the concrete floor like an exploding volcano. I scrambled forward, pulling Taylor out of the way as I screamed out Trace's name. But he couldn't hear me.

Or he was choosing not to.

He rammed into Dominic over and over again, like a bull shark with a taste for blood. Dominic absorbed each of Trace's hits with a grin. A sick, masochistic grin that made the bile in my stomach churn. I didn't know how much Dominic could withstand or the kind of damage he was capable of inflicting, and not knowing only pulled me deeper into my nightmare without end.

"Is that the best you can do?" laughed Dominic.

Trace's back stiffened. Fury and vengeance collided over his face and then exploded through his clenched fists. He hammered down onto Dominic harder, faster, his fists moving at the speed of light until Dominic's arrogant smile tapered into a line of nothingness.

Hope ignited in me as I watched Trace gain the upper hand, pinning Dominic under a torrent of front-knuckle punches.

The structure trembled with each of his hits, spitting out debris from the cracked ceiling above us like victory confetti.

"Get him, Trace! Rip his head off!" I hardly recognized the murderous scream as my own.

Dominic growled in response, a deep, unnatural roar that was neither animal nor human. His form suddenly began flickering, vibrating as a thick opaque blackness overtook his arms, legs, and face, making it impossible for Trace to land a hit. It was as though he were melting away or—

"Shit!" said Trace, jumping off Dominic.

"Oh my God!" My mouth fell open as the soldering picture became clear.

Dominic was morphing—*shifting* right before our bulging eyes. Within seconds, a black wolf-like creature emerged from the dark miasma. His eyes sharp as knives, his mouth a hostile snarl, baring his teeth like a promise of death.

Trace raised his hands to him, palms out and pleading. "Alright. Okay. Let's talk about this for a second."

Dominic pounced on Trace, clawing at his face as he took him down in a mess of blood and fur. Trace swung out at him wildly, but it was no use. They were the desperate hits of an overpowered man. Dominic was faster in this form. Stronger. *Deadlier.*

Jagged teeth and feral claws ripped at Trace's body and chest, tearing away at him as though he were made of sand. Blood poured from his wounds like water, pooling on the ground around him as his body snapped back and forth in unnatural ways.

"Stop it! You're killing him!" My deafening screams were futile. Morgan's vision was coming alive right before my eyes and I hated her even more for it.

"Run, Jemma!" Trace's voice came out choked and hoarse. "Get out of here!"

"I won't leave you here," I shouted back, tears spilling over my cheeks.

"Go...NOW!"

I had to do something. I couldn't let this happen. But what? What could *I* do? All I had was my partial training and some Protective necklace that was supposed to keep me—

That's it! *The Amulet.*

Without a second thought, I yanked the necklace from around my neck and closed my trembling hand around it. This was it. My one shot. I screamed out his name like a lovesick prayer, "Trace! Look up!"

As soon as our eyes connected, I drew my arm back and threw the necklace across the room at him. His hand punched up through the air and caught it.

Dominic, who had been crouched over him in his wolf-form, yelped out in pain and then shot backwards through the air; almost as though he'd been shocked by an electrical fence.

Or touched a magical barrier.

Dominic retreated into the corner, away from Trace and the Amulet, and then shifted back to his human self.

Yes! It worked!

Trace jumped to his feet, the necklace fitted securely in the palm of his hand. He was smiling to himself. A beautiful, victorious smile that ignited a fire inside my heart.

"Alright, Romeo, good job. Now hand it over to me," said Dominic, wiping the dust off his shirt.

Good job? I shook my head, certain I heard that wrong.

"Actually," said Trace, dimples blazing. "I think I'm going to hang on to it for a while."

Dominic quickly stepped to him but Trace moved back, seemingly one step ahead of him, in more ways than one.

"We had a deal," roared Dominic.

Trace laughed in response.

A *deal?* "What the hell is going on?" I shouted, even though it was painfully obvious. Trace was in on it.

"You don't want to play this game with me, boy," said Dominic as he pulled Taylor over to him like a human shield. "I'll rip both their heads off before you make it to the door." Flames of fury raged in Dominic's eyes as he watched Trace dangle the Amulet, taunting him with his victory.

"Knock yourself out," said Trace, backing away. "I got what I came here for and there's nothing you can do to stop me. I'm protected and we both know it." He turned his back on him— on *me*—and barreled off towards the exit.

What the hell was he doing? How could he do this to me? How could he just leave me here?

"Trace!" I heard myself cry out his name, a desperate last ditch effort to wake him up—to make him come to his senses and turn around. But it was all in vain.

He didn't even so much as offer a glance in my direction as he tossed my heart to the meat grinder and left the church with my Amulet in hand.

43. UNNATURAL BORN KILLER

Bitter tears of betrayal stung my eyes as the ugly truth nestled itself inside my soul. Trace had set me up. Everything we'd been through, everything he said to me...it was all a lie. It meant nothing to him. *I* meant nothing to him. He used me to get what he wanted and when he got it, he threw me to the wolf.

Through blurred vision, I looked up at Dominic. He was still holding Taylor by her neck, seemingly shocked by the sudden turn of events. God only knew what he would do to Taylor and me once the shock wore off. He would blame us for this, for all of it. Heck, we were the only ones around *to* blame.

Dominic's head twisted at the sound of my choked sob.

I shook my head at him as though attesting to my innocence—to the fact that I had nothing to do with this. As though silently begging him to have mercy on me.

His expression changed suddenly; faltered. For the faintest of seconds I thought I saw something *human* in his eyes. Something sympathetic. Maybe he wasn't all monster after all. Maybe there was still some feeling—some humanity—buried somewhere deep inside of him and he would let us go.

"How very pitiful of you."

"This isn't my fault," I quickly defended.

"I was referring to your choice in men. You certainly know how to pick them."

I felt the sting on my palm even before I registered what I'd done. I *hit* him. I hit Dominic Huntington right in the face.

I held my breath for what felt like an eternity as I waited for him to delve out the consequences for my massive misstep. But none came. He barely flinched nor did he say anything. My eyes moved to his hand still wrapped around Taylor's porcelain neck. I wondered if he was pressing down. If he was slowly strangling her to death. And then suddenly, as if responding to my thoughts, he released her from his grip.

"Go." His dark eyes bore into hers. "Forget everything that happened here tonight and go home."

Taylor turned on her heels and started off towards the door. I immediately tried to follow suit but Dominic snagged my wrist and pulled me back.

"Let me go, Dominic. Please, I'm begging you."

"Oh, I intend to," he said, his tone harsher now. "I have no desire to walk in the wake of the death and misfortune you leave behind." He stared down at me, watching me with his dark eyes as though trying to read me. "Utterly infuriating."

I shifted under his unrelenting stare, uncomfortable by our proximity. By his words. By the fact that I was alone with a soulless vampire who had no empathy or self-restraint.

He took a step towards me, surprising me. His hold on my arm tightened as he inched closer to me, moving as though he were going to kiss me. As though he were invited. The very thought of it sickened me, enraged me.

I shoved him back with both hands, freeing myself from his grip. He let out a sharp mocking laugh, showing me once again that this was all a game to him. *I* was a game.

But I would not be played any longer. Not by him. Not by

Trace. Not by anyone.

I reached around and grabbed the chair from behind me and smashed it to the ground in a fit of rage. My strength surprised both of us. I looked down at the scrambled pieces and without even making the decision, I reached down and snagged a piece of jagged wood from the wreckage. Long and pointed, just the way I needed it to be.

I looked up at him, makeshift wooden stake in my hand and lifted it into position.

"You won't do it," he said, so sure of himself and of me. "You don't have it in you, angel."

"Yes I do."

"You would have already done it." He took a step towards me, and then another, putting himself right in my line of fire.

A moment of deadened silence passed between us as we stared each other down in remnants of the old church. Me with the wooden stake in hand and him with that lopsided smirk that made my blood boil. I hated that smirk. I hated him. The world would be better off without Dominic Huntington existing in it.

So then why wasn't my arm moving? Why wasn't I doing the one thing I swore I'd do if I ever had the chance?

A bustle of men burst into the room, jolting me upright. Dominic snatched my elbow and pulled me to him, stepping in front of me as if to hide me, to protect me. I looked up at him baffled; one minute he's trying to kill me and the next minute he's protecting me? This man, this godforsaken thing, was not only depraved, he was obviously insane, too.

Let me handle this, said a balmy voice inside my mind. It wasn't my voice. It was a man's voice. Dominic's voice—familiar and sultry. Either he just spoke to me through my mind or I was going crazy…again.

"Dominic, my friend," said the leader of the pact. He was much smaller than the men that followed but there was something alarmingly unsettling about him. His long dark hair was slicked all the way back, accentuating his disproportionally large forehead. "I trust you have what we're looking for."

"There's been a slight problem, Engel."

Engel? The Engel? My eyes zeroed in on him.

This was the man that has been tormenting my sister for months, haunting her like a nightmare, and yet there didn't seem to be very much to him. In fact, he looked rather sickly— thin framed, pale skin—especially in comparison to the other men around him.

I took each of them in, assessing their strengths and weapons, and noticed the long blond locks amidst the group.

Taylor.

The tall, burly man standing behind Engel had her by her arm, holding her against her will. They must have grabbed her on their way in.

"A problem you say?" Engel's pale eyes glowered with supremacy.

"The Reaper has the Amulet," explained Dominic. There was a definite nervous pitch to his voice.

"Tsk, tsk." Engel shook his head in a scolding manner. "I'm disappointed in you, Dominic. You had *one* job."

"He had his own agenda. I didn't know—"

"And this one?" interrupted Engel, ticking his head at me (or what he could see of me as I cowered behind Dominic). "Why is she still alive?"

"We need her."

"She no longer holds the Amulet therefore no longer serves a purpose. You were told to dispose of her."

The massive knot in my stomach tightened as Engel moved in closer to me, his long fangs visible from behind his grimace.

"Don't come near me..." I meant for it to come off as a threat, a warning, but it came out like a pathetic plea.

He reached over and yanked me away from Dominic as though I were nothing more than an insignificant commodity.

"Ah, the blood of a Slayer," he said, sniffing the air around me like a rabid hound. "Truly an exhilarating aroma, though sadly, yours is quite faint."

I tried to pull away from him, writhing as best as I could, but it was no use. The frail looking little hobbit was shockingly strong. "Let me go you sick—"

His sharp teeth pierced through my neck before I could finish the words. I let out a faint scream though it quickly died in the back of my throat.

In an instant, his otherworldly venom was coursing through my veins, working hard to subdue me, to turn me into a useless bag of bones. Even in my mounting haze, I knew he wouldn't let me survive this. I knew I was on my own again, and I'd have to save myself. I just didn't know how I was going to do that.

Engel's men murmured in the background, their voices scrambled and distant. I tried to focus on what they were saying, tried to hear if they were planning on contributing to the dissolution of my existence, and then everything went quiet. Nothing but the deafening silence of a grave.

Is this it? Am I dead?

My pulse responded, pounding loud in my ears as my heart stopped and started in my chest. My eyes circled the room and found stillness. They were all standing motionless like wax figures; frozen in time—exactly like my first night at All Saints. Whatever had happened that night was happening again. Only this time, I didn't stop to question it.

In a fog of thinly veiled awareness, I twisted my body into Engel's, bringing myself as close to his paralyzed body as I could get. I tightened my grip on the stake and brought it to my side just as the room surged back to life. It took every drop of strength I had to trudge forward, to fight the mounting urge to succumb to the sweet poison and surrender all hope. He growled loud and ravenous as though I had offered myself up, and I responded by lifting the stake from my side and plunging it into the center of his cold undead heart.

Engel stammered back several steps, clutching at the stake in his chest as everyone in the room gasped in disbelief.

I waited for him to immobilize, to drop to the ground and cease to exist. But it never happened.

The seconds ticked by like molasses and with each one that passed, he remained very much moving and very much alive. All of which were not supposed to happen. It was painfully clear that something had gone horribly wrong.

"Boss?" asked a slender man from behind him.

"Well, I'll be damned," said Engel, eyes wide with amazement. "How peculiar."

Dammit, angel. "Only you would stake an ancient Rev and miss his heart," muttered Dominic as he stealthily pulled me back a step.

"Ah, but it appears she did not miss," replied Engel, looking down at his chest, stunned. "I can feel the wood burrowed in my heart, fiery and aching, yet here I stand."

"That isn't possible," scoffed Dominic.

"Indeed," agreed Engel as he wrapped both hands around the stake and pulled it out of his heart. "Yet here we are."

Audible gasps broke out behind him.

"Get her!" yelled one of his men.

Engel held his hand up, halting his herd of undead. A morbid curiosity filled his expression as he took me in. "Veni foras, genus."

"Huh?"

"What exactly are you, child?"

"I'm a g-girl...a Slayer," I stuttered.

"On the surface it appears that you are, yes, but your

blood..." he trailed off, wiping the corner of his mouth as he searched his mind. "It speaks of different origins. An Ancient I have not encountered for many centuries."

"An Ancient?" I flinched at the word. "I'm seventeen years old. There's nothing ancient about me."

His eyes thinned as he took that in. "Interesting."

"Why is that *interesting?*"

A cunning smile formed on his mouth, tugging at the corners like a dirty secret. He knew something—something about *me*—and by the looks of it, it was something big.

I stepped in closer. "Tell me what you know. Right now."

His expression darkened. "You stake me so callously yet you dare stand in my presence and make demands?"

"It was an accident—a knee jerk reaction," I lied.

"One that you will pay for with your life!" shouted the man holding Taylor hostage. Cheers broke out around him. They were out for blood. *My blood.*

Engel held up his hand once again to silence them. "It appears the crowd desires restitution."

I swallowed hard.

"Surely you didn't expect to leave here with your *life?*" he said, kneading his palm over his puncture wound.

"Well I didn't exactly think it through."

"Clearly," huffed Dominic.

I shot him a surly look. It was obvious he had no intention of helping me get out of this mess. Heck, he was probably enjoying every minute of my impending demise. I was in this alone and I had to think fast.

There was only one thing to do. I needed to make myself useful to him again. If he thought I was dispensable, he would dispose of me without question and I couldn't let that happen.

I turned back to Engel, my eyes forged in remorse. "I'm no good to you dead," I pointed out self-servingly. "I can make it up to you. I can make it worth your while."

"I'm listening."

"You came here for the Amulet, right? Well I know where it is. I can get it back for you." I knew I was making a deal with the devil but I was desperate. "That's what you want, isn't it?"

"It is," he nodded. "And to acquaint myself with you, of course."

"Why?" I flinched back, disturbed by this unfortunate turn of events. "I'm nothing. I'm just a girl."

"That is as far from the truth as one could get. A rare magical being is amongst us," he crowed, turning to the men behind him now. "One whose blood can cease death."

His men cheered in excitement.

"What makes you so certain it was because of her?" argued Dominic. "I've tasted her blood before. There was hardly anything exceptional about it."

Liar, I thought. I clearly remembered him blissfully staggering around like a complete drunk.

"I've dethroned more than my share of Slayers," said Engel, proud of his past conquests. "I know a Slayer's blood, and that, old friend, is not one."

"Then you know what she is?" asked Dominic.

He smiled secretively. "Time shall do the telling."

"So you're not even sure?" I jumped in, grasping at what little hope remained. "This could all be some random coincidence and have nothing to do with me *or* my blood. There's a million possibilities—"

"All of which I intend to explore."

"Okay. So—" *Wait.* A new level of panic hit me as I wondered how exactly he *intended* on doing that. "If I hold up my end of the deal and bring you the Amulet, I get to go free, right? You're not going to kidnap me and turn me into some magical lab rat, are you?"

"Do you take me for a savage?" he asked, insulted by my insinuations. "I hold no one against their will. My subjects come to *me*."

"So I have your word then?"

"Indeed, you have my word." He dusted off the shoulder of his sleek black jacket. "You will be free to go once I am in possession of the Amulet...if you so choose to do so."

As if I'd ever choose anything else, I thought to myself as a brief pang of relief kissed my insides. My curiosity over what he thought he knew about me—about what I was (and if it was related to the strange time freeze I kept experiencing)—paled in comparison to my desire to never see his face again.

"You have one fortnight to bring it to me."

"A fortnight?" I shook my head. "That's not enough time. I need to get close enough—"

"One fortnight is all you have."

"And if I can't do it?" I asked, already feeling defeated. "What happens if I fail?"

"Then I take matters into my own hands, though I assure you, it will be much better for this town and your schoolmates if you succeed. It has been a long time since the rivers ran red with blood. Let us keep it that way."

My eyes shifted to Taylor. She was a wreck. She hadn't said a word and was barely even moving. How much more of this could she take? I needed to get her home.

"Your comrade stays," said Engel, noticing the direction my eyes had taken. "As insurance, of course."

"But you said you don't keep anyone against their will!"

"I was speaking of higher beings, child. Those who cannot have their will manipulated. She is but a mere human. She has no *true* will." He nodded to her capturer who proceeded to escort her out of the room. "Fret not. She, too, will go free if and when you return the Amulet to me."

"I won't fail," I promised, though it was more of a promise to myself than to him. I had to believe I could do this. I had no other option. "I'll get you the Amulet."

"It is in your best interest to do so. I wouldn't want to soil your hands with the blood of the innocent."

"Aww," moaned Dominic. "But think of how much fun that would be." His steely eyes were as serious as cancer.

I wanted to carve them out of his head with my fingernails.

"One fortnight," reaffirmed Engel, dismissing me with the flick of his pale hand.

And with that, I was gone.

44. END GAMES

The cool night air encompassed my skin like an oil slick as I left the church alone, my mind fragmented from the weight of the encumbrance placed on my shoulders. I was alive, yes, but for how long? And at what cost?

The truth was cloaked in darkness and tainted with the bitter deceit of everyone I thought I knew. Trace, Tessa, Uncle Karl, Dominic—they were all puppeteers and I was but a puppet in their show, ready to dance on command and I didn't even know it. The stage was an illusion; the smoke and mirrors too thick for me to see through. Everything was a lie, right from the start.

But I would be a puppet no more.

I was in this thing alone and that was okay with me. It had to be. My friend's life depended on it. *My* life depended on it. I was going to figure out a way to get the Amulet back from Trace and get Taylor home safe and sound. Some way, somehow, I would do what needed to be done. And after that, all bets were off. Jemma Blackburn as I knew her would be no more. I'd seen too much, been hurt too much, to ever go back to the girl I used to be. That girl was dead and gone.

She *had* to be.

In that moment, as plumes of fog lifted off from the ground to meet me—to guide me home like my own army of vagrant ghosts, I silently vowed to gut this town from the inside out. To find out all of its secrets and lies and then watch it all crumble to the ground like a falling house of cards. Some way, somehow. There would be hell to pay.

And Trace Macarthur was first in line.

Bonus Material

For excerpts, teasers, character POV's, and deleted scenes,
check out the author's website at:

www.biancascardoni.com

ANAKIM INDEX

SLAYERS *(Warrior Angel Descendants)*
Jemma
Tessa
Gabriel+
Karl
Thomas*
Jaqueline*

REAPERS *(Transport Angel Descendants)*
Trace
Peter
Linley*

CASTERS *(Magi Angel Descendants)*
Nikki
Caleb
Carly

SHIFTERS *(Guardian Angel Descendants)*
Dominic+
Ben
Julian

SEERS *(Messenger Angel Descendants)*
Morgan

* Character is deceased
+ Character is a Revenant

ACKNOWLEDGEMENTS

Thank you Emma Le Bon, Tricia Simpson, Heather Watson-Crawford, and all my Tribe mamas for giving me the courage to publish this book. I have never known a more supportive group of women. And a big thank you to my amazing beta-readers Brittny, Amanda, and Shayna.

A goliath thank you to my step-dad, Jason, my dad, Victor, my sister, Melissa, and the rest of my wonderful family for supporting me in all my crazy endeavors.

A big thank you to my other half, Jeffrey, for putting up with the messy house and dirty laundry. You've seen *all* the parts of me—the hideous, asymmetric, imperfect parts—and you love me in spite of them. Thank you for showing me the kind of love people write novels about. I seriously love you…like *s'match*.

My biggest *thank you* goes to my mom, Anna, for her unconditional love and unwavering support. Thank you for loving me when I was utterly unlovable and for believing in me when I was incorrigible. I am stronger, faster, taller, smarter, and more beautiful in those fleeting moments when I catch a glimpse of myself through *your* eyes. For all that you are, and all that you have done for me, this one is for you. Love you lots.

And, last but certainly not least, I would like to thank my son, Jaxon, without whom this book would probably be just another one of my unfinished stories collecting dust on a shelf somewhere. I love you to the moon and back and more than all the stars in the sky. You are my reason for *everything*.

ABOUT THE AUTHOR

BIANCA SCARDONI is a paranormal fiction writer who resides on the East Coast of Canada with her family. She graduated from college with a degree in web design and went on to build an online writing community in 2004. When she isn't writing, she spends her time reading, watching vampire shows, eating junk food, and staying up too late.

For upcoming book releases, bonus material, and additional information on the author, please visit her website: www.biancascardoni.com

91384503R00234

Made in the USA
Middletown, DE
29 September 2018